LIVE AND LET SPY

Book 17 of the NEVER SAY SPY series

Diane Henders

LIVE AND LET SPY

ISBN 978-1-927460-69-6

Copyright © 2022 Diane Henders

PEBKAC Publishing Inc.
P.O. Box 67, Station Main
Qualicum Beach, BC   V9K 1S7
www.pebkacpublishing.com

This book is a work of fiction. Names, characters, places and incidents are either the product of the author's imagination or are used fictitiously, and any resemblance to actual persons, living or dead, business establishments, events or locales is entirely coincidental.

First printed in paperback October 2022 by PEBKAC Publishing Inc.
v.4

Books in the NEVER SAY SPY series:

More books coming! For a current list, please visit
www.dianehenders.com
Or sign up for my New Book Notification list at
www.dianehenders.com/books

Humour by Diane Henders

Since You Asked...

People frequently ask if my protagonist, Aydan Kelly, is really me.

Yeah, you got me. These novels are an autobiography of my secret life as a government agent, working with highly-classified computer technology... Oh, wait, what's that? You want the *truth*? Um, you do realize fiction writers get paid to lie, don't you?

...well, shit, that's not nearly as much fun. It's also a long story.

I swore I'd never write fiction. "Too personal," I said. "People read novels and automatically assume the author is talking about him/herself."

Well, apparently I lied about the fiction-writing part. One day a story sprang into my head and wouldn't leave. The only way to get it out was to write it down. So I did.

But when I wrote that first book, I never intended to show it to anyone, so I created a character that looked like me just to thumb my nose at the stereotype. I've always had a defective sense of humour, and this time it turned around and bit me in the ass.

Because after I'd written the third novel, I realized I actually wanted other people to read my books. And when I went back to change my main character to *not* look like me, my beta readers wouldn't let me. They rose up against me and said, "No! Aydan is a tall woman with long red hair and brown eyes. End of discussion!"

Jeez, no wonder readers get the idea that authors write about themselves. So no, I'm not Aydan Kelly. I just look like her.

Oh, and the town of Silverside and all secret technologies are products of my imagination. If I'm abducted by grim-faced men wearing dark glasses, or if I die in an unexplained fiery car crash, you'll know I accidentally came a little too close to the truth.

I hope you enjoy the book!

For Phill

Thank you for being my technical advisor and the most tolerant husband ever. Much love!

To my beta readers/editors, especially Carol H., Judy B., and Phill B., with gratitude: Many thanks for all your time and effort in catching my spelling and grammar errors, telling me when I screwed up the plot or the characters' motivations, and generally keeping me honest.

To everyone else, respectfully:
Canadian English is an unholy hybrid of British and American English, so I apologize if spellings in this book look odd to you. But if you find typos, please send an email to errors@dianehenders.com. Mistakes drive me nuts, and I'm sorry if any slipped through. Please let me know what the error is, and on which page. I'll make sure it gets fixed as soon as possible. Thanks!

CHAPTER 1

"Tell me you found something."

Despite the apparent optimism of the request, Agent Greg Holt's tone was devoid of hope.

Muttering obscenities, I ignored him and hugged my splitting head. I had made it safely out of virtual reality, but I still felt as though billions of terabytes of data were surging through my aching brain.

Never one to take a hint, Holt raised his voice. "Come on, give!"

"Shut up!" I hissed, squeezing my eyes closed so my eyeballs wouldn't explode.

"Just give her a minute." Spider's youthful voice was accompanied by his gentle fingertips massaging my temples. "Aydan, try to relax," he encouraged. "Just breathe."

The sound of sudden movement made my eyes snap open, only to involuntarily clamp shut once more against the pain. Holt's hands shoved Spider's aside and wrapped roughly around my head. Powerful fingertips ground into my pressure points.

The explosion of agony and relief yanked an inarticulate cry out of me as my spine arched, then released.

"*That's* how you do it," Holt said with satisfaction as I collapsed bonelessly on the sofa in my office.

Prying one eye open, I squinted up at the smug grin creasing his craggy features. "Thanks," I croaked. "Asshole."

His grin widened as he wiggled his fingers lasciviously. "Magic hands."

"Save it for your girlfriend."

I regretted the thoughtless words as soon as they left my mouth. Holt's stab of unhappiness was concealed almost instantly behind his impassive cop face, and I almost added 'Sorry'. But he hated sympathy.

"So I'm guessing you didn't find anything," he said flatly.

"No." A long sigh escaped me. "I swear I've checked under every virtual rock in the whole damn internet. That weapons expert is a friggin' ghost."

Holt's brows drew together. "Maybe he never existed at all. Maybe Kane and Stemp were lying about him, and it was just an excuse for Stemp to take the death ray out of the country last year." Holt's scowl deepened. "I bet Stemp took the original weapon to Volslav, and that's how they developed the second prototype. Hell, I still say Stemp *is* Volslav."

Indignation jerked me upright despite my still-aching head. "Kane was the best agent in the Department, and Stemp is the best damn Director we've ever had. They'd never sell out! And besides," I added with belated logic, "We know Tawny Harchman was Volslav, along with Dawn White and Yana Orlov. And Kane and Stemp both passed lie detector tests, so we know we can trust them."

"Speak for yourself," Holt growled. "I don't trust anybody."

"No shit, you paranoid bastard."

He gave me a superior smirk, his equilibrium apparently restored by our usual insults. "Kane only completed a standard exit interview, and Stemp only did a standard requalification. Neither of them was questioned directly about Volslav under the lie detector."

I shook my head. "Requalification and exit interviews ask whether you've violated your oath as an agent, so that covers it. You've been listening to Dermott's conspiracy theories again, haven't you?"

I couldn't quite prevent myself from glancing at the doorway as I spoke. If Dermott happened to overhear me, it would shatter our six months of precarious civility.

"You know I'm right," Holt needled. "Someday that blind trust of yours is going to turn around and bite you in the ass."

The thought of anyone putting me and trust in the same sentence jerked a snort of amusement out of me. I lowered my voice. "You know Dermott's got an agenda. He's just panting for the chance to get rid of Stemp and take over as Director."

This time both Spider and I glanced at the door. Spider's boyish features scrunched into an anxious expression, while Holt looked thoughtful.

"That's true," Holt agreed. "But at least Dermott doesn't sneak off to Europe and disappear every time somebody whispers the name 'Volslav'."

"Stemp doesn't..." I began hotly.

But Stemp *did* sneak off to Europe and disappear every time there was a new development with Volslav. And I couldn't tell anyone that he was protecting his secret wife and child.

"Okay, he does," I amended. "But you know he's only going off-grid so he can protect the contacts he had when he was working as an agent over there."

Holt grunted. "You say 'contacts'; I say 'sleazeball arms dealers'. I still say he's up to-" His words hitched almost imperceptibly as the man himself appeared in the doorway. "...something," Holt finished smoothly, looking as innocent as a cynical lantern-jawed agent could.

Director Charles Stemp's customary emotionless façade remained undisturbed except for the fractional elevation of one eyebrow. "Developments?" he inquired.

"No," Holt replied. "Kelly still can't find anything." Desperation edged his voice. "We need to get out in the field! We're not accomplishing anything sitting here day after fucking day!" His gesture at my office looked like a barely-controlled explosion.

Stemp's response was dry. "What do you expect to find in the field, when Agent Kelly has access to every scrap of data..." He hesitated uncharacteristically before amending, "...almost every scrap of data in the internet?"

Uh-oh. I didn't like that hesitation. Or that amendment.

Holt's fists clenched. "I won't know until I try. But we're sure as hell not getting anywhere here." His voice rose. "It's been damn near *six months* since we got that flash drive from Volslav. And we've found *nothing* since then!"

"Hardly 'nothing'." Stemp eyed my tired slump and glanced at his wristwatch. "Get some lunch. Briefing in my office at thirteen hundred." He withdrew.

Slouching lower on the sofa, I groaned. "A briefing. What fresh hell will this be?"

Holt straightened, hope rising on his face. "Finally! Something besides endless update meetings where he asks 'What did you find' and we say 'fuck-all'." His steel-blue eyes lit up. "Maybe we're getting another mission."

With a tremendous effort of will, I managed not to curl into a fetal ball. "Hooray." The word emerged with all the animation of a week-old corpse.

Holt shot me a contemptuous look, but he was grinning. "You're such a pussy. See you at the *briefing*." His grin widened as he emphasized the word, and he strode out with a spring in his step.

Another groan escaped me.

"Is your head still hurting?" Spider asked. "I could-" A tiny electronic ping cut across his words, and he jolted as though he'd been poked with a cattle prod. He dove for the phone on my desk. "I have to call Linda!" Halting, he flushed. "Um, I mean... is it okay if I...?" He gestured toward my phone but before I could answer, he spun for the door. "Never mind, I'll-"

"Use my phone," I interrupted.

"Thanks!" He snatched up the receiver and dialled, his bony fingers flashing over the keypad.

He jittered from foot to foot while he waited for the call to connect, his free hand drumming a rapid tempo on my desk. Despite my discouragement, his anxious anticipation made me smile.

He stiffened, his eyes widening. "Sweetie? Is it time?" His shoulders slumped. "Oh. Sure, that sounds great. Okay, see you then. I love you, too. 'Bye." He let out a long breath as he replaced the receiver in its cradle.

"False alarm?" I asked.

He gave me a sheepish smile. "No alarm at all. But soon..." Blowing out a shivery breath, he hugged himself as his smile widened. "Oh, Aydan, I'm so excited! Today is Linda's official due date. Any day now I'll be a dad!"

I got up and went over to give him an affectionate side-hug. "You started being a dad about nine months ago."

"I know, but... I'll be a *real* dad. I'll get to meet my daughter for the first time and hold her in my arms, and oh,

Aydan! It's going to be *so awesome!*"

He bounced in sheer joy, and I gave him another squeeze before letting him go. "You and Linda will be amazing parents. Have you picked a name yet?"

"We have some ideas, but we want to meet her first." His eyes sparkled. "We want to see if she's a 'Sophia' or a 'Lily' an 'Isabella' or..." He broke off. "Sorry, I know babies aren't really your thing."

"It's okay," I assured him. "If you're happy, I'm happy. Let's go and get lunch, and you can talk about babies all you want."

I hadn't realized exactly how much an excited father-to-be could talk about babies. By the time we returned from the Melted Spoon, my head was aching as much as it had earlier. It was a relief when we sank into chairs in Stemp's office and Spider fell silent at last.

Holt was already seated, every line of his body telegraphing alert readiness. My abysmal posture was probably telegraphing, 'please just let me stay safely in my office forever'. Or more likely, 'I'm too old for this shit'.

That was enough to make me straighten up. At forty-eight... hell, almost forty-nine now... it was a point of pride for me to be the oldest female agent to pass the physical qualification for active duty. And not just a point of pride; a point of self-preservation. If Command decided I was unfit for active duty, I'd be living and working in the underground secured area for the rest of my life.

Hiding my shudder, I pasted on what I hoped was an expression of attentive competence.

Stemp eyed me with a small frown. "Agent Kelly, are you

feeling unwell?"

Apparently my 'attentive competence' looked a lot like indigestion. I forced a smile. "I'm fine. Just the usual headache."

"Ah." He leaned back in his chair, steepling his fingertips in precise alignment. "In that case, you will be pleased to hear that you will be getting a break from your daily network surveillance."

I did my best to look pleased. That expression might not have been convincing, either.

Stemp cast me a dubious look and continued, including Spider and Holt with a glance. "Despite your earlier assertion that you have found 'nothing', your progress is acceptable. Tracing the financial connections between the three players in Volslav was helpful, and the government was able to seize their accounts." Stemp dipped his chin toward me. "And Command appreciated the twenty million dollars Volslav transferred to your cover identity. The funds from the proceeds-of-crime seizure go into the government's general revenue, but the twenty million went to the Department's operational funds."

"So what?" Holt demanded. "That was months ago. So we fattened the coffers, big deal. Shutting down the lab that made the death ray prototype was small potatoes, too. Another lab will just take over. The weapons expert we're hunting will know which labs can make another; and he'll have intel on Volslav, too. Maybe enough for us to take down their whole operation." His fist clenched. "We *need* that fucking expert!"

"That would be optimum," Stemp agreed. "Which leads us to this briefing. Agent Kelly-"

"We need to re-interview everybody who interacted with

the weapons expert," Holt interrupted. "This time, under the lie detector."

Stemp eyed him. "Including me?"

For an instant I thought Holt might back down, but I should have known better.

Holt thrust out his chest in his classic alpha-male posture. "Yes."

Stemp nodded coolly. "I believe it is available, and I have time immediately following this briefing. Agent Kelly can contact John Kane, too, and arrange for him to come in at his earliest convenience." He transferred his attention back to me with a level gaze that felt like a challenge.

I met it with my best casual tone. "Sure. I'll give him a call as soon as we're finished here."

Stemp nodded. "Very well. Returning to our briefing... Agent Kelly, it is my understanding that you have exhausted all available leads online."

Uh-oh.

My pulse ticked up. "Um, yeah, so far... but it's the whole internet. There are new connections every nanosecond. The problem is, sometimes the connections shift and I end up 'way the hell on the other side of the planet swimming through data in foreign languages I can't read. It might be exactly what we need, but I'd never know."

"Indeed. I believe we have a solution to that." Despite his customary lack of expression, a tiny crimp of satisfaction appeared at the corner of Stemp's mouth. "Rebecca Stile."

I couldn't help wincing.

CHAPTER 2

"Rebecca? Can... help?" Spider's voice was uncertain as he glanced over at me.

Rebecca Stile. The sibling rival I'd never even known I had.

Even now, seven months after discovering my mother's lies and criminal activities, it still hurt to know that she had faked her own death and abandoned my father and me thirty years ago. The fact that she'd treated Rebecca like a surrogate daughter while pretending I didn't exist was just the creamy shit frosting on a triple-layer shit cake.

I put on my best poker face. "That's great. How can Rebecca help?"

"I thought she was still living in the U.K.," Spider put in. "I thought we weren't going to tell her anything about the Department or the virtual reality network or-"

"Or anything about the fact that she can read any digital data regardless of encryption or security measures," Stemp summarized Spider's recitation. "Correct."

"But how...?"

"Ms. Stile's original contract with Sirius Dynamics guaranteed her a job until age sixty-five. Now that Agent Kelly's mother is deceased and Sirius U.K. has been seized by the British government, the only remaining branch of Sirius

Dynamics is this one. And Ms. Stile is entitled to another seventeen years of employment."

"Tough," Holt snapped. "She's useless. All she's done for the last thirty years is a bit of reception work. If Kelly can't find anything, Stile sure as hell won't be any help. She couldn't find her own ass with both hands."

"Ms. Stile will not be searching for anything," Stemp countered. "Webb and Dr. Travers can create a network key that will allow us to use Ms. Stile's consciousness to search the internet without her knowledge. As long as Ms. Stile is physically present in our office and receiving a paycheque, the terms of her contract are met. And..." His satisfied expression returned. "Ms. Stile is multilingual."

Holt sat up straight. "What languages?"

"She is fluent in English, French, German, Spanish, Russian, and Mandarin; and competent in Portuguese, Arabic, and Farsi. She also has a smattering of other languages. So her consciousness will automatically translate any of those languages into English for her handler in the network."

A short stunned silence greeted that revelation.

Then Holt grinned. "When does she get here? We'll throw her a nice welcome p-"

"No!" Spider's protest cut across Holt's words. Spots of red burned on Spider's cheeks as he sputtered, "That's... it's just *wrong!* It's a creepy invasion to take over Rebecca's mind without telling her, and it's completely unethical to just secretly... *use* her! I won't be part of this!"

My heart sank. I admired Spider's lofty principles and I was amazed at how well he dealt with the gray areas in the Department's clandestine operations; but sometimes...

Stemp met Spider's outburst with no expression beyond

the lift of one inscrutable eyebrow. "Ms. Stile's work would be no different than Ms. Mellor's. And you accepted Ms. Mellor's presence and purpose over a year ago."

Spider flushed redder. "That was different! Aydan had accidentally been inside Tammy's mind, and she knew Tammy would be happy to help if we could tell her what we needed."

Stemp's flat gaze swiveled to me. "Agent Kelly has been inside Ms. Stile's mind, too." He fell silent, eyeing me; and his psychic command wasn't difficult to pick up: *'Fix this.'*

Caught between Stemp's deadly gaze and Spider's imploring one, I opened my mouth to say who-knew-what. All that came out was, "Um..."

I added, "Sorry, I have to think about it. That was over seven months ago, and I was pretty messed up at the time."

Like a pair of unprepossessing Rockettes, Spider and I synchronized a shudder. Even Holt looked momentarily rattled.

"That was so awful," Spider quavered. "I still have nightmares about seeing your arms torn off..." He gulped and shuddered again.

"Yeah, not one of my happier experiences, either. I'm just glad it was virtual reality and not the real thing." I crossed my arms and sank my chin onto my chest as though deep in thought.

Hell, I wasn't acting. My mind raced, searching for an answer that would satisfy everyone.

How would Rebecca react if she knew what we were proposing? When I had collided with her consciousness in the network, I had been too busy making sure she didn't access any of my memories to bother looking through hers. My general impression had been of a pleasant but malleable woman, surprisingly innocent for her forty-eight years.

Then again, compared to the horrific shit in my mind, just about anybody would seem innocent.

"Aydan...?" Spider asked tentatively.

Realizing my face had twisted, I smoothed my expression and muttered, "Sorry, just trying to remember."

I was pretty sure I knew how Rebecca would react if we were truthful about what we wanted: *'Hey, can we slip inside your mind where we can see all your private thoughts, and use your brain to commit espionage every day for the next seventeen years?'*

Hell, yeah. Who wouldn't go for that?

I sighed.

But it didn't really matter. Stemp wouldn't be deterred. Rebecca would work for us no matter who protested or what the collateral damage might be. All I could do was try to make Spider feel better about it.

But I couldn't lie to him.

Prodded by the stinging of my conscience, I sighed again and opened my eyes. "I don't know about Rebecca," I admitted. "With Tammy, I was sure. She's so..."

"Cooperative." Stemp spoke into my momentary silence.

That was a much nicer description than 'gullible and submissive', which were the only words that had come to my mind.

"Um, right," I agreed. "Rebecca's more sophisticated than Tammy, but she's not ambitious. Her clerical job at Sirius U.K. was perfect for her."

"As this one will be," Stemp said.

"But we'll be lying to her," Spider protested. "What are we going to tell her when she doesn't remember anything but arriving at the office, eating lunch, taking coffee breaks, and leaving? She'll think she has a brain tumour or Alzheimer's or something."

Stemp looked thoughtful. "That could work."

"No!" Spider shot me a desperate glance. "It's *wrong!*"

Turning to me, Stemp inquired, "In your opinion, would Ms. Stile enjoy filing?"

"I don't see why not. She mostly answered the phones at Sirius U.K. They were only keeping her employed so they could secretly use her to skim data from the internet. She did an easy nine-to-five at the office, and then went home and studied languages for fun."

Holt spoke with his usual confidence. "Then she'll love this job. If we give her a stack of digital files in the morning and they're gone by the time she leaves at the end of the day, her mind will just fill in the blanks. She'll think her workday went the same as it's gone every day for the past thirty years."

"And we'd still be lying to her," Spider insisted.

Stemp massaged the bridge of his nose, looking suddenly weary. "Webb," he said with surprising gentleness, "We lie to everyone. That is the definition of 'clandestine operations'. Sometimes people would cooperate to the fullest if they knew what we wanted; other times not. We cannot know which, because we cannot reveal our purposes. Or even our existence."

Spider slumped, his brow furrowing.

"I don't want you to compromise your principles," Stemp went on. "However, I do ask that you weigh the relatively minor personal consequences for Ms. Stile against the extensive potential benefits to Canada and our allies. The information that Ms. Stile enables us to gather could save thousands of lives. Perhaps millions."

Spider sighed. "I guess. Who would be her handler?"

If Stemp felt triumph at the implied concession, it didn't show in his face or voice. "I believe Ms. Belling is due for a promotion. Although as her team lead, the final decision is yours."

Hope dawned on Spider's face. "Trish would be a great choice. She's crazy-good at her job; and she's so nice, I know she wouldn't snoop on Rebecca's personal thoughts." He let out a breath. "You're right, Trish totally deserves a promotion. And she'll love surfing the internet with Rebecca. It's such a cool experience."

"The substantial increase in security clearance and pay grade will undoubtedly be welcome, too," Stemp put in dryly. "Very well. Webb, offer Ms. Belling the promotion and if she accepts, set it up with HR."

"When should I tell her the job starts?" Spider asks.

"Immediately. As soon as her security interviews are complete and her clearances have been upgraded, brief her on the project. She will also need to visit Dr. Travers to record her baseline brainwave scan. Since we already have the network keys that were coded to control Ms. Stile, reprogramming them to Ms. Belling's control should be a relatively quick process. Tell Ms. Belling to be ready to begin her new role as early as Friday. Ms. Stile's flight arrives in Halifax on Wednesday morning. Holt and Kelly will fly to Halifax tomorrow so they can discreetly supervise her passage through the Halifax airport and subsequent connections." Stemp turned to Holt and me. "Your tickets, hotel vouchers, and itinerary will be emailed to you this afternoon."

My shoulders relaxed. Not a dangerous new mission. Just two gloriously boring days of sitting on airplanes and trudging through airports. Perfect.

Holt's cranky objection shattered my pleasant thoughts. "Why the hell would you send two top agents to escort Stile? Nobody knows who she is or what she's worth to us. She's flying to Canada from the U.K. without an escort. What difference does it make if she just makes her connection in Halifax as planned and flies here herself?"

"An excellent point," Stemp agreed. "Ensuring that Ms. Stile arrives safely is important, but it is not your primary purpose in flying to Nova Scotia."

All my earlier relaxation fled. I should have known it was too good to be true.

Stemp went on, "You will also rendezvous with Agent Rand from MI6."

Holt and I exchanged a glance that might as well have been an eye roll.

"What the hell does that twisty asshole want?" Holt demanded.

Although Stemp's expression didn't alter, he somehow managed to convey a mixture of mild annoyance and tolerant amusement. "With Agent Rand, one is never certain. However, he assured me that he had important information to impart."

I blew out a breath. "So why didn't he damn well tell you the information? Why do we have to meet him in person? And if he wanted to meet in person, why didn't he just fly here?"

Stemp's shoulders rose in one of his infinitesimal shrugs. "Unknown. All I know is that Rand has requested a personal meeting with you and Holt, and he also requests that you come disguised and be prepared to shift your appearance several times. He will contact us tomorrow with a rendezvous time and location, which we will pass on to you via secured phone."

"He requested Kelly and me, specifically?" Holt asked.

"Yes."

"Maybe he's found some new scam Kelly's mother was running," Holt speculated.

I grimaced. "That wouldn't surprise me. Hell, nothing would surprise me about Mommy Dearest anymore. But Rand might just be making shit up again because he's bored and looking for some entertainment. He lives to yank my chain."

Holt shot me an exaggerated leer. "It's not your chain he wants to get his hands on."

This time I didn't bother to suppress my eye-roll. "Maybe it's your chain he wants to pull. I hear he's pretty open-minded in his preferences."

Stemp gave us a quelling glance. "Holt and Webb, you are dismissed. Kelly, stay."

My stomach clenched.

Holt rose. "Remember to call Kane as soon as you're done here," he reminded me.

"I will," I mumbled.

As the door closed behind them, Stemp reached into his desk drawer.

I tensed. The last time he'd reached into his desk drawer without explanation, he'd pulled out a gun and shot me. With a tranquilizer, not a bullet; but still.

The fat file folder he withdrew and laid on his desk didn't reassure me. Fat file folders usually caused more misery and inconvenience than a mere twenty minutes of unconsciousness.

Stemp eyed me with a bland expression before pushing

the folder across the desk toward me.

I didn't reach for it. "What is it?" I growled.

The corner of his mouth quirked up in an uncharacteristic smile. "Some legal documents requiring your signature."

"I'm not signing anything without a lawyer."

The quirk of his mouth turned into a full-blown smile.

Stemp.

Smiling.

Oh, shit.

He leaned back in his chair, the smile still in place. "That is a prudent policy," he said. "Particularly for the new owner of Sirius Dynamics."

CHAPTER 3

"Wh-" My mouth formed the word, but no sound came out. I tried again, managing a hoarse whisper. "What did you say?"

Stemp's smile widened. "The government has rescinded their seizure of Sirius Dynamics and its capital assets. The estates of your mother and stepfather have been probated, and you are the sole heir. Congratulations." He nudged the folder a little closer to me. "You have only to sign the appropriate documents."

I eased my chair backward, eyeing the folder as though it contained a venomous snake. "But I told the lawyer to drop that lawsuit, months ago. The government can have Sirius. I have enough on my plate without..."

I waved a hand to indicate his office, all the surrounding offices, the secure underground labs and holding areas, the secret tunnels and bunkers and God only knew what else.

Somehow I suppressed my groan and finished anticlimactically, "...this."

"But it makes you a very wealthy woman."

"Maybe on paper; but it's actually just a big chunk of unsellable real estate with a huge property tax bill. And there's not enough money in the world to make me want to-"

I broke off at the sight of an unprecedented twinkle in

his eyes.

Sagging back in my chair, I let out a breath. "You're messing with me, right? This is just a really tasteless joke."

"Not a joke," Stemp countered. The spark of humour still glinted in his eyes. "However, I do admit to amusement over the fact that you react with such horror to an inheritance most would consider a dream come true." His smile faded into his usual gravity. "This will require nothing more from you than an occasional consultation with the management company which has been operating Sirius Dynamics efficiently and profitably for over forty years. In return for your very limited participation, you will receive a generous monthly stipend."

I groaned. "Yeah, that sounds great; but I can't just sign a bunch of random papers. I'm a bookkeeper, for shit's sake! You know how anal I am. I'm going to have to read every single damn word..." I waved a bitter hand at the file folder gloating at me from his desk. "...and make sure I understand it and go over it with a lawyer before I sign anything. And then I'm going to have to look into the building operations and the management company and-"

Stemp's palm-out 'stop' gesture made me break off in mid-whine.

"My condolences," he said dryly. "Nevertheless, you are now the owner of Sirius Dynamics; along with a considerable portion of the town of Silverside. Command has requested that you sign the Department's lease agreement immediately." He raised a calming hand as I began to protest. "After you have retained legal counsel, of course."

I sighed and accepted the folder at last. "Sorry. I know I'm being stupidly ungrateful. I'll look at the leasing agreement first. I just hope there's something in there that says nobody can sue me if Reggie blows up the Weapons Lab and takes out half the town."

The twinkle was back in Stemp's eyes. "I believe you will find the indemnity clauses satisfactory. May I reassure Command that their lease will be renewed?"

I stared at him. "Of course. What, they thought I'd kick them out? What would I do with all these buildings if..." A horrible thought swelled into my mind. "Oh, shit. They're thinking of pulling out and moving everything to the Calgary facility, aren't they? No wonder the damn government is giving me Sirius Dynamics; they don't want a giant white elephant in the middle of nowhere-"

"Kelly." Stemp's single flat word silenced me. "Your paranoia is showing."

I scowled. "It's not paranoia if they really are out to get me."

He shook his head. "Your suspicion is understandable, but misplaced. This facility will remain in operation indefinitely. Regulations prevent us from undertaking weapons development or testing within Calgary's city limits." He gave me a thin smile. "You did not hear that from me, although a small amount of research will confirm it for you. Command would not thank me for giving you leverage for a rent increase."

My answering smile was mostly relief. "Thanks. I won't gouge them."

"I knew you would not." His usual emotionless façade descended again. "Dismissed. If Holt is loitering outside, please inform him that I am available now for my lie detector interview."

I eyed him with concern, but I couldn't think of any words to express it: '*Jeez, I hope your lies don't catch up with you*'? Not exactly supportive.

Rising, I said, "I'll tell him", and let myself out.

Stemp's surmise was spot-on. When I walked into my office, Holt was sprawled on my sofa with his feet propped on my coffee table.

"He's ready for the lie detector whenever you are," I said.

Holt rose, looking smug. "Good. Honey's on her way up with it right now."

"She prefers 'Jack'," I reminded him.

"Doesn't suit her. And Honey's her legal name, so..."

"Don't be an asshole. How would you like it if I called you by your middle name just because I liked it better?"

Holt shot me an irritable look. "It's 'Allan', in case you're wondering, and you can call me that instead of 'asshole' any day."

"I calls 'em like I sees 'em. Act like a 'Greg', and that's what I'll call you."

His scowl deepened and I braced for his retort, but the arrival of a voluptuous blonde angel in my doorway lightened his expression.

Dr. Honey Jacqueline Travers gave us her usual luminous smile and hefted the small case she was carrying. "Here you go. Would you like me to set it up?"

Holt flashed me a quick side-eye before returning her smile and accepting the case. "No, that's okay. Thanks, Jack. I'll get it back to you as soon as I can."

After she left, I said, "Thanks, Greg. I knew I could count on the real you."

"Stop trying to handle me," he growled, but he didn't sound too upset. He added, "Do you want to sit in on the interview with Stemp?"

Surprised and relieved, I replied, "Yeah. Thanks. I'll call

John while you're getting set up. I'll be right there."

Holt nodded and left, and I picked up the phone.

John answered on the second ring with his usual brisk, "Kane."

"Hi, it's me."

"Hello." I could hear a smile in his voice. "I was hoping that blocked number was you. Is this a social call?"

"Not really," I replied, conscious of the unsecured connection. "I was just wondering if you had time to come up to the office sometime this week."

"I can be there in two hours, if that works for you."

"It works, but it's not that urgent," I demurred. "You don't need to rush up here."

"Now is a good time for me to come. Is there anything you need me to bring?"

"No, we just need to pick your brain."

"Then I'm on my way. See you around three-thirty. Can you join me for dinner at Fiorenza's at five-thirty?"

"Sure, if we're done by then."

We said our goodbyes, and I returned the phone receiver to its cradle thoughtfully. Kane was always decisive and efficient, but this speedy reaction seemed like more than that.

I pondered. It wasn't likely personal. Sure, it had been a while since we'd seen each other; but he wasn't the type of guy to moon around hoping I'd call. If he'd wanted to see me, he would have come up to Silverside or invited me down to Calgary.

Well, whatever. I'd find out in a couple of hours. I had enough to worry about right now. Holt would be fair in his questioning, but he would be thorough.

I just hoped my faith in Stemp hadn't been misplaced.

CHAPTER 4

When I arrived in Stemp's office, Holt had already fastened the band of electrodes around Stemp's forehead.

As I took a seat, Holt turned to Stemp and gestured to the tiny camera lens glinting in the corner of the room near the ceiling. "I'm recording this session via the security system. Do you consent?"

When Stemp nodded, Holt prompted, "State 'yes' or 'no' for the lie detector. Do you consent to having this session recorded?"

"Yes."

The green light on the lie detector shone its confirmation, and Holt went on, "I'm going to ask you for explanations and then confirm your answers with the lie detector by converting the information you give me into yes or no questions. You're not being arrested or detained. You don't have to answer any questions, and you can call a lawyer anytime you want. Would you like to call a lawyer now?"

"No," Stemp replied. "And it will not be necessary for you to recite the complete Police Warning."

"You waive your right to hear the complete Police Warning?"

"Yes."

Holt eyed Stemp. "I'll also remind you that if you refuse

to answer, or make any statement that registers untrue on the lie detector, it's grounds for immediate suspension pending a full inquiry by the National Security and Intelligence Review Agency. If they decide legal proceedings are warranted, anything you say here can be used as evidence. Do you understand?"

Something flickered in Stemp's expressionless amber gaze, but it vanished before I could identify it.

"Yes," he said. The green light shone its approval.

Tension wound up in my shoulders. Shit, Holt was dotting all the 'I's and crossing all the 'T's. Despite our near-constant trading of insults, I had a lot of respect for his skill as an agent. If there was anything to be discovered, he'd find it. And it would be witnessed, documented, and admissible as evidence in court.

Please don't let him find anything...

Holt leaned back in his chair. "Okay. Tell us everything you did, starting when you got the call from Kane saying he wanted to show the ultrasound death ray to a weapons expert."

"As soon as I received Kane's call, I contacted Upper Command and received approval to take the weapon out of the secured area and to the meeting with the expert," Stemp began.

"Do you know the expert's name?" Holt interrupted.

"No."

The green light corroborated Stemp's answer, and Holt frowned. "Have you ever heard a name associated with the expert? Do you have any idea who he might be?"

"That is two questions," Stemp reminded him. "Which would you like me to answer?"

"Do you have any idea what the expert's name might

be?" Holt asked.

"No."

"Can you think of any way to identify him?"

"No."

Green lights all the way.

Holt sighed. "Okay, that would have been too easy. Go on."

"I put on the disguise I had used in my cover as George Harrison in Bulgaria seven years ago..." Stemp paused and clarified, "Seven years ago at that time. Nearly nine years ago, now. I had previously created a profile for George Harrison in our security system. I went to Sirius Dynamics, accessed the secure weapons lab using George Harrison's credentials, and took the weapon. I then deleted George Harrison's credentials from the security system. When I arrived at the meeting with Kane, I realized that the expert was a man I had previously encountered in my George Harrison cover, and he likely recognized me. This could have caused significant risk to some of my contacts in Europe, so after allowing the expert to examine the weapon, I took the weapon to Europe without further contact or approval from Command. Once there, I showed the weapon to contacts who confirmed the expert's opinion, and also provided critical additional information. I gave the information to Interpol and they made multiple arrests in Volslav's organization. I then got in touch with some other contacts whom I knew to be potentially at risk from Volslav. I relocated them and provided them with new identities. Then I flew back to Canada, bringing the weapon with me, and contacted Command at my first opportunity. I returned to Sirius Dynamics and replaced the weapon in the weapons lab."

Holt eyed Stemp in the silence that followed. "Is that a true and complete account of everything you did?" he asked.

"No."

The green light shone its agreement.

"What the hell?" Holt ground out.

Stemp's eyebrow lifted a fraction. "It was a true account of what I did. It was not a complete account."

Holt blew out a breath. "Okay. Was that a true account of everything you did?"

"No."

Before Holt could explode, I spoke up. "The problem is the phrase 'everything you did'." I turned to Stemp. "Was everything you just said true?"

Stemp gave me an approving glance. "Yes." The green light shone.

"So it wasn't a *complete* account of everything you did." Holt took over again with an irritated glance at me.

"That is correct," Stemp agreed.

"Yes or no," Holt growled.

"Due to the phrasing of your question, answering yes or no could both be construed as the truth, which would be potentially misleading," Stemp countered.

Holt glowered at him. "Did you give us a complete account? Yes or no."

"No." Green light.

With exaggerated patience, Holt asked, "What did you leave out of your previous account?"

"I left out all mentions of eating, sleeping, grooming, bodily functions, and travelling."

"Is that true?"

"Yes." Green light.

"Is that a complete account of everything you left out?"

"I do not know."

Holt's eyes narrowed. "Yes or no?"

Stemp shrugged. "Yes."

The yellow light flashed. Invalid pairing. None of Stemp's brainwaves had proved or disproved his reply.

"No," Stemp amended.

The yellow light flashed again.

"As you can see, the lie detector confirms that I truly do not know," Stemp said. "I have given you an accurate account of what I remember. However, human recall is unreliable at best; and two years after the fact there is an excellent chance-"

The door slammed open, making us all jump. My hand was halfway to my concealed holster before I realized there was no threat.

Well, no physical threat.

In the doorway, Brent Dermott's meaty features flushed with pique. "What the hell are you doing, interviewing him without me?" he demanded.

Holt's hand dropped away from his holster, too. He scowled and demanded, "Have you ever heard of knocking?" Before Dermott could retort, Holt added, "I told you in my message that I'd be recording the interview." He gestured at the camera. "And I am. We just got started. All he's done is confirmed the facts in his original report."

Looking somewhat mollified, Dermott closed the door and took a seat.

Holt turned back to Stemp. "You were saying?"

"I have reported the salient events around my acquisition, possession, transportation, and subsequent return of the ultrasound weapon two years ago. My statements were all accurate, to the best of my current recollection."

Dermott crossed his arms, giving Stemp a skeptical sneer. "Is that true?"

"Yes." Green light.

"So you don't know who the weapons expert is," Dermott prodded.

Before Stemp could split hairs about the phrasing of the question, Holt spoke up. "We asked that already, but we'll try it again." He turned to Stemp. "Do you know who the weapons expert is?"

"No." Green light.

Dermott gave Holt a 'shut-up' look and eyed Stemp with the eager contempt of a bully about to attack. "Can you guess who the weapons expert might be?"

Stemp hesitated. "Yes," he said, and the green light shone.

Triumph bloomed on Dermott's face. "Who is it?" he demanded.

"I have no idea."

"You just said you could guess," Dermott snapped.

"I can."

"So guess!"

"You, Brent Shirley Dermott, are the weapons expert," Stemp said coolly. As Dermott's mouth dropped open, Stemp added, "Or perhaps the Pope is. Or Ryan Reynolds, the actor. Or possibly-"

Dermott flushed purple. "Don't fuck with me!"

"I am not. You asked if I could guess. I truthfully answered that I can. Given a complete list of the planet's inhabitants, I am capable of making well over seven billion guesses."

"Okay, let's try a different question," Holt said loudly

over the obscenities Dermott was beginning to sputter. Holt glared at Stemp. "Are you Volslav?"

"No." The green light shone its blessing, and I eased out a breath of relief.

"Do you know if the weapons expert is or was associated with Volslav?"

"No."

"Are you associated with Volslav in any way?" Dermott interrupted.

Stemp hesitated, and my heart sank.

"Yes," Stemp replied.

Green light.

Oh, God, no.

"But not in the way you are implying," Stemp added. "I am associated, in that I spent over a year investigating Volslav when I was an agent nine years ago. And I am associated again by the actions I described earlier in this interview. Also, as the Director of Clandestine Operations, I am by necessity involved in all investigations pertaining to Volslav, which creates yet another connection. Those are the only associations I have with Volslav."

"Is that all true?" Holt asked.

"Yes." Green light.

"Before we discovered the evidence six months ago, did you know Tawny Harchman, Dawn White, and/or Yana Orlov formed either all or part of Volslav?"

"No."

Holt and Dermott took turns asking variations of the same questions, and Stemp fielded them with cool confidence. I slowly relaxed again. Shit, this was almost as bad as being in the hot seat myself.

"Okay," Holt said at last. "Let's move on. Who are these

contacts you mentioned overseas?"

I tensed all over again. Would Stemp finally admit that he had a wife and daughter?

Stemp gave no indication that the question was loaded. His face and voice were as expressionless as ever as he replied, "The contacts are listed in my official report. Their names have been redacted for their own safety, and the complete reports are available only to Upper Command."

"Is that true?" Dermott demanded.

"Yes." Green light.

Whew.

But Holt was smarter than Dermott. "Did you list all your contacts in your report?" Holt asked.

"All contacts pertaining to our investigation of Volslav are listed in my report," Stemp confirmed.

Shit. I knew weasel-words when I heard them. I was betting Holt did, too.

"Is that true?" Holt asked.

"Yes." Green light.

Holt moved in for the kill. "When you were overseas with the ultrasound weapon, did you get in touch with contacts that you didn't list in your reports?"

Stemp hesitated.

Shit, shit, shit! If he said no, the lie detector would catch the lie and he'd be suspended. Maybe even convicted and imprisoned.

But if he divulged the existence of his wife and young daughter, it could cost their lives.

I held my breath, my pulse thumping in my ears.

What would he say?

CHAPTER 5

Stemp sat silent. No evidence of his inner turmoil showed on the expressionless planes of his face, but his pupils had dilated.

My hand clenched on the arm of my chair, my knuckles popping loudly in the silence.

Holt repeated, "Did you make contact with anyone else that you didn't list in your reports?"

A nasty grin spread over Dermott's face. "You did, didn't you?" he taunted.

"Yes," Stemp said quietly. The green light illuminated his defeat.

"Who?" Dermott barked. "And how many?"

"Two contacts," Stemp replied.

"Is that true?" Holt's question was emotionless, but I could see disappointment in his eyes. He might tease me about my trust of Stemp, but apparently I wasn't the only one who wanted to believe in him.

"Yes." Green light.

"Did you contact anyone else besides those two contacts?" Holt asked.

"No." Green light.

Maybe Holt would let it go. My vision darkened around the edges and I eased out the breath I'd been holding.

I sucked in another involuntary breath as Holt asked, "Were either of your contacts ever associated with Volslav?"

Stemp met his gaze steadily. "Yes."

"Ha!" Dermott's bark of triumph made me twitch. "Arrest that asshole!"

Holt gave him a 'shut-up' glance and returned to questioning Stemp. "How were those two contacts associated with Volslav?"

"Only one of them was associated with Volslav. The other was personally connected to the first."

Couldn't get much more personal than mother and child. I held my breath again, sending Stemp psychic support in his delicate dance with the truth.

Stemp went on, "At great personal risk, my contact supplied me with translation services while I was gathering intelligence about Volslav. When I was wounded and had to be extracted from Bulgaria nine years ago, my contact went underground. I consider it my personal responsibility to ensure the safety of these contacts. Identifying them in any way would compromise their safety."

"Is that all true?" Holt asked. I could tell he was trying to sound dispassionate, but hope edged his tone.

"Yes." Green light.

Holt's shoulders settled as if in relief, but he asked the next question without hesitation.

"Has your contact ever provided intelligence to Volslav about our operations?"

"Any answer I could provide would be speculation," Stemp replied calmly. "I am not aware of all my contact's activities. I can only speak for myself."

Dermott's voice broke the silence. "So that's a 'yes'. You've been selling us out all along, you slimy piece of shit."

He turned to Holt. "Arrest him."

Holt ignored Dermott, but his next question came out in a voice as taut as my muscles. "Did you ever supply intelligence about our operations to anyone?"

"I supplied information to my contact in order to have it translated; and also to gain trust," Stemp replied carefully. "Some of that trust-building information was verifiable fact which could technically be considered 'intelligence'. I did not reveal my association with the Department. I provided no intelligence which would not have already been known or inferred by my contact. I did not disclose any classified information."

"Is that all true?" Holt's voice was urgent in spite of his obvious attempt to stay cool.

"Yes." The glorious green light shone, and I slumped in my chair.

"He just admitted to selling us out," Dermott snapped. "How much more do you need to hear?"

"He admitted to doing his job as an agent," Holt said tiredly. "And probably doing it well." He turned back to Stemp. "Have you ever revealed information that could be harmful to our country or our national security, or that could have aided Volslav in any way?"

"No." Stemp's reply was firm and confident, and the green light shone its blessing.

"Good, then we're done here," I said, and dragged my stress-stiffened body up from the chair.

"Not quite," Dermott said nastily. He gave Stemp a narrow-eyed glare. "Who are these contacts?"

"As I said before, their identities are redacted to protect them."

Dermott waved a hand at our group. "Everybody here

has top-level security clearances."

"Nevertheless, it would be irresponsible of me to divulge identities while our interview is being recorded. I have no control over who might view the recording."

Dermott leaned forward, eyes narrowing. "Sounds to me like you're hiding something. Like maybe somebody's paying you big bucks for a coverup."

Stemp met his gaze steadily. "I have not been offered, nor have I received, any tangible compensation from anyone other than the Department; nor have I been coerced or persuaded by anyone to protect these identities."

"Is that true?" Dermott demanded.

"Yes." Green light.

I stared at Dermott's forehead, beaming a psychic command at him with all my strength. *Drop it. Just drop it, for fucksakes.*

"Who are these contacts to you?" Dermott snapped.

My heart plummeted.

Stemp met Dermott's gaze without an iota of expression. His bland colouring and amber eyes reminded me all over again of a rattlesnake. Not the most venomous snake in the world, but don't ever step on one.

Somehow I managed not to clench my fists in desperate hope. Maybe Stemp still had an ace up his sleeve. Maybe he could-

"I have provided all the information I can supply without endangering the lives of my contacts," Stemp said in a voice as precise and dispassionate as a scalpel incision. "I will answer no further questions on this topic."

Dermott's unholy grin lit up his entire face. "Refusal to answer a question during a lie detector interview," he breathed. "Automatic suspension pending full inquiry."

Drawing himself up, he began, "Charles Randall Stemp, I'm relieving you of duty-"

"He already said it'll put his contacts in danger if he identifies them!" I stared Dermott in the eye. "That question has already been answered."

Holt raised his voice. "Shut up, both of you!" In the momentary silence that followed, he directed one final question at Stemp. "Would revealing the identities of your contacts provide us with any information that could potentially help us investigate or identify Volslav or any other criminal organization, any of their members, or any part of their operations?"

"No." Stemp answered without hesitation, and the green light confirmed his answer.

Holt rose. "Okay, that was my last question. We're done."

"Like hell we are!" Dermott's voice snapped out like a whip. "I outrank you, Holt." He turned his sneer on me. "And I outrank you, too. As second-in-command to the DCO, it's my responsibility to relieve him of duty if I have doubts about his competence or reliability. And regulations state that refusing to answer a question in a lie-detector interview is an automatic suspension and NSIRA inquiry." Puffing out his chest, he turned to Stemp. "Charles Randall Stemp, I'm officially relieving you of duty. Give me your weapon, badge, and security fob. You'll be notified when your hearing has been scheduled."

"Very well," Stemp said without inflection. "Holt, please disconnect me from the lie detector, and I will remove myself from the premises."

"After you give me your badge and gun." Dermott smirked.

"Of course," Stemp agreed, as though they were discussing nothing more important than the weather. "Holt? If you would?"

Holt had been watching Dermott with a speculative expression. At Stemp's second request, he went over and unhooked the headdress of electrodes.

Looking up at the security camera, I said, "Let the record show that I disagree with this course of action."

"Noted," Dermott snarled. "Now get the hell out of here. I'm escorting Stemp out."

"I'll serve as a witness," I said as coolly as I could manage while holding back a spate of profanity that would have singed the eyebrows right off Dermott's smug face.

Dermott shrugged. "Suit yourself. Stemp, give me your weapon and badge. Now! I won't ask again."

"It was unnecessary to ask the first time," Stemp observed as he rose and unfastened his holster. "I am familiar with the suspension procedure."

"Is there anything personal from your office that you want to take home with you?" I asked.

"Thank you for asking, but no," Stemp replied as he moved toward the door. Dermott gripped Stemp's elbow like a self-important bouncer as we emerged into the hallway.

I swallowed dark amusement at the thought of how quickly and easily Stemp could dispatch Dermott in hand-to-hand combat if he chose. I'd pay good money to see Dermott flat on his ass. Especially right now, in the middle of the corridor, under the curious stares of the other office denizens.

As we passed Spider's office he shot me an anxious look, and I gave him a tiny headshake and mouthed 'later'.

"I'll wait in your office," Holt told me.

I followed Stemp and Dermott to the end of the hall and downstairs to the main lobby, watching with distaste while Dermott clutched Stemp's elbow and swelled with conceited victory. Stemp's quiet dignity made Dermott look even more idiotic than usual.

At the security wicket, Stemp handed over his fob to Leo the security guard, and accepted the sign-out sheet in return. As Stemp signed, Dermott announced with unnecessary volume, "Stemp's suspended. Seal his office and rescind all his clearances and security access, effective immediately."

Leo's hand froze over the lever that would rotate the sign-out sheet back to his side of the bulletproof barrier. He shot me a 'what-the-hell?' look, and I gave him a tiny shrug and nod in return.

"Uh... okay," Leo said as he reclaimed the sign-out sheet and Stemp's security fob. He raised his voice to match Dermott's volume. "Have a nice vacation, Director. Enjoy the warm weather."

"Thank you, Leo," Stemp replied. "I shall." With a polite inclination of his chin to Leo and me, he disengaged Dermott's clinging hand as though brushing an insect off his sleeve, and strolled out the door with his usual imperturbable composure.

Dermott turned to glare at me. "Get back to work."

I turned my back on him without a word and climbed the stairs.

By the time I completed the short trip to my office, my phone was already ringing. The sight of Leo's extension made my lips quirk up despite my worry for Stemp.

Holt was sprawled on my sofa, feet on my coffee table. I shot him a look as I picked up the phone and said, "Hi, Leo."

"Aydan, what the bleep's going on?" Leo demanded in a

hushed voice, and I imagined him glancing around the silent lobby and hiding his lips behind his hand.

"Dermott got Stemp on a technicality," I replied quietly. "I hope it's nothing serious, but it looks as though the National Security and Intelligence Review Agency will probably conduct an inquiry."

"What kind of technicality?"

I shook my head, smiling in spite of myself. "Sorry, I know gossip is your lifeblood; but I can't tell you."

"It's not gossip," he countered. "It's timely information that I need in order to do my job effectively."

"Good one, Leo. Let me know if that actually works on anybody."

He chuckled. "It was worth a try. Never mind, I'll find out somehow."

"I'd be shocked if you didn't." Hanging up, I turned to Holt and lowered my voice. "What did I tell you?"

He frowned. "About what? Putting my feet on your coffee table?"

I waved that away. "I don't give a shit. I meant, about Dermott having it in for Stemp. Which way do you think NSIRA will jump?"

Holt shrugged. "Nobody knows. They write their own rules. But if they don't have some underlying agenda, and if Stemp can convince them that his contacts' lives are in danger if their identities are disclosed, they'll probably reinstate him."

Letting out a long breath, I flopped into the chair across from him. "That's what I'm hoping." After a moment, I added, "You did a good job with the interview. Dermott looked like a-"

Too late, I remembered they were friends. I clamped my

mouth shut.

"...fucking moron," Holt finished my sentence morosely. "I wish he'd quit doing that. He's not stupid. He just gets caught up in the moment and runs his mouth without thinking. No filters."

I shrugged and attempted diplomacy. "At least you always know where you stand with him."

Holt grunted. "Got that right." He squared his shoulders. "But he's right, you know. Refusal to answer a question under the lie detector is an automatic suspension and NSIRA inquiry."

I couldn't stop the snarky comment that popped out of my mouth. "Yeah, you'll stand up for Dermott and his stupid technicality, but you wouldn't stand up for Stemp even though he'd already proved he was innocent and he'd given a good reason for not answering."

"Stemp doesn't need me to stand up for him." Holt glowered at me. "He doesn't need you to stand up for him, either. NSIRA doesn't give a shit what we think; and all you did was piss off Dermott."

"Probably true," I agreed, subsiding with a dismal sigh. "And now he's in charge."

CHAPTER 6

Preoccupied by my worry over Stemp, I was half-heartedly dealing with routine emails when my phone rang.

With a glance at the call display, I picked up. "Hi, Leo."

"John Kane's here to see you."

"Thanks, I'll be right down." I hung up the phone and hurried down the hallway to poke my head into Holt's office. "John's here. I'll get him signed in and bring him up." Hiding my worry behind a casual tone, I added, "Do you want to do the interview here or in a meeting room?"

"Meeting room," Holt decided, getting to his feet. "Do you want to ask your boyfriend any relationship questions while he's hooked up to the lie detector?"

I gave him my best frosty stare. "I'm not even going to dignify that with-"

"I'm not trying to be an asshole." Holt's gaze wavered, then dropped. "I'm just saying. A couple of simple questions under the lie detector would have saved me a lot of grief." As he pushed past me toward the door, his next words were barely audible. "And my partner's life."

My heart contracted with sympathy. "Sorry," I said softly to his retreating back. "Thanks."

He nodded and kept going. I followed him out, turning in the opposite direction to head for the stairs. As I descended, my lips turned up in a wry smile. This must be what it was like to have a brother. Holt was irritating as hell sometimes, but he had my back when it counted.

My smile widened as I stepped into the lobby and spotted six feet four inches of magnificent male standing at parade rest beside the security wicket. Kane relaxed into a smile and came over to meet me.

Our hug was short and probably looked platonic to Leo, but Kane's hard-muscled back scorched my palms and set off a chain reaction in other, more interesting parts of my body. I drew back before I could give in to the temptation to grope him.

"Wow, you're hot." The words popped out before I could consider them.

A teasing smile crinkled the sexy laugh lines around his grey eyes. "Should I say thank you?" he rumbled in his panty-vibrating baritone.

I managed a casual-sounding laugh. "I actually meant temperature-hot; but both ways are true. So, you're welcome."

Kane chuckled. "I stopped in at the Melted Spoon, and it was such a nice day I decided to walk from there." He gestured at the T-shirt stretched deliciously across his broad chest and bulging biceps. "Black shirt in the sun."

"Yeah, it's great," I breathed. Tearing my gaze off his sculpted cotton, I amended, "Um, the weather. Nice and warm." I spun and headed for the security wicket, adding over my shoulder, "Come and sign in. We'll be in the second-floor meeting room."

After completing the formalities at the security wicket, Kane and I headed for the stairs.

As we climbed, Kane lowered his voice. "Who's 'we'?"

A shiver of misgiving shook me. What if his interview went sideways like Stemp's had?

Matching his volume, I replied, "Holt and me. Dermott might sit in; I don't know. We're still trying to figure out how to find that weapons expert you consulted a year and a half ago. I'm sorry I couldn't tell you over the unsecured line, but this is a lie-detector interview. Holt's idea."

Kane's years as a top agent stood him in good stead. He didn't stiffen or change the tempo of his stride, and his expression stayed casual. Only the sharpening of his eyes betrayed him as he asked, "What is the scope of the interview?"

"Only that one mission."

His easy nod looked as though the answer meant nothing to him, but I knew better.

"We'll just confirm the facts in your report and see if there's anything else you can tell us," I went on. "I'm sorry you had to drive four hours round trip for what'll probably be a ten-minute interview. It really wasn't urgent."

I damn well hoped it would be a ten-minute interview. God, what if John was hiding something?

Well, something *else*. Besides the fact that he'd murdered the man who had kidnapped his son.

But that wouldn't come up in this interview.

Please don't let it come up...

"No problem," Kane replied as we gained the top of the stairs, causing me a moment of confusion while I tried to remember what I'd last said. "I'm happy to help if I can; and I wanted to come up to Silverside anyway. The timing worked well for me."

When we entered the conference room Holt looked up from beside the lie detector, his steely gaze an arrogant challenge. "Kane."

John eyed him steadily, cool amusement quirking the corner of his mouth. "Holt."

Holt thrust out his chest. "Have a seat."

Kane sat, and Holt strapped the headdress of electrodes on him.

When everything was connected, Holt said, "We'll be recording this interview via the security system." He indicated the glowing red light under the tiny camera in the corner of the ceiling. "Do you consent to having this interview recorded?"

"Yes," Kane said.

This time, Holt recited the entire Police Warning word for word, confirming Kane's waiver of his right to a lawyer and his understanding that everything he said could be used as evidence.

I gulped. There would be no NSIRA inquiry if this interview went to hell. John was a civilian now. He'd be arrested on the spot.

Holt eyed Kane in silence, apparently hoping to establish dominance. Kane met his gaze without discomfort, his strong square features composed in the unreadable expression I called his cop face.

"Tell us everything that happened after Dawn White contacted you a year and half ago," Holt said.

Kane responded, "After Dawn contacted me using an old telephone code, I replied using the same code to tell her the coast was clear. Then she came to my house in Silverside. I had faked a relationship with her when I had been undercover as an arms dealer seven years earlier, and she said she wanted to resume our relationship." He stared straight at Holt, focused on his report.

Or maybe he was avoiding my eyes.

"In order to maintain my cover, I went along with it," Kane went on. "Once Dawn was confident that I was still interested in her, she revealed her guess that I had killed Yana Orlov in order to acquire the ultrasound death ray weapon from Fuzzy Bunny. Dawn offered to broker a deal between me and Volslav to sell the weapon. She said that in order to gain Volslav's trust, the weapon would need to be evaluated by a weapons expert she knew. I agreed to that, hoping the expert would be able to tell us where the original weapon was constructed and who had the prototype drawings."

Holt held up a hand to halt him. "Is everything you've said so far true?"

"Yes." The green light shone, and I tried not to slump in relief.

Dammit, Kane wouldn't lie about any of this. And Holt wouldn't have any reason to ask anything but mission-related questions. Everything would be fine...

The door swung open and Dermott strode in.

Oh, God, not again.

Flopping into one of the chairs, Dermott studied Kane with a sneer. "Any lies yet?"

"No," Holt said shortly. He turned back to Kane. "Go on."

"I contacted Stemp for instructions," Kane said. "He got permission from Upper Command to bring the weapon to the meeting. Dawn, the expert, Stemp, and I met in an automotive shop in Drumheller late in the evening after the shop was closed. We believe the expert recognized Stemp in his George Harrison cover, but he also provided some useful information about the weapon. Immediately after the meeting, Stemp took the weapon out of the country and I continued to work with Dawn, hoping to gain more intel."

"Is that all true?" Holt interrupted.

"Yes." Green light.

Holt made a 'go on' gesture, and Kane resumed his account. "I didn't realize at the time that Volslav was an organization, not an individual. And I didn't know then that Dawn was part of Volslav."

Dermott interrupted this time. "Is that all true?"

"Yes." When the green light shone, Kane went on, "I also didn't know that Dawn had arranged a meeting with Fuzzy Bunny's men later. They abducted us and tortured us, trying to get information about the weapon's whereabouts." His face tightened. "I thought at the time that Dawn was trying to play both sides by selling me out to Fuzzy Bunny. Now I realize she was probably using me to try to gain intel about her competitors."

He fell silent, his jaw clenching. When he spoke again his voice was emotionless, but ghosts darkened his eyes. "They started by torturing Dawn. When she couldn't reveal the weapon's location, they started on me." He met my eyes at last. "That's when Aydan rescued me."

"Tried to rescue you," I said tightly, fighting off the blood-soaked memories. "Too late to keep you from getting shot."

"Just in time to step in front of the bullet that would have killed me," Kane countered.

"Aw, that's sweet," Dermott snarled. "I'm all choked up. Was everything you said true?"

Kane eyed him without expression. "Yes." Green light.

"Did you have any further contact with Dawn White?" Dermott demanded.

"No." The green light shone its agreement, and Kane added, "She died of her injuries."

Holt took over again. "Before we discovered the evidence six months ago, did you know Tawny Harchman, Dawn White, and/or Yana Orlov formed either all or part of Volslav?"

"No." Green light.

"Have you ever been associated with Volslav in any way?"

Kane frowned. "N... Uh, yes...?" The green light shone, and he added, "I investigated Volslav quite a few times. I guess that counts as being associated with Volslav."

"Other than your investigations, have you ever been associated with Volslav in any way?" Holt sounded like he could ask these meticulous questions all day long.

I, on the other hand, was pretty sure I was on the verge of a stroke. My heartbeat thumped in my ears.

"No," Kane said, and the green light agreed.

"Have you ever revealed information that could be harmful to our country or our national security, or that could have aided Volslav in any way?"

"No." Green light.

While Dermott and Holt asked question after question, I willed them to stay focused on Volslav. Concentrating on my breathing, I did my best to fake relaxation.

After an endless time that I didn't dare monitor by checking my watch, Holt and Dermott ran down.

"Is there anything else you can tell us about the weapons expert?" Holt asked with a touch of hopelessness.

"No," Kane replied. The green light shone, and he added, "I'm sorry. I only met the expert that one time. Dawn never mentioned his name or how she was connected to him. I could try to recreate his face in virtual reality, but after this long, I don't know how helpful it would be. I might come close; but probably not close enough for our..." He bit off the pronoun that was no longer accurate and substituted, "...your facial recognition algorithms to use."

Holt brightened. "That's worth a try. We could get Stemp to do the same, and that would give the algorithm a range to work in."

"Except Stemp is suspended," I pointed out.

Holt and I both glanced at Dermott.

Dermott stood up, scowling. "Nice try, Kelly." He transferred his truculent gaze to Holt. "Get Kane a temporary fob. Make sure he doesn't get into anything else while he's in the VR network. And keep Kelly out of the network until he's gone. I don't want them collaborating."

With that vote of non-confidence, he strode out.

Holt rose, looking irritable. "End recording," he said loudly. The tiny red light on the camera blinked off, and he added, "I'll be back in ten minutes with the fob. Ask your questions, Kelly." He left, closing the door behind him.

I let out a long breath, sagging in my chair.

Kane eyed me curiously. "Are you all right?"

"Fine." Even though I could see that the camera wasn't active, I couldn't help peeking into my ever-present waist pouch to consult my bug detector. Its light glowed a reassuring green, and I showed it to Kane before returning it to its berth. Letting out another gust of air, I added, "That was just... really nerve-wracking."

"Why?" A flash of hurt darkened his clear grey gaze. "Did you think I had falsified my reports?"

"No, of course not! I just... fuck it, never mind." I got up and went over, reaching for the headdress of electrodes. "I'll take this off you."

His big hand closed gently around my wrist, stopping me. "What questions do you want to ask me?"

"I don't have any questions. Holt was just being an asshole."

John searched my face. "I don't think so. He was serious. What is this about?"

"Nothing!"

I tried to free myself, but Kane laced his fingers through mine and studied me, seeing too much as usual.

"You're defensive and angry," he observed. "That means you're feeling threatened." His hand tightened on mine. "Is Holt threatening you?"

"No, of course not! Holt's fine. He's just..." Giving up, I blew out a breath and flopped into the chair Holt had vacated. "Look, Holt got burned by bad intel in a mission a few years ago. The intel cleared a woman who was pretending to be his girlfriend, and then she double-crossed him. The op went to hell, Holt got injured, and his partner was killed." I muttered the next sentence as quickly as possible, my face burning. "So he thinks I should ask you relationship questions to make sure you aren't lying to me."

I dared a glance at Kane's face, expecting him to look as uncomfortable as I felt.

Kane looked thoughtful. "I see." After a moment, he added, "I think that's an excellent idea."

CHAPTER 7

"I'm sorry-" My apology was already half-uttered when Kane's words registered. "You *what?*"

Kane smiled. "I think it's an excellent idea. Ask me anything you want. And for once in your life, you'll be able to believe everything I tell you."

I drew myself up, hiding my fear behind affronted dignity. "I most certainly am not going to grill you like a criminal about our relationship. Or lack thereof. That's pathetic. And it's an insult to you." I made another attempt to reach for the lie detector's clasp.

Kane didn't let go of my hands. "When you need answers, asking questions is never pathetic. And it's no more insulting than the fact that you don't trust me in the first place." Before I could reply, he added gently, "And that's not insulting at all. My life used to depend on my ability to lie convincingly. You'd be insane to trust me without some kind of corroboration." He hesitated. "It would really mean a lot to me if you'd do this."

Torn, I stared at him in silence.

I should do what he wanted.

No, *fuck* that. Doing what a man wanted was how I had gotten trapped in that long-ago marriage with my abusive ex.

And my questions would tell John too much. If he knew

what mattered to me, he could use it against me. I shivered at the memory of the dark satisfaction in my ex's eyes, his vicious words battering the weak vulnerable places I should never have revealed.

"Aydan?" John's voice caressed my ears, and I realized I had squeezed my eyes shut. "Aydan, please. Ask me."

My spine bowed under the weight of old pain and the fear of new.

John's voice firmed. "Aydan, I love you and I want you in my life. The only time I've ever lied to you was when I said that all I wanted was casual sex with you. I want more than that, and I won't lie to you again. But no matter how our relationship changes..." He hesitated. "Or doesn't change... I won't be angry with you or blame you. I won't try to manipulate you. I would never intentionally do or say anything to hurt you. I envy the closeness of your relationship with Arnie, but I would never interfere with it. I would give my life for you, and for him." After a short silence, John added, "I think that covers it. Please ask me if everything I just said was true."

My throat closed.

What if he'd slipped a lie in there? I couldn't bear to pick apart his statements and ask him which were true and which were false.

But what if it was all true? Where did that leave me?

Fucking terrified, that's where.

"Aydan?" I could hear the resignation creeping into Kane's voice.

A rap at the door and the click of the latch made my eyes pop open.

Holt strode in. "You done here?"

"No," Kane snapped. "Please ask me if everything I just

said was the truth."

Holt's gaze bounced from Kane to me and back again. His voice was hard and level as he demanded, "Was everything you just said true?"

"Yes." Kane's single word was filled with relief.

Unable to look away, I stared at the bright green glow on the lie detector's panel.

All true.

Oh God.

"Kelly?" Holt stooped, frowning into my face.

I opened my mouth, but nothing came out.

Holt turned a thunderous scowl on Kane. "What did you tell her?"

"The truth," Kane said.

"You fucking-"

At last my muscles obeyed me, and I laid a hand on Holt's sleeve. My words came as if from a long distance away. "He didn't tell me anything bad. I'm just... just... thinking."

Holt's frown deepened. "You look like you're going to puke."

I shook my head. "I'm fine."

Lucky I wasn't hooked up to the lie detector, because that was a lie of galactic proportions.

Avoiding Kane's gaze, I focused on Holt. "Got the fob?"

Mercifully, he took my cue. "Yeah." He handed the network access fob to John, then removed the lie detector's headband from John's temples and took a seat. "Kane, I'll come into virtual reality with you. Don't bother finding a sim room. Just do it in the portal so I can supervise you and still make sure Kelly doesn't come in."

John nodded. His eyes took on a thousand-yard stare

and his shoulders slumped as he entered the brainwave-driven virtual reality network, and a moment later Holt did the same.

I sat staring at the two blank-faced men while my mind raced in a frantic attempt to process Kane's declarations.

It was no use. When they both snapped back to reality and sat up a few minutes later, my heart was still hammering my ribcage.

I summoned a smile. "How did it go?" By some miracle, I sounded normal.

"Fine, I think," Kane replied with an answering smile as he handed the fob back to Holt. "I did my best, anyway. If Stemp adds his recollections, it should give the algorithm enough to go on."

"Thanks," Holt said. Standing, he picked up the headdress of electrodes and advanced on me. "Your turn, Kelly. I need to cover all the bases."

A deluge of icy adrenaline spurred my pulse into a ragged gallop.

Dammit, that was completely irrational. Holt was only going to ask about the weapons expert. I hadn't lied about that. Calm the fuck down.

Kane rose. "I'll wait outside."

"No, stay," Holt said. "I want a witness, and you'll do as well as any. I'm not going to ask anything outside your knowledge or former security clearances." He picked up the phone. "Yeah, Leo? Holt here. Activate the recording camera in the meeting room again, and give me voice command override." The red recording light blinked on, and Holt added, "Thanks", and hung up.

I sat like a statue while he attached the lie detector to my temples.

Don't-panic-don't-panic-don't-panic...

"Do you consent?" Holt's words interrupted the yammering voice in my brain.

"Uh... What?" My dry mouth barely formed the words.

Holt frowned. "Do you consent to having this interview recorded," he repeated slowly.

"Oh. Um... yes." The green light shone.

Apparently Holt was having doubts about my ability to focus. He cautioned me about suspension and an NSIRA inquiry if I lied or refused to answer, and repeated the entire Police Warning loudly and slowly. I waived my right to a lawyer without a qualm. No lawyer in the world could help me if Holt asked the wrong questions.

Holt flopped into his chair with a glance at the closed door. Was he hoping Dermott would stay away? Or hoping he'd return to ask the questions that would destroy me?

"Okay, just a few quick questions," Holt said rapidly. "Did you ever see or meet the weapons expert?"

That was an easy one. "No."

Green light.

"Do you have any idea who he might be?"

"No." Another green light.

"Have you ever hidden, deleted, altered, or failed to accurately report information you discovered in the internet?"

"No."

When the green light shone, Holt's shoulders relaxed. I gave him a half-smile, knowing that had been one area where he couldn't quite bring himself to trust me.

"Have you been doing your best to find information about the weapons expert?" he asked.

"Yes." Green light.

"Okay, that's it." Holt glanced up at the camera. "End recording."

The red light blinked off.

"One last question," Holt said with another glance at the door. "Off the record."

"What does that mean?" I asked.

He scowled. "It means it's a personal question and you don't have to answer."

He glanced at Kane as if debating whether to ask him to leave, but turned back to me instead. Holt's gaze was as hard as ever, but his question showed a vulnerability I'd never thought he would reveal.

"Have you ever lied to me?"

I gaped at him. Partly I was replaying our past interactions so I could answer accurately; but mostly I was awed by his courage. He had just done what I couldn't. And he'd done it in front of Kane, with whom he'd been jockeying for dominance. The guy had balls of steel.

And now I felt like a pathetic coward.

Shaking myself back to the situation at hand, I stammered, "Um... I don't know. Maybe? I can't remember everything I ever said to you."

Holt made an impatient gesture and began to speak, but I kept talking. "I've never lied to you about anything work-related or mission-related. And I've never lied to you about anything that could turn out to hurt you personally or professionally. I would never do that."

His gaze bored into me. "Is that all true?"

"Yes."

He glanced at the green light and smiled. "Thanks." He got up. "That's it for my questions. Kane, she's all yours." He let himself out the door.

In the echoing silence that remained, I sat frozen in shock.

Kane's eyes were wide, his usual cool composure gone. "I..." He swallowed and tried again. "I can't quite believe he just... left you..." He made a tentative gesture toward the lie detector. "...like this. With me."

I couldn't believe it either. I had thought I could trust Holt.

I'd been wrong.

Kane blinked. "Well. I..." He broke off, his face softening. "Aydan, don't look so terrified. We're not doing this." He got up and came over. "Here, I'll take that off you."

Stiffening my spine, I managed words even though they came out in a croak. "That's not fair to you. You answered my questions. You get to ask yours."

He hesitated, his hand poised over the fasteners at my temple.

"Do it," I grated. "Ask."

John stood as if frozen. Only a tiny tremor in his fingers betrayed him.

He sucked in a breath and let it out slowly. "Aydan..."

A long pause stretched between us, tightening the air. Tightening every muscle in my body with the effort to stay seated instead of leaping up, bursting out the door, and sprinting far, far away.

When John spoke, his words were so quiet I had to strain to hear.

"Do you want me out of your life?"

Of all the questions he could have asked, that was one I'd never expected.

"No!" The answer burst out before I even had a chance to consider it. "Of course not!"

The green light shone, and Kane's rigid posture relaxed so fast he had to steady himself with a hand on the table.

His swallow was audible, his voice husky when he spoke. "That's all I need to know." He unbuckled the lie detector's headband and tossed it onto the table as if ridding himself of a snake.

We were staring at each other in the ensuing silence when a rap at the door heralded Holt's return. He strode in without waiting for a response again, his too-perceptive gaze evaluating us in an instant. My face felt cold and numb, and John was looking a bit pale, too.

Holt's lip curled in a sardonic smirk that didn't quite hide the concern in his eyes. "You two don't deal with the truth very well, do you?"

Kane's composed façade returned instantly. "Are you finished with your mind games?"

"For now." Holt repacked the lie detector in its case and changed the subject. "Hey, Kelly, did you look at our airline reservations yet?"

Switching mental gears with an effort, I mumbled, "Um, no. Haven't had time."

"Departure is at one o'fucking-clock in the morning," Holt complained.

That was enough to jerk me back to reality. "What? *Tonight?*"

Holt snorted. "Technically it's 'tomorrow', just like Stemp promised. That asshole."

"Shit. So I'll have to leave home no later than..." I did some rapid mental math. "Nine-thirty tonight to get to the Calgary airport by eleven-thirty."

Holt nodded. "Yep. Want to carpool?"

"If you're driving."

"I wouldn't ride in your piece of shit when I could be driving my Quattro. I'll pick you up at your place at nine-thirty." He strode out carrying the lie detector.

CHAPTER 8

Before awkwardness could descend between Kane and me again, Spider tapped on the open door of the meeting room, his brow furrowed.

He gave Kane a quick uncertain glance before turning to me and lowering his voice. "Aydan, what's going on? I heard..." He glanced at Kane again and didn't finish the sentence.

"I'll wait for you in the lobby," Kane said. "If you'll be wrapping up for the day soon?"

I checked my watch. Nearly five o'clock. "Um... yeah, I guess. Go on down, and-" I broke off with a sigh. "Shit, I keep forgetting you don't have clearances anymore. I'll walk you down and sign you out. Spider, I'll be right back."

"I'll be in my office," he agreed, and withdrew.

The awkwardness returned full-force while Kane and I walked down the corridor. I kept my eyes trained to the front, torn between the urge to sneak a sidelong glance at him and the almost-overpowering desire to turn tail, hide in the women's washroom, and pretend none of the past half-hour had happened.

Kane cleared his throat. "Aydan..."

I didn't turn to look at him, but my pace might have increased a bit.

Kane hurried after me, laying a gentle hand on my arm. "Stop panicking. Nothing has changed between us."

"Okay, good. That's good. Good to hear." I cornered hard into the stairwell and jogged down, arriving in the lobby with breathlessness that had little to do with exertion. Sucking in a lungful of air, I pasted on a casual expression and headed for the security wicket as Kane caught up.

We completed the signout process in silence. As I spun the clipboard back to Leo behind the bulletproof glass, I finally summoned the courage to look Kane in the eye.

Okay, fine; I looked him in the chin. Courage is relative.

"I'll be down in a few minutes," I said, my voice still about half an octave too high. "See you later." Giving him a dorky half-wave-half salute, I scurried for the stairs.

At the top, I strode down the corridor, powering past the open door of Spider's office with a jaunty wave and an excuse. "Bathroom break; be right back."

Safely locked into a toilet cubicle at last, I hunched over, wrapping my arms around myself and fighting to control my breathing.

Okay, calm down. John said nothing had changed from his point of view. Everything's okay. We're just friends. Friends with benefits, now and then. Nothing more. Nothing's changed.

Everything had changed.

"Oh, God." My quiet groan bounced back at me from the tiled walls.

I straightened. Fuck this. I was nearly forty-nine. Not the messed-up twenty-two-year-old who'd married a narcissistic abuser. Not the even-more-messed-up thirty-something who'd married the next liar that came along, because I'd believed I didn't have a choice.

John wouldn't force me or manipulate me. I knew that now. I *knew* it, goddamn it. It was a fact. Proven by infallible technology.

Technology I'd managed to game in the past...

"Shut up!" The echo of my too-loud words made me wince, but I squared my shoulders and left the bathroom with my head held high.

Inside Spider's office, I swung the door shut and sat.

"What's going on?" he demanded. "I heard Stemp got suspended, and Holt and Dermott were questioning you and Kane under the lie detector. Is there... is this some kind of witch hunt?"

"No, it's okay. Stemp has been suspended, but it's just a technicality." Crossing my fingers to dilute what might turn out to be a lie, I went on, "I'm sure NSIRA will reinstate him as soon as they have a chance to interview him. And Holt just wanted to question Kane and me with the lie detector because he has trust issues. I think he feels better now that he knows nobody's lying to him."

"Oh." Spider's anxious gaze searched my face. "What was the technicality? Do you think..." He glanced toward the door and lowered his voice. "Is this just another of Dermott's tries at getting promoted to Director?"

"Yeah, I think so." I put on my most confident voice. "But I don't think it'll work. Stemp refused to answer a question under the lie detector, so it was an automatic suspension and inquiry; but he'd already made it clear that lives would be at stake if he answered. Holt questioned him really thoroughly, and Stemp wasn't lying about anything. He only refused to answer that one question, and Dermott shouldn't have asked it in the first place."

"Oh." This time Spider's single syllable came out on a

breath of relief, and he slumped back in chair. "Good. Any word on when the inquiry might be?"

"No idea. I hope NSIRA will be quick about it, but who knows?" I sighed and rose. "I guess I'd better go and see if anything in my email is about to blow up."

Spider jumped up, too. "I'm heading home."

I glanced at my watch. "On the stroke of five. That's a first. I think you do more overtime than your whole department put together."

"Usually I love my work and I lose track of time." He moved toward the door, bouncing on the balls of his feet as though he might break into a run. "But the last few days have felt like the longest days *ever*."

I chuckled. "Get going." As he spun and hurried out, I raised my voice. "Say hi and good luck to Linda for me. By the time I get back, you might be holding a new baby."

"That would be *so awesome*!" His excited voice drifted back to me, but by the time I made it to the doorway he was already disappearing down the stairs.

Smiling, I strolled back to my own office. As I pulled up my email, I half-hoped to find something urgent that would keep me until, oh, maybe... nine PM? But for once my inbox was devoid of emergencies.

I should look at the likeness of the weapons expert Kane had created in virtual reality, though. Leave no stone unturned. A good agent would be thorough like that.

I ignored the small perceptive voice in the back of my mind that muttered 'That's an avoidance tactic, and you're a chickenshit'.

Thank goodness I could use my security fob to pop into the VR network pain-free, instead of using the tiny secret network circuitry that gave me such crushing headaches.

Leaning back in my chair, I slipped into virtual reality and headed for the file repository.

The 3D image showed a middle-aged man. Maybe in his early forties, he was white with short medium-brown hair graying at the temples and thinning on top. Behind thick glasses, his eyes weren't blue enough to be blue or gray enough to be interesting. Average height; average build; soft around the middle without quite burgeoning into flab.

"Smile," I commanded the construct.

Its lips drew up, revealing completely ordinary teeth. Shit. It would have been nice if he'd had a distinctive gold tooth or something.

"Rotate."

I hadn't expected anything out of the ordinary, and that was exactly what I saw. Just an average-looking middle-aged guy from the front, back, and sides.

Kane's accompanying description didn't help. No limp, no apparent mannerisms. Hell, I would have been happy if the guy even had obnoxious body odour, but the only thing Kane had noted was that the expert had seemed intensely focused on the weapon and avoided eye contact. Hardly surprising for a guy who was examining a stolen classified weapon.

With a sigh, I banished the simulation and returned to the real world.

So. That had used up fifteen whole minutes.

Switching back to my email, I printed my travel documents. Departure at 1:05 AM from Calgary, with a fifty-minute stopover in Montreal. Total flight time of six and a half hours, which would land us in Halifax at about ten-thirty AM local time after travelling all night. Joy.

At last I couldn't rationalize any more dawdling, and I

dragged my reluctant feet out the door.

In the lobby, Kane rose with a smile. "It's not even five-thirty. That wasn't too bad."

"It's a nice change to be leaving on time." I kept my body language relaxed as I headed for the security wicket.

"Are we still on for Fiorenza's?" he asked as I signed out. Maybe noticing the flinch I thought I'd hidden, he added tactfully, "I know you have to get ready to leave tonight. It's fine if you're too busy."

Booting my inner coward in the ass, I summoned a smile. "You know I'm never too busy to eat. Do you want a ride over?"

"Thanks, but I'll drive myself. I have an appointment at seven PM so I'll need my wheels." He held the door for me as we left the building. I sidestepped abruptly, letting out an involuntary grunt as we crashed into each other.

"Sorry," I mumbled, my cheeks burning. "Habit. I always..." I made an ineffectual gesture. "I was preoccupied and I just..."

Kane chuckled. "I know you always make random sidesteps when you're exiting into an exposed position. I should have confirmed so I knew which way to sidestep myself." He fell into step beside me. "No need to apologize."

"Thanks." I gave the small-town street my usual once-over, automatically checking for threats before turning toward my car. "See you there," I threw over my shoulder.

Kane gave me a wave and strode down the street toward the Melted Spoon, and I got into my car wondering if I should just head for the highway and keep on driving.

But I didn't. Sitting in Fiorenza's parking lot, I gave myself a pep talk while I waited for Kane's SUV to appear.

It was long past time I got over my commitment phobia.

If I didn't want to be in a relationship, I only had to say 'no'. It was stupid to freak out. I was fine.

When the big black Expedition pulled into a parking space, I got out and went over, concentrating on the warmth of the sun on my shoulders and trying to ignore the tremor in my knees.

Kane swung out of the driver's seat and smiled down at me. "You're here. I thought you might make a break for freedom."

"Of course not."

He quirked an eyebrow, and I abandoned the pretense. "Okay, I considered it."

"But here you are." His voice softened. "Your courage is one of the many things I admire about you."

Hiding my surge of combined pleasure and fear, I gave him a grin. "I hate to admit it, but it's not courage. Just hunger."

"That'll do." He dropped an arm lightly across my shoulders, turning us toward the restaurant but keeping his distance so the gesture didn't feel smothering. "Let's eat."

Getting settled in our booth and deciding on our entrées used up several minutes. After the waitress had departed with our orders, it took all my will not to squirm while I avoided Kane's gaze.

God, how was I going to get through this meal?

"Aydan." John touched my hand, but didn't grasp it. "I'm sorry I blindsided you. I certainly didn't come up here planning to blurt out all those things. I know how phobic you are about relationships and commitment, and I should have handled the situation better."

I managed to meet his eyes for a moment before dropping my gaze. "It's okay. I don't see how you could have handled it any differently. I'm sorry for the way I reacted. And I'm going to smack Holt, first chance I get."

"You don't need to apologize." I could hear the smile in his voice. "And I don't think you should smack Holt just yet. I know how traumatic this was for you, and I am truly sorry for that; but I'm also..." He drew in a breath and let it out slowly. "Glad that you can finally believe me. And relieved that you haven't been secretly wishing I'd just go away."

"I'm sorry I've given you such mixed messages," I mumbled.

"Aydan..." He reached over to gently raise my chin. When I reluctantly met his gaze, he repeated, "You don't need to apologize. You don't owe me anything. And I don't expect you to trust me."

I scowled. "Well, I damn well should, after all we've been through together. And I'm not delusional enough to think you somehow fooled the lie detector."

"No, of course not. I know you believe me now. But trust is earned. It takes a long time." John gave me a bittersweet smile. "It might not even be in your power to give, and that's all right. I meant it when I told you nothing has changed between us."

Swallowing hard, I searched his face for lies and hidden agendas. "So... that's it? No expectations? No... demands?"

"No." He sighed. "I'm sorry for all the times I've made demands on you in the past. My family counselling sessions with Alicia and Daniel have helped me recognize some of my entitlement issues, and I've been working with a counsellor on my own, too. Not because I'm trying to force things to work between you and me, but because I need the clarity to go forward with... life. A career change." He made a frustrated gesture. "Everything."

I seized the opportunity to steer the conversation to safer ground. "Right, so what have you been up to lately? Still volunteering at the Red Cross?"

CHAPTER 9

With that uncomfortable conversation out of the way, the meal passed easily while Kane and I caught up with each other's lives and enjoyed Fiorenza's famous lasagna and garlic bread. A couple of times Kane eyed me as though he wanted to broach some difficult topic, but each time I successfully steered the conversation elsewhere.

When at last we stood outside the restaurant in the lengthening rays of the sun, he smiled down at me. "It was great to see you. There are a couple of things I'd like to talk to you about..." He held up a calming hand as I took an involuntary step backward. "I recognized your avoidance tactics earlier, and I understand you need some time to process. We can talk another time. Meanwhile..." He held out his arms. "Hug from a friend?"

"Absolutely." Relieved, I moved into his embrace, enjoying the strength of his arms and the pressure of his muscular body against mine.

John nuzzled my ear, sending a hot shiver down my spine. "Kiss from a friend?" he murmured.

"Maybe," I mumbled against his T-shirt. Delivering a little nip to the base of his shoulder, I traced my lips up the hot skin of his neck and across the erotic roughness of his five o'clock shadow.

Our lips met, and I forgot my own name.

Several heated moments later, I pulled away, breathless. "It's a good thing Fiorenza's is a family restaurant. Otherwise I'd be climbing you like-"

I broke off when a couple with two small children came out of the restaurant. As the parents shepherded their offspring past us, Kane finished my sentence with a mischievous glint in his eye. "A monkey after a banana?"

I grinned. "Nope. A plantain." The family moved off, and I added, "They're bigger and harder than bananas."

His voice dipped into a sexy rumble. "Any time you feel like climbing my tree, I'm available."

The memory of his magnificent wood flushed heat through my entire body, and I suppressed the urge to smack myself. Why the hell was I flirting with him?

My baser self spoke up. Because he's sizzling hot, and he's mind-blowing in bed. Let's get some of that. *Lots* of that.

But my better self reminded me that shit happened whenever John and I hit the sheets, and it was usually because I should have thought things through instead of jumping him.

I forced myself to step backward. "Unfortunately, I have to go home and pack. For what, I have no idea. Damn Ian Rand."

Kane's flirtatious smile vanished. "You're working with Rand again? Where are you-" He bit off the question. "Sorry, I shouldn't ask."

"It's okay. We're flying to Halifax. And as usual, Rand is jerking us around. He wants to meet but he won't say why. Or even when or where." I aimed a short vicious kick at a pebble, sending it skittering across the parking lot. "He gets on my last goddamn nerve."

Kane's mouth quirked up. "Most women find him irresistible."

"Most women haven't had to work with him. I guess if I only wanted to screw him, everything would be fine."

"That implies screwing him might be somewhere on your priority list," Kane pointed out cautiously.

"Oh, I want to screw him all right," I snarled. "Right up the ass with my Glock. Sideways."

Kane winced. "And on that note, I'll head for my meeting." He took me in his arms again and pressed his lips gently to my forehead. "Good luck. Stay safe."

"Thanks." I hugged him back and pulled away before the horny devil on my shoulder could convince me to do something extremely enjoyable but ill-advised.

Back at my farm, I frowned at the open suitcase on my bed with Stemp's words replaying in my memory.

'Come disguised and be prepared to shift your appearance several times'.

How much of a disguise did I need, and for what? If I had enough time, I could make alterations to my appearance that could confound even a facial-recognition scanner. But that was no damn good if Rand wanted quick-change tactics to evade a tail. For that, I needed to be able to duck into a washroom and emerge less than a minute later with enough superficial changes to convince a human observer that I wasn't the person they were following.

And if that was what he had planned, it meant our lives could be on the line. Which Rand would consider a delightful lark.

Damn him and his love of subterfuge.

His sparkling moss-green eyes with their heavy fringe of dark lashes hovered in my memory. Combined with his chiselled physique, cut-glass British accent, and effortless charm, it was no wonder women found him irresistible. Hell, half the time he managed to make me smile even while I was contemplating ways to murder him and make it look like an accident.

But if his damn shenanigans ended up killing me, I'd come back and haunt the bastard forever. I blew out an irritable breath and started shoving clothes into my suitcase.

When my surveillance system pinged on the dot of nine-thirty, I checked my wrist monitor to see Holt's red Audi Quattro turning into my lane. I met him in the driveway, slinging my carry-on bag into the back and taking my place in the passenger's seat.

We drove in silence along the dusty gravel road, with Holt flinching each time an upflung stone banged the car's undercarriage.

"That damn gravel knocks fifty bucks off the value of this car every time I drive to your place," he complained as we reached the highway and turned west.

"You offered to drive."

He scowled and snapped the sun visor down to block the red-gold rays of the setting sun. "So how do you figure Rand's going to screw us this time?"

"Whatever it is, I'm sure it'll be creative," I replied gloomily. "This disguise thing makes me nervous. He never gives me the whole picture. Only enough to keep me from actually dying while he entertains himself watching me flail."

"It's not just you," Holt growled. "He always wants to be the fucking star of the show, so he never gives anybody enough intel. Someday he's going to withhold the wrong information and it'll blow an op. Probably kill him to boot."

I shrugged. "As long as it doesn't take us with him."

"Got that right."

We fell silent.

An hour later I was blindly watching the yellow lines spooling past on the dusky highway when Holt's voice jolted me from my thoughts.

"Talk to me."

"Uh... about what?"

"I don't give a shit." He yawned and scrubbed a hand over his face. "I'm falling asleep here."

"I can drive if you want."

"Fuck no. Nobody drives my car."

"So you'd rather crash your fancy car because you can't stay awake?"

He shot a glower at me before returning his attention to the road. "No, I'd rather my fucking passenger makes herself useful and talks to me."

I grinned. "See, you're already more awake. Annoying you is my super-power."

"Fuck off."

Recognizing the not-too-heated words as Holt's version of a conversational gambit, I replied, "I had a look at Kane's sim. That weapon expert is so forgettable, I doubt if I could even pick him out of a lineup; let alone spot him in a crowd."

"Yeah. I'm hoping Dermott will bring Stemp in to add to the image. Then Webb can start combing the internet with facial recognition software."

"He won't."

Holt frowned. "Webb won't?"

"I meant, Dermott won't bring Stemp in." I bit my tongue before I could add, 'He's too insecure to back down'.

Holt blew out a breath. "You're probably right."

Silence fell again.

What the hell could I talk to Holt about? I had no idea what he did in his spare time. He was a martial arts expert, so he obviously worked out a lot. Beyond that, all I knew about him was that he liked flashy cars, single-malt scotch, and expensive designer clothes. And watching hockey on TV.

How pathetic. I'd been working with the guy for nearly two years.

Holt's abrupt voice interrupted my internal recriminations. "If Kane's hiding something, you shouldn't cover for him."

"What?" I gaped at Holt. "What makes you think I'm covering for him?"

"You looked pretty shell-shocked this afternoon after your lie detector session."

I grunted, but didn't reply.

Holt gave me a sidelong glance. "If he told you something that bad, it's your duty to report it."

"I told you this afternoon, he didn't tell me anything bad," I snapped. "And it had nothing to do with the Department. It was just personal shit. And he didn't tell me anything I didn't already know."

Holt drove in silence for a few moments before remarking, "Knowing the truth for sure, is a hell of a lot different than just thinking you know it."

And that was what made him a top agent. He rarely bothered to turn his skills on me, but he definitely knew how to use them: The perceptiveness; the open-ended statements followed by attentive silence, engineered to make his subject volunteer information.

I said nothing.

The silence stretched into minutes, and I guessed that was the end of our conversation. Smothering a yawn, I crossed my arms, settling my chin on my chest.

"Christ, Kelly!" Holt's sudden bark made me twitch.

"Jeez! What the hell?" I demanded, clutching my chest in an attempt to slow my thumping heart.

"Don't you ever let anybody in? It's no wonder you keep two boyfriends; you have to play them off against each other to make sure neither of them gets too close!"

"What the..." I stared at his rigid profile, unable to summon words. Giving my head a shake, I tried again. "Okay, obviously I'm missing something here. What are you trying to say?"

Holt shot me a ferocious glare. "I'm your fucking partner, and we're going into an op with an asshole we can't trust. If you don't have your head in the game, we could both end up dead. So if there's something you're trying to deal with, tell me. Maybe I can help. Or at least I can listen while you figure it out for yourself."

I blinked at him, shocked and inexplicably touched.

"Um," I said after a moment. "Thanks. Sorry. I wasn't trying to..."

Okay, yeah, I was trying to shut him out. But it was only fair to offer him some reassurance. After all, his ass was on the line, too.

Blowing out a breath, I attempted an abridged version of the truth. "I have trust issues..."

"No shit," he muttered, but I pushed on.

"...and I'm phobic about commitment. John told me

how he feels about me this afternoon." I gulped. "Under the lie detector. I already knew, but hearing it out loud freaked me out. But we talked afterward and everything's fine, so you don't have to worry. I have my head in the game."

Holt drove without speaking for a while. Maybe he was assimilating what I'd told him, or maybe hoping I'd keep talking just to fill the silence.

"That's it?" he asked at last.

"Yep."

Holt shook his head. "You're an idiot. Do you know what I'd do for that kind of relationship? Knowing you can completely trust-" He bit off the sentence with a scowl. "Fuck."

I touched his arm. "I'm sorry."

"Forget it." After a moment, he added, "You must have gone through some bad shit if it messed you up so much you can't even trust a guy who passes a lie detector interview."

My throat went tight. I didn't reply; mostly because I couldn't speak.

Holt's voice softened. "So I probably triggered the hell out of you, leaving you there for Kane to question. Sorry."

"Forget it." My voice came out in a croak, and I cleared my throat and tossed out a lame diversion. "Are we there yet?"

"You better not tell me you forgot to pee before you left home," he groused, switching to the safety of our usual insults.

"That's why we're taking your car," I rejoined. "You've got leather seats, so I can pee right here and it'll just run off."

"If you piss in my car, I will fucking end you."

Relaxing, I grinned. "You won't even know I've done it until we get back from Halifax. By then it'll have cooked in the sun for two days. Your car will reek for the rest of its life."

"Anybody ever tell you you're an evil bitch?"

"All the time." After a moment, I added, "Anything else on your mind?"

"No." He hesitated, then offered a subject change of his own. "What did you bring for disguises?"

"I've got some makeup and prosthetics, but who knows whether there'll be time to use them. Other than that, I've got a couple of hats, different sunglasses and bags, reversible jacket, shorts I can wear under a skirt; quick-change stuff like that."

Holt nodded. "Me, too."

Grinning, I teased, "Shorts you can wear under a skirt?"

He shot me his superior smirk. "We're going to Nova Scotia. I brought my kilt."

"Your... kilt." I didn't quite know what to do with that. "Okay. I didn't realize Holt was a Scottish name."

"It's not. But my mother's maiden name was Mackenzie and I have five uncles who are proud wearers of the tartan. I had my first kilt before I could walk."

Imagining a tiny tartan-swaddled Holt, I grinned. "That's awesome. But... don't you think you might, um... stand out a bit if you're wearing a kilt? Even in Nova Scotia, I don't think they wear kilts regularly."

Holt the Magnificent eyed me with lofty superiority. "That's the whole point. If somebody's watching a guy in pants and he goes into a bathroom, they're not going even going to glance at a guy who comes out wearing a kilt."

I couldn't argue with that.

CHAPTER 10

The flight to Halifax felt interminable. Holt fell asleep immediately but I fought for a comfortable position, dozing and waking. As the hours dragged on, I had to fight the urge to kick him in the shin just so he could share my misery. When we landed in Montreal I got off the plane to stretch my legs, but the short-lived freedom made returning to my cramped seat even worse.

At last I managed to fall into a deeper sleep, only to be woken seemingly minutes later by the 'fasten seatbelts' announcement. I cheered up a bit when I realized that I'd actually slept for almost two hours, and we were on our final descent into Halifax.

Holt stirred and stretched, rasping a hand across his stubbled chin. He glanced over, but didn't say anything stupid like 'good morning'.

As we entered the terminal, he finally spoke. "Let's get separate rental cars. Meet you at the hotel for lunch."

I nodded and we split off to different rental counters. The helpful clerk offered directions to the nearby hotel, and I headed for the parking lot grateful that I wouldn't have a long drive in my sleep-deprived condition.

When I got out of my car in the hotel parking lot, Holt was leaning against a shiny SUV. He eyed the sedan I'd rented and gave an approving nod. "Good, we're covered no matter whether we need power and cargo space or anonymity. I figured you'd go for the boring econobox."

I considered demanding what the hell he meant by that, but I was too damn tired. By the time I had finished processing the thought, he was speaking again anyway.

"I called in. Rand just made contact. He wants us to meet him in front of the Tim Horton's in the food court at Mic Mac Mall in Dartmouth, at noon. He wants us in disguise, ready to do a quick change. He'll be wearing a red windbreaker."

"Noon!" I consulted my watch with alarm. "It's already after eleven! How long a drive is it from here?"

"About twenty minutes."

"Shit!" I shot a despairing glance at the hotel. "We'd better see if we can check in early. If we can't, I guess I'll have to change my clothes in a gas station bathroom. And I'm starving, so I'll have to grab something from a vending machine to eat while I'm driving. Did he give us any other information?"

Holt snorted. "Are you kidding?"

"For shit's sake! So we don't know whether he wants to hand off a slip of paper or get backup in a shootout!"

"The analyst said he sounded rushed, so he probably wasn't in a location where he could talk for long." Holt shrugged. "Guess we'll find out. What's your first disguise?"

"Old lady. Big baggy dress, gray wig with a kerchief to hold it on, and those sunglasses with the full sides that fit over top of another pair of glasses. Under that I'll wear another shorter dress, and under that I'll have shorts and a tank top. I'll put my hair up so I only have to whip off the wig for the second change, and then I'll let my hair down for the last change. And I've got different sunglasses, totes, the usual."

"Okay, good. I'll do an old guy for my first disguise, too. Windbreaker, fedora, same big-ass sunglasses as you've got. Baggy pants with my kilt and shorts underneath. The kilt is the second change, and we can both finish up with the summer-shorts look." He headed for the hotel lobby. "Come on."

To my surprise, we were actually allowed to check in early. We got adjoining rooms, and I was tying a drab kerchief over my wig when there was a tap at the connecting door.

When I opened it, Holt eyed the sagging hem of my voluminous grey dress and burst out laughing.

"Bedroom slippers?" he demanded.

I dropped a curtsey. "They're perfect. They're so big I can wear my running shoes inside them. The Velcro lets me whip them off in seconds, and they flatten easily to hide in a tote bag." Stooping slightly, I limped over to the mirror to slick on some unflattering flesh-coloured lipstick, then donned my sunglasses, pulled my mouth down into a dismal thin-lipped grimace, and turned to Holt with a 'ta-da' gesture.

"Christ, Kelly, you're scaring me."

"Look who's talking. It looks like you're wearing a giant diaper under there." I gestured at his baggy pants with their frayed cuffs and worrisome brown stain on the ass. "Your fly is open."

He grinned. "I know. So nobody will be looking at my face. Do you know where we're going?"

"Yeah, I checked the satellite map and the mall interior map. If I park in the southwest corner and you park in the southeast corner, we'll be equal distances from the food court and have some options if we have to move fast one way or the other."

"Sounds good." Holt joined me at the mirror to put on his fedora, carefully arranging the wispy strands of the gray wig that was attached to it. Sliding on his full-coverage sunglasses, he offered me his arm.

I picked up the cracked plastic handbag that held my Glock G26, waist pouch, lipsticks, flipflops, and a couple of folding tote bags, then took his elbow while we toddled out to our respective vehicles.

Following the prompts of the onboard navigation system, I drove with one hand and gobbled vending-machine snacks with the other. The closer I got, the faster my heart thumped.

Surely Ian wouldn't have told us to meet in a food court if he thought there would be any danger. So this should be safe.

Safe-ish, anyway.

Pulling into a parking slot at the mall, I took a few slow breaths that were supposed to be calming. In three minutes I'd get out of my car. Another five minutes to get to the food court.

Then what?

My pulse picked up and I drew in a few more long slow breaths while I mentally reviewed the floor plan of the mall. At least if I screwed up, Holt would be ready to take over.

But I wouldn't screw up. Everything would be fine.

Because things always went smoothly for me when Ian Rand was involved.

I barked out a short bitter laugh and climbed out of my car, clutching my handbag like the lifeline it was. As I limped slowly across the parking lot, my fingers tightened on the bag. Just a simple snap closure on the top. I could have my Glock in my hand in a second.

The humid sea-scented air and hot sun caused an unpleasant prickle of sweat under my three layers of clothes. When I stepped into the coolness of the mall, I let out an involuntary sigh.

A middle-aged woman held the interior door for me, remarking in a cheery Maritime twang, "Warm one, innit dear?"

I nodded and mumbled my thanks as I limped past her, keeping my back bent and my head down. Nearing the food court right on time, I slowed, rubbing my back and scanning for Ian.

Sure enough, his red windbreaker was easy to spot. He stood in front of the Tim Hortons kiosk, studying the menu sign above it.

Hobbling closer, I suppressed the urge to look behind me for Holt. He'd be there. Keep your head in the game.

I scanned the food court but didn't spot anyone who seemed to be watching Ian. Wandering closer, I plotted an erratic course while feigning rapt interest in the menu signs.

Just a few more steps...

Gazing up at the Tim Horton's sign, I trod on Ian's foot and stumbled, letting myself pitch forward.

The bastard didn't catch me.

I landed on my hands and knees with a pained grunt, and Ian immediately bent over me. "Ma'am, are you all right?"

"Orion, you're an asshole," I muttered in case he hadn't recognized me.

Raising his voice a touch, he said, "That was a nasty

tumble. Let's get you up." He slowly assisted me upright, whispering, "I'm being followed. I'm parked in the southeast corner of the lot, silver Honda Accord with an Avis rental sticker. In half an hour I'll go to my car. Fall back and follow me. I'll draw them into a dead end and you can box them in."

Ian eased me into a seat, and I waved him off.

"Stop fussing, young man," I croaked. "Thank you for your help, but I'm quite all right."

"Are you certain?" he asked, raising his voice for the audience. "Is there someone I can call for you?"

"No, no. My husband will be along in a minute. Go on with you, now."

Ian nodded and withdrew, making a beeline for the Tim Horton's lineup. I didn't turn to watch him. Instead I scanned the food court as though looking for my fictitious husband.

A few nearby people eyed fallen-old-lady-me with concern, but I couldn't spot anyone who seemed to be paying any attention to Ian. If he was being followed, his tail was a professional. Or maybe they were watching his car instead.

Tray in hand, Ian took a seat on the other side of the food court with his back to me. Holt still hadn't made an appearance. Where the hell was he?

As the thought occurred, he plodded into view. Just a sad stooped old man, wandering aimlessly.

I waved.

He ignored me.

I waved again but aborted the gesture, wondering if he was intentionally ignoring me because he wanted to stay separated. Dammit, I should have asked before we came in.

A young woman glanced between me and Holt, then

hurried over to him.

Holt raised a shaky hand to his ear as she spoke, and when she tried again her raised voice was audible from where I sat.

"Your wife had a fall, sir. She's sitting over there-"

"There's no need to yell," Holt shouted testily. "I'm not deaf, young lady!"

The woman spoke again at lower volume.

"What's that?" Holt cupped a hand behind his ear again. "Stop mumbling!"

The woman gave Holt a patient smile as she touched his sleeve and pointed in my direction.

I waved again.

Holt nodded his thanks to the woman and limped over. Easing into the seat beside me, he bellowed, "Are you all right, Martha? That young lady said you fell! I told you to bring your cane!"

Matching his volume, I shouted, "I tripped! That silly cane couldn't have helped! And I told you to wear your hearing aids!"

"I'm not deaf!"

Shaking my head as if in resignation, I said loudly, "Let's get some ice cream."

"Why would you scream? I told you, I'm not deaf!"

I pointed at the Dairy Queen kiosk. "Ice... cream!"

"Why didn't you say so?" Holt made a show of rising slowly before hobbling over to the Dairy Queen counter. The resulting transaction could be heard across the food court as Holt bellowed his request for two small cones. Then he paid for them using pocket change, counting painstakingly aloud.

When he returned, I thanked him at the same volume, and we ate our ice cream in merciful silence. The traffic in the food court looked completely normal. Nobody seemed to be paying any attention to us or Ian. Studying the crowd, I was pleased to see that several women were wearing fashionable dresses with running shoes. Hooray for the practical Maritimers. My next disguise would fit right in.

Ian finished his meal, dropped his tray at the pickup station, and strode out of the food court. A few people drifted out after him, but none seemed to be following him.

When we had munched the last of our cones, I laid my hand on Holt's arm and pointed to the washrooms. He nodded and rose slowly, bracing himself against the table to help me up and offering his arm as we limped to the washrooms.

We split off to the men's and women's. Inside, I chose a stall at the far end next to an empty cubicle. As soon as the door was bolted behind me I took a sleek black tote out of my handbag. Whisking off my slippers, I stowed them at the bottom of the tote and quickly topped them with the big sunglasses, wig, kerchief, and old-lady dress. The plastic handbag went in last, and I unfastened it so my Glock was easily accessible in the top of the tote. Choosing a conservative shade of lipstick, I ran it blindly over my lips and adjusted my large but fashionable sunglasses before shouldering the tote and stepping out of the cubicle.

After a moment at the sink to wash my hands and touch up my lipstick, I headed for the exit with the hem of my flowery dress fluttering around my knees.

Strolling down the mall, I took out my phone and checked the time. Ten minutes left. Nobody was close enough to hear me. Matching my pace to the surrounding shoppers, I hit the speed dial for Holt.

He answered on the first ring. "Yeah?"

"Can you talk?"

"Yeah."

"Rand says he's being followed." I relayed the message, finishing, "He says he's going to draw his tail into a dead end and he wants us to box them in."

"Fucking marvelous," Holt growled. "There's nothing I like better than being the barricade in a shootout."

I sighed. "Yeah. I'll drive around to your side so I'm ready to move. Do you want to take point, or should I?"

"Does your car have a nav system?"

"Yes."

"Then I'll take point. Stay back a few blocks, and I'll give you directions by phone. If Rand's got a team on him, I don't want us both boxed in when the next car comes up behind us."

"Okay. Good luck."

CHAPTER 11

As I drove around the corner of the parking lot, Holt emerged from the mall. He was easy to spot, partly because of the striking blue-and-green tartan he wore, but mostly because of the gaggle of admirers trailing him. Apparently well-built men in kilts were an irresistible attraction for elderly women.

Pulling into a parking space, I grinned in spite of my tension. Holt was getting manhandled. Or, more accurately, woman-handled. One of the women pinched his ass while another slipped her fingers into the wraparound edge of his kilt.

Most of Holt's features were obscured by his fashionable dark glasses, but I could see his smile as he shook his head teasingly and disengaged the wayward hands. Then he blew the group a kiss and strode away.

For a moment I thought they'd follow him, and I snickered at the thought of Holt's discomfiture if I had to rescue him from a mob of sexed-up seniors.

Apparently they'd had their fun, though. They went back inside the mall, allowing Holt to get to his SUV.

As soon as he settled behind the wheel, I dialled his number again.

"Yeah."

"Did they tuck lots of big bills into your sporran?"

Holt snorted. "That wasn't my sporran they were groping. Next time I'm around little old ladies, I'll wear it on my hip so they don't have an excuse to fondle my junk."

"At their age, they don't need an excuse. They just go for it." When he groaned, I added, "And don't try to bullshit me. You loved every minute of it."

"Hardly-" He broke off. "Rand's moving. Putting you on speaker."

I toggled my phone to speaker, too, and dropped it into the cupholder so I had both hands free.

Ian's silver rental headed for the exit. After a short delay Holt followed, keeping several vehicles between them.

"See anybody following?" Holt asked.

"Too much traffic to tell." I eyeballed the distances. "I'm going to let you get onto the road before I pull out."

"Give it a bit longer," Holt countered. "If Rand's got more than one car on him, they'll be doing the same as us. I'd rather you show up too late than too early."

"Unless you're bleeding to death."

"Still rather have you show up later and be able to call an ambulance. No damn good if we both get shot."

On that cheery note, we fell silent.

Fighting the urge to follow, I watched Ian's car and Holt's SUV turn and disappear into traffic.

A couple of minutes later, Holt spoke. "Okay, come after us. We're eastbound on Route 111, Highway of Heroes." I had barely made it to the exit when he added, "Looks like we're turning already. Route 318, Waverly and Braemar."

Pulse picking up, I hit the brakes when the traffic light turned red. "Shit. I'm stuck at the light. How fast are you going?"

"Eighty klicks."

I blew out a tense breath. "You'll get too far ahead. Does it look like anybody's following Ian? Or you?"

"Too soon to tell. Several vehicles exited with us. Okay, we're on Braemar and the speed limit's only fifty. You should be able to catch up."

My light turned green at last, and I accelerated through the intersection and changed lanes, heading for the highway.

Holt spoke again. "Rand's turning right on..." He hesitated, apparently not able to read the street sign yet.

I merged onto the highway and hit the gas. Already the Braemar exit was in view.

"...Maple Drive," Holt reported. "Two cars turned after him, a white sedan and a red SUV... Damn, nearly lost him. He turned right again. Still two vehicles following. The street is..."

Merging onto the Braemar exit, I sucked in a breath and let it out slowly, trying to ease my shoulders down from around my ears.

"...Fourth Street. Shit, there he goes left. The street name's..."

As I navigated the cloverleaf and emerged on Braemar, Holt added, "...Major Street. The SUV just turned off. The white sedan is still... nope. It turned off, too." A moment later, he went on, "Black sedan just pulled out between us, maybe it's the next tail. White SUV behind me. Where are you?"

I consulted the onboard navigation. "Coming up on Maple Drive."

"Pull over!"

Holt's sudden bark surged adrenaline into my veins. I tapped the brakes instinctively, but there was nowhere to stop.

"I can't, it's single-lane!" I cleared my throat and added in a calmer pitch, "I'll swing onto Maple and-"

"He's turning right," Holt interrupted. "Onto the main highway, going west again."

"Shit!" I took the corner fast and nosed into the first driveway.

There was no place to hide on the short lane of the small residential lot. The homeowner looked up from mowing his lawn, and I swore softly as he headed my way.

Powering my window down, I waved and called, "Sorry, I'm just a bit lost. I needed to pull over and look at my map."

I had been hoping he'd go back to his mowing, but no such luck. Damn helpful Maritimers.

"Where're you goin'?" he asked. "I can give you directions."

"Main Street," Holt said loudly.

"It's okay, I've got my friend helping me," I told the homeowner, lifting my phone as proof and trying not to clench my teeth.

"Main Street, y'say?" the man drawled. "Well, now, you could keep goin' the way y'are and turn right on Fourth Street and follow it down along Major, or you could-"

"No, dammit, Waverly-Braemar again!" Holt shouted. "Stay where you are!"

Straining every muscle in my face, I summoned my sweetest smile for the puzzled homeowner. "Sounds like I'm about to be rescued. I don't want to take up any more of your time, but would it be okay if I just stay in your driveway for a few minutes? My friend should be here to get me soon."

"Sure, honey, that's fine. You just let me know if you need any more help."

"Thanks." I held onto my smile and gave him a wave as he turned back to his lawnmower. Powering up my window again, I hissed into the phone, "He's gone. Where are you?"

"Retracing the same route. Rand should be passing your position pretty soon. Stay put until I tell you. The black sedan didn't follow him through the last turnoff, but the white SUV is still behind me."

Craning my neck, I spotted a silver sedan heading north through the intersection. "Rand just passed."

Holt let out a breath. "Okay. Give me a good head start before you follow."

Checking the quiet street, I backed out and headed for the intersection as Holt's SUV drove through, closely followed by the white SUV.

Was that SUV following Rand? Or Holt? Surely they wouldn't hang on Holt's bumper like that if they were following him.

But who knew?

Counting seconds that felt like minutes, I fought the urge to pull out right on the tail of the white SUV.

Thirty long seconds later I eased up to the intersection, signalling right, and let a car and a motorcycle pass through before I turned.

"I just turned onto Braemar," I said.

"Okay. We're still heading north. Still got the white SUV behind me. Unless they've got a hell of a team, that's the only possible tail I can-" He broke off. "Rand's turning left."

Heart thumping, I peered ahead but couldn't see past the vehicles ahead of me.

"Locks Road," Holt added.

A glance at the navigation system confirmed my position, and I went back to peering fruitlessly ahead.

A few seconds later, Holt said, "I'm turning now. And... the white SUV didn't. Do you have a visual?"

"Not y... Okay, yeah." Tension seized my shoulders. "A motorcycle turned in behind you."

"The road curves so I can't see behind me, but I'll keep my eyes peeled."

Checking the navigation system again, I added, "There are only two ways off Locks Road, both right turns. Lorway is the last one. If Rand doesn't take it, this is our dead end." Pulling into the turn lane, I braked and signalled left. "I'm going to close the gap."

"Roger that." Holt sounded calm, but I could hear the edge in his voice. "If shit's going to happen, it'll be soon. Anybody on your tail?"

I made the turn and accelerated, my knuckles whitening on the steering wheel. "Not that I can tell. Nobody followed me when I turned from Maple, so if there's somebody back there, they picked me up later."

My mind whirled through the twists and turns we'd taken. Could a team have successfully followed Ian, identified both Holt's and my vehicles, and managed to sneak up on us? It seemed far-fetched, but there was still that worrisome motorcycle...

"Rand just drove past the last right," Holt snapped. "This is it."

"On my way." I accelerated a bit more, tensely gauging the narrowness of the tiny residential street and the potential danger to its inhabitants. "If I can get there in time, I'll block the street just past Lorway."

"We're pulling into a park turnaround," Holt reported. "Rand's going around. I'm stopping on the other side. I see the motorcycle now..."

I held my breath, my gaze glued to the street and my teeth clenched on fear.

"Motorcycle went by me," Holt said. "Coming up on Rand... Rand's pretending to park."

Yanking the wheel around and slamming on the brakes, I screeched to a halt in someone's driveway and reversed hard, placing my car crosswise in the road.

"Road's blocked!" I snapped.

"Bike's coming at you!"

Holt's warning was superfluous. I could hear the throaty roar approaching as I threw myself out of the driver's seat and ran for cover behind a nearby parked car.

The motorcycle's engine slowed to a rumbling idle. Gripping my Glock inside my tote, I crouched and peered through the parked car's side windows. The slim rider glanced around, revealing a long shiny braid and red lipstick.

Ian's sedan accelerated out of the park. The rider's head snapped around, noting the vehicle bearing down on her and the one blocking her path. The bike snarled and laid rubber as the rider launched her bike up over the curb, through the shrubby underbrush beside the street, and down the road to freedom.

"Shit!" Straightening, I emerged from behind the car.

Ian got out of his vehicle and strode to meet me, his body language that of an indignant motorist impeded by an idiot.

I did my best apologetic cringe as he muttered, "Meet me in the lobby of the Halifax Westin." He raised his voice to an irritable shout. "Well, move it, then!"

Doing my best to look cowed, I hurried back to my car and did a three-point turn to drive toward the park turnaround. Ian cruised away in the opposite direction, flashing me a rude gesture.

"Asshole," I mumbled as I pulled into the park, past Holt's SUV.

"What's happening?" Holt's voice crackled over the phone, reminding me that I hadn't taken the time to hang up before I'd bailed out.

"Ian wants us to meet him in the lobby of the Halifax Westin," I replied as I parked on the opposite side of the lot. "I'm going to go for a walk here, to look normal and make sure nobody followed me."

"I'll do the same. Stay in phone contact so we both have backup."

"Okay." I got out and headed for the water. Glancing at the sign and pathway beside it, I added, "I'll walk along the canal."

Holt swung out of his SUV and strode in my direction, ignoring me as he replied over the phone, "Good. I'll take the path that parallels it. That way we won't be more than a few seconds from each other."

Carefully placing my phone in the top of my tote without hanging up, I shouldered the bag and strolled down the canal pathway. My hands were trembling, and I concentrated on taking slow deep breaths and letting them out evenly.

Calm. Breathe.

Birds sang, the wind played softly in the leaves, gaily coloured kayaks paddled up and down the canal, and pedestrians and joggers dodged each other with practiced ease on the narrow path.

Hyperaware, I concentrated on every footfall behind me. I stopped frequently to gaze out over the canal as though admiring the view, tensing when people approached and easing out a breath when they passed without incident.

After a short walk I came to a footbridge on my left, but

before I could decide whether to take it, Holt rounded the corner from my right and strode toward me.

Okay, decision made.

Ignoring him, I headed in the direction from which he'd come, turning onto the path he'd vacated. Hiking back toward the parking lot, I finally began to relax.

No bloodshed. So far, so good...

While I kept an obsessive watch on my rear-view mirror and the vehicles around me, the navigation system guided me across the tall bridge over the harbour, into Halifax, and through narrow one-way streets to the grand historic building that housed the Westin. I found a parking spot between two trucks and used the relative privacy to strip off my sweat-damp dress and let my hair down. The dress went into a large brightly-flowered tote that also accommodated my former black tote and its contents. I donned a pair of funky wire-rimmed sunglasses with bright blue reflective lenses, and swung out of the driver's seat.

As I strode across the parking lot, the warm brine-scented air kissed my bare arms and legs, swirling my hair around me. If I tried really hard, I could pretend this was a vacation.

Except I was so famished that my stomach was growling audibly. My hands quivered with a combination of nerves and hunger.

Straightening my spine, I pasted on a smile. A hotel as nice as the Westin probably had an amazing restaurant. And Ian owed me.

Holt arrived from the opposite direction as I approached the main doors. He had changed into his shorts, too: A well-fitting pair of khakis, topped with a short-sleeved collared T-shirt that emphasized his muscular physique. Female heads turned as we stepped inside.

Across the high-ceiling lobby, Ian rose from a lounge chair where he'd been sheltering behind an open newspaper. With barely a glance in our direction, he turned and headed for the elevators.

Holt and I followed without looking at each other. Inside the elevator we stood without speaking, staring blankly at the illuminated floor display like strangers.

When Ian disembarked, we followed. He stopped at one of the doors and flashed his trademark brilliant smile as he plied the cardkey. Throwing the door wide, he motioned us forward with the grand gesture of a man unveiling a priceless treasure.

Hand hovering near my Glock, I stepped inside and snapped a glance around the luxurious suite, alert for the slightest movement.

Holt did the same. Then we turned to face Ian as he closed the door behind us.

Holt frowned at him. "So it's a hotel room. Big fucking deal."

Ian scanned the large open area, his smile fading. Then he hurried into the adjoining room, and checked both bathrooms before turning back to us wearing an expression of consternation.

"Oh, bollocks!" he said.

CHAPTER 12

"What the hell is *that* supposed to mean?" Fuelled by stale adrenaline, my words came out in a hostile bark.

Ian gave a guilty start and avoided my glare by concentrating on a small electronic screen he'd pulled from his pocket.

Holt strode across the room to whisk a notepad off the table. He read aloud, "*I took your advice. Thank you. Goodbye.*" Lowering his dark glasses to give Ian the full force of his steely blue stare, he added, "Spill it, Rand."

"There's no time," Ian objected. "We have to..." He trailed off as he studied his electronic gizmo. Then he sank into a chair and massaged his forehead. "Oh, bollocks," he repeated quietly.

Stalking over to stand in front of him, I somehow managed not to grip him by the throat. Instead, I peeked into my tote and activated my bug detector. Green light. Clear. But just in case...

"Can we talk?" I demanded, accompanying the question with a rotation of my finger indicating the surrounding room.

"I've secured the room as best I can," Ian muttered.

"Okay." My voice came out soft but ice-cold. "Why are you here, who was here with you, why did they leave, and why did you bring us in here like you thought you were doing us a huge favour?"

Ian took out his cell phone, tapping and swiping. "Do you recognize this man?" he asked, turning the screen toward me.

Staring at the forgettable features of the man in the photo, I muttered, "Oh, for shit's sake. Is he dead?"

"No!" Ian gave me an affronted look. "He was sleeping. I could hardly ask him to pose for a photo, could I?"

Holt came to peer over my shoulder. "That looks like the damn weapons expert." When Holt focused on Ian's face again, his expression made me take a quick step backward to get out of his potential line of fire. "Rand," Holt said dangerously. "Explain."

"I will, I promise, but we have to find him. He can't have gotten far."

"Send that photo to this number," I snapped, and reeled off my burner number. When the phone vibrated a moment later, I forwarded the photo, then dialled Spider's direct line.

When he answered on the first ring, I rapped out, "Hi, Spider, I just sent you a photo. Fire up every facial-recognition algorithm you've got. We need to find this guy, pronto. He's somewhere within a..." Pausing, I fixed my glare on Ian. "What time did you see him last?"

"Five AM."

"Fuck." Turning my attention back to the phone, I went on, "...nine-hour radius of the Halifax Westin."

"I'm analyzing the photo and uploading the parameters right now," Spider assured me.

Returning my attention to Ian, I demanded, "Any idea where he might have been headed? What did he mean, 'he took your advice'? What the hell was your advice?"

"I... don't actually know." Ian gave me a self-deprecating smile. "I gave him quite a bit of advice, over the past week. I didn't think he was listening."

"The past week? You've had this guy for a *week*?" My voice rose to a near-shout. "*And you told him to DISAPPEAR?*"

"Aydan?" Spider's tentative voice dragged me back from the precipice of homicidal rage.

Getting a grip on my temper, I lowered my voice again. "Sorry, Spider, I didn't mean to yell in your ear. Check everywhere. I'll get more information."

Turning back to Ian, I asked, "What's his name?"

"I thought you'd know." Ian flinched at my glare and added, "He was using the name Rupert Weiss."

I relayed the information to Spider.

"I'm running algorithms on the public channels already, but I can start tapping into CCTV feeds, too, if this is top priority...?" Spider made it into a question.

"If you've got anything higher than 'top', this is it." I hesitated. "No, scratch that. It's not life or death. I hope." I covered the phone microphone so he wouldn't hear me growl, "Except for *Ian's* death", before uncovering it again to finish, "So don't drop anything that might put somebody at risk. It's high priority, not top."

"Okay. Are you and Holt safe?"

"Yeah, we're fine. Any baby news yet?"

His sigh rattled the phone speaker. "No. This baby is taking her time."

"Hang in there, then, and good luck. Talk to you soon." I disconnected and gave Ian the evil eye.

He returned a sunny smile, and I reflected sourly that being furious with Ian was like being mad at a helium balloon. He just kept brightly bobbing up again no matter how angrily I lashed out.

A gun or a knife might put a leak in his buoyancy, though...

"Penny for your thoughts?" Ian inquired.

"I'm deciding whether to stab you or shoot you," I growled, and stuck out my palm. "Where's my penny?"

Ignoring my hostility, he gave me a concerned look. "Storm, you don't look well. Your hands are shaking. Do sit down." He ushered me to a chair. Suddenly aware of my complete exhaustion, I sank down gratefully.

"Low blood sugar," Holt diagnosed. "Have you got snacks?"

"Yes." Ian scurried over to the mini-bar and returned with a bag of chips and a can of soda to each of us. "This should help."

I didn't have enough energy to hold onto my pique, and it was pointless anyway. "Stop calling me Storm," I said wearily, and gulped a mouthful of ginger ale.

The carbon dioxide made a prompt return in the form of a window-rattling belch, and I tore the chip bag open and stuffed a handful of chips in my mouth.

"Christ, Kelly," Holt said. "Way to embrace your inner pig."

I flipped him my middle finger and swilled more ginger ale, this time releasing the excess CO_2 in a sustained low-frequency rumble before gobbling more chips.

"Good God." Ian peered at me with fascination. "It's like Dr. Jekyll and Mr. Hyde."

Holt snorted. "Trust me, she's all Hyde. The Jekyll's just an illusion."

"But what a gorgeous illusion it is." Ian gave me his

flirtatious smile. "That untamed edge is positively... titillating."

Holt groaned and threw himself into a chair. "Stop trying to butter her up. It won't work. Now tell us what the hell's going on."

"I wasn't trying to butter her up," Ian protested. He arched a teasing eyebrow. "Though I would dearly love to butter her crumpet."

Emitting a growl, I reached into my tote and took out my Glock.

"All right, all right," Ian said hurriedly, even though he had to know I would never point a gun at anyone unless I intended to fire.

Then again, maybe he wasn't sure whether I intended to fire. I sure wasn't.

As I returned the weapon to my bag, he went on, "This is a little embarrassing, to be honest."

"Just start at the beginning," I advised with resignation, and tilted the chip bag above my mouth to capture the last crumbs.

"All right. Last week I was... doing my job," he began, and I suppressed an eye-roll.

Less than ten words in, and already the lies and evasions were starting.

"I had been working at a particular task for some time," Ian went on. "Ever since your esteemed Director dropped in for a visit last January."

Now we were getting somewhere. So Ian had been hunting Volslav on his side of the pond. I gave him a 'go on' gesture.

"However, I had been reassigned. Then, in the course of my travels, I encountered our mutual friend. I was just getting to know him when things got a bit sticky and I was forced to..." Ian hesitated. "...make a quick decision. Leaving Rupert behind seemed counterproductive, so I booked us a passenger cabin on a freighter that was departing from Liverpool within the hour." He inclined his chin toward me. "Hence my sustained contact with him over the past week."

I read between the lines. The situation must have been dire indeed if the high-flying Agent Rand had been forced to flee on a cargo freighter.

"So you've been on a slow boat all this time," I summarized. "Didn't that...limit your options a bit?"

"It did. And it necessitated some rather brisk activity when we disembarked at three AM this morning."

For the first time, I really looked at Ian. Despite his usual charming smile, he was pale and there were dark smudges of fatigue under his eyes.

Sympathy flooded in, and I forgave Ian for being himself. Again. He might be annoying at times, but he was a damn good agent. If he had lost control of the situation, likely nobody could have done better.

"Did you get done what you needed to do?" I asked.

"Yes. After some necessary evasive manoeuvres, we checked in here at five AM. I told Rupert to wait while I completed some... other activities, but apparently..." Ian sighed. "He developed some initiative. I really am terribly sorry."

I sighed, too. "It's okay. So what advice do you think he was following?"

"Honestly, I have no idea." Ian frowned. "He's a very... strange chap. Routine is everything for him. I was trying to prepare him for the kind of quick changes we might need to make if we were being pursued. He lives by detailed step-by-step instructions, so I left nothing out. But he was very resistant to the whole plan, so it never occurred to me..." Ian fell silent.

Holt finished his sentence with biting sarcasm. "It never occurred to you that you were giving him everything he needed to escape from you. Smooth move, MI6."

"He wasn't my prisoner. And in any case, I still have a tracking device on him." Ian hefted the small electronic screen. "He's simply out of range."

"What's the range?" Holt demanded.

"About twenty kilometres."

"It'd be pretty damn pathetic if he couldn't cover twenty kilometres in nine hours," Holt growled. "He could fucking *walk* it in that."

"Yes, well, I didn't intend to be gone for so long," Ian snapped.

"So why did you call us?" I asked. "Why not just call your Command and request an extraction team to meet your ship as soon as it docked?"

Ian gave me his sparkling smile. "But then I would have missed seeing you, Storm. I so enjoy our times together."

Giving up on ever getting him to use my real name, I focused on the issue at hand. "Yeah, whatever. And?"

He shrugged. "And Rupert mentioned that he wanted to get in touch with George Harrison. I thought you might oblige."

My stomach dropped.

Stemp's cover identity. Shit.

As soon as Stemp found out somebody was asking about George Harrison, he'd go overseas to protect his family. And that would make it look as though he was avoiding the

NSIRA inquiry. He'd look guilty as hell.

I hid my dismay behind a calm tone. "Why did Rupert want to talk to George?"

"I haven't the foggiest."

Holt hit the speed dial on his burner phone.

"Who are you calling?" I asked, trying to hide my alarm.

Holt scowled. "Who do you think?" A reply crackled from his phone, and he snapped, "Rupert Weiss is looking for George Harrison. Weiss could be on the way to Alberta by now. Check the airport security cameras, notify Dermott right away, and get eyes on Stemp." He hung up, looking grim.

Shit.

If I'd had a few minutes to think about it, I might have been able to figure out some kind of damage control, but now it was too late. Damn Holt's decisiveness.

"You got a problem with that?" Holt inquired evenly.

CHAPTER 13

"Of course I don't have a problem," I lied. Trying to hide my worry over Stemp, I changed the subject. "So, Ian, have you made any progress on Volslav?"

Ian flinched and glanced furtively around the hotel suite.

Infected by his paranoia, I activated my bug detector again. Still a green light.

I blew out a breath that was half relief, half annoyance. "You said you cleared the room. I just checked it again. It's fine."

Ian went over and turned on the television, then lowered his voice to match its volume. "Sorry. Habit."

"It's okay, I get it. So tell us what you've found out about Volslav."

He grimaced. "Nothing more than what your Department supplied six months ago. All trails seem to be cold in the U.K. and Europe."

"Not all trails, obviously. You found Weiss."

"He found me," Ian countered. "Earlier in the year I had spent quite a bit of time seeding bait in various places, but never a nibble. I had been on my other assignment for six weeks; and just as everything went pear-shaped, Rupert turned up. Hence our glamorous trip here." He shrugged. "At least nobody followed us."

"But you told us they followed you here," I pointed out.

"Ah." Ian avoided my gaze. "Yes. Well... not exactly."

More fucking lies.

Squelching my temper, I held my voice level. "What does that mean? *Exactly*."

"I *was* being followed." Ian gave me one of his brilliant smiles.

"But..." I prompted cynically.

"Not by anyone related to the op I left behind."

"So if it wasn't related to your op, it must have been related to Weiss," Holt interpreted. "Who was following you today? And why would they follow you instead of staking out this hotel to watch Weiss?"

Anxiety tightened my throat. "Shit, what if Weiss didn't leave of his own accord? What if he was taken? You said it would be uncharacteristic for him to-"

"No, no." Ian made calming gestures. "I'm quite sure he was safe here. Nobody followed us from the ship, I'm certain. Nobody knew where he was."

"Then how did your tail pick you up when you left here?" Holt demanded. "And if you knew you were safe here, why the hell did you leave?"

"That's confidential, my dear fellow," Ian said with another blinding smile. "But not to worry. We lost the tail, so all's well that ends well."

"If losing the man we've been hunting for six fucking months is your idea of 'ending well'..." Holt growled.

The suspicion that had been niggling at the edges of my mind flared into certainty.

"You were screwing around, weren't you?" I demanded.

"What?" Ian blinked at me, looking hurt. "Why, Storm, how could you even-"

"*Weren't you?*" My question came out like a whipcrack.

Ian opened his mouth, then took a closer look at my expression. He put on a sheepish face that might have been endearing if I hadn't been on the verge of murder.

"You do realize it's extremely inconvenient that you can always tell when I'm lying," he chided.

I said nothing; mainly because if I opened my mouth, all that was likely to come out was a shriek of fury.

"Yes, well..." Ian hesitated. "You have to understand, it was a very *long* week cooped up in that cabin with Rupert. The man has all these bizarre rituals-" His persuasive campaign choked into silence as Holt drew his gun and pointed it at Ian's knee.

"Kelly's too much of a soft touch to shoot you," Holt said conversationally. "But I will. And I can spin it so I get a fucking medal for it. Kelly will cover for me. Now, in five words or less, who was following you?"

Ian slumped. "My lover." Then he had the audacity to wink. "Or one of the many, at any rate."

Holt's other hand flashed upward. I barely glimpsed his tranquilizer pistol before he fired.

Ian dodged the instant Holt moved, but he was too late. His momentum carried him out of the chair to sprawl unconscious on the luxurious carpet.

Holding my breath, I jumped up and followed Holt into the adjoining bedroom. Holt swung the door shut behind us and we both drew in a breath of air untainted by tranquilizer vapour.

"What the-" I began.

"It was either that or a real bullet," Holt snapped. "And I wasn't sure you'd back me up."

I dropped onto the bed, hunching over to prop my

aching head in my hands. "I would, but the lie detector would trip us up."

The bed dipped as Holt took a seat, too. "Yeah, that's the only thing that stopped me."

After a minute of silence, I rose. "The aerosol should be dissipated by now. We've got at least fifteen minutes before he shakes off the injected trank, so what do you say we get set up to pry the full story out of that asshole?"

An evil smile spread over Holt's face. "What do you have in mind?"

Fifteen minutes later, I smirked down at the bathtub where Ian's unconscious body lay, restrained with Department-issue steel reinforced zip ties and naked except for his sexy bikini briefs.

Upending a bucket of ice cubes over his crotch, I grinned wolfishly. "I've wanted to do that for months."

Holt flinched. "Remind me not to piss you off."

"I'm going to get more ice." I headed for the door, still grinning.

By the time I returned with my brimming bucket, Ian was tugging at his bonds and mumbling slurred obscenities with his eyelids at half-mast.

Taking a seat on the toilet lid, I selected an ice cube and tossed it onto Ian's bare chest.

He twitched, toppling the pile of ice from his crotch. The cubes poured over his bare skin and into the bathtub, and he let out a yelp. My sadistic amusement mounted as he thrashed and squirmed, trying to avoid the cold in his semi-conscious state.

At last his eyes focused on me and he stopped struggling.

"Shtorm," he slurred. "S'not funny. Lemme go."

I laughed. "I don't know; I think it's funny as hell. Holt? Funny as hell, am I right?"

"Fuck, yeah. Funniest thing I've seen all year."

"Wha'..." Ian broke off as a violent shiver interrupted his words. "...d'you wan'?"

"The truth. But take your time." I dropped another ice cube on him. "I know how much you enjoy spinning out your stories. We've got nothing else to do today." I offered the bucket to Holt.

He selected an ice cube and lobbed it lightly at Ian's forehead. "That's worth two points," he observed as it bounced off.

"Left nipple is five points." I lobbed a cube of my own, but it landed an inch away, slithering over Ian's sculpted pec. "Damn. Missed. Your turn."

"Easy." Holt scored a direct hit on the nipple. "I call belly button. Ten points." He made his toss. "No fair, he moved."

"Them's the breaks." I flicked my ice cube, landing it with unerring accuracy. "Ha!"

"You've got a better angle from there," Holt complained.

"All right, all right," Ian interrupted, his slurring less noticeable as the last of the tranquilizer wore off. "Point taken; very funny. I'll talk. Let me out of here."

Ignoring him, I turned to Holt. "You're the one who called belly button in the first place, so stop bitching. I call..." Ian heaved in the tub, scattering ice cubes as he flipped onto his side. "Butt crack!" I cried with delight, and pegged an ice cube.

"You missed!" Holt taunted.

"Did not!"

"Did so! It bounced off. It didn't actually go down his butt crack. Watch this." Holt stepped to the head of the tub and fired an ice cube with a sidearm flick of his wrist.

"Ow!" Ian protested. "Leave off, you nutters! I said I'd talk!"

"And yet, he isn't talking," Holt pointed out. "This is fun. Left ear."

"Well, you could hardly miss," I groused as the ice cube landed. "You're standing right over him."

"Fine." Holt retreated a couple of paces. "Left knee... damn. Stop thrashing, Rand."

"All right, I admit it," Ian said loudly. "I left Rupert here and went to see a dear friend whom I haven't seen for quite some time..."

"Torso," I specified, and dumped half the bucket of ice on Ian.

Holt scowled. "Cheater. Give me more ice cubes."

Ian raised his voice. "When I left her house she wasn't ready for me to leave but I was quite worn out, so I- *eek!*"

"Now who's the cheater?" I berated the grinning Holt. "You can't just stuff a handful in his underwear like that."

"Says who?"

"Says the rules."

"I was a little distracted when I left," Ian said in a rapid high-pitched voice as he bucked and squirmed in an attempt to dislodge the ice. "I didn't realize she'd followed me until I was halfway back to the hotel, so I took evasive manoeuvres and then called your Department to arrange for your help."

"Because we've got nothing better to do than help you whenever you trip over your own dick!" This time I sent an ice cube winging at him with some shoulder behind it.

"Ow!" Ian yelped, beginning to shiver in earnest. "I'm s-sorry, but honestly, you w-weren't in any danger. I w-was almost certain I'd lost her by the time I g-got to the shopping centre; I j-just had to be positive. We had to m-meet anyway; and we had to m-make sure we weren't followed to the hotel. W-We wouldn't have d-done anything differently wh-whether or not you'd known the t-truth."

The fact that he was right did nothing to lessen my irritation.

"Was that your lover on the motorcycle?" I demanded. "Because if it was, she managed to outfox all three of us. Who is this woman? If you've put us in danger just because you can't keep your prick in your pants..."

Holt grabbed my wrist just as I whipped another ice cube at Ian full-strength. The cube fell short of the tub, and I blew out a breath of shame at my loss of self-control. I gave Holt a sheepish grimace, and he returned a shrug of absolution.

"That w-wasn't her," Ian assured us. "I'd n-never seen her b-before."

"Then why was she following us? And why did she run?" Holt demanded.

"I d-doubt if she w-was following us. It's a n-nice day. Perfect for a little motorcycle c-cruise to the p-park." Ian shrugged, shivering harder. "And you can h-hardly blame the poor g-girl for running. L-Look at it from her p-point of view."

Frowning into space, I replayed the nerve-wracking pursuit. The motorcycle hadn't appeared until late in the game. Professionals might have managed to follow us, but if there hadn't been any professionals in the first place...

"I'd have done exactly what she did," I admitted grudgingly. "A roadblock in front and some unknown idiot roaring up behind me? I'd have been out of there, too."

"R-Right," Ian agreed. "N-Now, I repeat: I'm t-terribly sorry. P-Please let m-me go."

Holt and I exchanged a glance.

"C-Come on, Storm. I'm g-getting h-hypothermic. L-Let m-me out."

I scowled at Ian's shivering goose-pimpled form. "Only if you promise to never jerk us around again. You tell us the whole story, up front. Always. If we ask you a question, you answer it directly, completely, and honestly. Every time. No more fucking head games. Agreed?"

"Of c-course. Storm, *p-please!*"

With a sigh, I leaned over and cut the ties. "Your clothes are on the vanity," I said and walked out without looking at him.

Holt followed me, swinging the door shut behind us. "You really think he'll keep his promise?"

As the shower came on behind us, I snorted. "That wasn't a promise, it was a lie. He won't hesitate to jerk us around. As much as he wants, whenever he wants, for as long as he wants."

Holt sank wearily into a chair. "I figured."

My burner phone vibrated, and I accepted the call with my usual generic greeting. "Yeah?"

"Spider here. I found Rupert Weiss."

Adrenaline singed my veins. "Where?"

Spider's resigned tone warned me that the news wasn't good. "We picked him up on the Halifax airport security cameras. He boarded a flight at 08:55 Halifax time. The flight landed in Calgary nearly an hour ago. When he got off, he had changed his clothes and he was wearing a hat that blocked facial recognition on the interior cameras; but we're having a chinook here and the wind is crazy. The algorithm picked him up when he stepped out of the airport and his hat blew off." Spider sighed. "But he left the airport on foot, and he didn't show up on any transit or taxi cameras after that. We lost him."

CHAPTER 14

Somehow I managed not to spit violent invective in Spider's ear. The phone emitted a small creak as my fist clenched, but I kept my voice calm.

"At least now we know which way he ran. I assume you've let Dermott know? And Stemp's prepared?"

"Yes, I told Dermott right away." Spider lowered his voice. "I called Stemp at home, too. I wanted to make sure he got the message."

"That's great," I said, even though it wasn't. "Thanks, Spider. Maybe your software will pick him up again."

"I've got the software watching every camera I can think of. Right now I'm checking ride-share activity in the area, but that's a really long shot."

I sighed. "Thanks, Spider. I knew you'd be on top of it. If you can't find him, nobody can."

When I disconnected, Holt eyed me morosely. "What's the bad news?"

"Weiss flew to Calgary, left the airport, and vanished an hour ago."

"Fuck!" Holt unleashed a vicious punch on the soft upholstered chair arm. "Fucking Rand!"

The bathroom door opened and Ian emerged, knotting his tie. His gaze bounced from Holt's scowl to mine.

"I thought we had no hard feelings," Ian said plaintively. "You had your fun; I apologized; we're square."

"Weiss landed in Calgary an hour ago," I spat. "And disappeared."

"Oh. That is unfortunate." Ian squared his shoulders. "Well, not to worry, I'll make it right. I'll check in with my Command and hop a plane this evening, and hunt him down with my tracker when I get to Calgary. Meanwhile, I know Aydan is desperately hungry. Let me buy you an early dinner." He gave us his sparkling smile. "Just to show I can let bygones be bygones."

Holt dropped his head into his hands. "You seriously think you're going to find him with your tracker? After half a day's head start? You moron, Calgary covers nearly a thousand square kilometres. *Just* the city of Calgary. Alberta is over half a million square kilometres. Your tracker is good for *twenty*! Twenty fucking kilometres!"

"Fortunately, the tracker is just a tool," Ian rejoined. "What I truly need to find Rupert is right up here." He tapped his temple. "Now..." Picking up the room service menu, he handed it to me with his most debonair bow. "Lady's choice."

I briefly considered whacking him with the heavy leather-bound folio, but I was too hungry. Opening the menu, I scanned it. "Greg, what do you want?"

"The most expensive fucking steak they've got," he growled. "And two glasses of most expensive single-malt scotch."

"Oh, that does sound appetizing," Ian agreed. "I'd love a scotch."

Holt gave him a death-glare. "They're both for me. Get your own."

I handed the menu back to Ian. "I'll have the steak, too. Medium-rare. And I don't drink when I have to drive, so you still owe me beer."

"I'll be happy to buy you all the beer you can drink, at the time of your choosing," Ian promised.

For once, I believed him. Not because he owed me, but because he'd seize any opportunity to put the moves on me when my resistance was low.

"The steak will do for now," I said.

Dinner should have been silent and awkward, but Ian was his usual scintillating self. Despite my best efforts to stay annoyed with him, I found myself laughing at his jokes and disarmed by his seemingly-sincere interest. Even Holt relaxed and joined in when the conversation turned to the inevitable shop-talk, peppered with the dark twisted humour that seemed to be shared by all agents.

At six o'clock we parted; Ian heading for the airport while Holt and I returned to our hotel. When I pulled into a parking space and got out, Holt strode over.

"I'm going for a run. Want to come?"

"In the gym or outside?"

"Outside, of course." Holt waved a hand at the clear blue evening sky and mellow sun. "This air is great. I love running at sea level. Makes me feel like a fucking hero when I'm used to working out at four thousand feet."

"Sounds good to me. A run would be perfect to blow off all the steam I've still got left from not strangling Ian. I'll just go up and drop off my stuff..." I hefted my flowery tote. "...and grab a water bottle."

We turned together for the hotel. As we strolled down

the corridor toward our rooms, Holt tucked an arm around my shoulders.

When I stiffened, he leaned in to speak softly. "Come in through my room. The old folks left through yours. We might want to use those disguises again."

I let out a breath. "Right."

He ushered me into his room, and I hurried for the connecting door. "Back in a sec."

After a stop in the bathroom, I strapped on my waist pouch and holster and donned a lightweight shirt to conceal the weapon. Then I hesitated.

Holt had a good point about coming and going through his room without our disguises, but did he have an ulterior motive? He'd propositioned me once before and I'd refused. It hadn't affected our working relationship, but what if he'd decided to try again? After all Ian's bullshit, the last thing I needed right now was to deal with another damn male ego.

Blowing out a breath, I squared my shoulders and tapped at the connecting door.

Holt opened it. "Ready to roll?"

"Yep."

He motioned me through, and I relaxed when we left his room without incident.

As we emerged from the hotel and swung into an easy jog toward the road, Holt glanced over. "You're safe with me, you know."

"Okay, good. I've got my Glock, too."

Holt shook his head. "No, I mean, I'm not going to harass you. The way you tensed up when I touched you..." He blew out a breath. "Look, I asked you once, and you said no. To me, that means 'no' forever unless you tell me otherwise. I might have to get handsy for a cover sometimes, but that's all it is. You can trust me, okay?"

My heart warmed. "Okay. Thanks." We jogged in silence for a few more paces, and I added, "I appreciate that. You're a good partner."

"Thanks." He pointed ahead. "Bet I can beat you to that rock."

"Bet you can't."

After a long run and a hot shower I was ready to melt into bed, but my stomach had other ideas. A ravenous growl reminded me that I'd only had two meals today; one of them inadequate and the other almost five hours ago.

When Holt answered my tap on the connecting door, I assured him, "Just passing through. I'm going down to get something to eat. Do you want anything?"

"Not at this time of night. I don't need to eat every two seconds like you do."

"Five *hours*," I protested, brandishing my watch at him. "And it's only eight-thirty."

He shook his head. "I'm good. Here." He handed me his cardkey. "Just let yourself in when you come back. If we're pretending to sleep together, it looks weird for you to knock."

"Right. Thanks." I accepted the card and headed for the restaurant.

I had just finished the last delicious bite when my phone vibrated. A glance at the call display made me smile. Hellhound.

Picking up, I purred, "Hi, Arnie. Long time no talk."

"Hey, darlin'." It was his typical greeting, but his sexy rasp lacked its usual easy warmth. Tension seized me as he went on, "I gotta tell ya somethin', but before I do... everythin's okay. Got it? Everythin's okay, so don't freak out."

I swallowed hard, my meal turning into a hard lump in my stomach. "What's wrong?"

"Kane got shot in the head half an hour ago..."

The room turned white and cold around me. Conversations and clinking utensils faded into a single shrill tone, the sound of a scream unuttered.

Frozen with the phone clutched to my ear, my hearing returned in sporadic bursts. Arnie, still talking: "Releasin' his name... next of kin..."

Greyness tunnelled my vision.

"Ya still there?" Arnie raised his voice. "Aydan!"

Breathe...

"Aydan, everythin's okay! He's fine, it barely grazed him. Are ya there? Say somethin', darlin'!"

Warmth and colour returned to the room and I sagged forward, gasping for breath.

"I'm... here. Sorry, I didn't get all that. Say it again." My heart hammered hard enough to shake my entire body.

"He's fine, darlin'. Somebody took a potshot at him in front a' the Red Cross buildin' where he volunteers. The bullet parted his hair an' he hit the dirt an' played dead. He decided to lie low, an' the news'll release his name an' say the next of kin have been notified. We didn't want ya to hear it an' think it was true."

"B-But... he was hit. *Shot.* In the head!"

"Just grazed. Scalp wound, that's all. Not even a concussion."

"But another fraction of an inch..." I wrapped my free arm around myself, shivering.

"Yeah." Arnie's voice was grim. "Only reason he ain't dead is 'cause he always does that little sidestep when he comes out a door, same as you."

"I learned it from him." My voice still wasn't working right. "Did he call it in to the police? Or the Department?"

"Cops're on it, but it was a drive-by, an' the car was stolen. They already found it ditched in a parkin' lot. An' Dermott ain't gonna do anythin'. Say's Kane's a civilian, an' it was prob'ly just a random shootin'."

Fury tightened my voice. "Dermott's such a-"

My burner phone vibrated, making me twitch.

Biting back my anger, I said rapidly, "Sorry, I've got another call coming in. I'll call you back as soon as I can."

"'Kay, darlin'. 'Bye."

He disconnected, and I picked up the burner. "Yeah?"

"It's Spider." He sounded shaky, and my already-pounding pulse picked up the pace.

"What's wrong?"

"How did you know..." He took a breath. "Somebody just tried to shoot Stemp."

"*What?*" I blurted the word so loudly that the other restaurant patrons turned to stare. Slouching down, I lowered my voice. "Somebody just shot John, too. At almost the same time. That's not a coincidence."

"Kane got *shot?*"

"Yes, but he's fine," I assured Spider. "He's pretending to be dead, but he's okay."

"Omigod, Aydan! What's happening?"

"I don't know, but I'm damn sure going to find out. Is Stemp okay?"

"Yes, somebody took a shot from a vehicle driving by his house, but they missed. He got a description of the car but there was no plate on it. The RCMP put up roadblocks and they're looking for the car."

"Fuck. Same as John. Call me if you get any new information. We'll be arriving in Calgary at a quarter after eleven tomorrow morning. I'll get an update from John when I get there. Then maybe we can figure out who's behind this."

"Okay." Spider hesitated. "Maybe it's good that you aren't here. Or Holt, either. Everybody knows you associate with Kane and Stemp. What if somebody's trying to kill all of you?"

I gulped as a horrible thought hit me.

Spider worked with us, too.

CHAPTER 15

"Um, Spider..." My throat was tight, and I cleared it before continuing, "...be careful, okay? Just in case. You work with Stemp and Holt and me."

"I know." His voice trembled. "I'm still at the office and I know I should be careful leaving, but... I don't really know what to do. I'm not an agent. And Linda..."

My stomach clenched. "Right, I forgot it's only six-thirty there. Can you stay inside Sirius? Maybe move into the secondary bunker for a few days?"

"I already asked Dermott, but he won't let me. Linda doesn't have a high enough security clearance."

"That fucking-" I bit off my incipient tirade as he spoke again.

"Aydan, I hate to impose, but... would it be okay if we stayed at your place tonight?"

"Of course, but..." I hesitated, not wanting to scare him any more than he was already.

"It's okay," Spider said quickly. "It's too much trouble. We'll be fine."

"No, that's not what I meant at all. You're welcome to stay at my place as long as you want. I was just thinking that it might not be much safer. I might be on the hit list, too."

"I know," Spider agreed. "But at least we'll get some

advance warning from your surveillance cameras. I can route the feeds to my phone."

"Okay," I agreed. "My neighbour, Tom, has a spare key. I'll get him to call you. Get the key from him, then check the monitors to make sure the house and yard are safe, and then go over and let yourselves in. Everything's the same as when you stayed with me for your wedding, so just make yourselves at home."

"Okay." He sounded relieved. "Thanks, Aydan."

"And don't follow a schedule. Go to work and leave at random times, and go through a different door each time. Use the tunnels at Sirius so you can come out at different places. Got it?"

"Got it. Linda's on maternity leave, so at least I don't have to worry about somebody getting her schedule. But I hate to leave her alone at home. Or even out at your place. It's so far from the hospital. What if..." His voice wobbled. "Oh, Aydan, this is so messed up!"

"Tom is right next door and he's a volunteer firefighter trained as a first responder," I promised. "And I'll call Margaret Young and see if she can stay with Linda while you're at work. You know she was a police officer for ten years before she switched to private investigation, right? Linda will be safe."

He cleared his throat, sounding watery, but when he spoke again his voice was firm. "Okay. Thank you so much. I feel better now."

"Good. I'll call Tom right away. He's usually home, and Margaret might be at his place, too. I think they're still dating. I'll get them to call you and you can get everything set up."

"Thank you," he repeated. "Thank you so much!"

After disconnecting, I dialled Tom's number.

His usually-pleasant voice sounded wary. "Hello?"

"Hi, Tom, it's Aydan. Sorry for the blocked number; I'm calling from a client's."

His tone warmed. "Well, hi, neighbour. How are you?"

Fighting the urge to snap out orders, I kept my tone relaxed while we exchanged a few pleasantries.

With those out of the way, Tom asked, "Can I help you with something?"

"I was wondering if I could ask you a favour."

"Of course. Any time."

I let out a small breath of gratitude. How had I gotten lucky enough to have him for a neighbour?

"I'm not sure if you've met my friends Clyde Webb and Linda Burton-Webb...?" I made it into a question.

"Sure, I know Linda from the Chamber of Commerce."

"Right, of course." I dove into the explanation of why Spider and Linda would be staying at my farm, and made the arrangements for them to get Tom's key before adding, "Oh, and is Margaret around?"

"Uh... she might be home." Tom's tone was cautious. "I haven't seen her in a while."

"Oh! I'm sorry, I thought you were... seeing each other?"

"We were for a bit, but we called it quits back in February. We're still friendly; just not... close."

Kicking myself, I apologized, "I'm sorry, I wasn't trying to pry; I just want to ask Margaret if I can hire her to stay with Linda while Spider's at work. They're a little edgy about her being alone out in the country with the baby due any day."

"Oh. Well, Margaret closed her private-eye business, but she'd probably be happy to help anyway. Would you like me to give her a call?"

"No, that's okay, I'll call her. Thanks, Tom. I really appreciate your help."

He chuckled. "It's not much of a chore to hand over a key, but you're welcome. And don't worry about your friends. I'll be here if they need anything before you get home. See you soon."

After saying my goodbyes and disconnecting, I hesitated over Margaret's name in my contacts list.

She'd be a great choice to guard Linda; and they knew each other, so that worked. But having Margaret in my home worried me.

As far as she knew, I was only a bookkeeper. She thought the assassin she'd unwittingly led to me last January had been a random stalker; but if she discovered my elaborate surveillance system, her cop instincts might lead her to dangerous speculations.

And anyway, calling to ask her for a favour was a bit embarrassing. I hadn't returned her friendly advances over the past months, and her calls had dwindled to an occasional invitation to join her and a group of other women for drinks or a movie.

But I liked her, dammit. Ex-cops shared the same dark sense of humour as secret agents.

I shook myself out of my unhappy reverie with a sigh. Let it go. Having me for a friend would only put her at risk.

Squaring my shoulders, I tapped in her number and hit 'Call'.

Margaret answered with a curt 'hello' that promised a speedy hang-up if I turned out to be a telemarketer.

Summoning a cheerful tone, I said, "Hi, Margaret, it's Aydan."

"Oh, hi! How are you?"

"Fine…" I hesitated. "Um, how's everything with you?"

Wariness crept into her voice. "Fine, thanks." An awkward silence descended.

Shit, I should have just cut to the chase. Now I sounded as though I'd only called because I wanted something from her and I was trying to pretend otherwise.

Which was exactly what I was doing.

I sighed. "Sorry, I'm no good at this. I'd like to chat, but I don't have time. May I hire you?"

Her tone turned brisk. "I'm not a private investigator anymore, so, no. But I might be able to help as a friend. What's the trouble?"

"Did you hear about the attempted shooting this afternoon?"

"I heard that shots had been fired. Who was the target?"

Shit, I should have phrased that differently. Once a cop, always a cop.

"I don't know," I lied. "I just heard there had been gunfire in town. Spider and Linda are feeling unsafe, so I invited them to stay at my farm; but I'm in Halifax right now and I won't be back until tomorrow afternoon. With the baby due any day, Spider doesn't want Linda to be alone out at the farm while he's at work. I was wondering if you'd mind staying with her tomorrow."

"I'd be happy to; but wouldn't she rather have her mother with her? Or a friend nearer her own age?"

"Her mother is busy tomorrow, and her friends all have to work."

Crap, I'd have to call Spider and get our stories straight.

"Well, if she's sure…" Margaret hesitated. "Does she actually know you're arranging this with me?"

"Of course," I said, relieved that at least that was true. "I'll give you Spider's number; he's expecting your call. And Tom said he'll be home, too, just in case you need a first responder."

"Oh. That's good." Her tone was unreadable.

I squirmed. "Um... I hope that's not too uncomfortable. I kind of put my foot in my mouth when I talked to Tom. I thought you and he were still dating. I'm sorry things didn't work out."

"It's no big deal. We were never really dating; just... friendly. He's a great guy, but not really my type. He's dating somebody else now, and I think they're pretty serious."

"Oh, good. I mean... I guess... *Is* that good? Or..." I thumped my forehead. "God, could I be any more socially awkward? Sorry."

Margaret laughed. "No problem. It sounds as though you have a lot on your plate right now, so give me Spider's number. Then you can take care of whatever it is that has you so frazzled."

"Thank you so much," I said with deep sincerity.

After a quick coordinating call to Spider I checked my secret phone numbers and dialled, grateful that Arnie and John and I had set up a communication protocol with burner phones.

Hellhound picked up with a brusque, "Yeah."

"It's me. Anything new?"

"Hey, darlin'. Nothin' new, I was just waitin' for your call before I head out an' pick up Kane."

"Don't go!"

Tension sprang into his voice. "Why not?"

"You might be a target. Somebody tried to shoot Stemp

around the same time as John got shot. It might be coincidence, or it might be somebody trying to clean up loose ends. If John's one of the loose ends, you and I might be, too."

"Shit! D'ya think I oughta move Kath outta my place?"

I hesitated. "Would she... *can* she move out?"

"Yeah, she's doin' a lot better with the agoraphobia now. Fuck, Aydan, what if somebody firebombs my place like they did hers?"

Squeezing my eyes shut, I shivered as I imagined his sister's trauma. "If she can go to a hotel, she should. But only if she can go alone. You don't want her caught in the crossfire if you go out together and somebody starts shooting at you."

"Yeah." His voice was grim. "I'll send her out the back door right now. An' then I'll do some scoutin'."

"Be careful," I implored.

"I will. You're back tomorrow, right?"

"Yes."

"Call me as soon's you're back, okay?"

"I will," I promised. "Probably around eleven-thirty. I'll have ditched this burner by then, so it'll be a different number. Will you keep using that one for a while?"

"Yeah, unless somethin' changes. Ya got the list, so if ya don't get me on this one, call the next."

"Okay." My hand tightened around the phone, wishing I could hold him instead. "Be safe. I love you."

"Love ya, too, darlin'."

Letting out a long shaky breath, I stowed the phones in my waist pouch and signalled for my bill. After paying, I vacated the restaurant and hurried upstairs to tap on the door to Holt's room.

He opened the door, frowning, and motioned me impatiently inside. "Why didn't you use the cardkey? That's why I gave it to you."

I handed it back to him with an irritable shrug. "I had other things on my mind. Shit just hit the fan back in Alberta."

"What happened?"

As I laid out the facts I knew, his scowl deepened.

"Fuck!" he snapped when I was finished. "It's got to be Weiss. Goddamn Rand, if he hadn't-" Holt bit off the useless recrimination and switched gears. "Have Webb and his team found out anything yet?"

"No, it only happened about an hour ago. If there's anything new, Hellhound or Spider will call me."

After a restless night of dozing and waking, I dragged myself out of the hotel wishing I could teleport back to Calgary instead of enduring hours of travel.

At the airport, we loitered near the gate until Rebecca arrived, then fell in behind her. Oblivious, she made her way to the boarding lounge and settled comfortably with a fashion magazine. I scanned the area and watched the other passengers, but didn't spot any threats. Across the room, Holt's alert scrutiny was disguised by his apparent absorption in his phone.

We boarded without incident, and as the aircraft climbed I let out a breath and eased back in my seat. The main burden of surveillance would be on Holt, who was seated a couple of rows behind Rebecca. I was a couple of rows ahead, so I only had to keep an ear open for disturbances and occasionally sneak a covert peek behind me, on the pretext of snapping selfies with my phone.

As the hours dragged by, my tension increased. Holt's knee-jerk reaction had been to blame Rupert Weiss, but Weiss couldn't be in two places at once. Somebody had hired a hitman. Maybe two.

Or maybe more.

I hadn't had a call from Arnie or Spider since last night.

What if they were already dead?

CHAPTER 16

By the time our plane landed in Calgary, I was vibrating with nerves. Still my phone stayed silent.

Easing my cramped body up from the seat, I put on a fake smile and snapped another selfie, checking that Rebecca and Holt were getting ready to disembark behind me.

In the arrival lounge, I sidestepped out of the flow of passengers and pretended to consult my phone while Rebecca and Holt went by. Rebecca went into the women's washroom, so I hurried after her.

When we emerged, Holt fell in behind again and we tailed Rebecca safely to the baggage carousel. There, I spotted handsome young Agent Richardson dressed in chauffeur's livery, bearing a sign with Rebecca's name.

She claimed her baggage and headed for the exit with Richardson, and I blew out a breath of relief as they disappeared out the doors.

Holt and I made for the parking garage.

"Any word?" he asked as soon as we were in his car and driving.

"Nothing." I pulled out a secured phone and hit the speed dial. "I hope Spider's-" I broke off as an unfamiliar voice spoke from the phone.

"Yes?"

"Is Spider there?" I asked.

"Transferring you now."

After a couple of clicks, Spider's 'hello' made me slump with relief.

"Hi, it's Aydan," I said. "I'm glad you're still okay. Hang on, I'm putting you on speaker so Holt can hear you, too." I hit the button, then added, "Okay. What's new?"

Spider sighed. "We still haven't seen Rupert Weiss. The police found the car that Stemp's shooter used. It had been stolen. Nobody spotted the driver when he dumped it, so there's nothing more to go on. Stemp's wearing a bulletproof jacket, but Dermott won't let him have his weapon back."

"That asshole!" I snapped, then stifled myself. "Sorry, go on."

"Stemp wouldn't go to a safe house," Spider said unhappily. "And until you two get back we don't have any spare agents to guard him. Kane called in yesterday to let us know what happened, but Dermott said it could have been a random shooting-"

"Not fucking likely," Holt interrupted.

"Probably not," Spider agreed. "But even if Dermott wanted to send somebody to guard him, we-"

"Don't have any spare agents," I said along with him. "Right. I'm going to check in with John and Arnie as soon as I'm off the phone with you. Maybe I can stay and guard them and Holt can go up and guard Stemp."

"That would be good," Spider agreed. "But I don't know whether Dermott will let you stay in Calgary. He wants both of you back here. Oh, and one more thing: Agent Rand from MI6 called to let us know he's here in Alberta looking for Rupert Weiss. I don't think it's a coincidence that less than a day after Weiss arrived looking for George Harrison, somebody tried to kill Stemp. But Rand says he doesn't think Weiss would do that."

Holt and I exchanged a glance. "I don't know," I said slowly. "Ian's usually a pretty good judge of character, but he's already misread Weiss once."

"Doesn't matter," Holt said. "Regardless of who's trying to kill Stemp, we need to get back to Silverside ASAP. Anything else, Webb?"

"No, that's it for now."

"We'll be there in two hours," Holt said.

"Maybe longer," I countered. "I want to see what John's planning before we leave Calgary. I'll call you back as soon as I can." I disconnected and looked up Hellhound's burner number as Holt signalled and changed lanes.

"Before you get on the phone, what do you want to eat?" Holt jerked his chin toward a Wendy's fast-food restaurant. "I'll hit the drive-through."

"Single burger combo with fries and a small chocolate Frosty," I said, and dialled Arnie's burner.

He answered immediately.

My voice came out on a breath of relief. "It's me. I'm so glad you're okay."

"Hey, darlin'. Yeah, I'm fine." He didn't sound happy.

Tension slammed back into my muscles. "What's wrong?"

"More'n I wanna talk about over the phone; but don't worry, everythin's okay for now. Can ya meet me somewhere?"

"Where and when?"

"Remember where you an' Kane an' Skidmark picked me up last winter?"

I hesitated, running back events in my memory and

shivering as I recalled him charging out of the snowy darkness with an armed man chasing him. "I remember."

"Can ya make it there by twelve-thirty?"

After quick mental calculation, I replied, "I think so... hang on." Turning to Holt, I asked, "Can you drop me somewhere before you head back to Silverside?"

Holt made a 'wait' gesture as he powered down the window to relay our food order into the drive-through speaker. Then he closed the window and turned to frown at me. "No."

My moment of surprise surged into irritation. "Fine," I snapped, and undid my seatbelt. An instant before I gripped the door handle, the power locks engaged with a clunk.

"Let me out." My voice came out in a feral growl.

"Would you take a damn pill?" Holt rolled the car forward as the line of cars moved closer to the pickup window. "In the first place, you need to eat, I just ordered your food, and you owe me for it whether you eat it or not. And in the second place, I was going to say..." He fixed me with a scowl. "...we'll go wherever you need to go, *together*." His scowl deepened as he made a testy back-and-forth gesture between us. "*Partners*. Remember?"

Heat rose to my cheeks. "Sorry," I mumbled without meeting his eyes. "Thanks."

Hellhound's voice crackled from the momentarily-forgotten phone. "Aydan! Ya there? What's happenin'?"

Returning the phone to my ear, I said, "Sorry. Everything's fine. We'll be there."

"Who's we? You an' Holt?"

"Yeah."

"Is he gonna be a problem?"

I sneaked a glance at Holt's craggy profile. He still

looked indignant.

A smile crept to my lips. "No, I don't think so."

Driving into the mall parking lot on a sunny summer day was far less stressful than the last time I'd been there. Hellhound was lounging on the grass in the shade of a tall fence, and I powered down the window and waved as we pulled up.

As he rose and ambled over, I enjoyed the view. His tattooed muscles were displayed to advantage in a worn concert T-shirt that stretched tightly over his bulky chest and hard midsection. His beard and moustache were clipped short as usual for the summer, and soft faded jeans showcased his assets very nicely indeed.

As he neared us, he lowered his dark glasses to study the car with a raised eyebrow. "Pretty fancy," he teased. "You're movin' up in the world, darlin'."

Holt leaned across me toward the open window and raised his voice. "Brush the grass off your pants before you get in."

Hellhound obeyed, then slid into the back seat. "Good thing ya didn't tell me to wipe the dog shit off my boots. That woulda been tougher."

Holt stiffened, but after a short inhalation he clearly realized Hellhound was needling him. "Where to?" he growled.

"Head for Hotel Village on Crowchild, an' I'll fill ya in while we drive." He glanced over his shoulder as we headed for the parking lot exit. "Ya checked for tails lately?"

"I always do," Holt replied. "I haven't seen any. Kelly?"

"No," I mumbled, choosing not to admit that I hadn't

been watching. Apparently I trusted Holt more than I realized.

"'Kay, good," Arnie said. "'Cause I'm pretty sure some asshole was set up to shoot me at my place last night."

CHAPTER 17

"*What?*" I whipped around so fast that my stiffened back muscles let out an audible crack. Anxiously eyeing Arnie in the back seat, I demanded, "What happened? Are you okay? How did you get away? Did you get a good look at him? What-"

"Slow down, darlin'," he admonished. "This's why I wanted to tell ya in person. I'm fine." He spread his arms. "See? No bullet holes."

"Cuts?" I asked suspiciously. "Bruises?"

He chuckled. "Nah. Soon's ya called me last night, I got Kath out the door an' then headed up to the roof. Spotted a guy in a black SUV that looked outta place, so I called the cops from one a' my burners. Gave 'em the plate an' description, an' told 'em I thought I saw a gun."

Holt grunted amusement. "Bet things got exciting for him after that."

Hellhound grinned. "Yep, cops were on him like flies on shit. But I didn't stick around to watch, just got out while the gettin' was good. Left the Forester in a downtown lot an' took transit to a hotel."

"Did you call it in to the Department?" I asked.

He shrugged. "Yeah, I told the analyst-on-call. But I ain't on a job, so Dermott won't give a shit."

"He'd better," I growled, and yanked out my burner phone.

When Spider answered, I rapped out, "A gunman was arrested outside Arnie's apartment in Calgary last night. Arnie called it in, but we haven't heard anything from Dermott. Can you find out if the police are still holding the gunman? And find out what kind of weapon he was carrying, and whether it matches the bullets that were fired at John and Stemp?"

A sharp intake of breath was followed by the rapid clicking of computer keys. "I see the call here," Spider said a moment later, sounding relieved. "Megan Novak took it. She's new, taking over from Trish Belling. Megan passed it on to Dermott right away..." He hesitated.

"And that's where it ended, right?" I inquired cynically.

"It looks that way."

I hissed out a breath of frustration. "If the Calgary police are still holding the gunman, arrange to have him blindfolded and transferred up to the secured area in Silverside. Requisition all the physical evidence, too, and tell them we'll run it through our lab and keep them in the loop."

"I'm on it."

We disconnected, and I growled and thumped my head against the headrest in frustration.

"Dermott's going to crucify you," Holt said. "It's the director's decision whether to take over a police case, and our lab needs his authorization to process the evidence."

"Dermott can take a long hard suck on my ass," I gritted. "If he wants the director's title, he'd damn well better do the job."

Holt eyed me in silence. Then he sighed and punched a speed dial button on his cell phone.

"Yeah, Brent?" he said. "Greg here."

He was ratting me out. *Asshole!*

Glancing at my murderous expression, Holt gave me a calm-down gesture and went on, "Hey, I just found out there might be a connection between Kane's and Stemp's shooters and the guy Helmand called in last night. What do you think about taking custody of the perp and running the evidence through our lab?"

He listened for a moment. "Okay, good idea. I know you're swamped, so I'll tell Kelly to get Webb and his team on it. Right. Catch you later."

He hung up and scowled at me. "And now your ass is officially covered. See how easy that was? Use your brain, Kelly. Pick your battles."

"It's easy for *you*," I snarled. "If I'd made that call, Dermott would have told me to fuck off, and then he would have dug in his heels and refused to take over the case just out of spite."

"Yeah," Holt said with exaggerated patience. "And I didn't say you should call Dermott. I said, use your fucking brain. Get *me* to call Dermott."

I blinked at him, all my irritation evaporating in the heat of embarrassment.

"I hate it when you're right," I muttered.

Showing considerably more tact than I expected or deserved, Holt limited himself to a small smirk before flicking his gaze back to Hellhound in the rearview mirror. "So what's your plan?"

"I wanna go collect Kane, an' then we'll head up to Silverside. We'll set up camp in the bush by the creek at Aydan's place. My gear's in my truck."

"Where's Kane?"

"Still hidin' at the medical examiner's office. I was gonna go get him last night, but I figured since ya were back today, it'd be easier to extract him with a team."

Holt shot him a frown. "We're not going into the medical examiner's office with guns blazing."

Hellhound shook his head. "Nah, I got a wheelchair, an' we can rent a coupla cars. I'll wrap up in a blanket, you wheel me in, then I'll go out the back an' you wheel Kane out the front."

"Not a bad idea," Holt said. "But we'll keep you out of it. You're a target, and by now whoever took out the contract knows you're still alive. If I were them, I'd be watching the M.E.'s office just in case you show up to ID Kane's body."

"I'll do it," I said.

An hour later, I fidgeted in the passenger seat of the rental car while Holt drove a complicated pattern through Bowness.

"See anything?" Holt asked as we came to the end of our evasive manoeuvres at last.

"Nope."

"Me, neither."

I let out a breath. "Now the only question is whether somebody's watching the M.E.'s office."

Holt shrugged. "One way to find out."

A few minutes later we pulled into a parking stall by the door of the medical examiner's office. Holt turned off the car but remained in the driver's seat, slowly unfastening his seatbelt and making a show of inspecting the ignition and straightening his fedora. I slumped in the passenger's seat in my layers of clothes, topped by a blanket around my shoulders. The sun beat unmercifully through the windows, skyrocketing the temperature in the car as soon as the air conditioning was turned off.

At last Holt opened his door, easing out first one foot, then the other. With a final heave he gained his feet, balancing precariously as he clung to the door before closing it behind him.

By the time he had doddered around to the trunk, extracted and unfolded the wheelchair, and wheeled it around to my side, sweat soaked my wig and trickled down between my boobs. When Holt finally opened the car door, I gasped in a desperate breath of cooler air.

While Holt puttered around lifting my feet up onto the wheelchair's footrests and tucking the blanket around me, I shot sidelong glances at the parking lot and surrounding area.

Nobody on the roof; nobody sitting in a vehicle. If anybody was watching, they were hidden in the highrise building across the street. No way to know about that, unless a sniper started shooting at us.

That thought did nothing to reduce my sweat.

Playing his elderly persona to the hilt, Holt struggled to roll the wheelchair up the slight incline to the door.

The air-conditioning inside the building was heavenly. While I slumped motionless in the chair, Holt limped over to the reception desk.

"I'm here to see Ben Salmer!" he shouted.

"I'll let him know you're here."

Holt leaned forward, cupping a hand behind his ear. "What's that?"

"He'll be right with you!" the receptionist replied loudly.

After a short wait, a paunchy middle-aged man came in

through a side door and paused, frowning. After an uncertain pause, he came over.

Pitching his voice discreetly low, he inquired, "Are you here for...?"

"What?" Holt yelled. "Speak up, son!"

"Are you here to identify someone?" Salmer shouted back.

"John Kane," Holt said loudly. "He's... He was... my..." His old man's voice cracked and wavered into silence, and I raised my hand to my mouth as though stifling a sob.

Salmer's frown deepened.

Shit, hadn't Hellhound told him we were coming?

"Come with me, please," Salmer said doubtfully, and led the way.

After a longish trip down a corridor, he opened a door and motioned us forward. Holt rolled me through, and Salmer crowded into the small windowless room, too, closing the door behind us.

An unpleasant chemical smell burned my nose. The walls were lined with shelves containing substances whose purposes I'd rather not know. Against the far wall, boxes were stacked almost to the ceiling.

Silence reigned. My breathing accelerated again in the stuffy air.

"So..." Salmer said nervously. "You're here for...?"

Something was wrong.

Under the blanket, I eased a sweaty hand into my handbag and gripped my Glock.

"John Kane," Holt said quietly. "Is there a problem?"

"Who told you he'd been brought here?"

Still moving with infinitesimal slowness, I withdrew the gun and mentally rehearsed the lunge to my feet and flip of the blanket that would clear my weapon for action.

"Arnold Helmand sent us," Holt replied. "Aren't you Ben Salmer?"

"Yes..."

A barely-audible rustle from behind the stacked boxes galvanized me into a leap from the wheelchair. I landed in a crouch, my Glock trained on the boxes. Holt shoved Salmer to the floor and whisked out his own gun, its deadly muzzle tracking the man as he sprawled with a yelp.

"Come out from behind the boxes or I'll shoot," I barked. "Three. Two-"

Kane's unmistakeable baritone spoke. "Aydan?"

I gulped a breath of relief mingled with worry. Was someone holding him hostage back there?

"Yes, it's me," I replied, my Glock still unwavering. "Come out where I can see you."

"I'm coming out now." He sidestepped out of the narrow space, his hands above his head.

"Why do you have your hands up?" I demanded.

He smiled. "Maybe because you're pointing a gun at me?"

But I wasn't. As soon as he had stepped out, I had shifted my aim to the boxes beside him.

Heart pounding, I flicked my gaze from him to the boxes and back again.

"Oh." Kane relaxed and lowered his hands. "It's all right. There's nobody else back there."

My breath left me in a whoosh as I lowered my gun.

"I'm sorry," Kane said. "I should have realized this was no time for joking."

"I should kick your ass." I flung my arms around him, holding him tight and hiding my face in his shoulder.

Mindful of our audience, I pulled away before I could cling to him. The sight of the wound on his scalp made my voice quiver. "Don't scare me like that. Ever again."

"I'll try not to." He gave my hand a brief gentle squeeze, eyeing Salmer's pale face and wide eyes. "Put your weapon away, Holt," Kane added. "Ben's on our side." As Holt holstered his weapon, Kane leaned over to offer Salmer a hand up. "Are you all right?"

"F-Fine," Salmer stammered. "I... I w-wasn't expecting..." He sucked in a breath and let it out slowly, and when he spoke again his voice was steadier. "Helmand told me to expect two people with a wheelchair, but they looked so... I thought... what if they weren't the right people? I could just imagine taking some sweet old couple who were here to identify a dead loved one, into the storage room and..." He made an ineffectual gesture.

"Sorry about that." I untied my kerchief and removed my big sunglasses and the sweaty wig, giving it a shake in an attempt to dry it a bit before Kane had to don it. "And we're sorry we scared you." My words came out muffled as I yanked the baggy grey dress over my head.

Salmer looked alarmed. "I can leave if you need to..." He gestured at my clothes, apparently afraid I was going to strip to my skivvies, or worse.

"No, it's okay," I assured him. "This is my next outfit."

"Okay..." He eased toward the door. "Um, I'll just wait in the hall."

"No," Holt snapped, making Salmer blanch all over again. "We need you to stay in here until we're ready to leave. Kane, put that dress on. Kelly, for Christ's sake, put some lipstick over top of that flesh-coloured shit. You look like the walking dead."

I flipped him a middle finger and retrieved my cracked plastic purse from the wheelchair. After applying a brighter but still conservative lip colour, I transferred the rest of the purse's contents to my sleek black tote bag.

Handing Kane the empty purse, I gestured at the wheelchair. "You're next on the throne. Sorry everything's so gross and sweaty."

"Not a problem," Kane replied as he held up the gray dress. "But I don't think this is going to fit."

"I can fix that." I whisked my sturdy lock-bladed knife out of my tote. Salmer flinched as light played along the razor-sharp edge.

After some cuts that turned the dress into an apron-like garment that covered Kane's torso, lap, and legs, he settled in the wheelchair. When we were finished applying the rest of his disguise he slumped forward, letting his head hang as I had done.

"All right," Holt said. "Salmer, you go out first. If there's anybody in the corridor, close the door behind you and stall until they're gone. Otherwise, we'll follow you to reception with the wheelchair, and Aydan will go out the back door."

"Okay," Salmer said nervously.

"I owe you, Ben," Kane said to his lap. "Thank you."

"No problem." Salmer slipped out the door, his sigh of relief audible. "Nobody's out here."

"See you at the pickup point," Holt said as he sagged into his old-man posture and plodded out pushing the wheelchair.

"Good luck," I replied, and strode off in the opposite direction trying to look as though I belonged there.

CHAPTER 18

As I neared the back exit of the medical examiner's building, a thought hit me and my step faltered. Dammit, I should have gone out the front with Holt and Kane instead.

What if somebody shot at them? Kane was unarmed, and Holt was pushing the wheelchair. He'd lose vital seconds getting to his gun.

I hovered indecisively. I could still probably sprint to the front door in time to cover them...

No. Their disguises were better than mine. Nobody had followed us, and nobody would suspect that the two old people emerging weren't the same two old people who went in. If I showed up and got recognized, I could get us all killed.

Stiffening my spine, I strode out the back door and power-walked toward Bowness Road. As I passed the parking lot, I flicked a glance sideways and breathed a sigh of relief. Kane was already slumped in the passenger seat of the rental, and Holt was just taking his place behind the wheel. No bullets flying.

So far, so good. And I could still provide covering fire if something went wrong.

Holt's vehicle turned onto Bowness Road and drove out of sight without incident. A few minutes later, Hellhound cruised by, too. I let my gaze pass over his car as my bus pulled up.

After riding for a few stops, I disembarked and headed for the small strip mall where we'd agreed to meet. Holt and Kane were parked at one end; Hellhound at the other. A quick survey of the stores decided my destination, and I ducked into a liquor store. A few minutes later I emerged with a six-pack, strolled over to Hellhound's car, and got in.

He shot me a grin. "Damn, darlin'. A sexy librarian with beer. All my dreams are comin' true today."

Leaning over, he slowly removed my glasses and dropped a light kiss on my lips. Then he drew back a fraction, holding my gaze as he eased out the wooden pin that secured my updo. As my hair tumbled down, he let out a raspy purr of satisfaction. "Oh hell yeah." Sliding his fingers into my hair, he leaned in for a slower, deeper kiss that left me panting.

As his fingertip traced down my neck to dip into the modest collar of the dress, I captured his hand. "You're not undressing me here."

I had intended it as a statement, but it came out sounding more like a question. One that begged for the answer, 'Why the hell not?'

Arnie grinned and drew back. "Only with my eyes, darlin'. But I got big plans for that librarian outfit later." His hungry gaze coasted over the frumpy dress and down my legs. "Never seen ya wear a dress like that before. Tell me what you're wearin' under there."

As I opened my mouth to reply, my burner phone vibrated.

"Yeah?" I answered it absently.

"Stop playing kissy-face and get your head in the game,"

Holt barked in my ear. "We're heading back to the hotel. Cover our asses." He disconnected.

"Holt's ready to move out now," I paraphrased.

Inside Hellhound's hotel room, Kane rose from the wheelchair and threw off the blanket with a breath of relief.

"Not so fast," Holt said. "You need to go back out to the car in disguise. And on the way up to Silverside, you can't be seen at all. If somebody spots Aydan with three other people and two of them are Hellhound and me, it won't be a stretch for them to figure out who you are. You'll need to lie down in the back seat all the way."

"He can't," I objected. "I'd be crippled if I did that for ten minutes, and he's six inches taller than me."

"I can lie in the back of Hellhound's SUV," Kane said.

"That'll work," Arnie agreed. "I got the blackout drapes for the back, an' if ya fold the rear seat down it's pretty comfortable." He caught my eye with a grin, and my cheeks heated with the memory of exactly how comfortable we'd gotten together in the back of that SUV.

"But you parked downtown," Holt said. "There'll be all kinds of people around in the middle of the day, plus surveillance cameras in the parkade. We can't let anyone see Kane getting in."

"I might have an idea." I hesitated, swallowing trepidation. "Arnie... is Weasel in or out of prison?"

"Out," he replied, his brow lightening. "Good idea, darlin'. We can do the switch at Weasel's place."

Holt and Kane exchanged a glance. "I'm not going to ask for details," Kane said firmly, and Holt nodded agreement.

Arnie pulled out his burner phone and dialled. After a

pause, he spoke. "Weasel? Yeah, Hellhound. I need your place at..." He consulted his watch. "Four-thirty. There's fifty bucks in it if ya clear out the back bay so we can fit two cars in, an' ya leave for an hour." He listened, then shrugged. "Okay, a hundred." A wheedling crackle came from the phone, and Hellhound said firmly, "Nah, that's it. That's all I got." Frowning, he listened some more. "I don't give a shit. Ya can have a hundred bucks, or nothin' at all. Your choice."

A lengthy crackle of words came from Arnie's phone, and I imagined Weasel making his case for more money.

Hellhound let out an irritated grunt. "Fuck ya, then. No skin off my ass. But Jane's gonna be pissed."

A slow smile spread across his face as he listened to Weasel's rapid reply.

"Nah," Hellhound said indifferently. "We don't need your place that bad. Lotsa other places we can use."

His smile widened at Weasel's response. He lowered the phone and spoke to me. "Weasel says we can use his place for free, anytime, as long as we want. Just say the word."

"Word," I said shortly.

Hellhound grinned and returned to the phone. "Yeah. Today between four-thirty an' five-thirty. An' if we see hide or hair a' you or anybody-" He broke off. "'Course I ain't shittin' ya. She's right here." He spoke to me again. "He wants to hear it from you."

Suppressing a shudder, I took the phone with my fingertips and held it several inches away from my face. "Weasel," I snapped. "It's Jane. You *will* be gone between four-thirty and five-thirty today. Completely gone. No peeking, no surveillance of any kind. Got it?"

His voice came faintly from the distant speaker. "Yes, Mistress! Anything you-"

I hurriedly handed the phone back to Hellhound. Holt and Kane eyed me, and I realized I was scrubbing my palm against the leg of my jeans. I desisted as Hellhound spoke into the phone again.

"Shut up, it's me. Fuck, no! Don't wanna hear it, won't *ever* fuckin' wanna hear it." He disconnected.

"Well, that was interesting." Holt eyed me with raised eyebrows. "Anything you want to share with the rest of the class?"

I scowled. "No."

To my surprise, everything went according to plan. On the long drive back to Silverside, Holt made a few attempts to pry into the details of my association with Weasel, but he gave up when I refused to respond to cajoling, insults, or any other form of manipulation.

At last we turned off the highway onto the gravel road to my farm. Holt swore and slowed the car as dust billowed up from the tires of Hellhound's SUV ahead of us.

"You owe me a car wash," he grumbled as the fine beige powder settled on the windshield and shiny hood of the Audi.

"You can hose it off at the farm."

"Deluxe wash," he growled. "In a touchless car wash. Pre-soak. Soap wash. Spot-free rinse. Wax."

"Bite m-" My retort was interrupted by the vibration of my burner phone. I whisked it out with my usual generic greeting. "Yeah?"

"It's me," Arnie said.

Something in his voice sent a chill down my spine. "What's wrong?"

"Just got a call from Weasel."

I groaned. "What does he want now? Wait, don't tell me. I don't even want to know."

"Think ya might wanna know this, darlin'." Arnie's voice was grave.

The cold hand of fear clamped around my guts. "What is it?"

"Ya know how ya had Weasel listenin' for word on the street about Arlene Widdenback last year? Well, he's been keepin' his ear to the ground ever since, hopin' to get in good with ya. An' he just heard that Arlene Widdenback's a cop."

I froze, and Arnie's next words registered in my brain as if from a hundred miles away.

"Your cover's blown to rat shit, darlin'."

CHAPTER 19

As my fist closed convulsively on the phone, I said the only thing that came immediately to mind. *"Shit!"*

"Yeah," Hellhound agreed. "Did ya check to make sure all the surveillance cams are up an' runnin' around your place?"

"I did; but hang on, I'll check them again." I laid the phone down and checked the small video monitor strapped to my wrist. After toggling rapidly through the views, I breathed a sigh of relief and picked up the phone again. "All clear."

"'Kay, good. I told Weasel to keep his ears open. Kane an' I'll get set up in our campin' spot an' keep our eyes peeled in case somebody tries to get through your perimeter."

"Spider should be able to route alerts from the security cameras to your phones," I said.

"Good. Tell him to send 'em to our current burners. We'll switch to our next numbers an' keep these ones just for surveillance."

"Okay. After it's dark, come up to the house and we'll do some planning."

As soon as I disconnected, Holt demanded, "What's wrong?"

"Word on the street is that Arlene Widdenback is a cop."

As he swore, I grabbed a secured phone and hit the speed dial. When the analyst-on-call answered, I asked, "Is Spider still there?"

"No, he just left."

"It's Aydan Kelly. I just heard from one of my informants that Arlene Widdenback has been outed as a cop. Check the chatter, see what you can find out. And keep your ears open for anything on Stemp, George Harrison, Holt, Kane, or Helmand. They could all be affected by this, too."

"On it."

I hung up and thumped the phone against my forehead.

"So, that's weird," Holt said thoughtfully as he pulled to a stop in front of my house. "If your cover's blown, why is our perp trying to kill everybody *but* you?"

I shrugged. "Maybe I'm on the list. I just wasn't here when they tried."

"But your surveillance system didn't ping. And if anybody had gotten close enough to see your house or yard, it would have. It's a big perimeter."

"Tell me about it. I get my exercise hiking around it once a week to swap out all the batteries." I considered for a moment, then added, "But I guess Arlene Widdenback doesn't really have many enemies left. Tawny and Lawrence Harchman were pretty much the last ones, and they're dead now, too."

Holt scowled. "Yeah. I was just hoping there'd be some connection."

"I still think the connection is Rupert Weiss. He's the only one who'd want to eliminate both Stemp and John. I was never in that picture."

"Yeah, I-" Holt began, then broke off. "Incoming."

I jerked around to follow his line of sight, my heart

thumping even though his relaxed tone told me there was no threat.

Linda's belly came out the screen door onto my porch, followed by Linda herself. She braced one hand on her lower back, smiling as she waved.

Holt's eyes widened. "Holy Christ, is she having a litter?"

"No. It's just that she's so tiny, the baby bulge is as big as she is." I waved back to Linda, not sure whether to smile or wince at her gigantic midriff.

As I got out of the car, Margaret emerged from the house, too. Her hazel eyes crinkled with a welcoming smile.

"Hi, Aydan!" she called. "I hope you're hungry. We've been cooking up a storm." She ducked to get a better look at Holt, still sitting behind the wheel. "Is your friend coming in? We could use some help eating all this lasagna."

Holt swung out of the car and stood, interest lighting his face. "Lasagna?"

"With fresh garlic bread," Margaret promised. "And caesar salad. And homemade apple pie for dessert."

Holt gave her one of his rare smiles, transforming his craggy features from dour to ruggedly attractive. "You had me at lasagna," he quipped.

Margaret's gaze flicked down his body and back up to his face so quickly I almost missed it, but I was sure she had registered his hard-muscled physique and sophisticated designer clothes. I couldn't imagine how he'd managed to keep a linen blazer looking that crisp throughout our long day of travelling. I looked as though I'd slept in my clothes for days. In a garbage dumpster.

Margaret's smile at Holt widened. "Well then, come on in."

"I'd love to," he assured her. "But I'm due back in Silverside."

I turned to face Holt and lowered my voice. "What for?"

Holt matched my quiet tone and discreet body angle. "Somebody has to guard Stemp."

"We should call him," I agreed, then turned back and raised my voice to speak to Margaret and Linda again. "Greg and I just have to make a couple of calls to work."

Holt and I got back in the car, and he called the Department's secure line while I dialled Stemp's home number.

Stemp answered on the first ring, his tone as brisk and expressionless as always. "Yes?"

I kept my voice low so I wouldn't interfere with Holt's call. "It's Aydan. Can you talk?"

"This line is public."

"I know. I'm just calling to see if you're okay."

"I am well, thank you. And you?"

I rolled my eyes and tried again. "What I meant was, Holt and I are back in town, and we can come over and stay with you. We're just at my farm now, but we can be there in fifteen minutes."

"That will not be necessary."

"But you're alone," I argued. "You should have-"

"Thank you for your concern, but it is unwarranted," he interrupted in a formal tone. "Should that change, I will contact the office."

"No; call me directly."

"That would be inappropriate," Stemp replied. "If you do not receive word from the office, you may be assured that I neither require nor desire your presence. Now, if you will excuse me, you are interrupting my crossword puzzle."

I blinked, feeling as though he'd slapped me in the face.

"Um... okay, then," I mumbled. "'Bye."

As the phone drifted down from my ear, I met Holt's inquiring gaze. Shaking myself back to reality, I said, "He's fine. He doesn't want a guard, and he says if that changes, he'll contact Dermott."

Holt shrugged. "It's his funeral. So, Rand's been in touch. He wants to meet up with us. I told them to tell him to come here at eleven tonight, when Kane and Hellhound will be coming in. I'll head home and come back at eleven, too."

"Don't you want to stay for dinner?"

He hesitated, and I glimpsed pride warring with interest behind his eyes.

I gave him my best scowl. "What, you're too good to eat at my table, you stuck-up bastard?"

"Christ, Kelly, it's all about you, all the time, isn't it? Fine, I'll eat your damn lasagna."

I couldn't quite stifle my smile at his fake irritation. He gave me a fleeting smile in return as he turned to get out of the car.

I led the way to the front porch. "Margaret, this is Greg Holt. Greg, Margaret Young."

"Nice to meet you," Margaret said, eyeing him with interest as she extended her hand.

He smiled and shook it, replying, "Nice to meet you, too", as if he was meeting her for the first time. He could hardly say, 'I already know you; I was watching while the police questioned you for hours.'

"So, you work with Aydan?" Margaret asked. "Are you a bookkeeper, too?"

"No, I'm a real estate agent." Slipping a sleek card case

from his breast pocket, Holt extracted a card and handed it to her with a smile. "I have my own business, but I'm on contract with the exploration group of Sirius Dynamics, for land acquisitions."

"Oh, that must be interesting work."

"Not really," he demurred. "Today was fun because Aydan and I went out to evaluate a potential purchase, but mostly it's just paper-pushing."

Diverting the conversation from our lies, I turned to Linda. "And Linda, you know Greg, right?"

Linda gave him her sparkling smile. "Sure. It's nice to see you again, Greg." She beckoned us toward the door. "Come on in." Her cheeks went pink. "I mean... I'm sorry, Aydan, it's your house. I just..."

"It's fine," I assured her. "My house is your house."

As we trooped inside and removed our shoes, my mind returned to my short chilly conversation with Stemp.

Dammit, I had thought we were friends. Well, not exactly friends; but his parents had virtually adopted me, for crying out loud. And Stemp had unbent when we were in the privacy of his home, revealing the warm-hearted man behind the reptilian robot.

His frosty words replayed in my brain, making my heart pinch with hurt.

I neither require nor desire your presence. Now, if you will excuse me, you are interrupting my...

"Shit!" I blurted.

Holt spun, his gaze flashing over me and the yard behind me. "What?" he demanded.

Linda and Margaret were eyeing me with alarm, too.

"Oh." I gave them a fake-sheepish smile. "Sorry, I just remembered. One of my bookkeeping clients emailed me an important document yesterday and I was supposed to deal with it as soon as I got home. You go ahead with dinner. I'll just zip to my computer for a few minutes."

"There's no rush," Linda assured me. "Spider isn't home yet, and anyway, we wouldn't sit here and eat while you're working. We'll eat whenever you're ready."

"Thanks. I won't be long," I said, and headed for the hallway.

Holt gave me an eyebrow-lift that asked 'Do you need me?', and I returned a tiny headshake.

He turned back to Linda and Margaret, and I hurried to my home office and plopped down in front of the computer.

Sure enough, as soon as I started the online crossword puzzle game, a tiny white square blinked in the bottom corner of my screen.

Alt-Shift-Click.

A text window opened, and I typed "*Status?*"

The cursor zipped across the screen. "*Secure for now. Need to talk.*"

"*When and where?*"

"*My shed at midnight?*"

"*Okay.*"

"*Come alone. Under surveillance.*"

My pulse picked up. Dammit. I didn't want to keep anything from John and Arnie; and I was beginning to depend on Holt's cranky but reliable presence to cover my back.

But Stemp never did anything without a good reason.

I sighed and typed, "*I'll be there.*"

CHAPTER 20

Despite the lively conversation over dinner and dessert, my mind kept circling back to all the worrisome loose ends.

Stemp, alone and unarmed, too proud to ask for help. Or, who knew; he probably had some elaborate plan already. He was always three steps ahead of everybody else.

Shit, what if he wanted me to cover for him while he slipped out of Silverside and flew overseas? If that came to light, my ass would be grass; and Dermott wouldn't just be a lawn mower, he'd be a bulldozer.

And how many hitmen were closing in on us? What if Volslav sent a team to attack my farm? My surveillance perimeter would provide a few minutes' warning; but what had I been thinking, inviting Spider and Linda out here where we could all get ambushed?

"Aydan?" Margaret's voice penetrated my unpleasant reverie.

"Uh?" I shook myself back to the present, realizing that the table had been cleared and Margaret was moving toward the door.

"I'm off." She shot a smile at Spider and Holt, who were standing at the sink. "Since those two won't let me help with the dishes, I guess I've outlived my usefulness."

"Thank you so much for staying with me," Linda said,

struggling to rise.

"No, don't get up," Margaret admonished. "Look how swollen your ankles are. You should put your feet up."

As Spider hurried over to pull a chair closer to Linda's feet, she sighed. "Every part of my body is swollen." As Spider tenderly lifted her feet onto the chair, she ran her hand over her huge belly and added, "Especially this."

I gave her a deadpan look. "Is now a bad time to remind you of how eager you were to have a baby bump, six months ago?"

Linda giggled, then winced and massaged her back. "This isn't just a baby bump anymore. This is a baby mountain. A baby Everest."

We all laughed, and Margaret turned for the door with a wave. "See you tomorrow at nine. Unless you're in the maternity ward by then."

"Oh, I hope so," Linda said fervently.

When the door closed behind Margaret, I went over to retrieve my bug detector from my waist pouch. As her car started and the tires crunched down my gravel lane, I showed the steady green light to the others, then brought Spider and Linda up to date, finishing, "Arnie and John will come in when it's full dark. Probably after eleven. And Ian will come, too."

Spider transferred the last dish out of the sink and onto the drainboard. "When we opened the closet in the guest room to put our stuff away, I noticed you had some board games. Do you mind if we get one out to pass the time?"

"Of course not, that's a great idea."

When he emerged from the hallway a few minutes later bearing my ancient Monopoly box, Holt hung the damp dishtowel on its peg and announced, "Guess I'll head out."

Spider frowned. "Don't you need to be here for the briefing?"

"Yeah, but..." Holt made an uncharacteristically awkward gesture. "I'll come back later."

There was that look in his eyes again. As though he'd like to stay, but didn't feel like he belonged.

His five tartan-wearing uncles flashed into my mind. A big family, but all in Toronto. All his friends lived there, too, except Dermott. And his childhood history with Dermott couldn't exactly be called friendship.

My heart squeezed. He must be so lonely.

"If you've got things to do, that's fine," I said. "But Monopoly's always better with four people. Can you stay?"

He hesitated, and I sweetened the deal. "I have single-malt scotch."

Holt's face lit up. "Really?"

"Not that super-expensive stuff you usually drink," I cautioned. "But it's pretty good. A twelve-year-old Macallan."

"Sold."

Halfway through a second cutthroat game of Monopoly, my wrist monitor and Spider's phone vibrated simultaneously. A tense silence fell while we checked the displays.

"That's probably Ian," I said, watching a car move down my lane. "Spider and Linda, stay here in the living room; Holt, stay with them." I drew my Glock and headed through the kitchen to the front door.

My wrist monitor's display was too tiny for me to recognize the driver's features when he got out of the car, but he moved with Ian's grace and assurance. Peeking out the fisheye lens in my door, I relaxed at the sight of Ian's face and holstered my gun. As he mounted the front steps I swung the interior door open and gestured him inside.

"How nice to see you again, Storm," he said with his charming smile. His avid gaze roamed my kitchen and dining room. "And how fascinating to observe you in your natural habitat."

Seeing my outdated kitchen and scuffed hardwood floor through the eyes of a man who stayed in the finest hotels and drank five-hundred-dollar champagne, I straightened my spine and lifted my chin. Fuck him if he thought my home was cheap and cheesy.

"Go on into the living room," I said. "Arnie and John should be coming in soon. Would you like a drink?"

Ian's gaze lit on the bottle of Macallan. "A scotch would be lovely, thank you. Two ice cubes, there's a love."

"Coming right up," I said through my teeth.

As I carried the drink into the living room a few moments later, my phone vibrated. Hurriedly handing the glass to Ian, I checked the text.

"It's Arnie and John," I said. "They're on their way in."

Everyone tensed when my wrist and Spider's phone vibrated simultaneously.

I shot a look at my wrist monitor. "They just triggered one of the perimeter cameras when they went by."

"Surveillance system?" Ian inquired, eyeing my wrist with interest.

"Yeah." I didn't show it to him.

Linda squirmed forward and attempted to lever herself up from the sofa. "I'll heat up some lasagna for John and Arnie."

Spider sprang up. "Don't move, sweetie, I've got it. Just rest."

"Thanks, sweetie, but I'll get the lasagna going and then I'm off to bed." She hauled herself to her feet with the help of Spider's outstretched hand.

The sound of the back door made me hurry in that direction. Arnie and John stood in my back entry, clad head to toe in black. I flung my arms around both of them, the coolness of their outerwear pleasant in the stuffy indoor air. They each put an arm around me in turn, and I cuddled into the three-way hug for a short but comforting moment.

In the living room, John surveyed the game board, drinks, and mostly-empty bowl of potato chips with a smile. "It looks like we missed the party."

"Sorry," I said. "But Linda's heating up some lasagna for you, and I can get you a drink. What would you like?"

As I headed toward the kitchen, I glanced back at the men lounging in my living room.

Dammit, John was right. It did look like a party in there. Not the kind of atmosphere that lent itself to a quick strategy session followed by everyone going their separate ways.

I needed to leave for Stemp's place soon, and I needed to do it alone. This wasn't going to end well.

After serving the lasagna, Linda said a general 'good night' and disappeared into the guest bedroom.

Eyeing Ian, Holt lowered his voice. "So, any luck with..." he hesitated with a glance at Hellhound.

"I can go outside," Hellhound volunteered.

After a moment of thought, Holt shook his head. "No, we'll bring you in on this." He brought Hellhound up to date in a few sentences, finishing, "So Weiss flew to Calgary, where he vanished. And a few hours later, the shooting attempts started."

"Well, if he's the guy from my parkin' lot, ya oughta be able to question him," Hellhound pointed out. "Cops're prob'ly still holdin' him."

"He's being transferred up here tomorrow morning," Spider said. "But I don't think he's Rupert Weiss. He doesn't look anything like the image Kane gave us."

Holt grunted. "But he might know something about Stemp's shooter. I bet Weiss left the Calgary airport and drove straight up here."

"You're probably right," Ian agreed cheerfully. "He's in Drumheller."

Holt jerked forward. "When the hell were you planning to tell us that? Where in Drumheller?"

"At his house. Have a look." Ian took his tracking device out of his pocket and passed it to Holt. "We're out of range now, but it's still showing his last known position."

"He lives in Drumheller?" I stared at Ian. "And it didn't occur to you to *tell us*?"

He gave me one of his sunny smiles. "The house is owned by a numbered company that Weiss owns, so I wanted to confirm that he actually lived there and was returning there." He gave me a virtuous look. "I'd hate to send you on a wild-goose chase."

Keeping my tone neutral with a supreme effort, I asked, "Have you made contact with him yet?"

"No. I thought it would be better if we give him some rope. See what he's going to do."

"He already did it," Holt snapped. "He tried to shoot George Harrison."

"I'm quite sure he didn't," Ian countered. "He's not the type."

Somehow managing to suppress my eye-roll, I said, "He's a weapons expert. He's the type."

Ian's eyebrows rose. "And you carry a small arsenal of weapons at all times. But you don't solve your problems by killing everyone who gets in your way."

"I'd sure like to solve *one* of my problems that way," I muttered, giving him the evil eye.

"We don't need to be on the alert unless Weiss approaches," Kane pointed out peaceably. "Rand, are you certain that the tracker is actually on him? Did you get a visual?"

"No," Ian admitted. "But we can stake out the location tomorrow. Weiss goes outdoors every day at exactly ten AM and three-thirty PM."

Reminded of time passing, I glanced at my watch. Shit, I had to leave in ten minutes.

"Okay," I said briskly. "So, John and Arnie, what's your plan?"

Hellhound shrugged. "Don't really have one. Just wanted to get outta town so Kath wouldn't get caught in the crossfire if somebody tried to off me. Figured ya might need a hand up here."

"Same for me," Kane agreed. "Alicia and Daniel will be safe if everyone thinks I'm dead. After you question the suspect tomorrow morning, we'll be able to form a better plan." He frowned. "Attempts on my life and Stemp's indicate a connection with Rupert Weiss and/or the ultrasound weapon; and probably Volslav. But why would Hellhound be on the hit list?"

Silence fell and answering frowns appeared.

"You're right, it doesn't make sense," I agreed. "Arnie only picked up the weapon and brought it back to Silverside after the plane crash where we first got it."

Hellhound shrugged. "Maybe somebody spotted me at the airport."

Holt leaned back, still frowning. "If somebody's trying to kill you because they saw you at the airport with Kane and Kelly, then they should be trying to kill Kelly, too. But nobody tried."

"I wasn't here," I pointed out. "And if they're connected to Volslav, they've known about my security system since last winter; so they wouldn't come close to the farm. They'll probably try to hit me when I'm in Silverside." I glanced at Holt. "They'll probably try for you, too, if they're making a clean sweep."

"Oh, lovely," Ian said. "So thanks to your gracious invitation, I'm now a target, too."

I shrugged, refusing to embark on his guilt trip. "You were likely a target the minute you hooked up with Weiss."

Holt gave Ian a dark look. "Or maybe he's safe because he's working with Weiss to murder Stemp, and he's been reporting our movements to Volslav."

Ian sat bolt upright, his green eyes flashing. "I'm not a traitor!"

"Sure," Holt said with a shrug. "I believe you. You've been so honest with us about everything else."

"I have given you as much information as I considered relevant and advisable, in my professional opinion," Ian said, his British accent sharpening the words to a razor edge. "And I assure you, if you were to ask me under your infallible lie detector whether I'm working with Volslav, it would prove my innocence."

Holt's steely eyes narrowed. "Good to hear. We'll do that first thing tomorrow morning."

Ian blinked, then squared his shoulders. "I'll look forward to it."

"Okay, then." I rose decisively, hoping the others would do the same.

They didn't.

Shit.

"Well, I have to go," I said casually. "Let's meet at the office tomorrow morning at eight."

"Go?" Holt eyed me. "Where?"

"Out."

"Do you need backup?" Kane asked.

"No, but thanks."

"Where are you going?" Holt repeated.

I gave him my sweetest smile. "I have a personal engagement."

Ian rose with a chuckle. "Holt, you should know a lady never kisses and tells. But I recognize a polite dismissal when I hear one. I'm off." He disappeared into the kitchen.

Holt and I got up and followed. As we rounded the corner, Ian tossed us a jaunty salute from the front door and let himself out.

Holt turned to me. "Were you just trying to get rid of him?"

"No, I really do have to go out." I glanced at my watch and tried not to clench my teeth. "Now."

"Okay. Call me if you need backup."

"Thanks. See you tomorrow."

As Holt headed for the door, I scurried down the hall to the bathroom.

By the time I returned, Holt was gone and John and Arnie were hovering in the kitchen.

"Ya sure you're gonna be okay?" Arnie inquired

worriedly.

"Fine. This should be safe," I assured him.

"Gonna be long?"

"Likely not." I hurried for the door, shoving my feet into my shoes and strapping on my waist pouch. "Would you mind staying in the house with Spider and Linda until I get back? You know the combination to the gun safe if you need it."

"'Kay," Arnie agreed. "See ya later."

I jogged to the garage and let myself in, activating my bug detector from sheer force of habit as I slid into the driver's seat of my car.

Red light.

I froze.

CHAPTER 21

I stared at the steady glow of my bug detector.

Solid red. Not even flashing. I was right on top of the damn bug.

Another thought hit me, kicking my pulse into high gear.

The bug detector didn't just detect listening devices. It would catch anything that was transmitting a signal. Like, for example, an explosive device that would blow as soon as I turned the key or shifted my weight on the seat.

Fuck, fuck, *fuck!*

That answered Holt's earlier question about why nobody had taken a shot at me. They hadn't needed to. They'd planted a bomb in my car instead.

The memory of my previous car exploding in a fireball tightened my chest and accelerated my breathing.

How could they have gotten past my security perimeter without triggering the cameras? And more to the point, why the *hell* hadn't I taken a few extra seconds to walk around my car with my bug detector as I usually did?

Trying not to make any sudden moves, I reached slowly into my waist pouch and took out my phone. It took a couple of tries for my shaking fingers to correctly type, "Please come to the garage" and send the text to Kane and Hellhound.

Only moments later, the garage door opened and both

men entered, dodging sideways and ducking for cover.

I texted, "Safe to come out." As they emerged, I held up the bug detector so they could see the red light, then switched back to texting. "Might be bug, or bomb. Check my car?"

Their expressions grim, they hurried over to sink to the floor on opposite sides of my car. I sat in silence, teeth clenched while they examined the chassis and wheel wells.

After minutes that felt far too long, they both rose with headshakes.

I pointed to my seat.

Hellhound crouched beside the open driver's door, studying the seat and leaning carefully over and around me to look at the back. Kane went to my tool chest and got my inspection mirror, and I gave him a grateful look. Thank God he'd done enough recreational wrenching with me to know where my tools were.

More minutes crawled by while he used the mirror to examine every surface around and under the seat.

Still nothing.

I sat perfectly still, my skin crawling with nerves. If there was a pressure plate in my seat, the whole garage could blow if I shifted position.

Hellhound motioned for me to pop the hood, but I texted them both, "Don't take the chance. Go back to the house now."

John and Arnie exchanged a glance, then shook their heads.

I frowned and mouthed, "Go!"

John's fingers flew across his phone. "We'll call the bomb squad."

I texted back, "You didn't find a bomb. Probably just a

bug."

Arnie scowled and texted, "So pop the hood."

We stared at each other. Impasse.

I really didn't want to die in a fireball, and I especially didn't want to kill the men I loved in the process. But calling the bomb squad for nothing would be embarrassing; and it would take a long damn time. I was already late.

Arnie and John had gone over the car and found nothing. It was probably just a bug.

But if it wasn't...

I texted, "I'll open the hood if you go outside first."

An instant after John's phone vibrated with my message, he was already typing his reply. "If you aren't willing to risk our lives, you don't get to risk yours." Even as the text popped up on my screen, he was typing a second one. "Open the hood and trunk, or we'll call the bomb squad."

I eased out a long slow breath. Be logical. Nothing had happened so far. The most likely triggering options would be turning the key in the ignition or a pressure plate in the driver's seat. They wouldn't bother hooking a detonator up to the hood or trunk latches, because I might not open those.

So it should be safe to open the hood and trunk...

Gritting my teeth, I hit the hood and trunk releases simultaneously. The thump of their opening made every muscle in my body clench, but nothing else happened.

Arnie and John split up, one to the hood and one to the trunk. I barely breathed until they both emerged, shaking their heads with relief.

Trembling, I eased out of the car.

Nothing exploded.

I hissed out my tension on a long breath as I walked around the car, bug detector in hand. The light stayed solid red.

The men and I exchanged a frown. Shit, had I just had a near heart attack because of an electronic malfunction?

I moved farther away from the car, then farther still. Halfway to the door, the bug detector still registered solid red.

Comprehension arrived in a burst of adrenaline-soaked anger.

I handed the bug detector to Kane and he took a few steps backward. The light flashed in a rapid cadence. As he moved farther away, its rhythm slowed.

Dammit, I was right. The fucking bug was on me.

Fury swelled higher inside me as I kicked off my shoes and removed my waist pouch, then padded in my sock feet toward Kane.

The red light's cadence didn't change.

Hellhound picked up my waist pouch and relocated it a couple of yards away, and Kane approached my shoes. When the bug detector didn't react, he turned and moved toward my waist pouch.

The cadence increased until the light glowed solid red.

Slipping my shoes back on, I picked up my waist pouch and upended it over the workbench. My usual accoutrements were tightly packed as usual so they stayed in place, but a tiny black device bounced free.

Extracting my reading glasses from the pouch, I peered at the bug. Or was it a tracker? I couldn't tell. John and Arnie each took a look and returned a shrug, too.

Simmering with rage, I selected my biggest pair of pliers and crushed the device. Then I lowered its remains to the concrete floor and fired up my propane torch. Moments later the garage reeked of burnt electronics, and all that remained was an ugly blotch on my formerly-pristine floor.

Arnie broke the silence. "Think it's done for, darlin'."

"Not half as done as Rand's going to be when I get hold of him," I snarled. "I'm going to give his balls the same treatment."

Hellhound flinched and cupped his crotch. "Tell ya what, darlin', why don't ya put down the pliers an' torch? My nuts're tryin' to climb up my asshole right now."

I laughed in spite of myself and put down my weapons. "Don't worry, all testicles currently in this garage are safe."

Kane gave me a smile. "That's a relief." Sobering, he added, "What makes you think that device was Rand's?"

"I did a bug check right after Margaret left around eight o'clock, and everything was clear. I'd left my waist pouch and shoes by the front door. Rand was the only person who went over there unsupervised, and he had enough time to drop that thing in my waist pouch before Holt and I came around the corner."

Kane frowned. "Rand was the first, but maybe not the only. Holt had opportunity, too, while you were in the bathroom."

My heart plummeted. "I... guess you're right. But I don't think..." I trailed off.

I didn't *want* to think Holt had bugged me. But if Dermott had given him a direct order...

"Fuck!" I shook my head. "I don't have time for this. I'm late already. Thank you for everything, and I'll be back as soon as I can."

I hugged and kissed each of them in turn, holding them a little longer than necessary despite the urgency pounding at me.

When I reached the dark highway a few minutes later, I

swung onto the pavement and accelerated. As the yellow lines whipped past, I stared tensely into the cone of visibility provided by my headlights.

Despite my reckless disregard for traffic laws, I was half an hour late when I pulled into the back lane behind Stemp's house. For the first time, I wondered whether I should have tried to contact him with a schedule change. But I couldn't phone him on an unsecured line, and even though I trusted John and Arnie with my life, I didn't want them to know about my secret communication system. What they didn't know, couldn't be construed as treason if the shit hit the fan.

And it might.

I sighed and reached for the door handle, then froze.

Stemp had said he was under surveillance. My car's dome light would turn on as soon as I opened the door, making me an easy target. I should scout the area for potential spies and/or assassins first.

Half annoyed that I hadn't thought of it sooner and half relieved that I'd thought of it in time, I idled down the alley.

All the surrounding houses were dark. Stemp's house was completely enclosed by a tall fence and sheltered by evergreen trees at the back, but it showed no sign of life from the front, either.

Alert for the slightest irregularity, I scanned up and down the street. Lots of windows were open to catch the cool night air, and I strained my eyes toward each dark screen. A sniper could easily lurk in any of those rooms, invisible until it was too late.

Stifling a curse, I drove away, zigzagging block by block until I was sure I hadn't been followed. I pulled over and retrieved my infrared / night vision goggles from my go-bag in the trunk, then returned to Stemp's street.

In my enhanced vision the houses glowed warm yellow-orange. No hot red body masses hunched by any of the windows, though a semi-horizontal blob indicated Stemp's frail elderly neighbour Bud Weems in his living room directly across the street. He must be ill again, dozing in his recliner. A flash of movement in my peripheral vision made me whip my head around, but the orange blob was too small to be a threat. The cool blue legs and tail identified it as a cat, slinking across the street on some nocturnal errand.

I eased out a breath and cruised around to the back alley again. There, I parked several houses down and switched the dome light off before pulling on the black hoodie from my go-bag and tucking my hair inside.

When I slipped out of the car, gravel crunched under my feet. I closed the door softly behind me and crept toward Stemp's gate, placing my feet cautiously to keep my footsteps as silent as possible.

Dammit, I was nearly an hour late now. Stemp undoubtedly had a good surveillance system, so he'd know somebody was skulking around in his alley; but would he still be expecting me? Or would he attack me as soon as I came through the gate, thinking I was an enemy?

Giving a mental shrug, I let go of that worry. Stemp was far too professional to kill someone accidentally. At worst, I'd end up with a few bruises and a short session of unconsciousness.

As I reached for the gate latch, another thought froze my hand in midair.

Shit, what if midnight had been a critical deadline and Stemp had left? If there was anyone other than Stemp on the opposite side of the gate, this meeting could be fatal.

Mouthing silent curses, I drew my tranquilizer pistol.

Then I flipped the latch, opened the gate just enough to accommodate me, and whisked through the gap.

An almost-inaudible '*pfft-thunk*' was the only warning I got.

The world slipped sideways and faded to nothingness.

CHAPTER 22

I swam slowly back to consciousness, but my eyelids wouldn't open.

Better not to let my captors know I was awake. I took stock as best I could. There was a hard surface under me, but the sensation was distant. I couldn't feel my arms or legs.

Panic flared. Was I paralyzed?

I must have made some involuntary sound or movement, because Stemp's precise voice spoke.

"Aydan, it's Charles. You are safe. You inhaled some tranquilizer gas, and you should regain full motor control in two to three minutes. Don't be afraid."

Relief flooded me. I couldn't get any more limp than I already was, but I mumbled "Thank God" so he'd know I'd heard and understood.

My words came out sounding like "Ahn-guh", which apparently wasn't enlightening. Stemp repeated his reassurances, and kept patiently repeating them until I managed to pry one eyelid open.

I mumbled, "'M'kay. Thangz."

He nodded and fell silent.

Even with the blurry vision of my one cooperating eye, I recognized the secret holding cell concealed in Stemp's backyard shed. I was laid out on the floor, while Stemp sat on the bench that occupied one side.

I was grateful he'd put me on the floor. That bench was carefully constructed at a slant that made it impossible to sit or lie down for more than a short time without discomfort. Not exactly a torture device, but diabolically designed to cause maximum unpleasantness. Once more I thanked my lucky stars that Stemp and I were allies, not enemies.

At last I got both eyes open and hauled myself into a slumped semi-seated position against the wall.

"My apologies for the unpleasant reception," Stemp said. "I was almost certain it was you; but caution seemed prudent."

"No problem." My tongue still felt thick, but at least my words were intelligible. A squint at my wristwatch showed that only about five minutes had elapsed. Stemp must have shot the dart at the fence to release the instant-acting aerosolized tranquilizer, instead of giving me the double whammy of the inhaled drug plus the dart's injectable payload.

"Can you stand?" Stemp inquired.

"Yeah." I struggled to my feet, accepting his proffered hand for support. After a wobbly moment I got my muscles under control. "Okay, I'm fine now."

"Take time to be sure," he advised. "We will be descending a short ladder. A fall would be unlikely to cause serious injury, but it would cause considerable discomfort."

"Okay..." I eyed him with a raised eyebrow, but he didn't elaborate.

Of course not. This was Stemp: Mr. Need-To-Know.

After another minute of pacing back and forth in the shed, I declared myself fit to climb.

Stemp nodded and came over to stand beside me, then withdrew a key fob from his pocket and pressed a button.

With a faint click, the bench and the portion of floor around it descended and retracted beneath us. Dim lights flicked on in the void below, revealing a ladder and the mouth of a concrete tunnel.

A really small concrete tunnel. Barely tall enough to traverse on hands and knees.

My chest seized.

"I apologize for the close quarters," Stemp said. "It is only a short tunnel to the basement of my house. Will you be all right?"

"Of course." My voice came out level despite the frantic banging of my heart. "Didn't you see in my psych reports that I've dealt with my claustrophobia?"

"I did see that in Dr. Rawling's reports." Stemp's piercing amber gaze coasted over me, seeing too much. He held up the remote control and pointed to two unmarked black buttons. "Should you need to escape..."

He surveyed me, and I did my best to look as though I was perfectly comfortable in a coffin-sized concrete tube eight feet underground.

"...the left button opens the access points; the right button closes them," Stemp went on without a change of expression.

"And I remember that the red button is knockout gas, the green button is surveillance, and the blue button is the exhaust fan to clear the knockout gas," I contributed, trying to sound matter-of-fact. "Does that apply to the tunnel, too, or only to the shed?"

"Tunnels as well," Stemp confirmed. "There is also a manual release lever inside each end of tunnel so you can escape even if the power fails."

"Okay, thanks," I said casually, hoping he didn't realize exactly how much I had needed to hear that.

But he probably did. Stemp knew everything.

He nodded and went down the ladder, then turned to give me an expectant look.

Clenching my teeth, I stepped onto the ladder. My knuckles glowed phosphorescent in the dim light. As I stepped onto the concrete floor, a clatter from behind made me spin with a gasp.

"Mechanic's creepers," Stemp said, pushing one toward me as he lay down on the other. "Much more comfortable than hands and knees for traversing the tunnels."

Not trusting my voice, I nodded and lay down, too. The bench and floor segment slid out again, and I clamped my eyes shut as a click from above signalled that the portal had locked back into place.

Trapped-trapped-*trapped*...

The hush of rubber wheels on concrete made my eyes pop open in time to see Stemp's feet disappearing down the tunnel.

I used the moment of privacy to give in to a few quick shallow gasps.

Not hyperventilating. I was fine. Just fine.

Breathe...

I couldn't force myself to go headfirst down the tunnel like Stemp. Instead I swung the creeper around and went in feet first, my trembling arms barely hauling me along by the handholds in the tunnel. As soon as my head was fully inside the tunnel, the lights in the chamber went out.

Sucking in a hiccup of pure panic, I propelled myself as quickly as possible toward the glow I glimpsed between my boots.

Motion sensor lights, that's all. I wasn't entombed down here in the stygian blackness. I was fine...

The tunnel was surprisingly short. In seconds I emerged into a concrete cubicle that was tall enough to allow me to stand. The soft sound of wheels on concrete ahead made me realize that this was only an interim chamber, and the low tunnel continued on the other side.

The chamber contained a single sturdy chair.

In a concrete cell. Hidden far below ground, where nobody could hear the screams.

Bloodstains on the floor and walls...

My stomach lurched and I dove for the tunnel, scrabbling along until I shot out the other end so fast that I nearly bowled Stemp's feet from under him.

All pretense of composure gone, I sprang up and gibbered, "Wh-What...?" My finger shook as I jabbed it back in the direction of the nightmare chamber. "Wh-What *is that?*"

"My panic room." A small frown creased Stemp's forehead in what was, for him, an unprecedented display of emotion. "An unobtrusive escape route from the house, and a defensible position if necessary."

"B-But the blood..." I sucked in a breath and forced my voice hard and steady. "Do you bring people down here to torture them?"

His incredulous stare eased my panic even before he replied. If emotionless Stemp looked that poleaxed, then I had definitely misinterpreted the purpose of that chamber.

Stemp closed his dangling jaw. "No, I do not." His words were stiff and clipped. "The chamber is a repurposed water cistern. The stains are rust."

I sagged with relief. "Shit, I'm sorry. I just... You have the prison shed with the knockout gas; and two creepers, one for you and one for an unconscious body; and an underground chamber with nothing but a chair in the middle..." I trailed off.

"The chair is for my own comfort." To my astonishment, a flush rose on Stemp's cheeks. "I am learning the violin. I practice underground, so that my lack of competence offends only my own ears. And I usually leave one creeper at each end of the tunnel to provide instant access in an emergency. Since I used the tunnel to access the shed tonight, both were at that end."

"Ohmigod." I hid my face in my hands. "I'm such an idiot. I'm so sorry!"

"Not at all." The hint of humour in his voice made me peek through my fingers to see him smiling. "On the contrary, it was a logical... albeit disturbing... deduction. Shall we?"

He motioned me forward, and I realized for the first time that we were in his basement.

As I stepped past the clothes dryer, Stemp pressed one of the black buttons on the fob. The washer and dryer, accompanied by a segment of wall behind them, slid smoothly in front of the tunnel entrance.

"Please have a seat." Stemp indicated a leather sofa in front of a small television. "May I offer you a drink?"

"Um, no. Thanks," I mumbled, completely rattled. "You go ahead if you want, though."

"Unnecessary." As he sat down in the armchair to my right, the phone rang and he added, "Please excuse me for a moment."

Before I could wonder who the hell was calling at one-thirty in the morning, he spoke. "Hello, Bud. I have confirmed that the vehicle is not a threat. Your troops can stand down." After a pause for Bud's reply, he responded, "Thank you again for your concern and dedication. Goodbye." He gave me a wry smile as he hung up.

I groaned. "I saw Bud in his recliner, but I didn't realize he was guarding your house. And he has troops?"

"Sadly, yes. Citizen's Reconnaissance And Protection Services is on the job."

"Oh, God. They're going to get themselves killed."

Stemp's mouth flattened into a grim line. "I most sincerely hope not. I have joined them for the express purpose of preventing that outcome."

"You joined CRAPS." After a moment of incredulity, I realized the wisdom of that. "Good idea. Maybe I should join, too."

"That would be beneficial." He sighed. "However, my membership is not entirely altruistic. The geriatric sleuths are an asset in my current situation. They know most of the town's inhabitants and are familiar with their vehicles, so they are better at spotting non-residents. They are unconstrained by the demands of work or family, they are insatiably nosy, and they have sufficient numbers that they can maintain effective surveillance around the clock."

"I guess you're right," I agreed. "I just hate the idea of them getting caught in the crossfire. And you know Lola and Pearl..." I hesitated. "Well, maybe you don't know them as well as I do; but they wouldn't think twice about pretending to be old, and doddering out in front of a speeding car assuming the driver would stop."

"They are not *pretending* to be old," Stemp said dryly. "Pearl is ninety-three. Nevertheless, I agree; and I am doing my best to control the risks. Dermott and I decided to have the RCMP announce that this was not a targeted attack; merely random shots. I don't want Bud to worry about me unduly. He can barely walk, but he would not hesitate to throw himself in harm's way to protect me. Or anyone, for that matter."

"Army guys," I said with a mixture of fondness, respect, and annoyance. "It doesn't matter how old they are, they're always army guys."

"Indeed. And being an 'army guy'..." A dip of Stemp's chin indicated air quotes around the words. "...Bud is mightily offended that anyone would threaten the safety of his neighbourhood. I could not prevent him, so I instead encouraged him to set up a command post in his home. There is a CRAPS member in his recliner at all times. They work in teams of four, spelling each other off. They have also set up two more command posts in other members' homes. I claimed the responsibility of coordinating intel."

"So they call you with everything they see. Brilliant."

"Unbeknownst to them, I have also installed an expanded surveillance perimeter." Stemp turned on the TV and several rows of dark squares appeared on the screen. "The cameras are motion-activated so there is little to see at this time of night, but I spotted your car as you drove in. Both times. Did you see anything unusual on your patrol?"

My cheeks heated at the memory of my indecisiveness after I'd arrived. "No. And I'm really sorry I was so late. Ian put a bug or a tracer on me; I'm not sure which. I had to get rid of it before I left."

Stemp sat up straight. "Rand is trying to surveil you?"

"I don't know if it's him..." An embarrassing thought occurred to me, and I hunched my shoulders. "I should have had Spider look at the device. He could have told me whether it was a bug or a tracer, and probably whether it was one of ours or MI6's. But I destroyed it. Damn. I was so stressed and mad, I wasn't thinking."

Stemp's eyes narrowed. "Why would it be one of ours?"

"I have no idea; but I don't trust Dermott, and the feeling is mutual. He might be trying to trip me up again. Holt and Rand were the only two people who had the opportunity to place the device, so I can't rule out Holt acting for Dermott. But my gut says it's Rand."

"Why?"

"I don't... know..." I thought out loud. "I've never trusted Ian. I mean, I don't think he's crooked; and he's a good agent. It's just that he's not a team player. If he has to screw somebody else to get what he wants, he doesn't hesitate. And his whole situation just seems... off. He said it was coincidence that he ended up in Halifax, and coincidence that Weiss decided to take off on his own; but now he's showed up here and inserted himself in the investigation..." I shook my head. "It could be all coincidence like he says, but I smell a rat. I haven't figured out his agenda yet, but I'm sure he has one."

"I concur. Have you discussed this with Dermott?"

"No. I'll brief him tomorrow morning." When Stemp raised an eyebrow, I shrugged. "This isn't urgent, and the analysts are on top of it. Dermott gets annoyed if I call him after hours with unnecessary updates."

For an instant Stemp looked as though he had bitten into a lemon, but the expression vanished before I could be sure. "Very well," he said. "I did not hear any of this, and you were never here. I have informed Dermott about my arrangement with CRAPS, so he will likely brief you in the morning."

"And I'll join CRAPS, too."

Stemp gave me an approving nod. "Now, the reason for my secrecy in summoning you..."

"Katya and Anna," I surmised.

"Yes. Although those are not their current identities." Stemp hesitated. "My suspension and the NSIRA inquiry are... troublesome."

I braced myself. "Are you planning to go overseas?"

"No."

I hid my relief as he went on, "As much as it galls me to remain here, my involvement would create unacceptable risk for my family; and undesirable consequences for me. Mother and Father have already departed in my stead."

"Your mom and... Karma?" I guessed. "Or Skidmark?"

A small smile touched Stemp's lips. "I still refer to Karma as my father, and Skidmark remains Skidmark despite our biological relationship. We are both more comfortable that way. While I treasure the opportunity to get to know the dedicated operative behind Skidmark's reprobate stoner cover, Karma is and has always been my father figure."

I smiled. "I'm so glad you've reconciled with them. If they need anything, or if you need to talk privately again, just get one of them to call me."

"I do not foresee your aid being necessary, but I do appreciate the offer." He opened a drawer in the side table and withdrew a small piece of paper, which he handed to me. "Should you need to contact Mother or Father, these are the burner numbers they are currently using. My burners are the bottom three numbers."

"Thanks. Let's hope I don't need them." I smothered a yawn. God, I was exhausted. "What do you plan to do if there's another hitman?"

"Dermott will brief you in the morning." Stemp rose. "Which will come all too soon. Go home and get some sleep. You may leave the creeper under the shed. After you pull the emergency lever to open the tunnel, you will have ten seconds to exit before it recloses automatically." He pressed the fob button and the washer and dryer slid aside.

"Okay, thanks." I lay down on the creeper and rolled toward the tunnel. "Good night."

The return trip wasn't quite as alarming as the first, but nevertheless I hurried up the ladder into the shed with a gasp of relief. Pulling up my hood again, I emerged cautiously from the shed and slipped through the back gate.

Focused on home and bed, I didn't see the dark figure lurking by my car until it was too late.

CHAPTER 23

I was already dodging sideways and snatching for my gun when the figure spoke in a familiar voice.

"Caught you!"

"Oh-for-fucksakes!" My words blew out on a gust of relief as I converted my grab for my holster into a scooping clutch of my chest instead. "Lola, what are you doing out here in the middle of the night? You scared the shit out of me!"

"Caught you red-handed is more like it," she said smugly. "CRAPS surveillance saw your car arrive half an hour ago. I thought you said you didn't get along with your boss. Called him a dickhead, in fact." Teasing and prurient curiosity mingled in her voice as she added, "I knew something was up when he invited you to his place for dinner with his parents. And now you're paying him a secret visit in the middle of the night, just long enough for a quickie. You've been holding out on me, you naughty girl."

I gaped at her small shadowy figure, shock and horror weighing my jaw down. "Christ, no! I'm not scr-"

I bit off the denial before I could complete it. If I wasn't screwing my boss, then how the hell could I explain why I was sneaking in to see him in the middle of the night? Impossible to explain it to Lola; catastrophic if I had to explain it to Dermott.

I sank my face into my hands. "Oh, God."

Lola dropped the tease immediately, hurrying forward to slip a motherly arm around my waist. "It's okay, Aydan, I won't say anything. And nobody else recognized your car. But... honey, is something wrong? Is he..." Her small body stiffened beside me. "Aydan, is he forcing you to have sex? Threatening your job if you don't?"

For shit's sake, this just kept getting worse.

"No, nothing like that. Don't worry," I assured her hurriedly. "It's just... embarrassing."

"Why? If you like each other, where's the harm? You're both adults. Unless..." I could hear the frown in her voice. "Are you keeping it a secret from Arnie and John? I thought the three of you had an open relationship. Do you think they'd be jealous? Or is there a workplace dating policy that could cause problems?"

Since slashing my wrists didn't seem to be an option, I straightened my spine and put as much certainty into my voice as I could manage. "Lola, please, just let it go. It's a private thing, and I don't want to talk about it. And I especially don't want anybody else to find out."

"My lips are sealed, honey." She bumped my hip with hers, and I could hear the mischievous smile in her voice. "Trust me, as the owner of the only sex shop in town, I keep all kinds of secrets. Yours is tame compared to some of the stuff I know."

I groaned.

Her tone turned brisk as she straightened and squeezed my hand. "Seriously, Aydan, your secret is safe with me. And if you ever want to talk about anything... just know that I'm always here for you. Okay?"

What could I say?

Half humiliated, half grateful, I pulled her into a hug. "Thanks, Lola. Now, you'd better get back to Bud's before they send out a search party. And you should stay inside. It's dangerous out here in the dark." Reconsidering, I added, "Come on, get in the car and I'll drop you off."

Lola snorted. "I don't need a ride. It's half a block."

"Which is half a block too far in the middle of the night. Get in."

"But then the rest of the team will see you," she pointed out. Her tone turned contemplative. "If they keep digging with the description of your car, they might figure out who you are anyway. We need a cover story so they don't look any further."

I nearly snapped, 'If I had one, don't you think I would have used it?' but instead I bit my tongue and said humbly, "That's a good idea, but no matter what I say I'm here for, you know what it looks like."

"So you were never here," Lola said. "Just go out the alley and turn down the next street so they don't see your car again. If anybody asks, I'll tell them I recognized the car and it was pizza delivery."

"It's two o'clock in the morning. Fiorenza's is the only pizza place in town, and they close at ten o'clock."

"But you can still get a pizza delivered if you know the right people."

"Bullshit."

"Oh, ye of little faith." Lola patted my hand. "If the owners like you, you can get pizza any time of the day or night. You just have to pay a little more."

I raised a skeptical eyebrow, forgetting that she couldn't see it in the darkness. "How much do they have to like you?

I'm pretty sure Mr. Rossi isn't harbouring a secret passion for my boss."

Lola laughed. "No, but your boss can probably afford to pay the premium. That's our story, and we're sticking to it: It was a pizza delivery. Tell Charles so he doesn't accidentally spill the beans. I'll tell Bartolo. He'll corroborate if anybody asks."

"Oh, it's Bartolo, is it?" I teased. "Does Mrs. Rossi know about this?"

"Bartolo and Fiorenza and I go 'way back." Lola's voice turned mock-severe. "And you, young lady, are in no position to make innuendos."

Chastened, I was about to apologize when Lola snickered. "That's a word that always makes me laugh. It's like The Godfather saying 'up yours'." She put on an atrocious Italian accent and made a graphic gesture. "In you end-o!"

My snort of laughter escaped before I could clap a hand over my mouth.

"You'd better skedaddle before somebody catches you," Lola urged. "You can drop me at the end of the alley if it'll make you feel better."

"Thank you. It does." We got into the car and I idled down to the next cross-street. There, I braked and turned to face Lola. "Thanks again. I really appreciate this."

"No problem, honey." She reached over and patted my cheek. "Just remember, if you ever need to talk, I'm here. No judgement. I'll always be on your side." She let herself out of the car before I could overcome the lump in my throat and thank her again. She strode off with a jaunty wave, and I watched her tiny but sprightly figure until she arrived safely at Bud's house.

By the time I got home I could barely keep my eyes open despite the many worries still nagging at me. I winced as I drove down my lane in the darkness. My vehicle would have tripped the motion sensors, and everyone would be on alert. Pulling into the garage, I texted, "It's just me, don't worry".

When I let myself into the house, Kane and Hellhound met me.

"Everythin' okay?" Hellhound inquired as he engulfed me in a hug.

"Fine. Thanks." I hugged him back, then repeated the process with Kane. "Sorry I took so long. I meant to be back earlier, but shit happened." Taking in their worried expressions, I hurriedly added, "Not dangerous shit, just annoying. Everything's okay. Do you want to stay in the house tonight?"

"No, I'll go back to the campsite," Kane said. "It'll be getting light in a couple of hours. I'd rather go out now in full darkness and sleep soundly until you trip the motion sensors leaving for work."

"I'll go out, too," Hellhound seconded, then hesitated. "Unless ya want me to stay?"

"Either is fine with me." I tried to stifle a yawn, and failed. "I can't go to bed yet, but you're welcome to if you want."

Both men frowned.

"What else do you have to do tonight?" Kane asked. "Can we help?"

"No, it's okay. Just some desk stuff I have to finish." I put on my most reassuring expression. "It won't take long, but it has to be done tonight."

"Awright, then, we'll get outta your hair." Hellhound dropped a kiss on my forehead. "G'night, darlin'. Give us a call if ya need anythin', no matter what time it is."

"Thanks." I hugged him. "Good night."

Kane offered me an equally chaste hug and kiss, and they slipped out the back door.

As I was heading toward my office my wrist monitor vibrated, and I heard a ping from the guest room.

Hurrying over, I stood outside the door and kept my voice low. "It's just Arnie and John going out."

Spider's reply drifted through the door, equally quiet. "Got it. Thanks, Aydan. Good night."

Emitting a yawn so huge it nearly turned me inside-out, I shuffled down the hall to my office. When I dropped into my chair, I wasn't surprised to find the tiny white square already blinking in the crossword puzzle game.

God, now I had to explain to Stemp how I'd screwed up and gotten caught. When he'd said he was under surveillance, I had assumed he meant by enemies, not by friends who knew my car.

But I should have been more careful regardless. This screwup was all mine.

I groaned and held Alt-Shift while I clicked on the square.

The text window bloomed and the cursor zipped across the screen. "You were intercepted. Report."

I sighed and typed, "Lola identified my car. She thinks you and I are having an affair, but she's covering for us. None of the other CRAPS members know my car, so she'll tell them you were getting a late-night pizza delivery, and my car was Bartolo Rossi's."

I hit send, then added, "Bartolo and his wife own Fiorenza's, and apparently they'll deliver pizza at any hour if you pay enough. Lola is friends with them, and she'll tell

Bartolo to corroborate our story if anyone asks."

After I hit send, the cursor blinked without moving for several moments. I winced, imagining Stemp processing the mortifying news.

At last the cursor moved. "Not optimum; but acceptable damage control. Anything else?"

"No."

The text window vanished, and I hauled myself upright and trudged off to bed.

Less than four hours later, the sound of my alarm jerked me out of slumber. Pumping a bullet into the offending device was a temptation, but unfortunately not an option. I silenced the alarm with an irritable swat, and dragged myself out of bed and into the shower.

At the breakfast table, Spider and Linda's bright morning faces compelled me to put on as cheerful an expression as I could manage. After gulping my peanut butter toast, I headed for the garage.

This time I circled my car warily with the bug detector, but the green light shone its blessing.

On the short drive to Silverside, my mind ticked over all the questions I wanted to ask the prisoner. But first I'd talk to the analysts and see whether they'd been able to dig up any useful dirt about him.

But before that, I had to get safely into Sirius Dynamics. With Stemp's shooter still at large, I had to assume we were all in danger. After trying and failing to kill Stemp, the killer might decide to try for someone else.

Should I park in the Sirius lot, and depend on Sirius's surveillance and security to protect me? Or park at the house/office above the secondary bunker and take the tunnel, in case someone was set up near Sirius ready to pick me off?

But the house had my name on the sign out front, so that would be a logical place for an assassin to lurk, too. Maybe I should go in through the secret bowling alley entrance.

And dammit, I needed a bulletproof jacket. But I couldn't get one until I got into Sirius...

By the time I got to town, my brain was buzzing with too many thoughts and too much adrenaline. Choosing the safest option, I parked a block away from the bowling alley.

Pretending normalcy but ready to dodge and run if bullets flew, I headed down the sidewalk. Varying my speed and occasionally crouching in the guise of tying my shoe or picking up litter, I tried to make myself as difficult a target as possible. When I let myself in the back door of the bowling alley at last, my heart was thumping as though I'd run a mile.

For once, being entombed underground was calming. By the time I emerged from the secured area into the Sirius lobby, I was almost ready to face Ian when he rose from one of the chairs.

"Good morning," he said cheerfully.

"Morning," I grunted as I headed for the security wicket.

As I signed in, Leo glanced at Ian, who had taken up a position at my elbow.

"Do you want a visitor's fob?" Leo asked.

"Not yet." Turning to Ian, I faked politeness as hard as I could. "Sorry for the delay. I have a few things to do before we can get started."

"No trouble at all." Ian gave me his debonair smile.

I managed a twitch of my lips in return, and hurried through the secured doors before I could yell or smack him.

As I climbed the stairs and turned toward my office, I attempted an attitude adjustment. Hell, maybe Ian wasn't even the person who deserved my wrath. If it had been Holt who stuck that tracker on me...

"Kelly!"

Holt's voice made me start guiltily, and I swung around to see him standing the doorway of the meeting room.

"I've got the lie detector set up here," he said as I approached. "I want to do Rand first. Then we can decide whether we want him to sit in on our interview with the prisoner."

"Okay. Have you talked to Spider's team yet? Did they find out anything more about the prisoner?"

"Haven't asked yet. I was getting set up here."

"Okay, I'll call them now." I cocked an eyebrow at Holt. "Do you mind signing Ian in and supervising him for a few minutes while I finish up?"

"Sure." Holt's too-observant gaze flicked over me. "He really chaps your ass, doesn't he? Why? Lover's tiff?"

I snorted. "In his dreams. Last year he bet Skidmark that he could seduce me. He lost, and now he's made it his life's mission to succeed. He doesn't really want me; he just can't bear to lose his bet."

"Huh. That pretty much sums up his whole attitude," Holt said thoughtfully. "Fuck anybody, as long as he gets something out of it."

"Yep." I turned toward my office. "Back in a bit."

When I returned to the meeting room, the electrodes of the lie detector were already fastened around Ian's temples.

As I swung the door shut behind me and took a seat, Ian said, "Just before we get started... I spoke with my superiors last night and they agreed that I could verify that we have the same objectives regarding Volslav. But those are the only questions I'm cleared to answer."

"Good enough," Holt said. "So, you know the drill. Answer yes or no. Are you supplying, or have you ever supplied information to Volslav or any of their personnel?"

"Not to my knowledge."

Holt rephrased. "Are you now knowingly supplying, or have you ever knowingly supplied information to Volslav or any of their personnel? Yes or no?"

"No."

The green light glowed, and Ian gave Holt a smug smile.

"Are you working with Volslav?"

"No."

Green light.

"Do you have any association with Volslav at all?"

"No."

Red light.

CHAPTER 24

Holt's eyes narrowed.

Ian frowned at the damning red glow on the lie detector. "I'm telling the truth. Why is it red?"

Despite my uncharitable desire to let him sweat a bit, I spoke up. "If you've investigated them, that's an association."

"Oh." Ian relaxed. "All right then, have another go."

Holt chose his words with care. "Other than your investigations, do you have any associations with Volslav at all?"

"No."

This time the green light confirmed Ian's reply.

"Were you involved in any way with the attempts on Stemp's and Kane's lives?" Holt asked.

"No."

Green light again.

Holt and I exchanged a glance, and he shrugged and changed tack. "Have you told us the truth about Rupert Weiss?"

Ian gave him a pleasant smile. "I'm sorry, that's outside the scope of the questions I'm allowed to answer."

"So you've been lying to us," I growled.

Ian's expression never changed. "It doesn't mean I've

been lying to you; it's simply outside the scope of the questions I'm allowed to answer."

My temper boiled up and over. "Did you put a device in my waist pouch last night, you slimy bastard?"

Holt stiffened, his brows snapping together.

"Storm." Ian gave me a look of pure hurt. "What a vicious accusation. I thought we were friends."

"I thought so, too," I growled. "Guess we were both wrong. Did you put a device in my waist pouch last night? Yes or no?"

"Well," Ian said haughtily. "I can see there's no trust here. I've answered all the questions I can, so we're finished. Take this device off me."

"Yeah, now you get all hoity-toity," I snapped. "Because you damn well did put that thing in my pouch, didn't you?"

Ian turned to Holt, gesturing imperiously toward his crown of electrodes. "If you please."

Holt glowered, but there was nothing either of us could do. Ian was far too cool-headed to blurt out any answers, and we had no grounds to detain an MI6 agent. He had already cooperated more than was strictly required.

Holt removed the headdress and stood. "Kelly and I will walk you out."

We marched down the hallway in silence with Ian between us. When the visitor's fob had been returned, Holt took Ian by the arm and escorted him to the door.

Leaning close, Holt spoke softly but with chilling clarity. "If you ever feel like telling the truth, give us a call. Otherwise, stay the fuck out of my way, or I'll slap you in handcuffs and deport your ass."

Ian batted his eyelashes flirtatiously and raised his voice. "Why, Greg, you kinky thing. I'm flattered. I never knew you had a bondage fetish."

Before Holt could explode, I seized his arm. "Anger management," I muttered as I half-dragged him away. "Trust me, he's not worth it."

Holt didn't reply, but I could hear his teeth grinding. I waved my fob at the prox reader and we climbed the stairs without speaking.

Inside the meeting room, Holt closed the door gently. Then he lashed out with a violent kick, striking the nearest chair with such force that it flew across the room and rebounded off the table with a crash.

Holt drew in a long breath and let it out slowly. "I see what you mean about Rand getting under your skin," he said mildly. "Why didn't you tell me he'd tagged you last night?"

Not trusting his apparent calm, I eased backward. "I didn't realize he'd done it until after you were gone; and by the time I found the device and destroyed it, I was late and there wasn't time." Sidestepping casually to put the table between us, I added, "Besides, I wasn't positive he was the one that placed it. You had the opportunity, too."

Holt stood stock-still.

Bracing myself with every ounce of courage I owned, I held his gaze.

After a long moment, he said, "Huh. Fair enough." He dropped into the chair beside the lie detector. Strapping the headdress around his temples, he added, "Ask me."

The desire to back down was almost overwhelming, but I kept my voice level. "Did you put a device in my waist pouch last night?"

"No."

The green light shone, and I couldn't prevent a breath of relief from whooshing out. "Thank God. I was sure it was

Rand, but..." I hesitated. "Sorry."

"No need. It was a fair question." It was Holt's turn to hesitate. "Look... I get that you have trust issues, so you probably won't believe me. But I don't lie to my partners." He grimaced. "Sometimes I can't tell the whole truth, or any of it, but I won't jerk you around if I can avoid it." He met my eyes. "Ask me if that's true."

I shrugged and gave him a smile. "I don't have to. Even when you had orders to screw me over, you still treated me as fairly as you could. I just thought you might have gotten an order to tag me last night."

His shoulders eased. "Okay. But I still want you to believe that I won't lie to you unless I do have orders. So ask me."

Fighting off the fear of vulnerability, I asked, "Was everything you just said true?"

"Yes."

The green light shone.

"Thanks," I said softly.

"You're welcome. Now..." Holt unhooked the lie detector and laid the headdress on the table. "Tell me about this tracker. Or bug, or whatever it was."

"I will, but I think we need to brief Dermott, too."

"Right. Let me get the lie detector packed up and we can go and see Dermott before we question the prisoner."

A few minutes later Dermott answered my tap on his door with a grumpy, "Yeah."

Holt opened the door and stuck his head in. "Got a minute? We've got an update."

"About time," Dermott growled, and jerked his chin toward the two chairs in front of his desk.

Biting my tongue so I couldn't snap back, I took a seat

and looked to Holt.

"Rand's up to something," he said.

Dermott scowled. "No shit. If that's your update, you're wasting my fucking time."

"Last night he planted a bug or tracker on Kelly," Holt replied with surprising patience. "He's not admitting it, but we know it was him."

Dermott's eyes narrowed. "Bug or tracker? Which was it?"

"I don't know," I admitted. "I destroyed it."

"That was fucking stupid."

I bit my tongue harder, then replied, "I realize that now."

Holt spoke up. "It doesn't really matter. We would have dealt with it the same either way. But the good news is, we know where Rupert Weiss is."

"Who?"

This time I bit my tongue and clamped my lips together for good measure.

If Stemp had still been in charge, he would have taken our update calls in person; and if he'd had to route them through the analysts, he would have read their reports the instant he had time. Dermott hadn't even bothered to catch up with our reports from two days ago.

"Rupert Weiss is the name of the weapons expert," Holt said expressionlessly. "He's at an address in Drumheller. He'll be outside at ten hundred and Kelly and I are going to be there when he shows."

"Good work, Holt," Dermott said. "Anything else?"

"We're going down to question the prisoner now," Holt replied. "We were originally thinking Rand could sit in, but I booted him out of the building when we found out he was screwing us over. We'll keep him out of the loop unless he gives us something first."

Dermott gave him an approving nod. "Good. Fucking Limeys. Never trust those bastards. Let me know when you've got Weiss in here for questioning. And you'd better crack the prisoner. I'm getting pressure to release him. The only charge we've got so far is auto theft and possession of an unregistered restricted firearm, and that might not stick. He swears he just lifted the SUV for a joyride and he didn't know there was a gun in it."

"Has the lab done the ballistics from the bullet that hit Kane yet?" I asked. "Any chance it might match the prisoner's gun?"

"If it did, we'd have more than a possession charge, wouldn't we?" Dermott snapped. "So make that bastard talk. And get Weiss in here and make him talk, too."

"What charge did you have in mind for Weiss?" Holt asked.

Dermott gave him a blank look.

"We don't actually have any grounds to arrest him," Holt said cautiously. "As far as we know, he hasn't committed any crime."

"Well, make something up! Just get him in here for questioning!" Dermott jabbed a finger at the door. "Get going! Kelly, stay."

Oh shit.

I did my best to hide my surge of adrenaline.

Holt hesitated. "Anything else I can answer for you?"

"If I wanted answers from you, I'd have fucking asked you." Dermott glared at him. "Get out."

Holt rose and left.

As soon as the door closed behind him, Dermott fixed me with a scowl. "Where's our fucking lease agreement?"

Relief eased my shoulders, but I hid that, too. Holding my voice level, I replied, "It's in my office. I'll get it signed as soon as I can; I just haven't had a chance to look at it with a lawyer yet."

Dermott's eyes narrowed. "Haven't found a way to screw us over yet, you mean. You and your fucking lawyers. Must be nice to have the Department by the balls."

"I tried to give Sirius back to the government, but they wouldn't take it. I'll make sure everything is fair."

"Oh, that makes me feel *so* much better." He leaned menacingly forward. "You think you're so fucking special. Well, I've got news for you, honey. I'm watching you. You put even a toenail out of line, and you're going down hard."

Using every ounce of restraint I owned, I didn't tell him exactly where I wanted to put my toenail: Inside a steel-toed boot, and straight up his ass.

Stay calm...

Somehow I managed to force my face into a cool smile. "Good. The Department needs somebody like you to make sure everybody's toeing the line."

Dermott blinked, then gave a self-satisfied nod. "Too fucking right. So get that fucking agreement signed. Get out."

Holding myself under rigid control, I stood and walked unhurriedly to the door.

When I let myself out and closed the door behind me, Holt straightened from where he'd been leaning against the wall.

Eyeing me worriedly, he asked, "Everything okay?"

I shrugged. "Sure. Let's go question the prisoner." As we strode down the hall, I lowered my voice and added, "I might just need to take a quick kick at a chair."

"Anything I can do?"

"No..."

I almost told him about the leasing agreement, but I didn't know whether my ownership of Sirius was supposed to be confidential. I made a mental note to ask Stemp. Or General Briggs. Or anybody in my chain of command, right on up to the Minister of National Defense. Definitely not Dermott.

"...nothing I can talk about right now, anyway," I finished.

Holt nodded, and we made the rest of the trip down into the secured area in silence.

In the small observation room next to the holding cells, we stood side by side eyeing the video screen. The prisoner sat in the interview room, manacled to the table. He looked unconcerned.

"Shit," I muttered. "He's a professional."

Holt grimaced. "Probably. While you were in with Dermott, I called the lab. They've prioritized the physical evidence and they've already got ballistics on the bullet that hit Kane, but it doesn't match this guy's gun."

Flopping into a chair, I scowled at the video screen. "So either he's not the same guy who shot John, or else he's professional enough to ditch his gun after a kill and switch to a clean one."

Holt nodded. "Yeah, the weapon was clean. No fingerprints, not even a partial. Serial number filed off."

I let out a growl. "So he knows we've got nothing solid except auto theft under five thousand." I glared at the image on the screen. "Have you got any ideas on how to shake him up?"

"All we can do is bluff. Tell him we found a partial print

on the gun. Or that we have a witness who spotted him at Kane's shooting."

"But we don't even know if he's the same guy who took a shot at John. If we go in with that and he didn't do it, he'll know we're full of shit."

"Yeah." Holt blew out a breath. "But nothing else is going to rattle him. Even if we did have a partial print on the gun, he'd still only be looking at possession, plus auto theft at the worst. If he's a pro, that won't even be enough to make him blink."

I sat up slowly. "Hang on. If he's so smart, why doesn't he have a lawyer here? Wouldn't a guy like that lawyer up instantly?"

"Huh." Holt crossed his arms over his chest, eyeing the monitor with a frown. "Wonder if he had a lawyer when he was at the cop shop in Calgary?"

"Let's find out." I dialled Spider's extension. When he answered, I said, "Hey, Spider. I'm putting you on speaker so Holt and I can both hear you. We're down in the secure area, about to do the interview with the gunman from Arnie's place. Can you find out if he had a lawyer when he was being questioned by the police in Calgary?"

"He didn't. And they couldn't shake him during questioning. He only repeated his name and the story about stealing the car for a joyride."

"That's weird. What else can you tell me about him?"

"His driver's license says he's Eldon Rice Swift, thirty-two years old. It's a fake ID, but he insists it's his real name. We haven't gotten any hits from the police database under that name. Facial recognition hasn't turned up anything yet, either."

I sighed. "So either he's a top-of-the-line assassin who's

never been caught; or he really is just a small-time idiot with no record, who stole the wrong car."

"Sorry, that's all we've got right now," Spider apologized. "The international facial recognition search is still working, though."

"Thanks, Spider."

I hung up and stared at the monitor again. The prisoner yawned and settled himself in the chair, stretching out his feet comfortably.

"There's no fucking way that guy's a small-time joyrider," I growled.

Holt snorted. "You know it, and I know it; and he probably knows we know it. Doesn't make a damn bit of difference."

I stood, scowling at the monitor. "Well, fine. Let's see if we can shake him up a bit. If we agree he's a professional...?" Holt nodded, and I went on, "...then we might as well go for broke. Let's tell him we found a partial print on the gun, and we found gunpowder residue on his clothes that makes him a suspect for a murder. We won't tell him which murder, or when it happened."

"That's lame. You can't match gunpowder residue to a crime scene. And he's probably washed his clothes since the last time he killed somebody."

"Yeah, but maybe he doesn't know that. And even if he does know, it might make him second-guess himself. Do you have a better idea?"

"Nope." Holt stretched and cracked his knuckles. "Do you want to be Good Cop or Bad Cop?"

A thought occurred to me. "Um... should we even be showing our faces?"

He shrugged. "What does it matter? Apparently

everybody knows Arlene Widdenback's a cop now anyway. But if he still thinks you're an arms dealer, that might shake him better than anything we say as cops."

"That works." I paused, thinking. "Okay, I have an idea. You can be Bad Cop, and there is no Good Cop. If we really want to throw him off-balance, then I'm going to be Weird Cop."

Holt grinned. "Never a dull moment with you." He gestured toward the door. "Let the weirdness begin."

CHAPTER 25

Outside the interrogation room, I drew in a deep breath and let it out slowly, then opened the door.

The prisoner glanced over, but didn't move from his comfortable sprawl. If not for the handcuffs tethering him to the bolted-down table, he'd look like a guy happily channel-surfing in his own living room.

I said nothing; just watched him.

He made eye contact with a small contemptuous smile, but I held my face expressionless and stepped inside, closing the door behind me. Keeping my pace unhurried, I strolled in front of him and continued around the table to take up a position directly behind him.

There I stood, still and silent. A long minute passed. Then another. The prisoner didn't move, and neither did I. When my mental count reached about four minutes, I leaned forward and blew a leisurely stream of air across the back of his neck.

He didn't change position, but his shoulders tensed almost imperceptibly. Unseen behind him, I grinned at the camera, knowing Holt would be laughing his ass off in the observation room.

I stood still again for the count of ninety. Then I leaned forward and blew on our captive's neck again.

This time his muscles bunched visibly before relaxing.

I waited fifteen seconds, then blew a sharp puff of air at his left ear. He rewarded me with a distinct twitch, but still didn't speak.

Grinning, I surveyed him for my next target.

After several minutes of silent air attacks, the prisoner sat up abruptly and twisted around as far the handcuffs' restraint allowed.

Sidestepping, I stayed out of his field of view. When he spun to the other side, I shifted in the opposite direction. Hide and seek.

He huffed out a breath and slouched in the chair again. I could practically see the thought-bubble above his head: '*Fine, I won't react*'.

Challenge accepted.

Reaching out, I brushed my fingertip across the back of his neck. I followed that up with feather-light touches all over his head, barely enough to move a few hairs. As I continued to alternate touching his head and neck and blowing on him, his muscles slowly grew taut.

I was definitely annoying the shit out of him. Just about ready for Holt. But first...

Drawing back, I clapped my hands together with a sudden sharp crack directly behind the prisoner's head.

His body convulsed and he spun. Once more, I dodged out of his field of view.

He settled in the chair again, staring straight ahead, but I could hear the breath hissing through his nostrils.

Time for some more air-and-fingertip torture.

He lasted another five minutes before barking, "What the hell do you want?"

I didn't reply; just continued my micro-irritations.

A few minutes later, he jerked violently at the handcuffs and twisted around again, trying to catch sight of me. "Cut it the fuck *out!* What the hell, you freak!"

I let him settle down again. Holt still hadn't appeared, so I guessed he wanted me to carry on; but a glance at my watch showed we needed to wrap this up if we were going to get into position in Drumheller by ten o'clock.

Maybe that was Holt's plan. Let our prisoner think about this bizarre little interlude for a while. As I leaned in to blow on him one more time, I froze without exhaling.

Our captive had dark roots. And was that a tiny scar near his hairline?

I eased back and silently drew my tranquilizer pistol. I wouldn't need him unconscious for long.

Holding my breath, I fired at the floor. The captive sagged, and I hurried for the door.

As I slipped into the hallway, Holt emerged from the observation room, grinning. "You know, you're one sick puppy. You must have driven your siblings crazy as a kid."

"I'm an only child." I pushed past him into the observation room. "I need some examination gloves."

Holt snickered. "Why, are you going to anal-probe him now?"

"Speaking of sick puppies..." I pulled on the gloves and headed back to the interrogation room.

"What's up?" Holt asked as he followed me in.

"I bet he's had plastic surgery. That's why we can't find him with facial recognition." I crouched beside the prisoner and raised his lolling head, checking around his hairline and under his chin, then opening his mouth and checking inside his upper and lower lip.

"Chin implant and cheek implants," Holt said, eyeing the

unobtrusive scars. "And probably eyelid surgery, too. That might give Webb and his team something to go on."

"And speaking of going..." I headed for the door. "We'd better hit the road if we're going to get set up in Drumheller by ten."

"Yeah." Holt followed me out. "Good catch with the plastic surgery. But you really are a freak. My kid sister used to do that exact thing to me when we were kids. Drove me fucking nuts."

I pulled off the gloves and sketched a bow. "Weird Cop aims to please. At least we've given Mr. Swift something to think about until we get back to him this afternoon."

"And you got him to react," Holt said with approval. "You can go in first next time, too. As soon as he sees you he'll be tense and off-balance. After you fuck with his mind a bit more, I'll come in and hit him with both barrels."

"And if Spider does some facial remodelling and runs him through the database again, we might even find his real identity," I agreed.

"Wouldn't that be nice."

As we turned away, I said, "I need a pit stop before we go. Can you call Spider and tell him about the plastic surgery?"

"Sure. And I'll tell Security to move Swift to a cell until we're back. Meet you at Stores."

As we stood outside Stores putting on our lightweight bulletproof blade-proof jackets, Holt turned to me. "I'll drive. Car's down in the main lot."

I gave him a side-eye as we turned and strode down the hall. "I'm surprised you parked there. Aren't you worried about being an easy target in your bright red Audi?"

He shrugged. "Maybe if I was driving the Audi; but I'm not. I requisitioned one of the surveillance beaters last night."

"Smart. Just so you know, I'll be sidestepping right when we go out the door."

We made it to the dirt-coloured Ford Focus without incident and got in. Eyeing the sun-faded dashboard and stained upholstery, I shot Holt a grin. "Are you sure you want to be seen driving this? It's a hell of a come-down from your fancy Audi."

"The whole point is for me to *not* be seen."

"True." Whipping out my phone, I snapped a photo of him behind the wheel. "There. Blackmail leverage, if I ever need it."

He stared at me open-mouthed for an instant before shaking his head. "Okay, now I have to kill you." He steered for the street.

"Maybe you could hold off until I actually try to blackmail you."

He smirked, and I changed the subject. "Should we make contact with Weiss? I don't think we should arrest him, no matter what Dermott says. Even if we only detain him, we're tipping our hand. We don't have any grounds to hold him, and as soon as we release him, he'll run."

"Maybe. Or he might stick around if he's still looking for George Harrison. Rand made it sound as though he was pretty predictable." Holt's lantern jaw tightened. "But we can't trust Rand, so..."

I blew out a tense breath. "Yeah. We don't even know if Ian actually did pick Weiss up on his tracker, or if that was a lie, too. He might just be sending us on a wild goose chase."

"And even if he was telling the truth about Weiss's location, there's no guarantee Rand didn't walk out of Sirius this morning and drive straight down to Drumheller. He might relocate Weiss just to fuck us over."

"Oh, for shit's sake." I thumped my head against the headrest. "What do you want to bet Ian just wanted us out of Silverside so he could snoop around there? He could have lied about Weiss's location *and* about his routine. I mean, seriously; do we ever get lucky enough to be looking for a guy who stays at his last known position, and goes outside at the same time every day without fail?"

Holt and I exchanged a look, and Holt accelerated with a growl. "We have to check it out, though. And that fucker knows it."

"Which fucker? Rand, or Weiss?" I asked gloomily.

"Probably both." Holt hesitated. "Why do you think Rand would be snooping around Silverside?"

"I don't know. But if he's sending us one way, then he probably wants to go the opposite way."

"He can't get into Sirius..." Holt said thoughtfully, "...but what *can* he get into?"

"Nothing that matters."

"Your place?"

"Not without setting off my monitors. And I don't know why he'd want to anyway." I hesitated. "Although he was rubbernecking pretty blatantly last night."

"Maybe he's looking for something. Investigating you."

"Why would MI6 investigate me?"

Holt stared out the windshield. "You never know."

Something in his voice made me turn to scrutinize him more closely. "What's that supposed to mean?"

Instead of replying, Holt dipped into his pocket and

brought out a bug detector. The green light glowed.

"And...?" I prodded.

"I guess it's okay to tell you now, but you didn't hear it from me. The Department was investigating you until about a month ago."

"Wha..." I gaped at him. "Why? And *who* was investigating me?" Suspicion rose. "You?"

"No, they had Brock and Mellor and a team of analysts on it. I didn't even know about it until it was over."

"But why?" Comprehension arrived an instant later. "Dermott, getting up my ass again, right?"

Holt kept his eyes on the road. "The order came down from the Minister. Maybe because of your mother's treason? I don't know; but a couple of weeks ago Dermott let it slip. He clammed up right away, so I only know they were investigating you; and now the investigation's over and you're cleared."

"But... if it was an NSIRA inquiry, why didn't they suspend me while they were investigating? Or ask me for testimony?"

"No idea." Holt gave me a sidelong glance. "It doesn't make sense to me, either, but I guess it's good that you're cleared."

"I guess. Just goes to show, don't expect loyalty from the Department."

"I wouldn't say that," Holt objected. "You can hardly blame Command for wanting to be sure you're on our side. It'd be a security disaster if you ever turned."

"Yeah..." Enlightenment struck and I sat up. "Shit, *that's* why-"

I bit off the sentence before I could complete it. Of course the government had investigated me. They were deciding whether to hand over Sirius Dynamics.

"That's why, what?" Holt prompted.

"Sorry, can't tell you. But some stuff makes sense now. Anyhow, we were talking about Ian. I can't imagine why he'd be investigating me. I think he was just fascinated with how the common folk live."

"Maybe it's something to do with the investigation into your mother's treason and murder charges. I bet they tore Sirius U.K. apart after they found out she owned it." Holt shrugged. "Maybe that's why the Department was looking into you, too. Helping the Brits with their investigation."

"Mm. Maybe."

That might make sense, too. If Ian had found out I was inheriting Sirius...

"Okay, that's the house up ahead on the left." Holt's voice interrupted my thoughts.

The blinds were down in Weiss's small house, but the slats were open. The street contained a few parked cars with heat waves already rippling off them in the hard bright sun. No pedestrians. Just the way I liked it.

At the corner, Holt turned right and circled the block, pulling over and stopping just before the final right that would carry us past Weiss's house again.

"Wonder whether he's as prompt as Rand said." Holt eyed his watch. "Five minutes. Go-time."

Glancing casually around, I got out and opened the trunk to extract a folding baby stroller complete with 'baby'. I bent over the stroller and adjusted its sunshade, hoping nobody had spotted me apparently transporting a child in the trunk of the car. No curtains twitched, and I let out a breath of relief.

Pulling my hair up into a high ponytail that I hoped

would knock a couple of decades off my age at a distance, I mentally rehearsed our simple plan. *'Walk past, follow Weiss and observe him, then walk away'.* What could possibly go wrong?

I blew out a tense breath. With my luck...

I wheeled the stroller up beside the driver's door and leaned down. "Are you sure you don't want to play Devoted Dad? I don't mind swapping places."

Holt grunted. "Not my scene."

"You think it's mine? I have all the maternal instincts of a sea turtle: Dig a hole, grunt out a few eggs, and walk away." I sketched a carefree wave. "Buh-bye, kids; hope life works out for you."

He frowned. "Bullshit. You mother everybody. Your farm is practically a refugee camp right now."

"That's different-"

He tapped his designer wristwatch. "Get going."

Blowing out a breath of annoyance, I hit my speed dial. Holt's phone vibrated and he tapped the button and answered, "Audio check."

"All good." Keeping the line open, I tucked my phone into my pocket and affected a bouncy gait that set my ponytail swinging.

A few houses down from Weiss's, I stopped abruptly and took out my phone, pretending to be reading a text. Typing my fake reply, I watched our target.

A minute to go.

I could see a sliver of the front door and most of the back yard. If Weiss stepped out the back door and stood against the house, he'd be invisible; but if he went through the back yard to the gate, I'd spot him.

I bent over my 'baby' and pressed its stomach, triggering

a recording of baby wails. Leaning in, I pretended to fuss with blankets and pacifiers.

Holt's voice spoke from my phone. "Ten o'clock."

Weiss's front door swung open.

A quick shot to the button in the doll's stomach silenced it, and I resumed my jaunty approach.

Weiss emerged from the house wearing a lightweight jacket, with a laptop case slung across his body on a shoulder strap. As he turned to lock the door I gave him a quick once-over. That jacket could hide a weapon, but I couldn't see any sign of one.

My timing was perfect. I'd be just a few yards behind him if he turned left at the sidewalk. If he turned toward me instead, I'd trigger the crying baby, allowing me to stop and observe him as he went by.

A few paces closer.

What the hell was taking him? He had locked both the deadbolt and the knob; but instead of turning away, he put his key in each lock again. Then again, dammit.

I dawdled to a halt, peering at my phone and muttering, "Christ, how many times does he need to check the damn locks?"

Apparently five was the magic number. As Weiss turned away from the door at last, Holt spoke. "Red minivan just turned the corner, coming up behind you."

The sound of tires approached as I set my stroller in motion again. Dammit, now my timing was off. But I couldn't plausibly stop again.

I was only a feet from Weiss when Holt's yell erupted from my phone.

"*Gun!*"

CHAPTER 26

Flinging the stroller toward the street, I dove at Weiss.

Tires squealed and two gunshots exploded as we hit the ground. The scream of an over-revved economy car was followed by a shattering crunch.

The other engine roared and tires squealed again as I rolled on top of Weiss, yanking out my gun in time to see the minivan fleeing. A dent in its rear matched the newly crumpled bumper on our Ford.

Holt was already out of the driver's seat, gun drawn. He fired three quick shots and the minivan lurched as its rear tire blew just before it skidded around the corner.

I gave Weiss a fast once-over but didn't see any blood. Grabbing a handful of his jacket, I hauled him to his feet. Holt ran to us and together we half-dragged Weiss to the car.

Yanking open the back door, I pushed him inside and barked, "Move over!"

Holt jumped into the driver's seat. Weiss sat frozen, his face chalk-white.

"*MOVE!*" I bellowed, hip-checking him as I shoved my way inside.

I had barely gotten the door closed when Holt accelerated hard. As we fishtailed around the corner in the wake of the vanished minivan, Holt demanded, "Have they got blockades in place yet?"

"I don't-" I began, before realizing that he was using his hands-free to communicate with our support team.

Apparently their reply wasn't to Holt's liking. He swore and yanked the car around another corner, then another, zigzagging through the quiet streets.

"We lost them! Tell those assholes to get their thumbs out of their fucking asses and set up a fucking blockade," Holt snarled at the hapless analyst on the other end of the line. He stomped savagely on the gas again and we squealed around another corner, the little engine whining in protest. "I'm driving a grid to see if I can pick them up," he added.

"Let it go," I urged. "It's too dangerous to drive this fast in a residential area."

"Fuck off!"

Before I could yell at him, Holt slammed his fist against the steering wheel and spat, "*Fuck!*" as he slowed to the speed limit.

I turned to Weiss. "Are you all right?"

Hunched against the opposite door as far away from me as he could get, he hugged his laptop case like a barricade in front of him, his eyes screwed shut. His hands twisted together over and over as though he was washing them, while his lips moved in a frenetic whisper.

I raised my voice. "Rupert? Are you all right?"

He flinched at my increased volume, and his own voice rose as if in defense. "...Glock 26, nine by nineteen Luger, standard ten mag, optional twelve, fifteen, seventeen, nineteen, thirty-three. Sig Sauer P224, nine by nineteen Luger, standard twelve mag. Walther PPK, nine by seventeen .380 ACP, standard six mag. Glock 26, nine by nineteen Luger, standard ten..."

Holt pulled over, frowning in the mirror. "What the hell?"

"I think he's reciting pistol specs." I touched his shoulder. "Rupert? It's okay, you're safe."

He shrank away, squeezing his eyes shut tighter. His voice rose. "...Walther PPK, nine by seventeen..."

"Forget it, he's checked out," Holt said. He steered back onto the street. "We'll give him a few minutes to calm down." Shooting me a look via the rearview mirror, he added, "You weren't kidding about your lack of maternal instincts. Even the fucking gunman swerved to avoid a baby in a stroller. Pushing it out in front of him probably saved your life."

I blinked. "Oh. Right. I just needed the stroller out of the way, but I guess a real mother wouldn't have shoved her baby out in front of a speeding car."

Holt barked out a laugh. "You think?" Continuing his grid pattern, albeit at a safe speed, he rounded a corner and stiffened. "There!"

The dented red minivan sagged at the curb on its flat tire.

"Fuck, he's gone," Holt snarled, surveying the empty windows.

"Or hiding in the back," I pointed out.

"I doubt it." Holt recited the address to our support team, then pulled over half a block away. "Cops are on their way. No point in taking a bullet if we don't have to."

The lights and sirens arrived only minutes later and surrounded the vehicle, which turned out to be abandoned.

After getting the all-clear, Holt said, "I'll go over and coordinate with them." He cocked an eyebrow at me in the rearview mirror. "Think you can handle him?" He jerked his thumb toward our unhappy passenger.

Weiss was still folded in on himself, dry-washing his hands and whispering with his eyes screwed shut.

"I think I can manage," I said dryly, but I didn't holster my gun. Just in case.

Holt got out, leaving me to listen to the litany of calibres.

I tuned out Weiss's repetitive muttering and watched while Holt flashed his identification and spoke with the RCMP constable. After a short conversation, Holt returned to the car and got back into the driver's seat.

"They're looking for the bullets over at the scene now. When they find them they'll ship them up to our lab, and they'll tow the minivan up to Silverside, too. I didn't want to interfere with their show, so I told them to bag the stroller and ship it up, too." He scowled. "The minivan's stolen and nobody reported any suspicious pedestrians around here, so our guy probably switched to another vehicle and drove away before they got the blockades up."

"So he's long gone. Shit." As Holt put the car in gear and pulled away, I added, "Could be worse, I guess. At least you didn't blow the airbags when you hit the minivan."

Holt muttered something that probably didn't bear repeating, then jerked his chin in Weiss's direction. "Any progress?"

"No. Do you think we should take him to the hospital? He's breathing okay and he doesn't seem to be in pain; he's just... like you said, checked out."

"If he hasn't snapped out of it by the time we get to Silverside, we'll take him to the hospital there."

"Okay." I leaned back, trying to block out the irritating sibilance of Weiss's whispers. "I wish he'd vary his routine a bit. I thought I might learn something, but he's just repeating the same specs over and o-" I broke off. "Hang on. Greg, you shoot a Sig, don't you?"

"Yeah, P224."

"With a twelve-shot magazine."

"Yeah." He frowned over his shoulder. "So what?"

"And mine's a Glock G26 with the standard ten-shot magazine, but you can get crazy-big mags for it if you want. Optional up to thirty-three."

Holt shot me a scowl. "Yeah, so what?"

"So he's just repeating the same three specs over and over. Glock G26. Mine. Sig Sauer P224. Yours. And Walther PPK."

Holt's eyes widened in the mirror. "If he's reliving the incident, maybe that's what the gunman used. It was about the right size for a PPK, but I wasn't close enough to be sure. Did you get a look?"

I shook my head. "He came up from behind, and I hit the dirt as soon as you yelled. By the time I got my head up he was driving away. But... Ian carries a Walther PPK."

"Fuck, really?"

"Yeah."

"You think Rand decided to off Weiss?" Holt's brows drew together in the mirror. "Or you?"

"N... no..." I hesitated. "A drive-by shooting doesn't seem like Ian's style. Plus, if he wanted to kill Weiss, he could have done it on the freighter and heaved his body overboard with nobody the wiser. And he's had lots of chances to kill me. Why would he try now?"

"Maybe something changed." Holt's frown still hadn't smoothed out. "Maybe Rand needs to silence you now. Or silence Weiss. How many people knew Weiss was here? He's only been here a day. And I bet the shooter knew Weiss would come outside right at ten o'clock and we'd be here. It's got to be Rand. Two targets for the price of one."

"But Ian's not that stupid," I countered. "He wouldn't shoot Weiss right in front of you and me. And if he'd wanted to shoot me, he could easily have done it last night. He could have just waited on my road and flagged me down when I left. I'd have recognized him and stopped, and he'd have had a clean kill with no witnesses."

"It's got to be him," Holt insisted. "A PPK isn't a common weapon over here; plus it doesn't hold enough rounds for a drive-by shooting. A professional killer wouldn't piss around with a PPK. But if that's the only weapon Rand has..."

"I can't see it," I argued. "Ian's a dickhead sometimes, but he's a professional. If he wanted to kill Weiss, he could have just knocked on his door, got invited in, and done the job without anyone ever knowing. No witnesses, no chance of getting caught."

"Unless Weiss knew he was a threat," Holt pointed out. "Maybe that's why he ran from Rand in Halifax."

"Hm." I rubbed the burgeoning ache between my eyes. "Okay, here's a different angle. What if this was just a distraction? Our shooter could have unloaded his whole magazine and had a better chance of hitting us, but he only took two shots."

"I rear-ended him and started shooting," Holt replied. "He didn't have time for more. But if it was Rand, just messing with us..." He scowled. "I could see him doing that."

"But why? If he was here shooting at Weiss, he couldn't be sneaking around doing anything else. And he would have recognized me with the baby carriage; and he knows I'd return fire if somebody shot at me. He wouldn't risk it." I sighed. "I just don't get it."

"Okay, so maybe it wasn't Rand at all." Holt shot me a look via the rearview mirror. "Maybe it was another hitman. Stemp, Kane, and Helmand have all had their first dance with a drive-by shooter, so it's your turn."

"That doesn't make sense. Nobody knew I was going to be here, and I'm pretty sure we weren't followed. We were both watching."

Holt's only reply was an irritable shrug, and I added, "Maybe we'll find out more when Weiss recovers."

Holt shot a dubious glance at our withdrawn passenger. "Maybe."

By the time we neared Silverside, Weiss had stopped wringing his hands. His eyes were open but he stared straight ahead, his lips moving silently while he hugged his computer case. If he had been anyone else, I might have guessed he was praying; but I was pretty sure he was still reciting gun specs.

Holt pulled over and stopped on the shoulder. "If we're not taking him to the hospital, we need to blindfold him."

"Rupert," I said gently.

He flinched, squeezing his eyes shut while his hands began to circle each other again.

I tried again, a little louder. "Rupert, can you talk to me?"

Weiss curled into a tighter ball and his hand-washing increased its tempo, but to my surprise he replied in a loud toneless voice.

"Yes. What do you want talk about?"

CHAPTER 27

Holt and I exchanged a look via the rearview mirror. Okay, then.

"Are you injured, Rupert?" I asked. "Do you want to be seen by a doctor?"

"No. No." His inflection didn't vary, and after a puzzled moment I realized he wasn't expressing an antipathy to medical care; he was simply answering both questions.

"Do you know who was shooting at you?"

"No." He hesitated, then added without opening his eyes, "Not Ian Rand."

Shit. I thought he'd been completely zoned out, but he'd taken in part of our conversation at least. Maybe all of it. My mind rocketed back over everything we'd said. Had we revealed anything we shouldn't have?

Probably not, I decided. Weiss hadn't been responsive while Holt was dealing with the police, so likely he'd only tuned in when the conversation turned to guns and Ian.

"What makes you think it wasn't Ian?" I asked. "Did you see the face of the person who shot at us?"

"It wasn't Ian Rand's hand. No."

I had asked two questions again. Got it.

"Let's finish this later," Holt said as he leaned forward, twisting to tug off his bulletproof jacket. "I'll give you my jacket to put over his head for a blindfold."

"No, I'll use mine," I objected. "You'll still have to park and walk." I turned to Weiss again. "Rupert, we need to blindfold you. I'm going to put my jacket over your head, and then we're going to ride for a while longer before we get out of the car."

"Restrain his hands first," Holt advised.

It was good advice, but I wasn't sure how Rupert would react. I reached for my tranquilizer pistol, and for the first time Weiss snapped out of his straight-ahead stare and tracked my hand's movement toward my holster.

Shit. I couldn't let a non-allied weapon expert see a classified weapon.

Fortunately Holt realized my intent. Keeping his hand low so Weiss couldn't see over the seat back, he drew his trank pistol and gave me a nod.

I took out a set of nanosteel-reinforced nylon hand restraints. Keeping my voice calm, I said, "Rupert, please turn away from me, and put your hands behind your back."

He stared at my chin. "Who are you?"

After an instant of indecision, I replied, "Arlene Widdenback."

If he'd heard Arlene Widdenback was a cop or noticed our earlier interactions with the police, he'd know I was with law enforcement. That might convince him to cooperate. But if he only knew Arlene Widdenback as an arms dealer, that could work, too.

Weiss showed no recognition of the name, but he'd been pretty much expressionless anyway. Best poker face ever.

"Do you know George Harrison?" he asked without making eye contact.

"Yes. I can arrange for you to meet with him if you want.

But you have to let me put these restraints on your wrists and my jacket over your head." Recalling his literal interpretation of my questions earlier, I added, "And you have to do everything I say."

Still staring at my chin, he responded to each of my statements in order. "Yes. Okay. I'll do as you say unless you tell me to do something bad." He added, "And don't touch me."

"Okay," I said cautiously, wondering what kind of minefield I was entering. "But I'll have to touch you a little, to put on the restraints and the blindfold, and to lead you when you're walking blindfolded so you don't fall or bump into anything."

"Okay. But if I say stop touching me, stop. If you respect my boundaries, I'll respect yours."

I didn't quite know how to respond to that. Holt gave me a 'get-on-with-it' jerk of his chin, so I repeated, "Rupert, please turn away from me, and put your hands behind your back."

He obeyed stiffly, his hands still twisting together.

I managed to zip the ties around his wrists without making skin-to-skin contact, and he didn't freak out. After slipping out of my jacket, I fastened it closed again and carefully settled it over Weiss's head like a hood.

"Can you breathe all right?" I asked, imagining all too vividly the strangling sensation of having my head enclosed by opaque fabric.

"Yes. Thank you." Paradoxically, his shoulders relaxed and his hands ceased their wringing.

Holt pulled onto the highway again, and we completed the last minutes of the journey to Silverside in silence. When we got to the bowling alley, Holt nosed the car into an alcove beside the door, protected by the wall on one side and a garbage dumpster on the other.

"Rupert, we're here," I told him. "When we get out of the car, I'll have to lead you where we're going."

He tensed up again. "Don't touch me."

Holt scowled and opened his mouth, but I waved him to silence.

"How would you like me to lead you, then?" I asked.

"Tell me how many steps. My stride is zero decimal eight four metres long." He hesitated. "But it will be shorter when I can't see where I'm going. So you won't know how many steps." Another short pause. "You can lead me by pulling on my computer case. The strap around my shoulders will tell me which way to go."

"Okay," I agreed.

Holt rolled his eyes, but it was more a gesture of relief than annoyance. He shot a glance at the deserted alley. "No witnesses. Go."

I hopped out and hurried around to open Weiss's door. With a final quick survey to make sure we were unobserved, I reached in and took hold of the computer case. "Okay, swivel. Feet on the ground. Stand."

Weiss obeyed, and I commanded, "One sidestep to your right."

As soon as he was clear of the car door, I swung it shut and pulled him gently forward. "Two steps. Stop." I unlocked the door and swung it open, then tugged him inside. "Two steps. Stop."

I closed the door behind us and Weiss stood still and silent.

Listening for clues to his location, or planning his escape? Or both?

Raising my voice over the din of the pin-setting machines, I told Weiss, "We're going to wait here for a few minutes."

"Okay." His voice was muffled by the makeshift blindfold, but he seemed calm.

That worried me. What was he planning?

Easing a couple of steps away, I drew my trank pistol.

A minute or two later, Holt slipped through the door and locked it behind him.

The trip to the secured area of Sirius via the underground tunnel was an exercise in concentration while I provided detailed instructions for Weiss's movements. By the time we got him seated at the table in the interview room, my head was aching.

Holt drew his tranquilizer pistol. "Okay, Weiss. We're going to cut your hand restraints. Put your hands on the table in front of you. If you do anything but that, or if you make any sudden moves, I'll shoot you."

I cut the ties and Weiss obediently moved his hands to the front. I handcuffed him to the table, and said, "Rupert, I'll take off your blindfold now."

As I reached for the jacket, he went rigid. "NO!"

His sudden volume made me twitch, and Holt's gun flicked up.

Hiding my surge of adrenaline behind a steady voice, I asked, "Do you want me to leave the blindfold on you?"

"Yes! Please. I'm overstimulated. The blindfold helps."

Doing my best to sound soothing, I said, "Okay, you can wear a blindfold for as long as you want. We'll get you a new one, though, because I need my jacket back."

Holt slipped out the door, returning in seconds with a standard blackout hood. He handed it to me, and I moved cautiously toward Rupert.

"Rupert, I have the new blindfold hood here."

"Please change it quickly." His hands knotted together and he began to whisper gun specs again.

I handed the hood to Holt, who went around to Weiss's opposite side. Gripping the jacket, I said, "On three. One, two, three."

The moment I whisked the jacket off, Holt popped the hood over Weiss's head.

"There, it's done," I said.

Weiss relaxed. "Thank you."

"We need to take your computer case now," Holt said.

Weiss tensed up all over again. "NO!"

"I'm afraid we have to," I said as gently as I could. "We don't know what's in it, so it's not safe for us to leave it where you can reach it."

"My laptop is in it. And my cordless mouse." His hands were twisting with anguish again. "I need my laptop. I can't let you take it."

"How about a compromise?" I proposed. "I understand that you need your laptop. I promise not to break it, and we'll give it back to you after-"

"Oh, for fucksakes, get over it!" Holt interrupted. He grabbed the case.

Weiss lunged to his feet. His hands were still tethered to the table so he was bent nearly double, but he twisted and lashed out with blind kicks, shouting, "NO NO NO!" in his expressionless voice.

Holt rolled his eyes, whipped out his trank pistol, and fired at the floor.

I only had an instant to suck in some air before the dart hit. Holding my breath, I sprang forward to catch Weiss's collapsing body before the shackles wrenched his shoulders.

Fortunately Holt grabbed him from the other side, and we lowered Weiss into the chair and laid his head on the table. I checked to make sure he had breathing space inside the blackout hood before hurrying for the door.

The instant it closed behind us I sucked big gulps of air, replacing the oxygen I'd used up in my exertion.

"Smooth move, asshole," I snapped after I'd caught my breath.

"I'm not his fucking mommy, and neither are you," Holt growled. "He's our prisoner, and we need to know what's in that laptop."

"He's not our fucking prisoner; he's the victim of a drive-by shooting attempt, and we just abducted him!" My voice rose with the effort of preventing myself from smacking Holt. "We don't even know if he's guilty of anything! He's scared shitless, he has no idea who we are or whether we're about to torture and kill him, and he was cooperating just fine until you got impatient!"

Holt shrugged. "You're Arlene Widdenback the arms dealer. You were being too nice to him. Trust me, the good-cop-bad-cop vibe will work when we start questioning him. Now, I'm going in to search him and get that laptop. I already called Webb to come and get it." Holt ducked into the room and wrestled the laptop case off Weiss's limp body, then patted him down thoroughly while I fumed.

Holt emerged a couple of minutes later carrying the case and wearing a self-satisfied expression. I was opening my mouth to say something I probably shouldn't, when Spider hurried around the corner and made a beeline for us.

"Is that it?" he asked, focusing on the laptop.

My weirdness-sensor quivered. It wasn't like Spider to

avoid eye contact.

Shit, had Holt told him I'd sacrificed a fake baby?

Holt handed him the computer. "How long will it take to make a copy of everything on there?"

"I won't know until I see it. If it's a big drive, it could take hours."

"We don't have hours," Holt snapped.

Spider shuffled his feet. "I'm sorry, but there's really no way to-"

"How long will it take to pull out the hard drive?" Holt interrupted.

"Um... it depends. Usually five or ten minutes. But if there's anything unusual..." Spider trailed off with an uncomfortable shrug.

Holt drew his trank pistol and opened the door to the interview room. The pistol spat its quiet report, and the dart lodged in Weiss's arm.

Holt turned back to Spider. "Take out the drive and start copying it. Put the laptop back together without it and give it back to us so we can use it as a prop. You've got twenty minutes until he wakes up."

Spider gaped at him. "Um... okay. That should do it..." His gaze dropped to his feet again.

"Spider," I said gently. "What's wrong?"

He flushed. "You're not going to like it."

"But I probably need to hear it anyway, don't I?"

Spider nodded unhappily, then blurted, "When we changed Swift's facial parameters, we got a hit in the database. He's been implicated in several murders, under the alias Arthur Ronald Walters. His fingerprints have been surgically altered, too."

"That's *good* news, Spider."

He grimaced.   "It would be... if we hadn't already released him."

CHAPTER 28

"*What?*" Holt's voice and mine mingled in an incredulous chorus.

"Why the hell did you release him?" Holt barked. "We were questioning him! We were making progress!"

Spider flinched. "I'm sorry! I knew you weren't done; I told Dermott not to-"

"*Dermott* released him?" Holt's voice was suddenly quiet and dangerous. "Did he say why?"

"Um..." Spider paled and eased backward. "Well... Swift had been in custody for so long without charges, and he finally called a lawyer. His lawyer pressured the police, and the police were pressuring Dermott..."

I stepped between the two men, intercepting Holt's icy gaze. "Never mind, Spider. We know there was nothing you could have done. We'll talk to Dermott and figure it out."

Spider's shoulders relaxed. "Thanks. Anyhow, we transferred Swift down to the Drumheller RCMP detachment via blindfolded prisoner transfer, so he won't be able to identify our building. They released him there. I notified Dermott and the Drumheller RCMP as soon as I got the hit from the database. Swift had only been free for an hour by then, so he can't have gotten far."

"Famous last words," Holt growled. "Gut that laptop.

We'll go and see Dermott." As Spider hurried away, Holt added under his breath, "And kill the fucker, slowly." With a sharp jerk of his chin at me, he snapped, "Come on."

Following Holt's rigid shoulders down the hallway, I reflected that it was nice to have someone else consumed by incoherent rage at Dermott for a change.

Not that it helped. We'd just lost the only lead we'd had.

My wrist monitor vibrated, and I managed to suppress my twitch. Between Kane and Hellhound moving around in the woods, Spider leaving for work, and Margaret arriving to stay with Linda, my surveillance system was getting a workout.

I peered at the tiny screen. "Asshole!"

"Save it for Dermott," Holt said grimly, not slowing his pace.

"No; Ian just drove up to my house."

"Shit!" Holt halted and turned to glare at my wrist, which I'd held out for his inspection. "What the hell does he want?"

"I wish I knew." Silently cursing the jamming devices that blocked cell phone signals in Sirius, I hurried into the nearest vacant meeting room. Grabbing the land line receiver, I punched in Linda's cell number.

"Hello?" she said breathlessly.

"Hi, it's Aydan. Can you-"

"Oh, hi! Can you hold on a second, please? Ian just drove up."

"I know. Don't let him in."

"Okay, but..."

The sound of the door and voices in the background provided audio for the video I was watching on my monitor, and I suppressed some particularly vile profanity. Margaret had already welcomed Ian into my house with her usual friendly smile.

"Margaret just let him in," Linda whispered. "What should I do?"

I sighed. "Try not to let him snoop around. Keep him in the kitchen if you can."

"She won't be able to," Holt growled from where he was listening over my shoulder. "He'll say he needs to use the bathroom or something."

I shrugged at Holt, equal parts resignation and irritation, and spoke to Linda again. "Just do the best you can. And don't worry, you're safe with him and it's not that big a deal. It's just that he's snoopy and I don't want him poking into my stuff."

"I'll do my best," Linda promised.

"Thanks. Talk to you later." I disconnected, hissing out a short breath between my teeth as I hung up.

Holt and I turned for the corridor together.

Three steps later, my wrist monitor vibrated again. I sighed and glanced at it with resignation, but the video made my stomach clench. Hellhound stood facing one of the cameras in the woods, looking worried. As I watched, he held up his phone and pointed at it, mouthing, 'Call me'.

"Shit!" I spun and scurried back into the meeting room. Grabbing the phone receiver, I dialled Hellhound's number.

He answered on the first ring. "Yeah."

"It's me; what's wrong?"

"Rand just showed up, did ya see him on your monitors?"

"Yeah. I called Linda to try to keep him out, but Margaret invited him in."

"Ya want us to go in an' keep an eye on him?"

I let out a breath of relief. "Yes. Thank you."

"On our way." He disconnected. Moments later, the vibrations of my wrist monitor tracked his and Kane's rapid progress through the woods and across the yard to my house.

Holt leaned into the meeting room, frowning. "What's wrong now?"

"Nothing. Arnie and John are going to keep an eye on Ian."

"I thought Kane was lying low during daylight."

I shrugged. "I guess he changed his mind."

"Works for us." Holt jerked his chin toward the corridor. "Let's try this again."

As we resumed our trip at a slightly less aggressive pace, I shot a sideways look at Holt's hard profile. "Don't lose your temper with Dermott. No point in having him pissed off at you, too."

Holt gave an irritable jerk of his shoulders. "Yeah, I know. Good thing he wasn't standing in front of me a minute ago, though."

I grunted agreement, and we completed our trip in silence.

By the time we got to Dermott's office, I was second-guessing the whole thing. As Holt reached out to knock on the door, I snagged his sleeve.

He shot me a scowl. "What?"

"Let's just forget it," I said quietly. "It's too late to change anything, and he'll just get defensive and pissed off."

"Oh, you mean as pissed off as I am?" Holt growled, and pounded on the door.

"I'll just be in the bathroom." I turned to hurry down the hall, but Holt grabbed my shoulder. Taking advantage of my momentary instability as I spun to face him, he slung an arm around my shoulder, opened the door, and marched us inside before I could escape.

Plotting his painful demise, I pulled free and shot him a glare; but it was too late.

"What do you want?" Dermott snapped.

"You released Swift." Holt's voice was even, but it held an accusing edge.

Dermott flushed. "Yeah, so?"

"So we weren't done questioning him."

"*Questioning* him?" Dermott's flush deepened to an unbecoming burgundy. "I watched the video. That wasn't fucking *questioning*! What if his lawyer got that footage?" Predictably, he turned his glower on me. "What the hell was that supposed to be? I told you to break him, not prance around like some fucking grade-school-"

"It was working!" Holt interrupted loudly. "She rattled him. Got him to react. As soon as we got back we were going to-"

"Going to what? Tell him he had cooties, and threaten to tattle to his mother? That was the most pathetic, incompetent travesty of-"

"It works!" Holt roared. "She broke a guy six months ago using exactly the same technique! Had him crying and pissing his pants!"

"Get out." Dermott's voice was cold and hard. "And if you don't get that weapons expert in here by the end of the day-"

"We've got him already!" Holt snapped. "Which you'd know if you ever read a fucking status update!"

Dermott turned purple and a vein throbbed dangerously in his forehead. "One more word, and I'll suspend your sorry ass! Both your sorry asses!"

Clapping a hand over Holt's mouth, I seized his collar and dragged him toward the door.

He put up a token struggle and some obscenities leaked out from behind my hand, but I was pretty sure he was only saving face. If he'd been serious about resisting, I'd have been unconscious on the floor in an instant.

Hustling him down the hall, I shoved him against the fire door push-bar and we stumbled into the stairwell. When the heavy metal door clanged shut behind us, I released him.

We stared at each other, breathing hard.

"So, nice anger management skills," I said.

"I'm going to kill that fucker."

"I didn't hear that." When Holt glared at me, I added, "Thanks for backing me, but you didn't do yourself any favours."

Holt crossed his arms, still scowling. "He cut Swift loose because you were the one doing the questioning. If I'd been the one in the interview room, he'd have been patting me on the back and telling me it was a smart technique." His fists bunched. "Goddamn it, I'm sick of his shit! Hell, I was sick of his shit when I was eight fucking years old. Three and a half decades later? I'm *so* fucking done! I'm going to-"

"Wait, you're forty-three?"

He blinked. "What?"

"You said 'three and a half decades'. After age eight. That makes you forty-three."

He shook his head as though trying to reset his brain. "So?"

"So, last winter you were bugging me about how you were ten years younger than me. You're only *five* years younger."

Holt's jaw dropped. "Seriously? That's what you're

getting out of this conversation?"

"You lied about your age." I shoved his shoulder. "Asshole."

"You knew I was yanking your chain. My date of birth is right there in my personnel file. Didn't you read it?"

"Of course not. It's none of my business."

He gaped at me. Then the tension released from his shoulders and a smile tugged at the corners of his mouth. A moment later he began to laugh softly, then louder, until he was doubled over pounding his fist on his thigh and gasping for breath between guffaws.

When he finally dragged himself upright, grinning and wiping his eyes, I said, "It wasn't that funny."

He chuckled. "It actually was."

"I'm not getting it."

"You *handled* me." As I opened my mouth to defend myself, he held up a silencing hand. "It's okay. That's why I was laughing. You took a pissed-off guy..." He cocked a thumb at his chest. "...who was seriously considering blowing up his entire career and probably going to prison just for the satisfaction of beating the hell out his childhood bully..." His expression darkened for a second, but he relaxed into a grin again as he went on, "...and you completely sidetracked me. With something so random and stupid..." He started chuckling again. "You didn't even snoop in your partner's personnel file when you had the chance? You're so fucking weird."

I relaxed and returned his grin. "Weird Cop aims to please. If you tell me your birthday, I might even buy you a birthday beer when the day rolls around."

"How about a shot of birthday scotch?" he bargained.

"Normal scotch. Not that overpriced shit you drink."

"Fine, I'll take the beer. November sixth. Scorpio."

"That explains a lot."

"Says the Leo."

I snorted. "So you snooped in my personnel file."

"Of course."

The clank of the door latch made us both spin. One of the civilian researchers hurried into the stairwell, halting abruptly to avoid us.

"'Scuse us," I said, and stepped around him to go back into the corridor. Holt followed, and when the door closed behind us I lowered my voice. "So, Laughing Boy, which one of us is going back into Dermott's office, to tell him we need Stemp to play George Harrison?"

Holt's face went blank. After a moment he said, "Shit."

I sighed. "Is there anybody Dermott actually likes? Or dislikes mildly enough that he can get over himself and help the investigation?"

"Maybe... Webb?" Holt offered doubtfully. "But Dermott'll eat him alive." He hesitated. "What if we went up a link in the chain of command? General Briggs is solid."

"Dermott would blow a blood vessel if we went over his head."

"We can always hope."

"Yeah, but we can't go to Briggs unless we've already tried with Dermott." I shrugged. "I'll go. He'll be extra pissed at you right now, but he's no more pissed at me than usual. And he knows releasing Swift was a colossal fuckup. I think he'll want to do something to fix it."

"Then you don't know him very well."

"Do you have a better idea?"

"Nope."

Holt trailed me back down the hall, then leaned against

the wall a safe distance from Dermott's door while I trudged closer to the lion's den.

Pausing outside the door, I drew a breath and let it out slowly. Be courteous. Be professional. Be a grown-up, for fucksakes.

God, if that was what it took, I was doomed.

I rapped on the door.

"Come!" Even muffled by the wood panelling, Dermott sounded as though he was chewing asphalt.

Squaring my shoulders, I opened the door and strode in.

"What the hell do you want?" he snarled.

"Sorry about Holt. We got shot at half an hour ago. He was a little keyed up."

"His problem, not mine. What the hell do you want?" Dermott repeated, but maybe he sounded a little less truculent.

I kept my tone polite and dispassionate. "We just brought in Rupert Weiss, the weapons expert. He says he'll cooperate if we set up a meeting with George Harrison." Before Dermott could say no, I went on, "This could work for us two ways: If Weiss keeps his word and cooperates with us, we're golden; and also, Stemp might be able to get some good intel from him by pretending to be George Harrison. Do you think Command will let us bring Stemp in, even though he's suspended?"

Dermott scowled. "I don't need their fucking permission. I'm the DCO, and I say get Stemp's ass in here and squeeze whatever you can out of Weiss."

Barely believing my luck, I was turning to flee with my victory when Dermott's irritable addendum halted me.

"I'm holding you personally responsible for Stemp while he's in here. If he steps even one toe out of line, you're going down for collusion and treason."

I bit my tongue so I couldn't retort, and used every ounce of my self-control to keep from flipping him a couple of much-deserved middle fingers.

"Got it," I said, and left.

CHAPTER 29

When I stepped out of Dermott's office, Holt detached himself from the corridor wall and ambled over, eyeing me. "I don't see any blood."

"It was fairly bloodless." I headed down the hall and Holt fell into step beside me. I lowered my voice. "We've got the go-ahead to bring Stemp in."

Holt's eyebrows climbed. "That quick? And without any yelling?"

"I asked him if he thought Command would let us."

Holt snickered. "So you handled him, too. Let me guess." He altered his voice to an approximation of Dermott's cranky grumble. "*I'm* the DCO. *I* decide."

"Nailed it."

"No insults? No threats?"

"Oh, I got the obligatory threat. I'm personally responsible for Stemp; collusion; treason; going down hard; yada, yada."

Holt paused at the door to my office, looking wistful. "I could still go in there and kick his ass."

"Yeah, but then I'd have to break in a new partner; and that's just a pain." I nudged him into the room. "Sit. I'll get the analyst-on-call to text Stemp. He'll likely call back in seconds."

I placed my call, then rounded the desk to take a seat opposite Holt. Ten seconds after my butt hit the cushion, my desk phone rang.

Shooting Holt a satisfied grin, I hurried over and picked up the receiver. "Kelly."

"It's Megan Novak, analyst-on-call. I have Director Stemp on a secured line for you."

"Thanks, Megan. Put him through."

"I'm connecting you now. Please go ahead."

"Hi." I hesitated, wondering if I should offer some pleasantry; but decided to stick to business. "We have Rupert Weiss, the weapons expert. In exchange for his cooperation, I said I'd arrange a meeting with George Harrison. And I got Dermott's permission for you to come in."

"Excellent. When would you like me to arrive?"

"Whenever you can."

"Very well." Stemp paused as if calculating times. "I can be there in half an hour."

"Perfect. I'll meet you in the lobby. And be careful. We've got at least two hitmen on the loose, maybe three."

"Acknowledged." He hung up.

"Half an hour," I said to Holt as I replaced the receiver on its cradle.

He frowned. "What you just said about three hitmen... maybe it's still only two. Swift was released in Drumheller. It could have been him shooting at us."

I flopped into the chair across from him. "Yeah, I guess. But where would he get a car and a weapon? He wouldn't have had either. He was arrested in Calgary and transferred up here."

We blinked at each other for an instant before springing

to our feet.

"He's got an accomplice!" Holt exclaimed at the same time as I demanded, "Who picked him up?"

I grabbed the phone and punched in Spider's extension. It rang once before the line clicked, indicated he'd forwarded it. It rang several more times before he picked up.

"Webb here." He sounded distracted.

"Spider, it's Aydan and Greg. I've got you on speaker. When you released Swift, who picked him up?"

"Um... hang on..." Rustling carried over the line. When he spoke again, his voice had its usual focus. "His lawyer."

"What was the lawyer's name? What firm?"

Computer keys clicked in the background. "Farrell Metz. The law firm is Metz, Metz, and Metz from Calgary."

Holt and I exchanged a glance. I sighed. "I'll bet you a three-hundred-dollar bottle of scotch that there's no such firm."

"No bet," Holt said glumly.

More key-clicking from Spider. "You're right! How did you know?"

"We finished questioning Swift and left here at nine-thirty. You said he phoned his lawyer right afterward. It's only eleven-fifteen now, and you said he was released an hour ago. So his lawyer got to Drumheller in forty-five minutes, but it takes over an hour and half to drive there from Calgary."

Spider sighed. "Right."

"Did you finish with laptop?" Holt asked him.

"Yes, I was just closing it up when you called. It'll take several hours to clone it. Do you want me to take it back to the interview room?"

"We'll meet you there," I agreed. "Weiss will be waking

up any minute, and I want to be there when he does. I don't want him to freak out if he wakes up alone, handcuffed and blindfolded. And would you please get the security footage from the Drumheller RCMP, and run Farrell Metz through the law enforcement and facial recognition databases?"

"I'll initiate the search now, and see you in a few minutes."

We disconnected and I headed for the door with Holt following. As we hurried down the corridor, Holt needled, "There's that maternal streak again. Why are you so worried about Weiss? We *want* him to freak out and tell us everything he knows."

I shot him a look. "I think he'll tell us anyway. And it seems to me that he's the victim here. First the poor guy has to spend a week cooped up in a freighter cabin with Ian; then he finally gets home and tries to go for a nice walk; and he doesn't even make it to the sidewalk before he gets shot at, tackled, abducted, and held in an undisclosed location. I'll be shocked if he doesn't sue our asses when we finally have to release him."

Holt shook his head. "He could try, but he'd lose. We're undercover; Arlene Widdenback is a badass; and we have reason to believe Weiss is involved with Volslav. Admit it, you're just getting all protective because he's neurodivergent. You're the biggest mother hen ever."

I halted, staring at Holt. "What?"

"You're a bleeding-heart-"

"No, I got that part," I interrupted. "I was just shocked that you actually knew the word 'neurodivergent' and used it correctly."

"Christ, Kelly, give me some credit! One of my friends in Toronto is on the autism spectrum."

"So why are you being such a jerk to Weiss?"

"Because... I'm... an... agent," Holt said as though addressing a simpleton. "I do my job regardless of my personal feelings. You should try it sometime."

"Bite me," I said mildly.

We completed the rest of the trip in silence. When we arrived outside the interview room, Spider was waiting with the laptop and Weiss was just beginning to stir.

I slung the laptop case over my shoulder, and Holt and I went into the interview room.

Weiss groaned and tried to sit up, but the tranquilizer hadn't worn off sufficiently. He managed to raise his head a few inches before dropping it back onto the table with another groan.

"Rupert," I said softly. "You're going to be okay. You were agitated and we gave you a sedative, but it will wear off in a couple of minutes."

He groaned again, but he must have understood. He stayed still, and exactly two minutes later he wavered upright in the chair.

"Do you want to keep your blindfold on?" I asked.

He hesitated as though taking stock. "No, take it off, please. But I might want to wear it again later."

"That's fine. If you want it again, just tell me."

When I lifted the hood off, he squinted as he adjusted to the brighter light. He looked like he'd been hit by a tornado, his hair standing on end in places and mashed flat in others.

After a moment of blinking, Weiss turned to give Holt's chin an accusing look. "You aren't very nice."

Holt snorted. "I don't get paid to be nice. What can you tell us about the person who shot at you today?"

Weiss eyed Holt's chin in silence. I thought he might not

answer, but after a long pause he said, "I promised I'd cooperate if you arrange for me to meet with George Harrison. After I meet with George Harrison, I'll answer your questions."

"That's fair," I said before Holt could pressure him. "George will be here in about half an hour."

"George Harrison?"

"Yes. Would you like a drink of water while you wait? Or do you need to use the bathroom?"

"I would like to urinate."

Holt cautioned Weiss not to make any sudden moves, unlocked him from the table, and ushered him out.

After they returned and Weiss was safely locked to the table again, I inclined my chin toward the door, and Holt and I stepped outside.

"Should we put the lie detector on him?" I asked.

"Can't hurt. None of this is admissible in court anyway, so we might as well make sure he's telling the truth." Holt headed for the observation room. "I'll call Honey... Jack... and see if the lie detector's available."

Fifteen minutes later, I met Stemp in the lobby. Or rather, I met George Harrison. Stemp's distinctive amber eyes were concealed by muddy brown contact lenses in tired, puffy face. A balding pate with wisps of too-long hair replaced his usual precise haircut, and a scruffy beard concealed his chin. The tubby roll around his middle made him look shorter, and he stumped across the lobby with no sign of his usual smooth athletic movements. His pants were baggy and a touch too long, and his shirt looked as though he'd slept in it.

"George, I presume?" I inquired.

His eyes crinkled with humour, but he didn't smile. "Yuh."

Shaking my head at his amazing transformation, I accompanied him to the security wicket. Leo glanced at him without recognition when I asked for a visitor's pass, and Stemp signed in as 'George Harrison' with an Alberta driver's license.

When I opened the door to the interview room, Weiss was already hooked up to the lie detector. He looked over as we entered, but as usual his gaze seemed focused around chin level.

"Rupert, I've brought George Harrison," I said, and stepped aside so Stemp could move forward.

Weiss studied him from toes to head, his gaze moving slowly upward until he paused at Stemp's chin. Then he jerked his gaze up to Stemp's eyes and quickly away again.

"Are you George Harrison, the arms merchant I met in Bulgaria, and saw again in Drumheller thirty-one months ago?" he asked.

"Yuh."

Weiss paused as if considering the laconic response. Then he asked, "What branch of law enforcement are you with?"

My heart stopped.

Stemp fielded the question with his usual cool composure, albeit in George Harrison's voice. "Why d'you think I'm a cop?"

Weiss's expression never changed, and he spoke with absolute certainty. "Because Aydan Kelly, a.k.a Arlene Widdenback, is with law enforcement, and you're working with her. Also this man..." He turned to Holt. "...who hasn't been introduced to me yet. Are you John Kane or Arnold Helmand?"

My pulse pounded harder. Dammit, he might know John's name as an associate of Arlene Widdenback; but he shouldn't have known Arnie.

"No." Holt's expression gave away nothing.

"I can't tell when people are lying," Weiss said. "But even if you're really not John Kane or Arnold Helmand, are you with the RCMP or CSIS? Or the CIA? I know you're all with law enforcement."

My guts clenched. Oh God. It wasn't just my cover that was blown; everything was blown.

Sky-fucking-high.

CHAPTER 30

"That's quite a theory," Stemp said casually, as though Weiss hadn't just dropped a gigantic and potentially fatal bombshell. "Where did you get that idea?"

"My sister told me that Aydan Kelly a.k.a. Arlene Widdenback, John Kane, and Arnold Helmand were all with some branch of law enforcement. I didn't realize you were with them until Aydan Kelly a.k.a. Arlene Widdenback said she knew you, and brought you here so quickly."

"And who is your sister?" Stemp inquired, still cool and composed.

"Dawn White was my sister."

I blurted, "That's the connection! White is the anglicised version of Weiss." Regrouping, I added, "I'm sorry for your loss."

"Why are you apologizing? Did you kill Dawn White?" Weiss asked in his detached tone.

I blinked. "Um, no. 'I'm sorry for your loss' isn't an apology or an admission of guilt. It's just an expression that means I'm imagining that you must be sad because she died, and I have sympathy for your sadness."

"Oh. Thank you for explaining. I am sad. I miss her." As usual, he uttered the words without an iota of emotion, but there was a subtle pinching at the corners of his eyes.

I tucked that into my mental file. Weiss might not make the vocal or facial expressions that I expected or recognized, but he did have expressions.

Fortunately, Stemp didn't seem to be as shell-shocked as I. He asked the next question without hesitation. "When did your sister tell you that?"

Weiss stared blankly forward.

After a moment, Stemp repeated, "When did your sister tell you that?"

Weiss squeezed his eyes shut and his lips moved silently.

Holt shifted impatiently, and I gave him a headshake and a 'settle down' gesture.

We stood watching Weiss in silence, and I wondered whether to put the blindfold on him again. Maybe he was too upset to ask for it.

Just as I was reaching for the hood, Weiss opened his eyes and spoke. "Approximately one year, seven months, and two weeks ago."

My jaw dropped. A small part of my brain noted that when Weiss screwed his eyes shut and recited gun specs, he was either thinking hard or trying to comfort himself. But most of my mind was reeling.

Volslav had known I was an agent ever since I'd started my cover as an arms dealer.

How had I stayed alive all this time?

Stemp's next question to Weiss jarred me from my unpleasant reverie. "Were you aware that your sister was working with Volslav, an international arms consortium?"

"Yes," Weiss said without hesitation, and the lie detector's green light underscored the truth. "She got me a job with them." He patted the table affectionately. "I'm very interested in weapons. Especially high-tech specialty

weapons. I'm the most knowledgeable expert in the world."
He hesitated, and his hands circled each other uncertainly.
"Is it impolite to say I'm the best? Sometimes telling the
truth makes neurotypicals think I'm boasting. But I thought
this is more like a job interview where it's good to tell the
truth about my qualifications. Is that correct?"

"This is a great place to tell the truth," I assured him.

Stemp took over again. "Were you aware that the
weapons Volslav supplied were used to commit crimes?"

Weiss hesitated. "No."

The yellow light flashed. Ordinarily that would mean
Weiss didn't know the true answer. But what if Weiss's brain
worked in a way that the lie detector couldn't process
accurately?

Weiss's hands circled each other, tugging awkwardly at
his bonds as they moved.

"Dawn White wouldn't do anything bad," Weiss added.
"Dawn White was nice. I loved her and she loved me. Dawn
White taught me how to interact with neurotypicals."

Holt broke in impatiently. "You can just call her Dawn.
We know who you mean."

Weiss glanced at Holt's chin. "I like to be accurate. I
always use first and last names. Otherwise you might not
know if I was talking about somebody else with the same first
name."

"All right, if you want to be so *accurate*..." Holt gave the
word sarcastic emphasis. "...then try this question again.
Did you know the weapons you were examining were illegal?
Yes or no?"

Weiss's hand-washing increased its tempo and the subtle
pinch appeared at the corners of his eyes. "No." The green
light corroborated his answer as he went on, "Every country

has different laws about weapons. I don't know about laws. I only know about weapons. People bring weapons to me, or show me pictures or schematics of weapons. I tell them about the weapons. Sometimes people ask me how to make weapons better, or ask me to design new weapons. I do that for them. I don't do anything bad."

"But you damn well know weapons are used to kill people," Holt snapped. "And killing people is a crime. Isn't it? Yes or no."

Weiss's hands twisted frantically and he squeezed his eyes shut. His answer was a toneless shout. "YES! NO!" The yellow light shone for both answers.

"Rupert," I said gently. "Would you like to wear the blindfold for a while?"

"YES! PLEASE!"

Moving slowly in an attempt to keep him calm, I came over and lowered the hood over his head. Immediately the tension eased from his shoulders and his hand-washing movements slowed.

"Thank you," he said. Then he added, "I want to ask the loud man a question."

"Go ahead and ask," I said, skewering Holt with a look.

"You carry a gun," Weiss said in his flat voice. "You said you would shoot me if I did anything wrong. Is it right or wrong for you to shoot me?"

Holt looked nonplussed. "It's wrong for me to shoot you for no reason. But if you're attacking me or somebody else, then it's right."

"That's why I can't answer your question accurately. If the same person can do both right and wrong with the same weapon, I have no way to determine which they will actually do. So I help everyone."

Holt opened his mouth to reply; but Stemp silenced him with an upraised hand and spoke instead. "This is George Harrison speaking.   Thank you for explaining that, Mr. Weiss."

"You're welcome."

"Why did you want to meet with me?" Stemp asked.

"Because I'm looking for a job. I thought you might want to hire me because I'm the best." Weiss hesitated. "I didn't realize until approximately half an hour ago that you were with law enforcement. But now that I know you are, I hope you can protect me even if you can't give me a job. I think Volslav wants to kill me. I don't want to die."

"You think the person who shot at you today was Volslav?" I asked.

"No."

I rubbed my aching temples.   "But you just said you thought Volslav wanted you dead."

"Yes.   But I don't think Volslav would kill me.   I think Volslav would hire someone to kill me."

"Right," I said tiredly. "You like to be accurate."

"Yes."

"Why do you think Volslav wants you dead?"

"After Dawn White died, Volslav said they would kill me if I talked. I have spoken to many people since then."

"They didn't mean for you to never speak again," Holt said. "They just didn't want you to tell anybody about your association with them."

"I deduced that," Weiss replied. "But I have told you and George Harrison and Aydan Kelly a.k.a. Arlene Widdenback about my association with Volslav, so I think Volslav will try to kill me."

"What's the name of the person who said they would kill

you?" I demanded.

"I don't know."

Stemp spoke up. "Is that true?"

"Yes."

The green light indicated Weiss was telling the truth, and Stemp went on, "It was our understanding that Volslav was made up of several people. Dawn White, Yana Orlov, and Tawny Harchman."

As usual, Weiss answered each part of the question separately. "Yes. Yes. I don't know that person." He hesitated, then added, "Dawn White told me four women own Volslav. Dawn White and Yana Orlov are dead, so the person who threatened to kill me must be Tawny Harchman or the fourth woman."

Four women. Shit. No wonder the consortium hadn't unravelled after Tawny Harchman's death. At least one quarter of Volslav was still alive and well.

Stemp's disguised features remained expressionless, but I could see my own unpleasant enlightenment reflected in Holt's eyes.

"Tawny Harchman wasn't the third woman's original name," I said. "She used to be Tanya Rumley."

"I don't know that person, either," Weiss replied. "I only met Yana Orlov."

"Do you know anything about the fourth woman?"

"Dawn White said four women own Volslav. She said one woman is in prison. That's all I know about the fourth woman."

Suddenly the pieces fell into place.

A deluge of adrenaline swamped my veins. "Thank you, Rupert." I cleared my throat so my voice wouldn't wobble with excitement. "We need to take a break now, so we're going to transfer you to a holding area. You'll be free to move around in there, and you'll be safe from Volslav. We'll have more questions for you later."

"Okay. Will you give my laptop back?"

"Not yet. But I promise we haven't harmed it. Would you like me to take your blindfold off so you can see to walk when you're being moved?"

"Yes. Thank you."

I lifted it off his head and handed it to him. "Here, you can keep it with you and put it on if you need it. We'll be back in a while with more questions. A guard will come and escort you to the holding area. As long as you cooperate, the guard won't touch you."

I headed for the door, followed by Stemp and Holt.

As soon as it closed behind us, I blurted, "Maria Harchman!"

Holt looked puzzled, but Stemp's steel-trap mind caught up with my thought process immediately.

"She does appear to be the most probable source of this intel," he agreed.

I knotted a fist in my hair and tugged. "Dammit! When we raided their place two years ago, I was so sure I had stopped all of her network messages before they got out." Defeat weighed down my shoulders. "Obviously I didn't." I stared at my toes, avoiding the well-deserved anger I expected in Stemp's eyes. "I'm sorry."

"There is no need for you to apologize," he said, the gentleness of his tone surprising me. "None of us can do more than our best. In any case, I consider it extremely unlikely that the dissemination of this information is due to those network messages. If it had been, we would have experienced repercussions two years ago. It seems more likely that something has changed, prompting Ms. Harchman to disclose intel she has kept to herself until now."

"Who's Maria Harchman?" Holt demanded.

Encouraged by Stemp's absolution, I dared to meet Holt's eyes and found no condemnation there either. I let out a small breath of relief. "That was before you were transferred here. It was the very first time we investigated Lawrence Harchman and found out he had brainwave-driven VR network technology. Maria was his first wife. Harchman was innocent, but Maria was using his business as a cover while she fed intel and resources to Fuzzy Bunny."

Holt frowned. "That doesn't make sense. If she was part of Volslav, she wouldn't give intel to her biggest competitor. It must be somebody else. We'll have to check prison records for women convicted and incarcerated in the past few years."

"Maybe..." I said slowly. "But I'm sure Maria was the only person who knew all that stuff. And remember, Dawn White and Yana Orlov pretended to be working for Fuzzy Bunny for a while, too. It made sense for them to be on the inside while they planned their takeover."

Stemp nodded. "If Volslav knew all along that we were law enforcement, keeping that intel to themselves was a clever strategy. Other players in the arms market would be fooled by Arlene Widdenback, and Volslav could simply wait for us to arrest their competition."

"So now her three partners are dead, and Maria's out for revenge," I speculated. "So she tells the world who we are, and puts out contracts on all of us." I turned to Stemp. "That might explain why she's out for your blood, too. When your cover as George Harrison got blown in Bulgaria, Volslav figured out you were an agent."

"Entirely possible," he agreed.

"And that's why Arnie's on the hit list, too," I realized aloud. "Maria knew he was working with me."

Holt straightened, his steely gaze kindling with predatory fire. "All right, then. Let's go and have a little talk with Maria Harchman."

CHAPTER 31

My stomach let out an audible growl and I clapped my hand over it.

Holt smirked and amended, "After lunch."

I turned back to Stemp. "Can you stay here at Sirius? It'll be safer for you, and we'll want you to interview Weiss some more in your George Harrison disguise. We can bring you back a sandwich from the Melted Spoon."

"Very well," Stemp agreed.

"Nope," Holt countered.

I turned a frown on him. "Why not?"

"*I'll* bring back sandwiches," Holt corrected. "Not *we*. Remember, you're personally responsible for Stemp. If he's staying here, you're staying, too."

I huffed out a short breath. "Right. Thanks. We'll go up to my office and wait for you there. I'll call Spider and get his team digging up everything they can find about Maria Harchman. She's probably still in the Edmonton Institution. And I'll get a guard to transfer Weiss to a cell and get him some lunch, too."

Holt nodded, and we headed for the time-delay chamber. After we emerged into the lobby, he split off to the front door while Stemp and I climbed the stairs.

As we strode down the corridor, Stemp asked quietly,

"What did Holt mean when he said you were personally responsible for me?"

"No big deal. Just Dermott being his usual self."

Stemp's voice developed a chilly edge. "I deduce that you told Dermott you required my input, and instead of taking responsibility for the decision, he intends to blame you if anything goes wrong."

I shrugged. "Same old, same old." As we entered my office I motioned him to the sofa. "Have a seat. I'll make those calls."

My first call was to Security. Assured that Weiss would be transferred to a cell and fed, I hung up and dialled Spider's extension.

He picked up, sounding glum. "Hi, Aydan. I guess you got my message."

Uh-oh.

I swallowed the sudden dryness in my throat. "No, I just got back to my office. I haven't checked my voicemail yet. What's wrong?"

His sigh carried clearly over the line. "The RCMP found Eldon Rice Swift, a.k.a. Arthur Ronald Walters."

"I'm not going to like this, am I?"

"No. He's dead. Shot."

"Oh." I spared a moment for some silent profanity, then refocused. "Okay, go hard after Farrell Metz, then. Whatever facial modifications you did to find Swift, do the same on Metz. Feed both his current appearance and the modified parameters into the facial recognition search. Did anybody get the make and model of his car when he picked Swift up?"

"No, but it doesn't matter. The car was stolen. The killer abandoned it in a residential area in Drumheller with Swift's body still belted into the passenger's seat."

"Fuck! These guys are one step ahead of us the whole way!"

"I'm sorry..." Spider began, but I interrupted.

"You don't need to apologize; you and your team are doing a great job as usual. Keep me posted on anything you find out about Metz. And... I'm sorry, I know how busy you are; but we also need as much information as your team can get us on Maria Harchman. Last I heard, she was in Edmonton Institution, so we'll go up and interview her there..." I consulted my watch. "Maybe even this afternoon, if they can arrange it at the prison. But it's a three hour drive, so we likely won't make it there before four o'clock."

"I'll check with them and get back to you right away."

"Thanks, Spider, you're the best." I hesitated. "Still no baby news?"

His sigh echoed down the phone line. "No. In a way, I'm kind of glad we're so busy right now. Otherwise I'd be a basket case." He sighed again. "More of a basket case."

"Hang in there. Talk to you later." I hung up and faced Stemp's concerned gaze.

"Adverse developments?" he inquired.

"Yeah." Flopping into the chair across from him, I broke the news about Swift's murder and Metz's escape.

"I see." After a moment of thought, Stemp added, "So if there were only two assassins, Farrell Metz is likely the person who attempted to shoot me."

"Probably."

"So whoever hired Swift decided to eliminate him when he became a liability by being arrested."

I sighed. "Whoever's trying to kill us has big bucks if they can hire two hitmen. And if Swift could afford to have all that cosmetic work done just to create a new identity, he didn't come cheap."

"Another reason to eliminate him," Stemp pointed out. "Perhaps Metz offered a better price."

"Well, if there are more of them out there, we can always hope they get distracted trying to kill each other." My phone rang, and I headed for the desk. "Kelly."

"Security here," said a male voice. "Your prisoner is in his cell, but he went nuts when we told him he'd have to change into scrubs and leave his personal property outside the cell. We had to trank him."

"Shit. Is he okay?"

"He isn't injured. We got him changed and laid him in the bunk. He should wake up in about fifteen minutes."

"Thanks for letting me know. I'll be there before he wakes up." Overcoming the urge to fling the receiver at the opposite wall, I lowered it into its cradle instead. "There's always something," I muttered, then addressed Stemp. "Weiss freaked out when they told him he had to change into prison scrubs and hand over his personal items. They tranked him."

"I suspected that would not go smoothly."

Wishing I had his ability to think three steps ahead of everyone else, I replied, "I didn't even think of it. I should have."

"If I had considered it important, I would have mentioned it. This is a better situation. It allows you to be Weiss's rescuer again, building more rapport with him."

I plodded over and threw myself into the chair. "That poor guy. I hate this fucking job."

Stemp's eyebrow rose fractionally. "Our interviews are not yet complete. Your sympathy for Weiss may be premature."

"Maybe, but my gut says he's innocent. I think he's just trying to get through life in a world that's confusing for him at best and hostile at worst. It's not his fault his sister decided to become an international arms dealer."

"As accurate as I know your instincts to be, I must nevertheless caution you to remain on your guard."

I grunted. "Yeah, I will. That's why I really hate this f-"

The ring of the phone interrupted me.

I sprang up and hurried over to answer. "Kelly."

"Megan Novak again. I have a call for you from Mr. Helmand."

A moment later, Hellhound's gravelly voice tickled my eardrum. "Hey, darlin'. We got Rand outta your house, an' we've got him cornered in the Silverside Hotel. Room 204."

"You've got him cornered." A grin tugged at the corners of my mouth. "I know there's a story behind this."

Hellhound's voice held an answering smile as he replied, "Kane and I went bargin' into your place, an' we got there before Rand even got past the kitchen. Kane walks in... ya know how he does that 'king a' the universe' thing..."

My grin widened, imagining Kane's imposing stature and commanding presence bearing down on Ian. "Yeah, and then...?"

"Kane goes, 'You're late, what took ya?', an' Rand goes, 'What the...', an' Kane says, 'Come on, hurry up, we can still make it'. He grabs one a' Rand's arms an' I grab the other, an' next thing ya know Rand's standin' beside his car, goin', 'What the fuck'. Kane says, 'Hurry up, I'll ride with you, an' Hellhound'll follow'; and out the lane we go, slicker'n owl shit."

I couldn't suppress a giggle of sheer delight. "You guys

are awesome. Then what?"

"Well, I dunno exactly what they said in the car; but the upshot of it was, Kane told Rand he was gonna stick to him like shit on a blanket, an' Rand played it cool like he wasn't up to anythin'. So now Rand's in his room, Kane's sittin' outside his door, an' I'm hangin' in the parkin' lot watchin' Rand's window. He ain't goin' anywhere without us knowin'."

"Have I told you lately how much I love you?"

His raspy chuckle floated over the line. "If you're feelin' all lovey-dovey, ya could put on that librarian outfit for me later."

"It's a date," I promised. "Thank you for taking care of Ian."

"No problem. If he moves, we'll keep ya posted."

"Be careful out there," I admonished. "And tell John to be careful, too. The hitmen are still in town. Somebody shot at us this morning in Drumheller."

The humour vanished from his voice, replaced by worry vibrating like high-tension wire. "Shit! You're okay, right?"

"Yeah. Anyhow, I have to go; I've got another situation here."

"D'ya need backup?"

"No, I'm fine. And thanks again."

As I replaced the receiver in the cradle, Holt strode in carrying sandwich boxes.

As he handed mine over, I said, "Thanks. You guys can eat here in my office if you want. I'm going down to the secured area. Weiss's transfer to the cell didn't go well, and he should be waking up from the tranquilizer any minute now. Oh, and Kane and Hellhound kicked Rand out of my house and escorted him back to his hotel. They've got him boxed into his room and under surveillance." As I spoke, I punched in the numbers to forward my calls.

Stemp rose. "I will join you in the secured area. We can continue our interview with Weiss when he recovers."

"Sounds good," Holt seconded, and we headed for the door.

"Ian Rand was in your home?" Stemp inquired quietly as we walked down the corridor.

"Yeah. I still don't know why he's snooping around me, but he's sure persistent." I lowered my voice with a glance around to make sure no civilians were within earshot. "Holt and I thought it might have been Ian shooting at us in Drumheller; but Weiss says not."

"What made you think-" Stemp broke off as we rounded the corner and came face to face with Trish Belling and Rebecca Stile.

Trish smiled. "Hi, Aydan; Greg; I'd like you to meet our newest employee, Rebecca Stile. Rebecca, this is Aydan Kelly from bookkeeping, and Greg Holt from land acquisitions." She hesitated, glancing at Stemp's disguise. "I'm sorry, have we met?"

"George Harrison," Stemp said gruffly. "I'm just here for a meeting."

"It's nice to meet you," Trish said politely before turning back to Holt and me. "Rebecca is a filing dynamo! It's great to have her on board; we're really making a dent in those daily reports."

"That's great," I said. "Rebecca, it's nice to meet you; and I hope you enjoy your new job. Trish, we'll chat later. We have to get to a meeting."

"See you later," she said cheerfully.

In the secured area, a burly security guard confronted us

as soon as we rounded the corner to the cells.

"Aydan Kelly?" he demanded, focusing on me.

Dammit, I'd been with CSIS for nearly two years, and the sight of a uniform still triggered an instant guilt complex.

I hid the lurch of my stomach in a cool professional tone. "Yes?"

"There's an urgent call for you." He pointed at the security phone beside the cells.

I handed Holt my sandwich box and beelined for the phone. "Kelly."

"Megan here. It's Mr. Helmand again. He says it's urge-"

"Aydan!" Hellhound interrupted. "Cops're arrestin' Kane!"

CHAPTER 32

"What? *Why?*" I demanded.

"Rand called the cops an' said Kane was threatenin' him; wouldn't let him outta his room," Hellhound replied.

"Fuck! Megan, are you still listening?" There was no reply, and I added, "Hang on, Arnie", hit Hold, and then punched in the analyst-on-call extension.

When Megan answered, I rapped out, "Aydan again. This is urgent. The police are at the Silverside Hotel, responding to call from a man named Ian Rand in Room 204. He told them a man in the hallway was preventing him from leaving his room. The man in the hallway is John Kane, and he's with a private investigator, Arnie Helmand. They're both working with me. Get the dispatcher to tell the constables it's a bogus call, and get them to detain Ian Rand for questioning instead of arresting John Kane. Got it?"

"Calling them now." Her reply was crisp and competent.

I hit Hold on her line and transferred back to Hellhound. "Arnie, hang tight. The constables are going to get an order to let John go and detain Ian instead, so don't let him sneak away."

"On it."

"Be right back." I switched lines again. "Megan?"

Dead air greeted me, and I waited. A moment later she came back on the line. "They've got the message. The dispatcher should be relaying it now."

"Thanks, you're the best! Tell them they can hold Rand and question him as long as they want, and when they're done, get them to transfer him up here."

Disconnecting from Megan's call, I switched back to Arnie. "Are you still there?"

"Yep. Kane an' I had a phone line open, so hang on a sec. I'll put ya on hold, an' switch back to Kane so I can hear what's goin' on." Silence blanketed the line, but soon Arnie was back with a smile in his voice. "Sounds like they got the order. They're cuttin' Kane loose and readin' Rand his rights instead. He's tryin' to weasel outta it, but they ain't lettin' him. Nice one, darlin'. That oughta put a kink in Rand's hard-on."

"Let's hope so. Once you guys get free of the scene there, can you come to Sirius? We have footage of one of the assassins, and I want you both to know what he looks like."

"Sure."

"And be careful!"

"Careful's my middle name." I let out a scoffing snort, and he chuckled and added, "See ya in a bit."

I hung up the phone and rejoined Holt and Stemp, retrieving my sandwich box from Holt.

"You're detaining Rand for questioning?" Holt asked. "About what?"

"Anything I damn well want." I took a savage bite of my sandwich, gulped it down, and added, "And if he pisses me off, I'll charge him with public mischief for calling the police and lying about a crime in progress."

"It won't stick. He has diplomatic immunity."

"I don't need it to stick. I just want him out of my business for as long as possible." I raised the sandwich, unhinging my jaw for another gargantuan mouthful. The savory tang of roasted peppers and garlic wafted to my nose and I paused. Inhaled, then exhaled slowly, letting my shoulders ease down.

"Thanks for the sandwich," I said, and took a smaller bite, actually tasting it this time. I chewed at a moderate pace, swallowed, and added, "What do I owe you?"

"You can get the next one."

"Deal."

Munching, I drifted over to Weiss's cell door. The transparent barrier revealed Weiss lying on the bunk, clad in orange prison scrubs. He was beginning to moan and twitch.

The sound of rolling casters made me glance up to see the guard helpfully dragging chairs over from a nearby meeting room.

"Thanks," I said, taking a seat and placing my sandwich box on my lap to give it my full attention.

Stemp, Holt, and I ate in silence, waiting.

At last Weiss opened his eyes. He lay staring at the ceiling for a few moments, flexing his arms and legs. Then he sat up, eyes downcast as usual.

His body contracted like a coiled spring. "No!" He squeezed his eyes shut, rocking violently and wringing his hands as his toneless voice rose to a shout. "*No!* NO! *NO!*"

"Rupert!" I had to yell to be heard. "RUPERT! PUT ON YOUR BLINDFOLD!"

He groped frantically for it with his eyes still squeezed shut.

"It's farther to your left," I encouraged. "That's it. You've got it. Just put it on and think of weapons."

He yanked the hood over his head, his knuckles white with the force of his grip as he held it closed under his chin. His cries of distress gave way to a torrent of words.

"556 Tactica, ADC, Adcor Defense, AEK, Arsenal, Arctiier, Baikal, Barrett, BB, BCM, Benelli, Beretta, Bergara, Bersa, Blaser, Browning..."

Not words; names. Firearm manufacturers of the world, in alphabetical order. The list went on and on, but by the time he got to 'Ruger' his tempo was slowing and his volume was closer to normal.

We waited patiently until he finished, "...Weatherby, Wilson Combat, Winchester, Zastava Arms." He stopped speaking.

"Can you talk to us now, Rupert?" I asked softly.

"Yes. I need to change out of these clothes. I can't wear orange. It's too loud. It hurts."

"We'll get you something else," I promised. "Are there any other colours that you can't wear?"

"Yellow. Red. Purple. Bright blue. Bright green-"

"Okay," I interrupted. "Beige or gray would work, right?"

"Yes. Beige and gray are quiet. I can think when I wear beige or gray."

"Okay. We'll get you a change of clothes as soon as we can. In the meantime, you can wrap up in the blanket. It's gray."

"Oh." His shoulders sagged with relief. "Yes. Thank you." He stood and struggled out of his pants, exposing pasty skin and pristine tighty-whiteys.

Holt let out a snort of amusement, but I gave him the stink-eye and he stifled himself.

The blindfold hood came off when Weiss yanked off the

scrub top, but he didn't open his eyes. He balled up the scrubs by feel and wrapped the blanket around the offending clothing.

"Is all the orange hidden?" he asked, looking pitiable in his underwear with his hair on end and his glasses askew.

"Yes, it's safe to open your eyes now," I assured him. "And we'll get you another blanket." I turned to gesture to the guard, but he was already ducking into the empty adjoining cell to get one.

When Rupert was safely wrapped in his fresh blanket, he sat staring at the floor with his lips moving silently for a few moments.

"There's a sandwich for you in the box over there," I prompted gently, pointing at the plastic shelf that served as a table in the cell.

Weiss eyed it. "What kind of sandwich?"

"Ham and cheese," the guard responded.

"Processed meats are high in nitrates, nitrites, sodium, and saturated fats. Grilled chicken would be a healthier choice."

The guard's lips pressed tight, but before he could retort Weiss went on, "But eating processed meat once in a while won't significantly increase my risk of cancer or cardiovascular problems. It's polite to eat what I'm offered, so I'll eat it. As long as it was prepared in an accredited commercial kitchen by people who have been trained in proper food handling techniques."

A muscle ticked in the guard's jaw.

I hurriedly said, "It was", hoping that was true.

"Thank you." Weiss eyed my chin. "May I have my laptop and my necklaces back now?"

"Necklaces?" I raised an eyebrow at the guard.

"He was wearing two necklaces under his shirt." The guard shot Weiss a disapproving look and jabbed his finger toward a paper on the table beside Weiss's sandwich box. "There's a complete inventory of your belongings. You need to read it over and sign it."

"I won't sign it unless it's complete and accurate." Weiss picked up the paper and scanned it. After a few moments of reading, he patted his thigh approvingly. "It's complete and accurate. I'll sign it. Now may I have my laptop and my necklaces back?"

"Not yet," I said. "I'm sorry."

His hands clenched on each other. "Where are they?"

"In a security locker," the guard said. "They're safe."

Weiss squeezed his eyes shut while his hands circled each other.

"Here comes another meltdown," the guard muttered.

To my surprise, Holt said quietly, "Cut him some slack. He's doing the best he can."

As if in reply, Weiss spoke. "Is this a secure facility?"

"Yes," Holt replied.

"Am I the only prisoner right now?"

"You're not really a prisoner," I comforted. "We're just figuring out what to do with you."

"If I cooperate, will you help me?"

Holt and I exchanged a glance with Stemp, but his disguised face was as expressionless as Weiss's. This was our call.

"We'll do our best," I equivocated.

"I will cooperate." Weiss hesitated, his hands flapping. "I understand that you've put my belongings in a locker for safekeeping. But I'm feeling very anxious about them." His volume increased and his hands moved faster. "I need to see my necklaces and my laptop! Please bring them to me so I know they're safe!"

"Okay." I nodded at the guard.

He hurried away, looking relieved to be departing. While we waited, Weiss clamped his eyes shut again, lips moving and hands wringing. We didn't bother to question him. It was obvious that he was barely holding onto control.

When the guard returned with a box, Weiss opened his eyes gingerly. The frenetic motion of his lips slowed as he studied the items in the box, but his hands still twisted in agitated circles.

"Would you please take them out of the box and put them on the floor right outside this barrier where I can watch them?" he asked.

"Okay." I took the laptop out and put it on the floor, then lifted out the two necklaces. Their chains were tangled, and I guessed that would upset Weiss. I spent a few moments separating the two items, reflecting that the large tiger-eye cabochon in its elaborate gold setting was an odd choice for a man, especially a beige-and-gray guy like Weiss. The sleek geometric silver pendant seemed as though it would suit him better.

That pendant reminded me of...

My heart gave a hard thump, making my fingers tremble on the chains.

"Rupert," I said as calmly as I could. "Where did you get these, and why are they so important to you?"

"They were Dawn White's. She told me that if anything happened to her, I should make sure to always keep the necklaces with me and never let them out of my sight. I promised her I would. I always keep my promises."

Holt and I exchanged a wide-eyed look.

Hiding my flare of excitement, I said, "Your sister was involved in a lot of things that you likely didn't know about. I don't know if she actually did anything bad..." I mentally crossed my fingers to negate the lie. "...but I do know that Tawny Harchman had a necklace that looked a lot like this silver one. It had a flash drive hidden in it, and there was important information on it about Volslav. I think these necklaces might have flash drives in them, too."

CHAPTER 33

"Oh." Weiss closed his eyes and his lips moved, but his hand movements slowed. Thinking.

I stayed silent.

After a long moment he opened his eyes and studied the necklaces again. "I think the silver necklace was Dawn White's. Dawn White showed me the silver necklace approximately seven years and five months ago. But she didn't show me the gold necklace until approximately one year, seven months, and three weeks ago. I think the gold necklace originally belonged to Yana Orlov."

I did some quick mental math. "Dawn showed it to you after Yana died."

"I don't know exactly when Yana Orlov died, but Dawn White packed Yana Orlov's belongings and sent them to Yana Orlov's parents in Bulgaria afterward. But Dawn White might have kept Yana Orlov's necklace if it had important information about Volslav hidden in it." His fingers knotted as he stared at the necklaces. "You're going to have to take them apart to find the flash drives, aren't you?"

"I'm afraid so. We'll try not to wreck them. Tawny Harchman's necklace was designed so that the flash drive could be taken out without harming the necklace, so they'll probably be okay. But we'll have to take them out of your sight."

Weiss stared at the necklaces, hands rotating. "I have a hard time understanding complex social mores. If the person I made a promise to is dead, do I still have to keep the promise?"

"No," Holt said.

I threw him a frown. "If breaking the promise to the dead person would hurt someone who's still alive, then it might be better to keep the promise. But it won't hurt anyone if you let these necklaces out of your sight for a short time, and it might help a lot of people. So it's all right to break this particular promise."

"That makes sense. You can take the necklaces. But I want them back when you're finished with them." Weiss squeezed his eyes shut, his hands picking up their tempo again. "I'm overstimulated. I need to concentrate on self-soothing. Please go away."

"Okay. If you need to talk to any of us, just ask the guard."

Weiss was already retreating to the bunk clutching the blackout hood, and didn't acknowledge my words. I threw the guard a nod of thanks; and Holt, Stemp, and I hurried down the hall toward Spider's tech lab.

We found him in his lair, his gaze glued to a computer screen while he scrolled text at breakneck speed. I tapped on the door frame and he twitched violently.

"What's up?" he asked, raking his fingers through already-rumpled hair.

"Sorry, I know how busy you are," I said. "But..." I held up the necklaces. "Remember how Tawny Harchman's necklace had a flash drive in it?"

Spider's eyes lit up. "Are those what I think they are?"

"Yep. Rupert thinks these belonged to Dawn White and Yana Orlov. And Dawn told him not to let these necklaces out of his sight."

Spider sprang up and hurried over, and I handed him the tiger-eye. Turning it this way and that as he studied the setting, he muttered, "I bet... this little depression..." He pressed in with his thumbnail and the cabochon popped out with a tiny click. Behind it a micro-SD card nestled in the gold setting.

I grinned. "You're a genius. I couldn't even see that without my reading glasses." Offering him the silver pendant, I added, "Two for two?"

He eagerly studied the necklace. "This one's too sleek to hide a latch like that. So..." Frowning, he turned it over and over, gently twisting and pressing. "Aha!" Grinning, he gripped the pendant by its top and bottom and squeezed. The bottom of the pendant detached, revealing a USB plug. "And we're in! I can hardly wait to see what's on these drives!"

"It's probably the same as what was on Tawny's," Holt said gloomily.

Infected by his pessimism, I added, "And no matter what it is, it won't be current. Dawn White and Yana Orlov have been dead for over a year."

"You're probably right," Spider agreed. "But I'll give it top priority, just in case."

A thought hit me, straightening my spine and filling my heart with hope. "Three women, three necklaces! What about the fourth? I bet Maria Harchman has a necklace, too. And I bet hers has all the current information on it. Like how many hitmen she hired, and who they are!"

"I doubt it," Holt-The-Downer replied. "She's in a

maximum-security prison. Pretty hard to hire hitmen from there."

"Um..." Spider began, but I overrode him in my excitement.

"Maybe; maybe not. I bet she's got somebody on the outside. If we can track down the people who've visited her in the past few months..." I trailed off at Spider's pained look. "What?"

"Um... I have some bad news about Maria Harchman."

I clutched my head. "Now what?"

"She's dead. She died in prison five months ago."

"*What?*" I stared at Spider as my theories collapsed into smoking ruins. "Maria Harchman was the only one left alive who knew all that stuff! So who the hell blew our covers? And who's trying to kill us?"

"I... I'm sorry, I don't..." he stammered.

"Shit, no, Spider; I wasn't blaming you." Massaging my aching temples, I glared at the floor. "I'm just..." The weight of my fear and disappointment forced out a gusty sigh. "Well, shit."

"What did she die of?" Holt asked.

"A drug overdose." Spider gave an uncertain half-shrug. "There were no signs of foul play; but there was no indication that Maria had ever taken drugs before, either. The medical examiner ruled it an accidental death, but it could have been a well-planned murder."

"How about her personal belongings?" I asked. "Can you find out what she had at the prison, and who claimed her stuff? And whether she had any friends inside, and who her recent visitors were..." I trailed off as Spider nodded along with my list. "Sorry," I added. "I know you're on top of this. I just... if we find out she had a necklace in her personal belongings, we'll know she was arrested wearing it. And if she didn't trust anybody else enough to have them come and pick it up and keep it for her, that could mean it's important."

"Or it could mean it was just a random necklace and she didn't care about it enough to have anybody pick it up," Holt pointed out.

"Well, yeah," I allowed. "But I just can't shake the idea that Maria is... was... the source of our security breach."

"You're grasping at straws," Holt said. Turning to Spider, he added, "Pull together a list of all the women who've been convicted and imprisoned in the past five years, and check them all for any connections to Dawn White, Yana Orlov, and Tawny Harchman."

I winced at the magnitude of the task, but Spider just nodded and agreed, "I'll get Megan to contact the prison and get the complete set of Maria's records right away, and I'll run an automated query for those convictions. We'll do a manual check for more nuanced connections, too; but the automation will flag any obvious matches within minutes."

"What would we do without you?" I marvelled.

As we withdrew to the corridor again, Stemp asked, "How long do you intend to allow Mr. Weiss to recover?"

I sighed and headed down the hall. "I don't know. Let's go and see how he's doing. I don't want to waste your time hanging around here all day, but at least it's probably safer for you here than at home."

"You are not wasting my time. This is my job." George Harrison's disguise concealed any hint of expression, but Stemp's tone was wry as he added, "Suspended or not."

"Thanks." Giving him a smile, I added, "If he'll respond, go ahead and ask him anything that comes to mind. You know as much about this case as we do."

Holt nodded. "I'll be the Loud Man if it's called for, but I think Weiss is more likely to respond to George Harrison's questions, with Arlene as his rescuer if he gets agitated."

Standing outside Weiss's cell, we eyed him through the barrier. He lay on his bunk wearing the blackout hood, blanket drawn up to his chin.

Stemp raised his voice. "Mr. Weiss?"

"Yes?" Weiss said without moving.

"George Harrison here," Stemp said. "I'd like to ask you some more questions now."

"Okay." Weiss hesitated. "I understand that neurotypicals want me to face them and make eye contact when we converse, but that's very stressful for me. I can answer more questions if I stay like this. Is it okay if I do that?"

"That's fine," I answered before Stemp could speak. "We'll have to ask you to take your hood off for a few seconds while we put the lie detector on you again, and after that you can lie down and wear your hood if you want."

When Weiss was hooked up to the electrodes and comfortably settled on his bunk again, Stemp said in George Harrison's voice, "Let's start at the beginning. Is your real name Rupert Weiss?"

"No."

Green light.

Holt and I exchanged a dumbfounded look. Shit, we'd missed the most obvious...

"My real name is Rupert Edgar Weiss," Weiss clarified. "Rupert Weiss is only my given name and surname."

Holt rolled his eyes, but Stemp's voice held no impatience as he replied. "Thank you. I appreciate your accuracy."

"You're welcome."

"What was your sister's real name?"

"Dawn Kimberley White. Her birth name was Dawn Kimberley Weiss. She legally changed her surname to White approximately..." He hesitated as though calculating time. "...seven years and nine months ago."

"Do you have any other siblings?"

"No."

"Are, or were, any of your other family members involved in any way with Volslav?"

"No. Only Dawn White and me."

Green lights all the way.

Stemp asked, "Do you recall the ultrasound weapon I showed you nearly three years ago?"

"Yes. Approximately thirty-one months ago."

Weiss's crossed arms moved under the blanket, and I realized he was patting himself on both elbows. Apparently when he was happy or interested, he patted whatever was under his hands. Good to know.

Weiss went on, "That was a particularly interesting weapon. It was the first of its kind to focus ultrasound into a destructive beam. The secret is in the-"

"Excuse me for interrupting," Stemp said. "We'll come back to that. I have some more questions."

"Okay." Weiss's toneless voice betrayed no hint of pique at being interrupted.

"Do you know who invented the ultrasound weapon?"

"Yes." The green light shone. Weiss said no more.

"Who invented the ultrasound weapon?" Stemp asked patiently.

"I did."

The security phone rang. The guard answered it, then beckoned to me.

I accepted the receiver from him. "Kelly."

"Hi Aydan, it's Leo. Kane and Hellhound are here."

"Great, thanks. I'll be right there." I hung up and spoke quietly to Holt so as not to disrupt the rhythm Stemp had established with Weiss. "You guys carry on with the questioning. John and Arnie just got here, and I'm going to show them the footage we got from the RCMP so they can identify Farrell Metz if he shows up again."

"What about Stemp?" Holt muttered. "You're supposed to be supervising him."

"We both know he's not a security risk. And you're here to supervise him, so we're not violating any policies. I won't be long."

Holt shrugged acquiescence, and I hurried down the corridor.

When I got to the lobby, Kane and Hellhound were chatting with Leo. The sign-in sheet only needed my signature, and I completed the formalities before leading the two men upstairs to a meeting room.

When the door closed behind us, Kane gave me a smile. "Thank you for the intervention earlier."

"You're welcome." I grinned. "I hope Ian is enjoying the hospitality of the Drumheller RCMP."

"They won't be able to hold him long," Kane observed. "He'll have diplomatic immunity."

"I know, but they'll hold him long enough to inconvenience him, and at least it'll keep him off my list of annoyances for a while." I entered my credentials in the meeting room computer, then browsed to the surveillance footage we'd received from the Drumheller RCMP. "Here's

Farrell Metz." I started the video.

We watched in silence. Metz was a generic-looking guy, and I wondered how many times I might have walked past him on the street without noticing him.

"Have either of you seen him before?" I asked.

Arnie shook his head. "Nope."

John frowned. "I don't think so. But he doesn't have any distinctive features. I might not remember if I had seen him in passing."

"But you'll recognize him now, right?"

John nodded, and I shot a grin at Arnie. "And I know you'll recognize him. You and your photographic memory. Sometimes I envy you."

He smiled. "It ain't always all it's cracked up to be, but it comes in handy sometimes."

I reached over and squeezed his hand, offering silent sympathy for the horrors he'd witnessed and could never forget.

He stood. "Well, guess we better get goin'."

As Kane stood, too, I asked, "Where? Home to hide in the woods, I hope." They exchanged a glance, and my heart sank. "You're planning to do something dangerous, aren't you?"

"Nah, not really," Arnie said at the same time John said, "It shouldn't be too risky."

I groaned. "Shit. Tell me."

"We're headin' back to your place all right," Hellhound said. "But I'm gonna drop Kane there an' keep on goin' to Drumheller. I'm gonna keep an eye out for Rand just in case they release him from there 'stead a' transferrin' him up here."

I turned to Kane. "I know better than to think you're

going back to my farm to hide at your campsite."

Kane shrugged. "The time for hiding is past. Alicia and Daniel left yesterday on a road trip through the Rockies to the west coast; and Dad is visiting friends in Ontario. Nobody will know how to find them or where to start looking, so they can't be used as leverage. If you don't mind, I'd like to borrow your street-and-trail bike. I want to do some reconnaissance. Maybe surveillance, depending on what I find."

Letting out a sigh, I rose, too. "Okay. I knew better than to expect you two to lie low and play it safe." I hugged them each in turn, then headed for the door. "I'll walk you down so you can sign out."

As we came down the stairs into the lobby, Holt and Stemp emerged from the secured area. Arnie's gaze passed over Stemp's George Harrison disguise without recognition, but John's eyes narrowed. He'd seen that disguise before.

"Later," I said quietly, and nudged him toward the security wicket. As he moved off, I went over to Holt and Stemp. "Done already?" I asked, keeping my voice low.

"Yes. Holt will brief you," Stemp said. "If you need me again, I will be available for the rest of the day, except for a short phone call I must make as soon as I arrive home."

Together we headed for the security wicket.

When Stemp, Arnie, and John had signed out, I gave them a wave and a 'See you later' as Holt and I turned for the stairs.

We were just walking into my office when a thunderous blast rocked the building.

From the direction of the parking lot.

Oh God.

CHAPTER 34

My mind frozen with horror, I sprinted downstairs with Holt keeping pace beside me. The garbled roaring in my ears resolved itself into Leo's firm voice speaking on the public address system.

"Everyone stay calm. The building is secure. Stay in your offices, away from the windows, until further notice. I repeat, stay calm, stay in your offices, stay away from the windows."

My Glock was in my hand. I didn't remember drawing it. Charging across the lobby, I fought nightmare memories of blood and dismembered bodies. I stiff-armed the door.

It didn't open.

Pain exploded in my hand and momentum slammed me against the door. I dimly heard a matching thump as Holt hit the other door at top speed. Reeling back, I sucked air and blinked away the points of light spangling my vision.

"We're in lockdown!" Leo's shout penetrated my pain and panic. "You can't go out!"

Clamping down on the hysterical urge to scream and kick the door, I limped rapidly to the security wicket, dodging armored tactical personnel as they streamed into the lobby from the secured area.

Leo's hands flew over his controls, toggling security

camera views while he barked information into his headset.

One of the views showed wreckage in the parking lot.

My guts twisted into a hard knot. Stemp's car, at the centre of the blast radius. There was a motionless lump in the driver's seat.

Only a lump.

No head or arms oh no no...

Fighting the mind-blanking horror, I tuned into Leo's voice again.

"Copy that. Coordinate with them; I'll update you ASAP." He punched a few more keys, transferring lines. "All teams: Door release in three, two, one..." He flipped four toggle switches. "Go!"

The tac team poured out the front doors.

Leo's hand hovered over the switches as his other hand pressed his earpiece. "Blue Team clear, copy." He flipped a switch back into position and a clunk from the front doors indicated they were locked again. As each team checked in, he confirmed them clear and flipped the switches back to their former positions. We leaned tensely forward, watching the video displays as black-clad figures spread out around the building.

Without taking his eyes from the screens or releasing his hold on his earpiece, Leo said, "Aydan, can't talk, I have to..." He motioned with his free hand at the screens. "Kane and Hellhound are okay. Call the analyst's line."

My knees weakened and I staggered back a shaky step, bumping into a hard body behind me. Holt's hands shot out to stabilize me, but I pulled away and ran to the lobby phone.

"Take it easy," Holt cautioned as I jabbed savagely at the buttons.

Ignoring him, I pressed the receiver to my ear, my

knuckles aching with the force of my grip.

When Megan's tense voice answered, I snapped, "Kelly here. Status on Kane and Helmand?"

"They had just driven out of the parking lot when the explosion happened. They spotted Farrell Metz driving away. They're following him and relaying his position to the RCMP."

"Are you in phone contact with them now?"

"Yes."

"I'll call you from my office and you can patch me into the call." I hung up and ran, taking the stairs two at a time.

Holt followed, and together we pounded into my office and skidded to a halt at my desk.

My shaking hands barely managed to hit the correct numbers on the keypad. When Megan answered again, I panted, "Kelly and Holt here. Putting you on speaker."

"Connecting you now," she responded. "Mr. Kane? I'm bringing Agents Kelly and Holt into the call now. Agent Kelly, go ahead."

"John?" My voice came out squeakier than I'd intended. "Are you okay? What happened?"

"We're both fine. We didn't see what happened. We were driving out of the parking lot when the explosion blew out our back window. Arnie slammed on the brakes and we turned back, but Stemp's car..." His voice went rough. I gulped down my own emotion as he cleared his throat and went on, "We spotted an SUV pulling out and identified the driver as Farrell Metz. We knew Security would get a team out right away to help Stemp, so I called 911 and we've been following Metz at a distance, relaying his position to the RCMP and coordinating with Megan. There should be a blockade..."

He paused, and his voice firmed into grim satisfaction as he went on, "There it is. Metz is braking... *dammit!*"

My heart drummed frantically as Hellhound spat a rapid-fire string of obscenities in the background.

"He spun a U-turn!" Kane snapped. "He's coming ba-"

His words were swallowed by tires squealing and Hellhound bellowing, "RUN!"

Staticky crackling took over, the sound of fast and violent movement.

"John! *What's happening?*" I demanded.

An apocalyptic blast rattled the phone's speaker.

Then silence.

"JOHN!" My shriek tore my throat. "ARNIE!"

Nothing.

Megan's voice trembled out of the phone. "I l-lost them..." She gulped. "I mean... the connection dropped. M-maybe... they'll... call back?"

A cracked ghost of a voice issued from my mouth. "Yeah. Keep me posted." I hung up and fell into my desk chair, staring at nothing.

CHAPTER 35

I was vaguely aware of Holt plodding over to sit on the sofa. His face was the colour of bleached bone, carved deep with lines that hadn't been there half an hour ago.

Cold numbness filled my soul.

My phone rang.

I pounced on it, my heart leaping into my throat. "Megan?"

"No, Leo."

Somehow I managed an appropriate response. "What's up?"

He rapped out quick sentences, obviously still handling the security fallout. "Stemp's alive. They're taking him to the hospital. No other casualties. Everything's secure."

Alive.

I should be elated.

But I couldn't shake the memory of the dismembered lump. I managed to ask, "How badly is he injured?"

"Don't know, but he's still with us." Leo didn't add 'for now', but I heard the words anyway.

"Thanks for letting me know." It took all my remaining energy to replace the receiver in its cradle.

When the phone rang again, my hand quivered above it for an instant before I braced myself and answered. "Kelly."

Megan skipped the formalities, her voice vibrating with relief. "Kane called back! They're fine! I'm connecting you now."

"Aydan?" Kane's deep voice punctured the wall of numbness around my heart.

"John!" I hugged the receiver to my ear. My voice trembled. "You're... okay?"

"Bruised and bit a deaf at the moment, but fine. Am I yelling?"

"Just a bit."

"How's this?" he asked, lowering his volume.

"Better. What happened? How's Arnie?"

"He's fine. As for what happened, Metz decided to run for it. And *somebody*..." He emphasized the word as if in reprimand, but I could hear the smile in his voice. "...forgot it wasn't up to us to stop him."

In the background Arnie said loudly, "Ya woulda done the same damn thing! I saw your foot stompin' on that imaginary brake pedal."

John went on, "Arnie hit the brakes and spun sideways to make a barricade, and we bailed out. Metz accelerated and made a run for it. I guess he thought if he clipped the end of our vehicle he could push it out of the way and get past. He miscalculated the rebound and dropped two wheels into the ditch. His car rolled and exploded. Judging by the damage, I'd say at least one fragmentation grenade detonated inside it, maybe more."

"Ouch. Is he dead?"

Arnie spoke up again. "If they get a shovel an' a squeegee, they might scoop up enough to fill a pail."

I shuddered.

In the short silence that ensued, Arnie added, "Sorry.

Bad taste." He sighed. "What's the situation there?"

"I just found out Stemp's alive. I don't know how badly he's injured. I'm going to head over to the hospital now."

"That's good news," John said, but his tone lacked conviction. He had likely seen what remained of Stemp, too. "Keep us posted," he added. "Hellhound's vehicle isn't driveable, but we're not far from your farm so we're going to walk back there."

"Be careful," I urged.

"We will; but I suspect hitmen will be scarce around here for a while, at least until word filters back to whoever hired them. We're likely fairly safe at the moment."

"Be careful anyway. And if you need a vehicle, the keys to the half-ton and the dirt bike are in my kitchen drawer. Just help yourselves."

"Thank you." Kane hesitated, and when he spoke again, teasing warmed his voice. "I notice you didn't offer us the use of your Corvette."

"What Corvette?" I asked with heavy nonchalance. He chuckled, and I added, "Seriously, though; if you need it, take it. Believe it or not, I love you guys more than I love my 'Vette."

"But not by much."

"No comment."

His laughter rolled out. "I'm flattered. I don't even like *myself* much better than a big-block '66 Stingray."

"Well, if it comes down to a choice between you and the 'Vette, sacrifice the car." My banter dried up at the thought of Stemp's shattered vehicle. I shivered. "Seriously, be careful."

"You, too." John hesitated. "I love you." He hung up before I could reply.

During the conversation Holt had regained his colour, and he sprang to his feet. "They're okay? And Stemp's alive?"

"Yes." I got to my feet with considerably less energy, my legs still shaking. "Come on, let's head for the hospital and I'll fill you in on the way."

"I left the Focus across the street," Holt agreed. "I'll drive."

Hurrying into the hospital a few minutes later, we strode straight for the secured wing. After clearing the security checkpoint, my steps slowed.

What if Stemp had died of his wounds?

How could I tell Moonbeam and Karma and Skidmark? It would break their hearts. And his secret wife and young daughter who hadn't seen him in months...

I gulped down the lump in my throat and held my voice steady as we arrived at the nurses' station. "How is Director Stemp?"

The nurse glanced up with a smile. "Ready to leave."

"Ready to..." I suppressed the urge to stick a finger in my ear and wiggle it around. "You mean he's... okay?"

"Yes." She motioned down the hall. "He's in the second cubicle. Go on in, he's dressed."

Holt and I exchanged an incredulous glance, then headed to the cubicle.

"Knock, knock," I said loudly, and peeked around the curtain.

Apparently the nurse had an elastic interpretation of 'okay'. Stemp looked like hell.

Half of his disguise had torn away, the latex edges curling disturbingly like flayed skin. Rusty stains and flecks indicated that his nose and ears had recently bled, and puffy shadows promised a pair of spectacular black eyes to come. His hands and arms were peppered with glass cuts, and one of his contact lenses was missing, exposing one piercing amber eye and leaving the other looking blind behind its muddy brown concealment.

But he had a head.

And arms, and legs.

And he was sitting in the chair, not even lying in bed.

He gave us one of his infinitesimal smiles.

"How...?" I stopped. Tried again. "I saw the security footage. How...?"

Stemp's smile widened. "AS YOU MENTIONED EARLIER..." he shouted. My involuntary flinch cued him, and he added more quietly, "My apologies. Both eardrums are perforated and my hearing is blunted. Is this an appropriate volume?" I nodded, and he tried again. "As you mentioned earlier, it's not paranoia if they really are out to get you. I purchased that car shortly after I was extracted from my mission in Bulgaria. I had it extensively customized."

I grinned. "Let me guess. Armour-plated?"

"Yes. It has..." He grimaced. "...had... military-grade armour plate on the underside and around the passenger compartment."

"So what happened?" I demanded.

"When I exited Sirius, I surveyed the area as usual and spotted no threats. But as I neared my vehicle, I heard something approaching. It proved to be a radio-controlled toy car with a payload that looked like a fragmentation grenade. It was travelling too quickly for me to outrun, so I jumped into the car and knelt on the seat." He mimed a fetal crouch with his elbows over his ears, hands protecting the back of his neck. "Fortunately, my door closed before the explosive detonated."

Letting out a gust of breath, I dropped onto the end of the bed. "*That's* what I saw on the surveillance camera. You were hunkered down on the seat. I couldn't see your head or arms or legs, and I thought..." I gulped. "Jesus. I'm really glad you're okay."

"Thank you. As am I."

I heaved another sigh, hoping to exhale the remains of my stress and trauma. "Well, I've got some good news and some bad news about your attacker."

Stemp raised an eyebrow. "Do tell."

"The good news is, we know it was Farrell Metz, and we know he won't get another shot at you. Or anyone. Ever again."

Stemp connected the dots immediately. "I presume the bad news is: He is deceased, so we can't question him."

"Yep. He tried to avoid the police roadblock, rolled his car, and blew himself up with his own grenades."

"Most inconsiderate of him."

"Yeah." I hauled myself to my feet. "So we're back to Square One. No idea who's trying to kill us; no idea whether there are any more hitmen after us; no idea who leaked our covers."

Stemp rose, too, frowning. "But Maria Harchman...?"

"Died in prison five months ago."

"Ah. That complicates matters. May I trouble you for a ride back to my home?"

"Sure."

As I spoke, my phone vibrated. Pulling it out, I checked the call display and grimaced.

"Problem?" Holt asked.

I spoke to Stemp instead. "It's Lola."

He closed his eyes briefly. "CRAPS in action. You might as well answer."

I tapped 'Accept' and said, "Hi, Lola."

"Aydan! I heard a car exploded at Sirius Dynamics! Are you..." She hesitated uncharacteristically. "Have you... heard about it?"

"Yeah, I was in the building," I said, my mind already rocketing through ideas for a cover story.

"Honey, I don't want to upset you, but... I heard... is Charles...? I heard it was his car."

"Don't worry, he's fine. Just a little banged up. They took him to the hospital as a precaution, and I'm actually bringing him home right now." I winced, realizing I was adding credence to her belief that Stemp and I were in a relationship.

"Oh, thank heaven! We were all so worried!" Lola's relief gave way to avid questions. "Somebody's trying to kill him, aren't they? First the shooting, now a car bomb?"

I held my voice steady as I churned out bullshit with as much reassuring confidence as I could fake. "I can't imagine why anybody would be trying to kill St-" I bit off the name and substituted, "Charles. He's just a normal guy with a normal job as a manager at Sirius. That gunfire was probably just some yahoo with too many drinks in him and not enough brains. And I heard one of the firefighters say there must have been a leak in Charles's gas tank. The catalytic converter is hot, and some gas must have leaked onto it and ignited. And if the gas tank was almost empty with lots of fumes instead of liquid gas, it'd go up like a bomb. So I'm pretty sure you can give the conspiracy theories a rest."

"Oh." Lola sounded vaguely disappointed. "Well, I guess you'd know about the car stuff, Ms. Mechanic." Her usual upbeat tone returned. "At least we don't have any crazy bombers around."

I almost replied 'Not any more', but fortunately I stifled the words before they could pop out. Instead I said, "Nope. I'm pretty sure it was just a mechanical problem and bad luck. Anyhow, if you wouldn't mind letting the CRAPS gang know that Charles is okay, he'll appreciate it. We don't want anybody spreading scary rumours."

"I will. I'm over at Bud's this afternoon, so we'll see you soon, I guess."

"Right." I hid another wince. The CRAPS team might have believed Lola's story about pizza delivery in the middle of the night, but when they spotted my car again, they'd recognize it. And since I was bringing Stemp home...

Fuck.

"See you soon," I mumbled, and disconnected.

Stemp had gone into the washroom while I talked to Lola, and he returned sans the remains of his facial disguise. His oversized shirt was tucked into his baggy pants in an attempt at tidiness, but it was far from his usual fastidious appearance.

"If anybody sees you, you'll have to tell them you borrowed somebody else's clothes after the explosion," I said. "And, turn around..." He complied, and I picked a few remaining shreds of latex from the back of his hair. "...okay, done."

He faced me again, cocking a philosophical eyebrow in my direction. "I doubt anyone will find my disheveled appearance remarkable, under the circumstances."

"Right, I guess n-" My phone vibrated again,

interrupting me. The number was blocked, and I hit the 'Accept' button with a twinge of trepidation.

"Yeah?"

A deep voice spoke. "Storm Cloud Dancer."

The connection went dead.

Oh shit.

"What's wrong?" Holt asked. "You look like you just saw a ghost."

"Um, nothing." I added a qualifier. "I hope."

Why would Karma Wolf Song be calling me?   Had something happened to Moonbeam or Katya or Anna?

Shit, shit, shit!

CHAPTER 36

Trauma involving his family was the last thing Stemp needed right now.

"'Scuse me," I said. "I just need to make a call."

I hurried down the corridor, my mind racing at the same speed as my heart. Something was definitely wrong, or Karma would have identified himself. That meant I needed to call back using a burner phone, from a place where I could talk freely.

I needed to be outside the hospital; but standing outside would leave me an easy mark for a drive-by shooting. I debated for only a moment before deciding to take the chance. We should be fresh out of hitmen for the moment.

I stepped out the hospital doors and dodged sideways, but no gunshots greeted me. Keeping a wary eye on my surroundings, I took my burner phone out of my waist pouch and dialled Karma's number.

The same deep voice answered with reassuring promptness. "Yes?"

"It's Aydan. What's wrong?"

"I hope, nothing." Karma sounded tense. "Can you talk?"

I glanced around again, but nobody was watching me. Just in case, I consulted my bug detector. Green light.

"Yes."

"Good. Are you aware of the current location of Cosmic River Stone?"

"Yes."

"He missed a check-in with us. Is he safe?"

"Um... yes..." I hesitated.

Worry sprang into his voice. "There's a 'but'?"

Moonbeam's soft voice spoke in the background, taut with anxiety. "*What's wrong?*"

"Don't worry, he's okay," I assured them. "His car got bombed but the armor plate worked. He's fine except for some cuts and bruises. And you may have to speak up a bit the next time you talk to him because his eardrums are ruptured."

"The attempts on his life are escalating." Karma was doing his best to hold onto his professional demeanor, but I could hear a father's desperate fear for his child. "Do you have any other ideas to safeguard him?"

"Only if I can keep him inside Sirius. He didn't want to do that, but maybe he'll reconsider now. I'll see if I can talk him into it."

"Thank you. Our minds are eased, knowing you are doing your best to keep him safe."

Guilt burned in my belly. Obviously I wasn't doing enough to keep him safe. I'd have to-

Karma interrupted my self-recrimination. "We have news."

I gulped. "By your tone, I'm guessing it's not good news."

"It could be worse; and with any luck it will lead to better things. There was an attempt on Katya's life."

"Shit! Is she okay?"

"Yes. We dealt with it."

I eased out a breath. Karma and Moonbeam's skill as covert operatives hadn't diminished with age.

"Good," I said. "So... what 'better things'?"

"We were able to obtain some intel from the would-be assassin," Karma began.

I shook off the small chill that skittered down my spine. Despite their peace-loving hippie alter-egos, I wouldn't want to be the person who threatened Moonbeam and Karma's family. Their method of 'obtaining intel' wasn't likely to have been pleasant.

Karma was still speaking. "It seems he was acting on instructions from a woman named Milena Georgieva Draganova-"

"Could you spell that?" I interrupted.

He obliged, then added, "If you can make discreet inquiries, that might be helpful; but she isn't a threat anymore."

I almost blurted 'You killed her, too?' but fortunately Karma went on before the words left my lips.

"She was murdered in a home-invasion burglary last week."

My heart sank. "So the assassin was lying about who hired him."

"Unlikely," Moonbeam put in coolly. "He was highly motivated to be truthful."

There went that shiver down my spine again. "So... what are you saying?"

"He said he had been hired five weeks ago, but it took him this long to locate Katya. Probably not coincidentally, Katya was recently in touch with her parents. We suspect their apartment is bugged, and we will deal with that issue as well." Moonbeam hesitated. "Usually Cosmic River Stone takes care of any inquiries discreetly through the Department. But now that he is suspended... are you in a position to do some undetectable research on Milena Georgieva Draganova? Don't take any chances, though. We don't want to get you in trouble."

I almost laughed aloud. If only I could tell them that undetectable research was my job.

"Don't worry," I assured them. "I'll look her up and nobody will ever know. Give me the assassin's name, too. I'll get back to you as soon as I have something, but it might not be today."

Karma spelled the assassin's name for me, and Moonbeam added, "Thank you, Storm Cloud Dancer. May the Earth Spirit guide and protect you." Her gentle voice was like a warm hug.

"You, too." Despite my worries, I was smiling when I hung up.

When I re-entered the hospital, Holt and Stemp were waiting.

"What's up?" Holt demanded.

"Sorry, can't tell you." Before he could argue, I added, "Let's get back to Sirius."

We emerged warily from the hospital and scattered, but no shots came our way. No radio-controlled grenades chased us as we headed for the car, and Holt and I both checked the Focus with our bug detectors before getting in.

In deference to Stemp's battered condition, I folded myself into the back seat. When we arrived at Sirius a couple of minutes later, I leaned forward and spoke to Holt.

"You go on in. I'll take him home."

"No, I'll do it," he countered. "You go in and check on

Weiss."

"No, I told Lola I was coming."

Holt shot me a frown. "So what? Change of plans."

I almost blurted that I was doing damage control over Stemp's and my alleged affair, but fortunately I bit my tongue at the last moment. Dammit, I was getting too comfortable around Holt.

"Okay," I said instead. Turning to Stemp, I raised my voice. "Holt will wait while you get whatever personal belongings you need from your house. Then you'll be coming back here and staying inside Sirius."

Stemp's eyebrow lifted. "Have you cleared that with Dermott?"

"He'll never go for it," Holt put in.

"Fuck Dermott." I clapped a hand over my mouth. Apparently I was getting too comfortable with Stemp, too. Removing my hand slowly so no other incriminating statements would jump out, I amended, "I'll clear it with him. It'll be fine."

"It won't," Holt argued. "You know damn well he-"

I silenced him with an outflung palm. "Talk to the hand."

Holt shrugged. "Care to make a bet on it?"

Making my tone as certain as I could, I said, "No bets. No arguments. Just do it, and get back here ASAP."

Stemp offered me a gracious inclination of his chin. "As much as I appreciate your concern, I must decline. I have business that cannot be conducted from within Sirius Dynamics."

My heart sank. Of course. He'd missed his check-in with Moonbeam and Karma. There was no way he'd stay inside Sirius, where he couldn't make and receive calls from his burner phones.

Holt gave him a suspicious look. "What kind of business?"

"Personal business." Stemp turned the full force of his impassive reptilian gaze on Holt.

"You're communicating with your contacts overseas, aren't you?" Holt demanded. When Stemp didn't reply, Holt snapped, "Okay, that's it. We're going into Sirius, and you're getting hooked up to the lie detector again."

"Let it go-" I began, but Stemp overrode me, his cool precise voice cutting effortlessly through my protest.

"I am afraid not, Agent Holt. As you are undoubtedly aware, I am not permitted to discuss any circumstances or occurrences related to my suspension, until the formal NSIRA inquiry." As Holt's face twisted into a scowl, Stemp raised a placating hand. "But I apologize for my evasiveness. I had arranged a telephone call with my parents, which I have now missed due to the explosion. They will be worried. I want to call them from my home. That is the personal business to which I was referring." Turning back to me, he added, "Since two assassins are recently dead, I believe my personal risk to be relatively low at the moment."

"Yeah, that's what John said, too; and it still doesn't make me feel any better." I sighed and got out of the car, leaning down to add, "Be careful, then. Both of you."

I hurried into Sirius, feeling as though I had a huge glowing target painted on my back.

As the doors closed behind me I sucked in a breath of relief, only to let it out again in a hiccup as I caught sight of Dermott glowering at me from across the lobby.

CHAPTER 37

"Well?" Dermott demanded.

"Well, what?" I asked, trying to keep the antagonism out of my voice.

Dermott's brows mashed together even harder. "How is he?" he ground out.

Taken by surprise, I asked, "Who, Stemp?"

"No, the fucking Easter Bunny! Of course, Stemp!"

"Oh. Sorry. He's fine."

Dermott rocked back on his heels. "F... Fine?"

"Yeah. His car was armour-plated. He's cut and bruised and partly deaf and probably concussed; and by tomorrow he's going to look and feel even worse; but he's fine. Holt's taking him home."

"Oh." Dermott blinked, seemingly at a loss for words. "That's... that's good."

Despite my combative history with him, my heart warmed a bit. He had been truly concerned.

A small cynical part of my brain countered that he might have been concerned; or he might only be disappointed that Stemp had survived.

Suspicion flared. Could Dermott be behind these attacks, and the leak of our cover identities? Dermott hated me, and he wanted Stemp's job. If we were conveniently out of his way...

No. That was too twisted to even contemplate. Probably Dermott was just trying to cover his-

"Answer me, or I'll have you up for insubordination!"

I blinked back to the ugly reality of Dermott yelling in my face. My fist twitched with the reflexive need to hammer into his nose, but I managed to keep my tone mild.

"Sorry, I zoned out for a second. It's been a tough afternoon. What did you ask?"

"I asked what the hell you were thinking, having the RCMP arrest Rand! Do you have any idea how much fucking paper I'm going to have to push because of your stupid little trick?"

Easing in a slow breath, I tilted my head toward Leo's avid face in the security wicket. "Let's talk upstairs."

Dermott grunted and spun to stomp toward the stairs. I followed, racking my brain for some reasonable excuse for Ian's arrest besides, 'He was pissing me off and I needed some space'.

By the time we reached Dermott's office, I was still devoid of inspiration.

"Well?" he demanded as he took a seat behind his desk. "This better be good."

I sighed. "Ian was snooping around my house while I wasn't there. I haven't figured out why he's still hanging around, and he won't tell me. I don't have time to deal with him and these murder attempts, too, so I was hoping to stall him at the police station and keep him out of my hair for a while."

"Well, they cut him loose. He has diplomatic immunity, which you knew damn well. So you wasted the RCMP's time,

and mine, too." Dermott's eyes narrowed. "Why are you so worried about Rand snooping at your place? What are you hiding?"

Biting back my temper, I drew in a slow breath and counted to five before replying, "I'm not hiding anything. I just think he's up to something."

"Get over it," Dermott growled. "He's an MI6 agent, so he's not a fucking security risk. If he is snooping, it's outside the Department's mandate, and you damn well know it. You've misused Department resources and RCMP resources, as usual, and I'm putting it on your official record." His lips twisted in a thoroughly unpleasant smile. "Expect a disciplinary hearing, and you're just lucky I'm not suspending you on the spot. Yet. Get out."

My last nerve snapped.

The frazzled remains of my sanity fought against the almost-overwhelming desire to draw my Glock and remove this irritant from my life once and for all.

"What are you, fucking deaf?" Dermott demanded. "Get the hell out of my office!"

If I moved a single muscle, I was going to kill him.

Pressure built inside my brain, my heartbeat thumping in my ears like a piledriver.

Dermott raised his voice to a bellow. "GET OUT, BITCH!"

I stood statue-still, staring straight ahead.

Breathe in. Don't kill him.

Breathe out. Don't kill him.

Breathe in...

Dermott stood up and stalked around his desk to stand glaring, inches in front of me. His hand came up in a threatening gesture as he opened his mouth to yell again.

I jerked forward, roaring all my rage and fear and trauma into his face at the top of my lungs.

Dermott jerked back a step, caught his foot on a chair leg, and fell on his ass.

My yell turned into a shout of shocked hilarity. Laughing helplessly, I turned and staggered for the door, barely able to walk but absolutely convinced that I had to get out of there. My tiny remaining shred of sanity whispered, 'And leave the building and keep on going, because there's no coming back from this.'

Somebody was blocking the doorway.

Still guffawing, I wiped my watering eyes and peered at the obstruction.

Shit. Dr. Rawling. Of course I'd completely lose my shit in front of the fucking psychologist.

I clapped a hand over my mouth, trying to stifle myself. Snuffles and snorts leaked out, making me laugh even harder. Tears rolled down my cheeks.

Hell, was I even still laughing? Maybe I was crying.

"Aydan." Dr. Rawling's quiet voice penetrated at last. He'd probably had to try a few times. "Aydan," he repeated. "May I help you to a chair?"

Still unable to catch my breath, I waved a dismissing hand. "M'okay," I gasped. "Sorry..." A snicker exploded out of me and I convulsed again, propping my elbows on my knees and bellowing with laughter.

Dr. Rawling dragged a chair around behind me. It only took his touch on my shoulders for me to collapse into it. I propped my head in my hands and gave in to the mirth.

I vaguely heard Dr. Rawling speaking with Dermott, but I didn't bother to listen. I already knew I was suspended.

Hell, not just suspended. Probably headed for a long

stay in the psych ward. If I was lucky. Prison, otherwise.

Well, to hell with it. I didn't have a single flying fuck left to give.

Spent at last, I fell silent with my face still in my hands. Might as well be comfortable while I waited for the guys with the straitjacket.

Dr. Rawling's mild voice spoke again. "Aydan?"

Get your shit together, woman.

I dragged myself upright. Dermott was sitting behind his desk, glowering. Rawling stood halfway between us, the third point of our triangle.

I drew a deep breath and let it out slowly before addressing Dermott. "I'm sorry." My voice was raw from the volume of my first yell and my subsequent shouts of laughter. "I hope you didn't hurt yourself when you fell. I didn't mean to laugh at you; I just..." Giggles threatened again, but I swallowed them. "It's been a tough day. Sorry."

Dr. Rawling nodded encouragingly at me and turned to Dermott. "Brent?"

Dermott shot him a hateful glance, then growled, "Sorry I called you a bitch." He glared daggers at me.

"And?" Dr. Rawling prompted.

After another dirty look at Rawling, Dermott grudgingly added, "It's been a tough day." When Rawling continued to watch him expectantly, Dermott muttered, "I'll work on respectful communication." As Rawling turned his benign smile back to me, Dermott mouthed 'bitch' at me behind his back.

"I'll walk you to your office, Aydan," Dr. Rawling said.

Taking his cue, I rose and headed for the door.

When we arrived at my office Dr. Rawling followed me inside, closing the door behind us.

"Let's talk," he said, gesturing me toward the sofa.

Taking a slow breath, I went over and sat. Body language open and relaxed. Polite, attentive expression.

Rawling took a seat in the chair kitty-corner to me, giving me his dangerously mild smile. "Please tell me what happened between you and Brent."

I shrugged. "No big deal. We were stressed. We both have hot tempers. We're both just trying to do our jobs as best we can."

"That is an astute observation." Rawling gave me the understanding smile that never failed to creep me out, and repeated, "So please tell me exactly what happened."

"We disagreed on a procedural thing. He accused me of using Department resources for my personal convenience and said it would go on my record, with a disciplinary hearing and a threat of suspension. He told me to get out. I was angry and trying to control my temper so I didn't move right away. He got angrier and started yelling. I yelled back, he backed away and tripped and fell..."

Recalling Dermott gaping up at me like a stunned goldfish, I stifled more laughter. My lips twitched despite my best efforts, and I finished, "Sorry, I know it's really inappropriate, but sometimes I laugh when I'm super-stressed. And it was just so... unexpected." Scrubbing a hand over my mouth to wipe away the last of the tell-tale smile, I repeated, "Sorry. It really wasn't that funny. I was just... really wound up. I guess we both were."

"Please tell me about what's stressing you."

"Um..."

The silence stretched, and I imagined him scribbling notes in his mental notebook: *Evasive. Uncooperative. Should be suspended and detained in the psych ward indefinitely.*

"I'm not trying to be evasive," I said hurriedly. "I just can't tell you any classified details, so I'm mentally editing. So... long story short, somebody's trying to kill John, Arnie, Stemp, and me; possibly Greg and Spider. John got shot a couple of days ago; somebody took a potshot at Stemp the same day; a gunman was captured outside Arnie's apartment; somebody shot at me this morning; and then somebody tried to blow up Stemp this afternoon and damn near succeeded. Meanwhile, we're trying to trace an international arms dealer, and an MI6 agent has been harassing me." I thought for a moment. "There are a bunch more things, but those are the ones I can tell you."

Rawling's professional composure never wavered, but his eyes had widened just a touch during my recitation. "I see," he said. "That certainly does sound stressful. How long has Brent been using abusive language toward you?"

I blinked.

"The door was open," Rawling said gently. "I arrived just as he mentioned the disciplinary hearing, and I witnessed the rest."

"Oh." I forced a casual shrug. "Well, it's no big deal. That's just the way he talks."

"So this has been going on for some time."

Too late, I saw the trap closing. God, all I needed was for Dermott to get a reprimand. I was already braced for a blood feud, but an official reprimand would make it much, much worse.

"Really, it's no big deal," I repeated.

"It is against the Department's policies regarding respectful communication."

"Well, yeah, but... sometimes tempers flare, right? I've

said inappropriate things, too."

"Anger is a common reaction when people feel stressed or threatened," Rawling agreed. "And despite our best efforts we all sometimes react in ways we regret." He gave me a small smile. "I am aware that you have occasionally had words with Charles. But I also know that in every case you apologized immediately and sincerely, and you share a mutual respect. That is a healthy relationship." His pale blue eyes looked through into my soul. "Do you have a similar relationship with Brent?"

"No..." I said reluctantly. "But Brent's job is a bit different. It's his job to ask uncomfortable questions and make sure nobody gets special treatment."

"It's admirable that you're able to empathize with him."

Silence fell between us. Just as I was about to ask if we were done, Rawling went in for the kill.

"What would you have done if he had struck you?"

"Beat the shit out of him." The words popped out before I could stop them, and I clapped my hands over my mouth.

I was *so* getting locked in the psych ward.

I hurriedly added, "What I mean is, I would have done whatever it took to defend myself. But I wouldn't have hurt him after he stopped being a threat."

To my amazement, Rawling chuckled. "That was an honest answer." As I stared at him, he added, "Responding to aggression with aggression isn't a reaction psychologists generally encourage; but I also realize that you've been trained to subdue adversaries when attacked. That was the answer I expected."

"Okay..." Eyeing him warily, I asked, "So, is that all?"

His usual accepting expression slipped, revealing weary resignation. A moment later, his professional façade returned.

"Aydan," he said gently. "Since I witnessed the exchange between you and Brent, it's my professional responsibility to discuss what happened with both of you. If there's anything in your interactions with Brent that makes you feel uncomfortable or unsafe, please talk to me or anyone in HR. Your wellbeing is our top priority." He eyed me keenly. "And if you fear reprisals, either personally or professionally, it's very important for you to speak up. I'm not here to judge you. I'm only here to listen and help."

A flippant dismissal flew to the tip of my tongue, but for perhaps the first time in my life, I hesitated. Why was I protecting Dermott?

The answers came without an instant's hesitation.

Don't complain; their retaliation only gets worse.

Don't ask for help; they'll use your weakness against you.

"Fuck, I need help." The words jumped out of my mouth.

I willed them back with all my might, but it was too late. Panic flashed through me. I would pay for this. With misery and suffering that would never end…

"I'll do my best to help you." Dr. Rawling's calm words broke into my spiralling thoughts. "What would you like to talk about?"

I held my voice steady with all my might. "Actually, you've helped already just by witnessing this incident. Dermott and I have been butting heads for a while. I understand that it's his job to scrutinize everything I do, but sometimes I feel as though he has a personal grudge against me. I'll talk it over with him, and if I feel as though I'm not getting anywhere, I'll come to you."

Rawling knew weaselly backpedalling when he heard it. I could see the disappointment in his eyes, but his tone was as accepting as ever. "If I'm not in my office, my answering service will forward messages to my personal phone. Don't hesitate to call at any time of the day or night." He rose, smiled his small smile, and let himself out.

I fell back on the sofa, heart pounding.

Hell, that had been close. Too close. I had almost...

A saner voice spoke inside my head. Almost what? Almost overcome decades of fear and distorted thinking?

"Shut up," I muttered.

Almost killed Dermott? How fucked up was I, if murder was my knee-jerk response to personal conflicts?

I squeezed my eyes closed. "Shut *up!*"

"You need help."

I levitated off the sofa with a barely-suppressed shriek.

CHAPTER 38

Holt took a rapid step backward. "Relax! It's just me."

"Shit! You..." Panting, I fell back on the sofa and patted my chest in an attempt to calm my hammering heart. "You..."

"Scared the shit out of you; yeah, I got that. Sorry." He gave me a quizzical look. "Why were you telling yourself to shut up?"

"Shut up," I growled. "Sit. Tell me what happened in Stemp's latest interview with Weiss."

Holt eased into a chair, still eyeing me warily. "Are you sure you're okay? Maybe you should talk to Doc-"

"I just did!" I snapped. "That's why I'm fucking talking to myself! Now give me the briefing on Weiss's interview."

"I thought talking to a shrink was supposed to make you feel better, not make you crazy. Well, in your case, crazier."

I gave him a long, icy stare.

Holt cleared his throat. "Right. So, it looks as though Weiss doesn't know anything more about Volslav than he initially told us, and he's exactly what he says: The Switzerland of arms experts. Completely neutral. He hasn't ever committed a crime as far as he knows. He has a strict moral code, but weapons are completely outside that. He just doesn't see them as anything but a tool. Not good or evil."

"I guess he's right, as far as that goes."

Holt shrugged. "I guess. But it also means he'll help our enemies just as readily as he'll help us."

"Hm." I leaned back, thinking. "Unless we hire him and ask him to sign a contract saying he'll only work for us. I bet he'd do it. And if he signs the contract, I bet he'll keep his promise."

"Huh." A slow smile spread over Holt's face. "I bet you're right. We should talk to..." He trailed off, his smile dissolving.

"Yeah. Dermott. That would be a bad idea. I'm persona non grata right now."

"What else is new?"

I grimaced. "This is new." As I described my run-in with Dermott, Holt's eyes gradually widened until I finished gloomily, "...and he fell on his ass. And I laughed."

"You... laughed?" Holt asked faintly.

"Yeah. Couldn't even walk, nearly peed my pants, laughed my stupid ass off. I just couldn't stop. And Rawling caught me."

Holt winced. "How are you not locked up right now?"

"Fortunately Rawling also caught Dermott yelling in my face and calling me a bitch and making like he was going to punch me. So Rawling had a *talk*..." I shuddered. "...with both of us. Then with me privately. And I assume, with Dermott privately, too."

"You're fucking doomed. Dermott's going to spend the rest of his life figuring out ways to make you pay."

"Yep." I sighed. "Anyhow, back to Weiss. I'll put together a written proposal for his employment and send it to the entire chain of command plus Reggie. That way you're in the clear. Dermott can't get any *more* pissed off at me, so it won't matter..." I trailed off as a thought struck me. "Hang on, I've got a better idea."

"Good, because that one sucked big sweaty balls."

I flipped him a casual middle finger. "I'm going to talk to Reggie, and get him to talk to Weiss. Then Reggie can propose to hire him. As the Weapons Director, Reggie's got clout with Command; plus I'm pretty sure Dermott's scared of him."

Holt snorted. "Most people are."

"With good reason. The guy spends every waking moment dreaming up better ways to kill people." I grinned. "Come on, let's go talk to him."

"You go ahead. I've got stuff to do."

"You're scared of him, too. Wuss."

It was Holt's turn to flip me the bird. "No; *I'm* actually working on solving some crimes instead of fluttering around Weiss like an old hen. I've got the police reports from the search of Swift's apartment, and our lab already has preliminary data on the evidence from all the stolen cars we have so far. Pretty soon they should be getting the wreck from Metz's explosion, too."

"Great, I'll drop by your office for an update after I talk to Reggie."

We parted company in the corridor, and I hurried down to the secured area. I let myself into the Weapons Lab, poking my head warily around the corner.

No foul smells; no swarms of deranged flies. So far, so good.

The door to Reggie's office was open, and I tapped on it and stuck my head in. "Knock, knock."

Reggie looked up from his computer, the unscarred side

of his face pulling into a grin. "To what do I owe the honour? I haven't seen you in weeks. My left nut has been pining away."

I grinned at our timeworn joke. "Hey, not my problem. You're the one who decided to shack up with the gorgeous Doctor Travers. Your nuts are her territory now. But if it'll make you feel better, I've got something that'll probably give you a hard-on."

"Oh, yeah?"

Lowering my voice seductively, I murmured, "Weapons."

"Mmm." Closing his eyes as if in pre-orgasmic bliss, he growled, "Keep talking, baby. You know what I like."

To Reggie's widening grin, I outlined our acquisition of Weiss, along with Weiss's qualifications. When I finished describing my idea for the employment contract, Reggie bounced to his feet. "What are we waiting for? Let's go talk to Weiss."

As we headed for the door, I observed, "You're very bouncy today. Are your regular legs out of commission?"

He nodded. "Just routine maintenance. I'm wearing my blades for the day."

"How's your training going? When do you leave for the Paralympics?"

"My training's right on the money. I'm ready." He grinned. "A month from now, I'll be landing in London, and a couple of weeks after that…"

"You'll be wearing a gold medal."

"That's the plan."

As we approached the holding cells, I said, "Just so you know, Weiss doesn't always understand social conventions. If he says something out of line, he probably doesn't mean to be rude."

"You mean if he screams at my freak-face?" Reggie's tone was dry as he gestured with his pincer-hand toward his missing ear, prosthetic eye, and the scar tissue that distorted half his face and neck. But I recognized his subtle tension as he braced himself for Weiss's reaction.

My heart hurt for him. "Reggie..." I touched his arm, not sure what to say. "I'm sorry. I hate that you have to deal with that shit."

He moved away just enough to disengage my touch as we continued down the corridor. "Forget it, I was kidding." He hesitated, not looking at me. "Thanks, though."

As we rounded the final corner to the cells, my shoulders tensed, too. If Weiss didn't respond well to Reggie's disfigurement, should I jump in and try to smooth things over? If provoked, Reggie was capable of invective that could make a drill sergeant cry. Would Weiss melt down entirely?

I drew a deep breath as we stopped outside Weiss's cell. He was seated on the edge of his bunk, still wearing the blackout hood.

Reggie shot me a 'what the hell' look.

"He wants to wear it," I explained quietly, then raised my voice so Weiss could hear. "Rupert, I've brought someone to talk to you."

"No more questioning," Weiss said tonelessly. "I'm over-stimulated."

"No more questioning," I agreed. "I've brought a weapons expert to see you. He'd like to interview you for a job. But he can come back later."

"I would like to have an interview with the other weapons expert," Weiss replied in his flat voice. "We can do it now. Does he want me to take off my blindfold?"

"Yeah," Reggie confirmed. "At least for a few minutes."

"Okay." Weiss removed the hood, his gaze downcast as usual. He blinked a few times as though adjusting to the light, then surveyed Reggie starting at the pads of his prosthetic legs. Weiss's scrutiny came up past Reggie's pincer-hand to his scarred neck and face, where Weiss made momentary eye contact without the slightest change in expression.

Dropping his gaze to Reggie's chin, Weiss said, "I like to be accurate and avoid misunderstandings. Before we start the interview, I'd like you to know that I have difficulty interpreting social cues. If you're feeling an emotion that you want me to know about, please tell me in words. If I say or do something that offends you, please tell me so I can change my behaviour. Also, I'm extremely uncomfortable making eye contact. I compromise by looking at people's chins, but I'll do my best to make direct eye contact if you require it."

"I don't," Reggie assured him.

"Thank you. Too much social interaction or noise or movement overstimulates me. I also get stressed when my routine is significantly disrupted. I'm very stressed today so I might need to put on this blindfold to self-soothe, but I don't mean to be rude. I always try to be polite. I'm an excellent employee. I'm accurate, prompt, conscientious, self-motivated, and extremely detail-oriented. I always tell the truth. I'm the world's most sought-after weapons expert, but I'm sorry I can't provide work references. My previous employer is dead and most of my clients don't identify themselves."

During the long recitation, the undamaged corner of Reggie's mouth had been slowly turning up in a smile.

Weiss added, "That was ten sentences, and I realize that

I should usually stop talking after five sentences to allow others to feel included in the conversation. I thought it would be okay to talk longer since this is an interview. But if that's not correct, please excuse me for monopolizing the conversation."

By this time Reggie was grinning. "It's okay," he said. "We'll waive the five-sentence rule for this interview. You can talk about weapons as long as you want. I'll tell you if I want you to stop."

Weiss gave his legs a satisfied pat. "Thank you. Which weapon would you like me to talk about first?"

Reggie appropriated one of the chairs we'd left outside Weiss's cell and shot me a grin. "You might as well go. This is going to take a while."

"Okay, I'll leave you to it." I tossed him a mock salute and headed down the corridor.

When I stuck my head into Holt's office a few minutes later, his attention was glued to his computer. His gaze flicked to me, then back to his screen. "Sit." He jerked his chin toward the chair.

"Woof, woof," I said, and obeyed.

He snickered. "At least you're housebroken. Okay, so the search of Swift's apartment turned up nothing, but when the team cracked an encrypted partition on his computer, they found banking records that showed a wire transfer from Volslav Dymt for half a million dollars, two weeks ago."

"What the hell? We shut down all Dymt Volslav's active accounts six months ago!"

Holt shrugged. "We missed this one. Probably because it's a Bulgarian bank; and it's not under Dymt Volslav, it's under Václav Dymt."

This time my ear caught '*Vahts-lahf*', not '*Volslav*'. I

gave Holt a quizzical look.

He elaborated, "Václav is a Slavic male given name." He spelled it, then added, "It means 'more glory'."

"Oh, for fuck's sake!" I knotted my fists in my hair. "Another anglicised name! God knows what Václav looks like in Cyrillic characters, so I'd never have found it. I wonder how many other bank accounts they have under that name. And of course Dawn, Yana-"

Realization struck and my mouth dropped open.

Holt glanced up sharply. "What?"

"I was going to say, 'of course they went for more glory', but I just realized..." I gave him a triumphant grin. "Dymt isn't a name, it's an acronym. Dawn, Yana, Maria, Tawny. D-Y-M-T." Unable to sit still, I sprang to my feet. "I told you Maria was involved!"

Holt raised an unimpressed eyebrow. "She's dead. Even if you're right about the acronym, the 'M' can't be her."

"She might not be the one sending the hitmen right now, but I'll bet she's the 'M' in Volslav!" I grimaced. "In Dymt. You know what I mean. We need to call Spider-"

"I'm here." Spider's voice made me jerk around to face the doorway.

I sucked in a breath. "Jeez, you scared me! I'm glad you're here, though."

"What's up?"

Holt said, "We just found out we've missed a Bulgarian bank account in Volslav's name." He explained the spelling, translation, and my acronym idea, then added, "Get Belling and Stile on it right away. This could open up a whole new angle."

"I don't think Rebecca speaks Bulgarian," Spider said. "But I'll tell Trish to surf the Bulgarian banks anyway.

Maybe there's a bit of crossover with Russian language. Rebecca might recognize something."

"She should recognize the name Václav if nothing else," I said. "I think the Bulgarian and Russian alphabets are similar. I looked them up when-"

I clamped my mouth shut. God, I'd almost told them about searching for Katya, and how her name in Cyrillic script looked like it started with a backward 'R'.

Holt eyed me, but when I didn't complete the sentence he turned back to Spider. "So, did you find something? Is that why you're here?"

"Yep." Spider grinned. "Aydan was right about the necklaces. There's a fourth one somewhere. There was nothing new in any of the files I found on Dawn's and Yana's necklaces, but when I compared the data from all three necklaces side by side, I discovered three file fragments. It gave me enough information to understand what's going on, but about twenty-five percent of it is missing. It needs a fourth fragment. And if we find that..." His face glowed with eagerness. "...I think it'll give us a database location and a decryption key."

Hope straightened my backbone. "All the secrets of Volslav's universe."

"I think so. And there was a necklace in Maria's personal effects at the prison. The designated contact named on Maria's prison records was her lawyer, Stephanie Maldova, who was also named as her executrix. Maria's personal effects were released to Stephanie after Maria died. We've left a message with Stephanie's office, so hopefully she'll get back to us today."

"I doubt it," Holt said cynically. "It's four o'clock. She's not going to open a can of worms like this if she thinks it'll keep her at the office past quitting time."

Spider shrugged. "Most of the lawyers I know are pretty hard-working. Anyhow, I haven't gotten to the big news yet." He paused dramatically, grinning. "Megan decided to check the police cases in the past year for any of the names associated with Volslav: Harchman, Orlov..." He rolled his hand in an 'and-so-on' gesture and continued, "...and guess what? Last month, Lawrence Harchman's heirs were cleaning out his house, and they discovered six cases of copy paper, still sealed. They donated it to a charity, and when someone at the charity opened the first package to put paper in their copier... it was money."

"Money?" I gaped at Spider.

His grin widened. "Yep. Three quarters of a million per case; four and a half million in total. The charity called the Harchman kids, and the kids called the police."

CHAPTER 39

"Whoa, wait!" I flung up a restraining hand. "The Harchman kids? Whose kids? Not Maria's or Tawny's; they weren't married to Lawrence long enough to have kids old enough to be making decisions about estates and donations."

"No, you're right," Spider agreed. "The heirs are from his first marriage. Lawrence and his first wife married right out of high school. They both came from big-money families, and apparently it was..." He hesitated, blushing. "A love match. Their daughter was born five months after the wedding, and their son was born a year after that, but they divorced soon after."

"She found out what he was really like," I guessed.

"He didn't even try to keep in touch with his kids, even when they were little!" Spider's cheeks took on a deeper hue. "I can't even imagine... how could you not want to be part of your children's lives?"

I shook my head. "Lawrence Harchman was a shallow, self-centred pig. They were better off without him."

Spider sighed. "Anyhow, he left his whole estate to them, so maybe that means something. But, back to the money: Those six boxes had only accumulated since Tawny Harchman died in January. According to the Harchmans' staff, a case of paper had been coming once a month for years."

"Who's the sender?" I asked.

Spider smiled. "It was a privately-owned stationery company called Glory Canadian Paper Products Limited."

I snapped to attention. "*Glory*?"

"Yep." His smile widened. "And the directors of the company were Dawn White, Yana Orlov, Tanya Rumley, a.k.a. Tawny Harchman... and Maria Harchman, whose maiden name was Maria Petrova Ivanova."

"Ha!" I did an enthusiastic and probably unattractive victory dance, grinning at Holt. "I told you Maria was involved! And her maiden name? I bet it's another connection to Bulgaria!"

"We need a copy of-" Holt began, but Spider was already nodding.

"Megan has asked the police to send us all the case documents."

"And we really need to talk to Maria's lawyer," I put in. "If she's Maria's executrix, I bet she already knows a lot about the stationery company. Now I have a whole bunch of questions for her."

"I've already requested a warrant, and they'll send it directly to her office. When she calls, I'll put her through to you," Spider promised. "Anyhow, those are the high points. I'll send you the full report so you get all the details."

After he left I turned to Holt, still grinning. "I finally feel like we're getting somewhere."

He shrugged. "Except for the fact that all our suspects are dead, and we still don't know who's sending hitmen."

Deflated, I flopped into a chair. "Yeah, except for that. But maybe Maria hired them before she died."

"Then who transferred half a mil to Swift's bank account

two weeks ago?"

"Shit."

"Yeah. Anyway, back to what we know: The lab is doing DNA analysis on some hairs found in the stolen cars-"

"That'll take weeks," I interrupted. "If we don't get this figured out in the next few days, it won't matter. We'll all be dead."

Holt shook his head. "You're thinking of the national lab. Our lab can sometimes get DNA results in a few hours. It depends on what kind of a sample they've got and what they're testing for. But here's something even more interesting: Police retrieved a Walther PPK from Metz's car, and it had two rounds missing from the magazine. And there was a burner phone that wasn't destroyed in the explosion." He grimaced. "It was in Metz's back pocket, so his body protected it. I wouldn't want to be the lab tech who has to clean it off."

"So it was Metz who shot at us this morning. And Spider might be able to work his magic on the phone."

"Let's hope. I told the lab to check the phone for fingerprints and swab for DNA first, and then give it to Webb right awa-" He broke off as Spider appeared in the doorway again. "Webb, good timing. I forgot to tell you, there's a phone coming your way as soon as the lab's finished fingerprinting. Came from Metz's car."

"Okay," Spider said. "Aydan, Kane and Hellhound are waiting in the lobby for you. And so is Ian Rand."

"Thanks, I'll head down."

Spider hurried away, and Holt and I exchanged a glance.

"I'll come down, too," Holt said. "I want to know what the hell Rand's up to."

As we exited his office, I replied, "That makes two of-"

The words died in my throat as we came face to face with Dermott. I took an involuntary step backward before reminding myself that I had as much right to be in the corridor as he did. Hell, more right. I owned the building. Or I would, as soon as I signed those damn papers.

Shoulders square, eyes front, I strode past his scowl.

"Hey!" His aggressive tone punched adrenaline into my veins.

I spun, my hands flying up to protect my head as I shifted my weight into a combat-ready stance.

Dermott took a quick step backward and his gaze darted sideways to Holt as though for reassurance. But when he spoke, he was as obnoxious as ever. "Stop jerking the Department around, Kelly! I want that leasing agreement signed and on my desk by the end of the day!"

Beside me, Holt murmured, "Breathe", barely loud enough for me to hear.

But maybe he wasn't talking to me. When I glanced over, he looked as though his desire to thrash Dermott had returned full force.

Taking Holt's advice, I eased a slow breath in and out again. Okay, so apparently my ownership of the building wasn't supposed to be a secret. Good to know.

I turned my best impassive expression on Dermott. "The lease doesn't expire until the end of the month. It'll be signed in plenty of time." Giving in to my inner shithead, I narrowed my eyes at him. "Unless *somebody* gives me reason to believe the tenants are going to be difficult. Then I might want to renegotiate the terms."

"You fucking conniving bitch! I knew you'd-"

Dermott broke off with a barely-concealed flinch as Holt and I moved fast and simultaneously. My hand shot out, gripping Holt's shoulder to hold him back as he did exactly the same to me.

Holt and I exchanged a startled look, and a laugh barked out of me. Turning back to Dermott, I said, "You'll be hearing from HR about your problems with respectful communication. And Dr. Rawling will probably want you in his anger management class, too. Don't burst a blood vessel, now." I gave him a little finger wave and marched away.

Holt followed, and I was glad to have him between Dermott and me.

Behind us, Dermott roared, "Holt! You asshole, get your fucking ass back here!"

I turned in time to see Holt stiffen.

"Anger management," I murmured.

"Damn right," he snapped. Turning, he faced Dermott. "HR will be getting a complaint from me, too. You need to go and sit in your office until you're calm enough to communicate respectfully."

We spun and strode down the hall, leaving ominous silence looming behind us.

We went down the stairs without speaking. In the lobby, Kane and Hellhound rose with welcoming smiles, but Holt gripped my shoulder and turned me toward the main floor corridor.

"HR first," he said.

I kept my voice low. "It can wait."

"No. You've been putting up with Dermott's shit for far too long. So have I. Come on."

I tossed a 'don't worry' wave over my shoulder at the newly-troubled expressions in the lobby, and fell into step beside Holt.

"Are you sure about this?" I asked quietly. "If you lodge

a formal complaint against Dermott, you're starting a blood feud."

Holt's jaw hardened. "Yeah. I know exactly what I'm doing: Something I should've done right after I got here and realized Dermott's still the same bully he was in grade school. My loyalty is to the Department, not him. And he's harming the Department."

Half an hour later we had completed the necessary paperwork and interviews, and it was all I could do to keep from telling HR that it was all just a misunderstanding; just delete the files and forget the whole thing.

As we emerged into the corridor again, Holt eyed my trembling hands. "That really pushed your buttons, didn't it? You faced Dermott like he was nothing, but the paper-pushers freaked you out. What's up with that?"

My over-stressed emotional defences sprang to DEFCON1. With a superhuman effort, I managed not to hiss '*Back off*'.

Something must have shown in my face, because Holt held up a placating hand. "None of my business." His voice softened. "Just let me know if I can help."

"Thanks," I said shortly, and strode away. "Bathroom break," I threw over my shoulder.

Inside the cubicle, I sank my head into my hands and concentrated on belly-breathing. In... two... three... four. Out... two... three... four. Slow like ocean waves...

Stiffening my spine, I squared my shoulders. Suck it up. This terror was only a knee-jerk reaction. The thoughts that caused it were lies I'd been conditioned to believe. I could change those beliefs, and I would.

I hoped.

When I arrived in the lobby, Kane and Hellhound rose

again, this time with a little less certainty. I gave them each a smile and hurried over to collect hugs. As I disengaged from Hellhound, Ian appeared at his elbow, holding out his arms with a seductive smile.

I snorted. "Nice try."

He batted his eyelashes at me. "But I'm all queued up like a good boy." He glanced from Kane, to Hellhound, to himself. "I was certain this was the hugging queue."

"In your dreams."

He let out a dramatic sigh. "Apparently."

"Why are you here?"

"To see you, of course."

"Right, whatever." I turned to John, putting my back to Ian. "So, why are you here?"

John smiled. "Well, apparently 'to see you' is the wrong answer. So... to give you a status update...?"

I returned his smile. "You're allowed to be here just to see me." Glancing beyond him to include Arnie, I added, "You, too. But a status update would be g-"

"Aydan!" Spider's cry cut across my words, and I spun to see him barrelling through the front door. Face drawn with worry, he skidded to a halt at the sight of our audience. "I need to talk to you!" he whisper-shouted.

CHAPTER 40

I hurried over to where Spider jittered near the lobby doors. "What's wrong?" I demanded.

His frantic words tumbled over each other. "I-got-the-phone-and-took-it-outside-and-"

I flung up a hand. "Whoa, slow down! What phone?"

"The burner phone from Metz's car; the lab was finished with it so I went down to collect it and I took it outside the jamming area to see if it could still receive a signal and..." He paused to pant a couple of breaths. "It rang. In my hand. I didn't know what to do and I... I answered it. I'm sorry, I wasn't thinking, I was just... I've been so frazzled lately and it was just reflex and I-"

"Spider." Gripping his shoulder, I gave him a gentle shake. "Take a breath. It's okay. What happened after you answered?"

"I... I just said 'Yeah'... like you do when you're answering a burner phone and you don't know who's on the other end."

"Okay, that's good. So then what?"

"Somebody said something." Spider scrunched up his face. "Some foreign language. And I panicked and hung up. I'm so sorry!"

"It's okay, don't worry." A slow smile tugged at my lips.

"Actually, this could work for us. Hey, Greg!"

Holt had been hanging back watching us worriedly, and he hurried over.

As he joined us, another thought occurred to me. "Hang on... John? Can you come here, too?"

"Oh, good thinking!" Spider exclaimed as Kane came over. "I'd forgotten he speaks almost as many languages as Rebecca."

Kane arrived in time to hear Spider's last sentence and deflect it with a modest smile. "I only speak three languages fluently."

"Right." I gave him a gentle shoulder-nudge. "And I've heard you converse in one of the other five languages you claim you can 'just get along' in, and you sounded pretty damn fluent to me." Before he could demur, I gave him a brief summary of Spider's report, then added, "Spider, can you remember anything you heard?"

Spider flushed. "No. It was just gibberish to me."

"How about the accent?" Kane asked. "Did it sound like this?" He spoke several phrases in a language I didn't recognize.

"I don't know," Spider said miserably. "I'm sorry."

"It's all right," Kane reassured him. "I'll just say a few words in all the languages I know. Don't worry if nothing sounds familiar."

He tried again in another language, and Spider hunched his shoulders. "I'm really sorry, I don't-"

Kane spoke again and Spider's face lit up. "Wait, yes! It could have been that! What language is it? And what did you say?"

"It's Russian, and I said, 'Have you done it yet? Meet me in an hour. Where's the money? You have another target. Is he dead? Where are you?'"

I grinned. "Phrases that somebody might be saying to Metz. Smart."

Kane returned my smile before turning back to Spider. "Let's try a few more."

After several more tries, Kane shrugged. "Those are all the languages I know."

"Russian was definitely the closest accent," Spider said. "But it doesn't really matter, because I have no idea what they said."

"Hmm." I stared into middle distance, thinking aloud. "But maybe... whoever was calling thinks Metz is still alive. How would you guys feel about trying a long shot?"

Holt frowned. "How long?"

"Really long. But if it works, we might be able to reel them in." I batted my eyes theatrically at Kane. "With the help of a guy who speaks Russian. If he's willing."

He smiled. "Of course. You're thinking I should call them back and pretend to be Metz?"

I nodded.

"You do realize that the chances are slim to none? There are over a dozen Slavic languages. Some words and phrases are similar, but they're all very different languages."

I grimaced. "I didn't realize there were that many that sounded like Russian, but I guess it doesn't matter. They're going to find out Metz is dead pretty soon anyway. If we're going to do this, we need to do it now."

"We've got nothing to lose," Holt agreed. "If you can bluff them, great; if not, there's no downside."

Kane shrugged. "All right, I'm game."

"Come on, let's go outside and call them back." I made for the door, then hesitated. "Sorry, John, why are you and

Arnie really here? Did you need me for something?"

"We were here to give a detailed report of what we witnessed at the explosion and car crash. Also, Linda asked us to let you know dinner will be ready at six and everyone's invited, including you, Holt." He lowered his voice. "And Rand. But we don't have to tell him, if you don't want him there."

I sighed. "Let me think about it. I don't even know if I'll be able to get home by six, but thanks for the message."

"You may want to try," Kane said as we went out the door, sidestepping in opposite directions. No bullets came our way, and we both studied our surroundings.

"Clear?" I asked, still scanning for threats.

He shot a glance around us. "As far as I can tell." Closing the distance between us as Holt and Spider arrived, John added, "There's a CRAPS meeting at seven."

"Right, we should go," I agreed.

Kane accepted the phone from Spider and retrieved the number from the call log. "What do you want me to say if I get an answer?"

"Just roll with it. You're a better agent than I'll ever be."

"You're far too modest. And I'm not an agent anymore." His last sentence was heavy, but before I could offer either comfort or commiseration, he toggled the speaker and hit the Call button.

An androgynous voice answered with a single word, and Kane responded with a short sentence.

The phone spat back a few syllables, then disconnected.

Kane blinked. "Well, it wasn't Russian."

Holt blew out a breath. "Shit. What language was it? Do you know what they said?"

"They might have said 'Who is this'. It was a Slavic

language, but I don't know which one."

"Could it have been Bulgarian?"

He gave a rueful grimace. "Yes. Or Serbian or Polish or..."

I sighed. "Or any one of a dozen others."

"I think I remember what they said. I'll look it up."

"So, you told them there was a problem?" I guessed.

"Yes." Kane eyed me. "I thought you didn't speak Russian."

"I don't. But it sounded like you said 'problem', only with a Russian accent."

He chuckled. "You're right; that word does sound similar in both languages." Sobering, he added, "I'm sorry. I blew it."

"Not your fault. We knew it was a long shot. Thanks for trying."

Spider appropriated the phone. "I'll see if I can trace the call." He hurried for the door.

As he reached for the handle, the door swung open. Trish and Rebecca came out, and inspiration struck.

"Hey, Trish, do you have a minute?" I asked.

"Sure." She turned to Rebecca. "See you tomorrow."

Rebecca agreed, "See you", offered the rest of us a vague '*I-can't-remember-your-names*' smile, and hurried away.

I glanced at my watch. "Sorry, Trish, I know you're off work now-"

She interrupted with a mock-affronted snort. "You're not cutting me out of the fun that easily! Working with Rebecca is cool, but there's nothing like those late-night calls when the manure hits the ventilator." Her smile went wistful. "I'm going to miss the adrenaline rush."

"I'm going to miss having you on the other end of the

line when the manure's flying," I assured her. "Do you mind heading up to my office? I'll be there in a few minutes."

"Sure." She gave me a smile and went back in the building.

Our group followed, and I waved Hellhound over to join us. Ian tagged along, too, and I didn't have the energy to dispute his presence.

"You guys might as well head home," I told John and Arnie. "And Spider, you should go, too." I hesitated. "Do you think it's better if you travel together or separately? If you're together, you can help each other if something goes wrong; but you're also giving any potential hitman three chances for the price of one."

Hellhound shrugged. "Don't think it makes much difference, darlin'. The shit can hit the fan either way."

"Agreed," Kane said. "Hellhound and I are driving together in Aydan's half-ton, so if any of you want to tag along in your own vehicles, it's fine with us."

"I'd like to follow you," Spider said timidly. "I don't know whether it's actually any safer, but I'll feel safer."

Ian flashed his brilliant smile. "I'll come along as backup. I'm armed, and I'm not a target as far as we know."

"Thanks, Ian," I said reluctantly. "Linda and Margaret have invited you to dinner, too."

His smile widened. "Lovely. I'll see you there, then."

Holt gave him a sour look and turned to me. "I'm staying until you're ready to go. I don't want to miss anything here."

I gave John and Arnie a smile. "Okay, see you at home, then." Hiding a shudder at how easily I could have lost them this afternoon, I hugged each of them tightly.

When Ian gave me a sad-puppy look and held out his

arms, I blew out a breath. "Oh, for shit's sake. You're pathetic."

I hugged him.

His arms came tight around me, his lips finding my ear. Before I could pull away, he whispered, "Need to talk privately."

My arms flew open and I jerked back.

"I could smack him for ya," Hellhound offered hopefully.

I forced a laugh. "Thanks, but if there's any smacking to be done, I'll handle it."

Ian waggled his eyebrows. "I certainly wish you would. Handle it, I mean." Heat kindled in those sparkling green eyes. "I'm not averse to a bit of light smacking, either."

"You're hopeless. And I'm busy." I waved a general goodbye, hiding my unease. "See you later."

When Holt and I returned to my office, Trish gave us an eager smile. "So what's up? How can I help?"

I flopped into one of the chairs, wishing I had a fraction of her energy. "How's it going with Rebecca?" I asked instead of answering her questions.

"Fine." Her smile widened. "Spider was right, it's *very* cool to be able to decrypt anything, anywhere." She hesitated. "It took a bit of practice to stay out of Rebecca's mind, though." Her gaze faltered and dropped. "I saw... quite a bit more than I intended to."

"Anything we need to know?"

She shook her head. "Nothing security-related. It's just... a little weird to be inside somebody else's head like that. Some things are meant to be private. I feel like kind of a creeper."

"I know what you mean," I agreed. "Are you going to be okay with it, though?"

"Oh, sure. I've figured out how to shield that stuff now." Her posture wilted a little. "Was that all you wanted to ask?"

"No, we were hoping you could get a little more specific with your searches, but I was just wondering... what's it like when you use Rebecca's mind to read a foreign language? Do you see the foreign characters and understand them, or does it just get translated to English for you?"

Trish straightened, her smile coming back. "That's the cool part! I see the foreign characters, and I understand what the letters and words mean and how they sound in their original language. Then when we come out of the network and I write my reports, my own brain does the translation to English." She grimaced. "I wish there was a way to port it directly to a file, though. I go in and out of the network a lot just so I can make sure I don't forget anything I've seen." Brightening, she added, "But at least it makes Rebecca's fake job seem a bit more convincing. Spider set up a program that creates a few thousand digital files every morning. Rebecca moves files while I'm writing my reports; then when we're in the network, Spider's program takes over moving files at the same pace. When we come back out again, Rebecca moves more files. She'll really think she's just doing digital filing all day long."

"That's great." Relieved, I gave her a smile. "So if a name like Václav was in Cyrillic characters, you'd be able to catch it, right? Even if the words around it were in a language that Rebecca doesn't actually speak?"

"Probably, as long as Rebecca recognized the name and the characters aren't too different between the languages." Trish's gaze sharpened. "So I'm looking for Václav? What else?"

I grinned. "Václav Dymt." After explaining our

discovery of the Bulgarian bank account and the Volslav / Václav pairing, I added, "And keep an eye open for Maria Petrova Ivanova, and any other Ivanovas that might seem related."

I almost added, 'And check for Milena Georgieva Draganova, too', but fortunately I stopped myself. God, I must be getting tired. Stemp would kill me if I blew his parents' covers.

A small chill trickled down my spine at the thought that 'he'd kill me' might not be a figure of speech.

Trish was replying, and I jerked my attention back to her. "...but you know her relatives won't necessarily be named Ivanova, right? A lot of Slavic people still use the patronymic naming system. So she and her mother and father might all have different last names. Even if she's got a brother, he might be Ivanov instead of Ivanova."

"Oh, for..." I blew out a breath. "Okay, you're far more on top of this than I am. Go play."

Trish shot me a grin. "Game on! If I get something, should I call you, or just shoot it to email?"

"Call. If I'm not here, my secure burner numbers are on the list."

"Will do." She bounced to her feet. "See you tomorrow."

She left with a light step, and I slumped in my chair with a small groan. "God, she's so young. We're dinosaurs."

"Speak for yourself, you old bat," Holt growled. "*I'm* young."

"Keep telling yourself that." Hauling myself to my feet, I added, "I'm going to go and grab my network key. I need a few minutes in the network."

"You sure that's a good idea? What are you looking for?"

I couldn't tell him I was looking for the dead attempted

murderer of a woman who wasn't supposed to exist, so I answered his first question. "Of course it's a good idea."

"It's nearly five thirty; you look bagged; you have to leave if you're going to go home, eat, and get to the CRAPS meeting by seven; and since Webb's already gone, you'll have to call to make sure Brock and Mellor's connection is throttled so you don't have a collision in the internet and self-destruct." He cocked a superior eyebrow. "Does any of that sound like a 'good idea'?"

I blew out a resigned breath and did my best not to shoot the messenger. He was annoying, but he was right.

"Fine. Let's go, then."

When we arrived at my farm, I couldn't help a small smile at the memory of Holt's earlier comment about a refugee camp. Cars lined my driveway, and Holt parked while I drove on into my garage.

Inside, my table was extended to its maximum and people milled around, pouring drinks and ferrying food to the table. Conversation and laughter filled the house.

My heart twisted.

Thirty years.

That was how long it had been since I'd had a group of friends around my table. At first I'd been grieving too hard for my supposedly-dead mother. Then too isolated by my abusive husband. Then too numb to care.

Arnie caught my eye and wove through the crowd. Slipping an arm around my waist, he leaned down to speak quietly. "Okay, darlin'?"

I leaned into him, swallowing hard around the lump in my throat. "Fine," I croaked. "It's great to have everybody here." Pulling away, I pasted on a smile. "I just have to check my email. Be right back."

Hurrying down the hall, I blinked rapidly to clear the moisture from my eyes. Get a grip. None of them would even be here if the alternative wasn't death.

My heart of hearts knew there were several flavours of bullshit mixed into that thought, but at least it quelled my foolish emotions. Plopping down in front of my computer, I concentrated on the screen.

I had barely moved the mouse when Ian slipped through the door. With a furtive glance down the hall, he eased the door shut, then faced me with his sexiest smile.

"What do you know about Stemp?" he demanded.

CHAPTER 41

Flummoxed by the mismatch between what I'd expected Ian to say and what he'd actually said, I gaped at him. "What?"

"What do you know about Stemp?" he repeated urgently. "For heaven's sake, Storm, I've been trying to talk to you privately since I arrived in Canada! Quickly, before we're interrupted again!"

I blinked. "What? All that bullshit and sneaking around, and the tracker you put on me... and you just wanted to *talk*? Why the hell didn't you just *say so*?"

"But where's the fun in that?" He glanced at the closed door. "And I could hardly walk up to you in front of your ever-present entourage and say, 'I have to talk to you privately'. What kind of questions would that raise?"

I glared at him. "They'd only ask one question: 'What was that about?' I'd tell them it was classified, and that would be the end of it! I can't believe you've been wasting my time trying to manoeuvre-"

"Well, it shouldn't have taken so long, should it?" Ian scowled. "Getting private time with a woman isn't usually this much of a challenge." As I stared at him, marvelling at the sheer magnitude of his ego, he urged, "Chop-chop! What do you know about Stemp?"

"Not much."

"Give over, Storm! You work with the man. You can do better than that!"

Alarm bells clanged in the back of my brain as I said slowly, "He's my boss. He doesn't hang out with anybody from the office. I've never seen him at the pub or in a restaurant or out with friends." I spread my hands in a 'search me' gesture. "I just don't know much about him. I don't think anybody does."

"That's rubbish! Moonbeam and Karma and Skidmark dote on you. There's no way you haven't gotten close to their son, too."

I shrugged. "I was invited to Stemp's house for dinner twice, both times by his mother. I didn't get to know him any better because he made the kind of small talk that you make with your parents' friends, when you don't particularly want to know their friends any better. That's it."

"Why does he come to Europe every time there's a development with the Volslav case?"

"He doesn't," I lied. "I mean, not as far as I know. It's not like I've been tracking his movements."

Lie, lie.

"Come on, Storm, you're not that dense!" Ian's accent clipped the words to razor sharpness. "He does. You know he does."

"For fucksakes, he *doesn't*! The Volslav thing is blowing up right now, and he's here! What the hell is this all about? Are you investigating him?"

"Do you trust him?"

"Of course! He's my boss!"

"And that's also rubbish," Ian said crisply. "We're agents. It's our job to mistrust people, even our superiors sometimes."

I hissed out a breath. "You're doing it again. Dancing around, playing cute, and not giving me any useful information. I'm going to ask you one simple question. If I don't get a straight answer, I'm going to go out there and tell *everybody* what you were asking."

Ian flinched. "For God's sake, don't do that! What's your question?"

"Why are you asking me about Stemp?"

Ian eyed me for a long moment.

"Quickly, before anybody comes looking for us," I prodded, with perhaps a touch of sarcasm.

He lowered his voice. "Are we secure?"

I whisked my bug detector out and showed him the steady green light.

He leaned closer and whispered, "Someone contacted MI6 and suggested that your Department might be leaking intel to Volslav, and they pointed a finger at Stemp. I'm asking you because you're the only person in CSIS that I trust."

I raised a sardonic eyebrow. "'Trust' seems like a bit of an overstatement."

"I trust you," he repeated firmly.

Letting my head fall back against the chair, I released a long sigh.

He'd been doing his best to communicate with me, and I'd been treating him like a particularly malodorous variety of shit.

"I'm sorry," I said to the ceiling.

"I'm sorry?"

"Yes."

Ian shook his head, pinching the bridge of his nose. "No,

I meant... never mind. Why are you sorry?"

"For treating you like an annoyance. I didn't know you were trying to talk to me. I've got a lot on my plate right now." Before he could reply, I went on, "Let me guess. Your intel came from Brent Dermott."

Ian's eyes narrowed. "Why do you say that?"

"Because Dermott wants Stemp's job. Has wanted it for quite a while. He also wants me fired, incarcerated, and/or slowly and painfully dead."

Ian stiffened. "He's trying to kill you?"

"No, I think 'dead' is more of a preference than a goal."

"But *someone* is trying to kill you." His green gaze was laser-focused. "And Stemp. Doesn't that seem... coincidental?"

I shrugged. "Not really. I did consider Dermott as a suspect; but nobody has actually tried to kill me yet." I hesitated. "Unless you count the drive-by shooting this morning; but I might not have been the target of..."

I trailed off at Ian's incredulous expression.

"Okay, fine," I conceded. "But that doesn't explain why Dermott would want to kill John and Arnie. They've never had a run-in with him. And they're no threat to his current job or to a potential promotion. It just doesn't add up."

"But Stemp is still the most plausible leak to Volslav."

"No, he's not. He was questioned under the lie detector. He denied leaking any information to anyone, and he specifically said he hadn't leaked anything to Volslav or any of Volslav's associates."

Ian's shoulders slumped. "He passed your infallible lie detector?"

"Yep."

"Bollocks. He must have an accomplice. Some way to

indirectly leak information that would still let him pass the lie detector test."

I was shaking my head before he finished speaking. "I was there. Holt and Dermott both questioned him really thoroughly. Trust me, Stemp isn't our leak. If we even have a leak. As far as I know, there's no evidence that we do."

Ian's jaw clenched. "Do you mean to tell me that gobby wanker falsified intel? To feather his own damned nest?"

"I don't know." I made a calm-down gesture. "I don't know what intel you got; I don't know whether it came from Dermott; I don't know if there's any other so-called evidence-"

A tap on the door interrupted me and Kane's deep voice asked, "Aydan?"

"Come on in-*umph!*" My invitation ended in a grunt as Ian lunged forward to embrace me. "Off!" I pushed him away as the door opened.

Ian straightened his shirt and faced Kane with a cheeky grin. "You'll be pleased to know that your girlfriend is loyal to you, even in the face of my..." He batted his eyes. "...*considerable* charm."

Kane raised an amused eyebrow. "I wasn't worried." Turning to me, he added, "Dinner is ready, but if you need a bit more time-"

"Nope." I stood. "Let's go."

Shooing Ian out the door ahead of me, I hesitated. By now, Stemp would have spoken with Moonbeam and Karma.

With a sigh, I motioned John and Ian toward the kitchen. "I just have to check one quick thing. I'll be right there."

As soon as I was alone, I dropped back into my chair and fired up the crossword app. Sure enough, the tiny white square blinked in the corner. A pang of guilt arrowed through me as I imagined Stemp waiting in front of his computer, bruised from the attempt on his own life and emotionally battered from the attempt on Katya's.

As soon as I entered the control sequence, the cursor zipped across the screen. *"Need to talk."*

I sighed. *"Same time & place?"*

"Yes."

"Confirmed."

The text screen disappeared, and I dragged myself up from my chair and went to join my guests.

I couldn't give the good food and pleasant company the appreciation they both deserved. Conversations eddied around me while worries swirled in my brain.

By now our enemies would know that John was still alive, and that he and Arnie were here. Stemp was alone, and the CRAPS surveillance wouldn't do a damn bit of good if he was attacked. Could I convince him to come and stay at my farm? At least nobody seemed to be targeting Holt or Spider so far; but we couldn't take their safety for granted...

"Aydan?"

"Uh?" I returned my attention to the kitchen table, discovering that Ian, Spider, Linda, and I were the only ones still seated. Kane and Hellhound were clearing the table while Margaret presided at the kitchen sink, with Holt once again wielding the dish towel.

Spider leaned forward and repeated, "Aydan, don't you think so?"

I shook my head. "Sorry, I was a million miles away. What did you say?" Taking a closer look at his strained features, I added, "What's wrong?"

"Nothing," Linda said confidently. "Everything's fine.

Perfectly..." She winced. "Ungh... Normal."

"She's in labour," Spider quavered.

CHAPTER 42

Spider gave me an imploring look. "Linda wants to go to the CRAPS meeting. Can you convince her to go to the hospital instead?"

"Oh, sweetie." Linda patted his cheek. "I know you're worried, but remember all those classes we took? You know this is just early labour. It can last for hours, sometimes more than a day. Especially for a first baby. If we go to the hospital now..." She drew in a slow breath, wincing again. "They'll just send me home. Trust me, I know."

"But wouldn't it be better to go anyway? Just to be on the safe side?" Spider turned a pleading look toward me. "Don't you think so, Aydan?"

"I have no idea. I never had kids of my own, and-" I bit off the words 'the whole process is horrifying' and substituted, "...so I have to defer to the expert." I inclined my chin toward Linda.

Hellhound had come over to take my empty plate, and he backed away staring at Linda as though she'd swallowed a bomb. "You're gonna pop? *Now?*"

Linda laughed. "No. Probably not until tomorrow. Maybe even as late as Saturday."

"'Kay..." He backed away a few more steps, giving Spider and Linda a look of mingled pity and horror. "Glad it's you an' not me, is all I can say."

"I envy you," Kane said softly as he returned to collect more dishes. With a quirk of a smile, he addressed Linda. "I don't envy *you* for the next day or so; but... I would have given anything to be there for Daniel's birth. And those precious first years..." He swallowed hard and clasped Spider's shoulder. "You're starting the biggest adventure of your lives."

"And it should start at the hospital, shouldn't it?" Spider begged.

Linda gave him a rueful headshake and raised her voice to be heard over the sound of dishes in the sink. "Margaret, you were right. I shouldn't have told him."

Holt and Margaret came over, Margaret reaching to dry her hands on the dishtowel Holt still held. "Now, listen, all of you," she said firmly. "This is a normal, natural process. Linda is in perfect health, she's taken all the prenatal courses, she's a nurse, *and* she's the one in labour. She calls the shots. Is that clear?" She cast an authoritative glance around room, lingering on each of the men to drive her point home.

Ian raised his hands in surrender. "Not my show. And definitely not my cup of tea." He rose. "I'm off. See you at the CRAPS meeting." He headed for the door.

"Not my show, either," Hellhound seconded hurriedly. "Lemme know if ya need anythin'; otherwise I'm buttin' out."

"Same here," Kane agreed.

Holt clapped Spider on the back. "Relax. I've seen lots of women in labour, and I guarantee Linda's nowhere close yet." All eyes turned to him. A flush climbed his neck as he surveyed the incredulous expressions and added defensively, "Three sisters. Cousins by the dozens."

Spider slumped. "Okay. I know you're probably right, I just..." Knotting his bony fingers together, he sprang up as though he couldn't bear to sit still any longer. "Holy crap, this is so *nerve-wracking*!"

Margaret chuckled. "If you think this is bad, wait until the first time your child goes off to summer camp. Or stays home alone for the first time. Or drives. Or stays out all night..."

Holt laughed. "You'd better stop." He touched her shoulder to turn her back toward the sink. "You're scaring the poor kid even more."

Shortly afterward, we departed for the CRAPS meeting despite more feeble protests from Spider.

Twenty geriatric sleuths plus our group made for tight quarters in Bud's house. Despite the open windows, the heat was stifling. Wedged between Kane and Hellhound, I alternated between fighting sleep and eyeing Linda's pained expression with concern.

My chin dropped to my chest and I jerked awake again for the umpteenth time.

"Nice head-bob," Hellhound murmured, grinning. Tucking an arm around me, he guided my head to his shoulder. "Stop fightin' it. If anybody says anythin' important, we'll tell ya after."

"No, I need to listen," I whispered back. "Plus, if I fall asleep, I'll snore."

He chuckled. "Prob'ly. But what ya don't know won't hurt ya."

"No, I want to hear this." Fighting my way back to alertness, I straightened and focused on Lola as she stood up to speak.

"So, our crack CRAPS-" she began, only to be interrupted

by titters.

"Wipe your crappy crack," one wag exhorted.

Another heckler from the opposite side of the room shouted, "Stand up; we can't see you."

"Smartasses," Lola said indulgently. "I can't get any taller unless I stand on your gigantic ego, Anthony." Raising her voice to be heard over the good-natured jeering, Lola went on, "Our crack CRAPS photographers have some faces for you to look at. If you know any of these people, sing out." She flicked on a projector to show a blurry photo taken from too far away.

The quality of the photos varied considerably, but I identified Metz in one of them. I kept that information to myself, and studied the rest of the strangers with as much concentration as my exhausted brain could summon.

The slide show went on and on, and despite my best efforts my eyelids drooped again. After Lola had asked 'Does anyone recognize this person?' for the umpteenth time, the heckler across the room spoke up once more.

"We don't know any of them! They're all damn tourists. We're never going to see them again; and even if we did, we wouldn't recognize them because we've just looked at photos of *dozens of other people!*"

Lola wilted a bit, but Stemp's crisp voice responded before she could. "It doesn't matter whether you know any of them. What matters is that you have a record of them. That will be invaluable to law enforcement should there be another incident." He moved to Lola's side and turned a quelling bruise-purpled gaze on the assembly. "CRAPS is doing excellent work. Lola, please continue."

She slipped a motherly arm around his waist and gave him a gentle side-hug. "Thanks, honey."

Shock stiffened Stemp's features for a bare instant before he recovered. Patting Lola's hand, he disengaged himself and added, "Do keep in mind that these people have a right to privacy; therefore you must treat these photographs as confidential." He returned to his seat with his usual poise, but I glimpsed softness in his expression.

At last the meeting ended, with Lola exhorting the members to stay alert and patrol in pairs.

In my car on the way home, I asked Kane and Hellhound, "So, did you see anybody you recognized in those photos?"

"Metz," Kane said without hesitation. "But that's all."

"Arnie?" I asked.

"Yeah, I saw Metz in there. Didn't recognize anybody else, but I'll know if I see any a' those people again."

"Thank God for your phenomenal memory," I said. "So if the two of you stick together, you should be able to spot any threats before they get to you."

"Maybe," Kane said. "But it's unlikely that a professional would get close enough for us to recognize. He'd just take the shot."

Despair weighed down my shoulders. "God, I hate this! I'm so paranoid, I'm even checking every damn toilet cubicle before I pee. In a secured building!"

Kane reached over to gently massage my shoulder. "I'm glad you're taking precautions."

I grunted and changed the subject. "So are you guys going to camp again, or do you want to sleep in the house tonight?"

The men exchanged a glance. "Camp," Kane decided. "You're inside the house to provide security for Spider and Linda, so it's best for us to be outside as the first line of defense."

"But you're unarmed, and a civilian..." I trailed off as he stiffened. "I know you can handle it," I added hurriedly. "And I can't think of anybody I trust more to defend us. I'm just saying it's not fair to put you in danger, after you quit being an agent so that Daniel could count on you being alive and available as his father."

"It's up to me to decide where my priorities lie, and weigh the risks accordingly." Kane's words were clipped.

I couldn't help flinching. "Sorry. You're right, it's none of my business."

Hellhound laid a protective hand on my shoulder. "Ya don't hafta apologize to him." Turning to Kane, he growled, "She's lookin' out for your fuckin' dumb ass, dumbass."

John let out a breath. "You're right. I'm sorry, Aydan. I'm struggling to balance my commitment to Daniel against my desire to protect you. I shouldn't have taken my guilty feelings out on you."

"It's okay." I changed the subject. "I have to go out again tonight. Could one of you stay in the house with Spider and Linda while I'm gone?"

"I'll hold the line at the campsite," Hellhound volunteered immediately.

Kane chuckled. "Are you sure that'll be far enough away from the scary impending baby? You might want to stay at the hotel in town, just to be on the safe side."

Hellhound shot him a look. "You're the dad; you can deal with bringin' life into the world. All I know how to do is take it out."

My heart squeezed. "Arnie, you're more than-"

"So where ya goin' tonight?" he interrupted, talking gently but inexorably over my attempt at comfort.

I sighed. "Can't tell you. It shouldn't be dangerous, though."

"Shouldn't be?" Kane frowned. "Take one of us as backup."

"It *probably* won't be dangerous," I amended. "And thanks, but I have to go alone."

"Will you be long?"

"Probably no more than an hour."

"Can you tell us where to look if you don't get back on time?"

Shaking my head, I gave him a smile. "No, but thanks for your concern."

"But you have a support team from the Department, don't you?" he persisted. "You're not-"

He fell silent as Hellhound cleared his throat, sounding like a rudely-awakened grizzly bear.

John shot Arnie a look. "Subtle." Returning his attention to me with a sigh, he added, "Please let us know if there's anything we can do to help."

"I will." I gave them each a grateful smile. "Thanks for having my back. Both of you."

Shortly before midnight, I parked a couple of streets over from Stemp's house. As I zigzagged toward his place, I spotted a pair of elderly CRAPS members strolling the sidewalk. They each carried a flashlight, and I suppressed a curse as the bright beams prodded every shrub and darkened doorway.

They were in no damn hurry, and my blood pressure rose as they dawdled along. It was nearly midnight, and I really didn't want to be late again. I already had a bruise on my butt from hitting the ground after Stemp tranked me last night. I didn't need another.

A chilly breeze curled around the corner of the fence where I was hiding, and I shivered and zipped up my lightweight bulletproof jacket. The CRAPS patrol drifted to a halt and stood chatting quietly, and I muttered, "Move it, for fucksakes!"

They must have had their hearing aids turned up to maximum. Two flashlight beams flicked up and skewered me.

Shit.

Pasting on a smile, I waved and went over to them. "How's it going? Everything quiet so far?"

The short bald man flashed his light into my face. "What's the password?"

My irritation overflowed despite my best efforts. "There isn't one!"

"Yes, there is. And if you hadn't slept through half the meeting, you'd know it."

I gripped the bright end of his flashlight and used all my self-control to press it down toward the sidewalk instead of shoving it up his ass. "And if you saw me at the meeting, then you know we're on the same side," I growled.

"She's got you there, Anthony," the other man pointed out.

Wrestling my temper under control again, I tossed them a jaunty salute. "You guys carry on. I'm going to check the alley." Without waiting for a response, I spun and strode away. Fortunately, they didn't follow.

On the stroke of midnight I lifted the latch of Stemp's gate and softly said, "It's me" before slipping into the back yard.

"Thank you for coming." Stemp's shadowy figure emerged from the spruce trees beside his shed. "Let's talk inside."

The doorway to the shed was a dark void, and I suppressed an involuntary shudder as I stepped into the profound blackness. The door creaked shut and Stemp flicked on a modified flashlight, providing dim red illumination.

"Would you care to sit?" Stemp inquired with a courteous gesture toward the bench.

"Thanks." I sank onto it, canting to adjust to its uncomfortable slope. "So what's up?"

"My parents wished to provide you with their next set of burner numbers." He handed me a slip of paper. "They also inquired as to whether you had any updated phone numbers for them."

"Thanks." I pocketed the paper. "And no, the original list I gave them is still good."

"Excellent. Did you have any luck finding Milena Georgieva Draganova?"

"Sorry, I didn't get a chance to check today, but I could drop in at Sirius tonight on my way home."

He shook his head. "Unnecessary. She is dead. She is merely a loose end, not a threat. Your sleep is more important."

"Okay, I'll try tomorrow. Is everything still okay overseas?"

"My parents are arranging a relocation, and there have been no more murder attempts. I don't wish to keep you any longer than necessary, so..." He withdrew an envelope from his pocket. "May I ask you to take this for safekeeping?"

"Sure." I accepted the envelope. "How safe? Are we

talking 'Keep it in your gun safe' or 'Keep it on your body at all times and shoot anybody who tries to take it'?"

"The gun safe will be sufficient. The contents are not a matter of national security; merely the keys to my house and safety deposit box, along with instructions that will be helpful if the next attempt on my life succeeds."

"Oh." I swallowed hard. "Then I really hope I never have to open it." I hesitated, then made up my mind. "Look, it's stupid for you to deal with this alone. Come and stay at my farm. I don't know whether it's actually any safer than your place, but at least you'd have backup."

"That is kind of you. However, it is best that I stay here, where I can communicate with my parents without the risk of being overheard." Stemp hesitated, his features unreadable in the near-darkness. "I do hope you realize how grateful we are for your efforts. Your care, concern, and..." He hesitated again, his voice softening. "...friendship... mean more than you will ever know."

Rattled by his uncharacteristic sentiment, I stammered, "Oh... um, I'm happy to help. I hope it all works out soon, so you can finally be together with your whole family."

He inclined his head. "That is my sincere hope also."

Retreating to safer ground, I asked, "Is there anything else I can do?"

Stemp rose. "Nothing of which I am currently aware. Thank you for coming."

I stood, too. "You're welcome. I'll let you know if I find anything tomorrow."

He turned off the light and I slipped out into the back yard, grateful that the dim red illumination had preserved my night vision. Typical Stemp, with every detail planned to perfection. It must be nice to be that smart.

Yawning, I managed to evade the CRAPS patrol and get back to my car without incident.

I fought sleep all the way home, but despite my grogginess I remembered to pull over just before my lane. As I took out my phone to text my guests that I'd be setting off the camera sensors soon, my wrist monitor vibrated.

When I peered at the tiny screen, my blood froze.

A dark figure pointed a weapon directly at the camera.

CHAPTER 43

With shaking fingers, I texted everyone, *'I'm home, got this'*.

My phone vibrated immediately.

John: *'Plan?'*

Me: *'I'll trank. Stay back.'*

I sprang out of the car and snatched my night-vision headset from the trunk. Securing it on my head, I bounded down the ditch embankment and up the other side. As I crawled between the strands of barbed wire fence, my wrist monitor vibrated again.

The figure was already aiming at the next camera. Closer to the house now.

At least I knew where he was and which direction he was going. Heart pounding, I dodged trees and pushed through undergrowth, trying to balance speed against silence.

The intruder was about an equal distance from me, the house, and the campsite. I knew better than to believe that Kane and Hellhound would stay put, so we'd converge on the intruder around the same time. I just hoped they wouldn't end up in the line of fire.

Something rustled nearby. More adrenaline surged into my veins. Did the intruder have a team? I flicked my headset to full-infrared and spun a three-sixty.

Nothing.

The next round of rustling came with a gust of wind, and I blew out a breath of relief. Switching back to combined night vision and infrared, I hurried on. At least the wind would camouflage the sound of my approach.

I intersected the game trail I'd been aiming for, and picked up my pace to a jog. As I veered onto the path that would lead me to my goal, my wrist monitor vibrated again.

The intruder was pointing his weapon at the final camera.

This time I was close enough to hear a small gunshot. Maybe a .22, probably silenced.

Half a dozen strides later the glow of the intruder's body appeared in my infrared. I could hit him with a bullet, but the wind and undergrowth would deflect a trank dart at this distance.

And I wanted answers from this bastard.

I panted open-mouthed, trying to be silent. My heart hammered so hard I was afraid he'd hear it.

Closer...

I sucked in an anxious breath as two more glows crept into view. John and Arnie converging on the intruder, *dammit!*

"Stay out of the damn way," I muttered under my breath as I sidestepped a shrub and raised my trank pistol.

Slow exhale, squeeze the trigger...

My pistol's report was no louder than a cracking twig, but the intruder spun, his gun hand arcing up.

Shit!

My finger pistoned on the trigger, snapping off more shots. One-two-three-four-

Gunshot and muzzle flash.

I hit the dirt, glimpsing movement in my headset as I dove. When I jerked my head up, three motionless glows formed a pile on the ground.

I sprinted.

Skidding to my knees beside the still bodies, I did another fast scan. Clear.

Switching to full night vision, I pressed trembling fingers to John's neck.

No pulse.

"*No-no-no...*" Stifling my breathless whimpers, I shifted my fingers and nearly collapsed with relief when I found his pulse, strong and steady.

Next, Arnie. This time I found the pulse point on my first try, thank God.

Arnie groaned and flopped over onto his back.

"All clear," I whispered. "We're safe."

After another quick scan around us, I ejected my magazine and fumbled out a dart with shaking hands. Pressing its point into the intruder's neck, I muttered, "And stay down, asshole."

John twitched and groaned, and I repeated my mantra. "All clear, we're safe."

"'Th' fuck?" Arnie mumbled as I frisked the intruder. "H'long w'z I out?"

"Only a few seconds. The wind must have carried most of the trank vapour away. That's why he didn't go down at first." I pocketed the gunman's weapons and bound his wrists and ankles with steel-reinforced zip ties.

Arnie hauled himself up onto his elbows. "Kane?"

John slurred, "M'fine." He sucked in deep breaths, clearing the drug from his system.

As he propped himself up, I admonished, "I told you

guys to let me handle this!"

"We were gonna," Arnie replied apologetically. "But when he started shootin' we figured he'd spotted ya. Couldn't see fuck-all, an' didn't know if you'd been hit. We didn't dare wait. Sorry, darlin'."

"It's okay, I'm not mad. Just glad you're both safe. Which reminds me..." I took out my phone and texted Spider, '*All clear, you're safe*'.

My phone vibrated a second later with his incoming call, and I accepted it. "Hey, Spider. Don't worry, everything's fine."

"Where are you?" he whispered frantically.

"At the edge of the woods behind my shed. What's-"

"Are you out of sight? Linda's mom will be here any second."

"Shit!" I shot a wild glance around us. "We'll handle it." I disconnected and demanded, "Can you guys walk?"

Both men struggled to their feet. "What's wrong?" Kane demanded.

"Linda's mom's coming! Drag this guy into the woods. I'm going to secure the driveway and the front of the house."

I ran, scouring the yard and the trees along the creek with infrared. As the sound of tires on gravel approached, I spotted a faint glow in the woods.

"*Fuck!*" I yanked out my Glock. No pissing around with tranquilizers in the wind. This asshole was getting a bullet.

Hunched over and zigzagging to make myself a more difficult target, I charged to the edge of the trees. As headlights slowed and turned into my lane, I ducked behind a tree and sucked air. Scanned the woods...

Red glow there.

As I raised my gun, the glow moved. A head came up

and four long legs glowed warm yellow, fading to cool blue in the undergrowth.

Deer. And if it was grazing, that meant no intruders were in the area.

Another scan of the woods showed only two vertical glows and one horizontal, marking the spot where Kane and Hellhound crouched over our prisoner. Panting, I let my knees collapse, sliding down the tree trunk to sit on the ground.

Linda's mother parked her car and got out, hurrying up onto my front porch without glancing around. As soon as the door closed behind her, I texted Arnie and John. '*All clear. Coming back now.*'

My phone vibrated immediately.

John: '*Bring truck*'.

I let out a long, quiet groan. He was right, of course. Our prisoner needed to go into lockup at Sirius; and I might as well take him. I'd have to question him anyway.

I texted Spider, '*Taking package to town in truck*'.

With any luck, Linda's mother would be too focused on the impending birth to notice my nocturnal wanderings. As I pressed Send, misgiving shook me. Spider would be just as flustered as Linda's mother; maybe more so. Would he come up with a plausible cover story?

Even as the thought occurred, Spider texted, '*Can u wait? Leaving for hospital now.*'

Blowing out a breath of mingled relief and worry, I replied, '*Will wait til you're gone. Good luck.*'

I texted Kane and Hellhound, then hunkered down beside my tree to keep an eye on the house and yard. Minutes dragged by, and I shot a worried glance at my watch. The prisoner would wake up soon. John and Arnie could probably handle him, but I didn't want them taking any more risks.

But I didn't dare leave my post. I'd never forgive myself if someone attacked Spider and Linda as they left.

At last my front door swung open. Spider hovered worriedly beside Linda, taking her elbow to help her down the stairs. She patted his arm and made calming gestures, but her posture was hunched, her expression strained. After a short discussion, Spider helped Linda into her mother's car. They drove off with Spider following in his tiny Smart car, and I let out a long breath and texted Kane and Hellhound, '*Coming now*'.

As I hit Send, a snicker burst out of me. I'd said those words to each of them before, under much more enjoyable circumstances. Sure enough, as I jogged toward the garage my phone vibrated.

Hellhound: '*thot u were just breathin hard ;-)*'

Grinning, I backed the half-ton out of the garage and headed for the woods.

John and Arnie hoisted the unconscious prisoner into the truck box, and I injected him with another dose of tranquilizer before we closed the tailgate and box topper.

"You guys might as well go to bed," I said. "That's probably all the excitement we're likely to have here tonight."

"Nope, I'm comin' with ya," Hellhound countered. "The kids're gone, so there's no reason for us to stick around here. I'll ride in the back in case our guy needs another dart."

"And I'll come along and pick up your car on the way by," Kane said. "Let's go."

"Okay," I agreed, too tired to argue. "I'm going to call Holt. He'll want to be there for the questioning." Taking out my phone, I hit speed dial.

"Holt." Even at one AM, he sounded ready for action.

"Caught a gunman at my farm," I said tiredly. "We'll have him at Sirius in fifteen minutes."

"See you there."

I handed Hellhound a couple of spare trank darts, and we took our places in the truck. As we drove down the lane, Kane glanced over. "You seem to be getting along better with Holt these days."

"Yeah. I guess we're getting used to each other."

"I'm glad. It's important to be able to trust your partner."

I shot him a look, but I couldn't tell whether he'd intended another layer of meaning.

As I pulled to a stop beside my car, I gave him a sheepish smile. "Good thing this isn't the big city. The keys are in the ignition, and the door's unlocked."

John chuckled as he got out. "At least that makes it easy for me. See you in town." He leaned in the open door and added, "Where do you want to meet? I'll help you bring him in."

"It's okay, you don't need to-" As his jaw stiffened, I bit off the demur and substituted, "Thanks. I'm thinking the secondary bunker. I can pull into the lane at the back of the house and we can take him through the tunnels."

When we arrived at the small converted house that masqueraded as my office in Silverside, I was thankful for Kane's muscular presence. As he and Hellhound hefted the prisoner into the house and down the stairs to the basement, I shook my head.

"I don't know what the hell I was thinking. Thanks, John. If it was just Arnie and me, I don't know how we would have gotten this asshole downstairs. He's a big guy."

Hellhound grinned as they lowered the limp body to the floor. "Put him at the top a' the stairs an'..." He mimed a vigorous shove with one foot.

"Yeah, except I actually want him to regain consciousness tonight." A thought struck me. "Oh, hang on. No need to make this any harder than it has to be. Be right back."

I took the stairs two at a time and grabbed one of the rolling office chairs. After cautiously carrying it down the narrow stairs, I rolled it over to the others. "This will be easier than carrying him three blocks."

I reclined the chair as far as it would go, and the men hoisted the prisoner into it. Opening the electrical panel, I leaned in and activated the retinal scan.

When the door to the time-delay chamber opened, the two men rolled the chair and its unconscious occupant inside. I joined them, trying not to flinch when the door thumped shut behind me. Squeezing past the men, I triggered the next retinal scan, then stood facing the exit door. Eyes clamped shut, I fought claustrophobia while I counted down the long thirty seconds.

When the door opened at last, I skittered out into the corridor with a distinct lack of dignity. Kane and Hellhound tactfully ignored my accelerated breathing, and we traversed the long corridors in silence.

When we rounded the final corner, Holt was waiting outside the interview room. He grinned. "How long 'til he wakes up?"

The prisoner twitched and groaned.

"Give him another shot," I said.

Hellhound tapped a dart into the prisoner's neck. "Twenty minutes," he deadpanned to Holt.

"Why the hell did you do that?" Holt demanded. "It's one-thirty in the fucking morning. I don't want to sit around here for another twenty minutes waiting for him to wake up."

I shrugged. "So go home. I can do the questioning; I just need time to get set up. I want to put the lie detector on him."

"Huh. Yeah, okay. I'll go and get it while you get him strapped in." Holt headed down the hallway.

Swinging open the door to the interrogation room, I gave Kane and Hellhound a sweeping gesture. "Gentlemen, if you please?"

Hellhound snorted. "I ain't no gentleman. An' if I did what I pleased, this asshole'd be in a fuckin' world a' hurt."

In short order, the prisoner was propped in the bolted-down chair and manacled to the table.

"Thanks, both of you," I said through a yawn. "You might as well go home to bed. If this guy's like the others, it'll be a long session. And he probably won't talk anyway."

"You'll need to escort us back to the bunker," Kane said. "The time delay needs your retinal scan."

A sigh escaped me. "Right. I keep forgetting. Let's go, then."

By the time I returned to the interview room, Holt was waiting with the lie detector.

"How do you want to play this?" he asked.

I sagged dispiritedly against the wall. "I doubt if it matters. He probably won't talk anyw..." I trailed off.

A smile tugged at the corners of Holt's mouth. "You must have an idea. I smell brain cells overheating."

"I do have an idea." Straightening, I rubbed my hands together and did my best evil-genius laugh. "Muwahahaha!"

CHAPTER 44

As the prisoner began to twitch and groan, I surveyed our staged setup with satisfaction.

Manacled to the table opposite the prisoner, Holt's steely eyes glittered through the tousled hair that hung over his forehead. His stubbled jaw bulged with anger. Orange prison scrubs revealed his rippling arm muscles, and his arrogant slouch growled 'Badass'. The lie detector's crown of electrodes made him look like an evil prince from some dark post-apocalyptic world.

He jerked at his bonds, snarling a string of obscenities that made my potty-mouth sound like a vicar's Sunday service.

"Keep it up," I advised in a hard voice. "If you piss me off enough, I'll fry your fucking brain."

Right on cue, the prisoner struggled upright in his chair, blinking heavy eyes. "Where'm I?" he slurred. "Who're you?"

Holt shot me a contemptuous look. "Don't tell that bitch anything. She's a fucking cop. We've got rights."

I narrowed my eyes at him. "You might not have as many rights as you think. Nobody knows you're here. I want answers, and that band around your head is a lie detector that's hooked up to your brainwaves. Tell me the truth, and you might get out of here with your brain intact."

Holt snorted. "Bullshit. You won't do anything to me. Bitch cop. Fucking bitch-pig." He spat at me.

"What's your name?" I demanded.

"King Cock." Holt thrust his pelvis in my direction. "Get on your knees and suck."

"I don't think you're hearing me," I said calmly. "You have two choices. You can answer my questions truthfully. Or you can keep pissing me off, and I'll send a charge through that headband that'll vaporize your frontal lobe. If you don't want to be a vegetable for the rest of your life, you'd better answer my questions."

"You're bluffing," Holt blustered, but he didn't sound quite so certain. "You're a cop. You can't hurt me."

"There won't be a mark on you," I agreed with a thin smile. "I promise."

He straightened, glowering. "Fuck off."

I stepped over to the lie detector case and ran my finger over the controls. "Let's try this again. What's your name?"

Holt smirked. "King Cock."

"That's one." Eyeing him, I touched the controls again. "Three strikes and you're out. Permanently. What's your name?"

"Emperor Dong."

"That's two." I gave him a flat look. "Just so you know: I don't actually need answers from you. You're completely expendable. So I'm going to give you one more chance. If you answer truthfully, you get to keep on-"

Holt let out a roar and jerked on his chains, muscles bulging. I couldn't help twitching, and he gave me a feral grin. "Come a little closer, bitch-pig. If you wanna keep flapping your lips, you can wrap them around my shaft."

"Last chance," I said stonily. "What's your name?"

"Suck my cock."

"Fry, asshole." I pretended to twist one of the controls.

Holt went rigid. His back arched, the cords in his neck tightening like bowstrings.

The prisoner's eyes widened and he eased backward in his chair.

Holt's face turned red, then purple. Every muscle stood out as though carved in granite. Then he suddenly melted like a plastic figurine in an oven. His eyelids drooped, his shoulders sagged, his back bowed. A rush of urine soaked his pants, dribbling off his chair into a pool on the floor.

The prisoner jerked back with a small sound of revulsion.

Advancing on the pathetic husk that had once been a man, I smiled. "How are you feeling now, King Cocky?"

Holt sagged wordless in the chair, staring blankly forward. A rivulet of drool trickled from his half-open lips and dripped from his chin.

Avoiding the puddle on the floor, I leaned over and removed the headdress from his temples, then unlocked his manacles. He sat unmoving.

"Stand up," I said.

Holt rose slowly, hunched like an old man, his eyes vacant.

"Go and sit in the corner." I pointed to the corner of the room.

Holt turned and shambled obediently over, sinking down to sit tailor-fashion facing the corner. Rocking repetitively, he tucked one thumb in his mouth. His other hand cupped his sodden crotch.

Turning my back on him, I smiled at the prisoner.

"Okay, your turn."

The man stared wide-eyed, his face bone-white. "A-Aren't you going to..." His gaze darted to Holt's hunched quiescent form. "Won't he...?"

"Nope. His frontal lobe's completely gone, along with all his free will. For the rest of his life, he won't do anything he's not directly told to do. If nobody says anything to him, he'll literally just sit there until he starves to death." I glanced over at Holt. "Stop playing with yourself."

Holt removed his hand from his crotch, but made no other sound or movement.

Turning back to the prisoner, I offered him a pleasant smile. "They used to do frontal lobotomies with an ice pick, you know. Just hammered it through an eye socket into the brain and wiggled it around." I clenched my fist on an imaginary ice pick and mimed a vicious joggling movement. "It only took about ten minutes, and they did thousands of them. Apparently they thought it helped some people, back before they had medications that worked."

I stepped closer, and the prisoner strained backward in his seat.

"It killed an awful lot of people, though," I went on conversationally. "This lie detector is much safer. No infections or brain hemorrhages. King Cocky will live a nice long healthy life." I smiled. "Assuming he's put in an institution where somebody will take care of him." Giving a carefree shrug, I added, "Oops. Guess he won't live long after all."

"B-But... you're a cop..."

I gave him a pitying smile and jerked my chin in Holt's direction. "That's what he said, and I didn't feel like arguing with him. I'm sure you'll be much more reasonable." I advanced on him with the lie detector headdress.

He jerked away, his voice rising half an octave. "Don't put that thing on me! I'll tell you everything I know!"

"Yeah. You will." I whipped out my trank pistol and fired at the floor, then hurried for the door as he collapsed.

After a couple of minutes in the corridor, I deemed it safe enough to return to the room. Holt was sprawled unconscious in the corner, and I winced. Avoiding the wet parts of his clothes, I moved his lax limbs to a more comfortable position. I was going to owe him big-time for this.

By the time the prisoner regained consciousness a couple of minutes later, the lie detector headdress was around his temples and my hand was hovering over the controls. As soon as he was capable of comprehension, he went rigid.

"What's your name?" I asked politely.

"M-Max Thorogood."

"Is that your real name?"

"Yes."

The green light shone, and I gave him a smile. "Too bad you didn't live up to your name. If you'd been thoroughly good, you wouldn't be in this fix. What were you doing at my farm tonight?"

His Adam's apple bobbed. "Um... I was supposed to... um..." His voice dropped to a whisper. "Kill you."

"Just me? Anybody else?"

"I j-just started with you."

"Bad choice. Who were the other targets?"

"George Harrison and Arnold Helmand."

I frowned. "Is that all?"

"Yeah..." The lie detector's yellow light flashed and Thorogood went paler. "I mean, there was another guy's name on the contract, but he's dead already. My partner did him."

"Who's your partner?"

"His last name's Swift. I don't know his first name, I swear."

I raised a skeptical eyebrow. "Really?"

"Yeah!" Thorogood shot an anxious look at the lie detector and relaxed a fraction when the green light glowed.

"Who was the guy he killed?" I asked.

"John Kane. I don't know if that was his real name."

"Is that true?"

"Yeah."

The green light shone.

I squinted at him, trying to ease the fatigue-induced grittiness in my eyes. "Tell me all the names on the contract."

"At first it was just John Kane and another guy called Hellhound. Arnold Helmand. But after Swift took out Kane, two more names got added. George Harrison, alias Charles Stemp..." He gave me a fearful glance. "And Arlene Widdenback, alias Arlene Cherry, alias Aydan Kelly. And, uh... we were s'posed to scare a guy called Rupert Weiss. That's all."

"Is that all true?"

"Y-Yeah."

The green light corroborated his statement, and I changed tack. "Who's Farrell Metz?"

"I d-don't know."

"Is that true?" I reached for the controls.

"Yes!"

The green light shone again, and I gave Thorogood a smile. "You're lucky I have this lie detector. I wouldn't have believed you otherwise. Farrell Metz got the same contract you did. He also got the contract to kill Swift, after Swift failed to kill Helmand. Swift's body showed up yesterday." I widened my smile to show a few more teeth. "I thought you might be interested in that. Since, y'know, you failed to kill me."

"Oh, fuck." Thorogood's shoulders sagged. "Listen, I'll do anything you want. Just let me-"

"Who took out the contract?" I interrupted.

"Some guy with a foreign name. Volkswagen or something."

"Try again," I said softly.

"I don't know, I'm sorry, I don't know!" Thorogood hunched his shoulders and ducked his head, frantically trying to dislodge the lie detector's band. "Don't fry me, please, I don't know! It was Volks-something! I didn't really want to know, you know? I didn't even talk to him, Swift did. And Swift handled the cash, I was just his helper, I was just supposed to steal the cars and pick him up after he did the jobs..." He trailed off into a whimper. "Oh, fuck, I'm so fucked!"

"Yeah, you really are," I agreed. "So, once more for the lie detector. Do you know who hired you?"

"Swift hired me! He said it would be easy..." He quavered into silence.

"So Swift hired you as his partner? Yes or no."

"Yes!"

The green light underscored his sincerity.

I sighed. "Do you know who took out the original contracts? Yes or no."

"N-No."

The yellow light shone.

"I told you, I don't know his name," Thorogood clarified hurriedly. "All I know is, it was Volks-something."

"For fucksakes," I muttered. "Okay, did Metz have a partner?"

"I don't know. I didn't even know who Metz was until you told me."

"Is that true?"

"Yes!" Thorogood stared imploringly at me. "You gotta believe me."

"I do." I shot a disgusted look at the green light. "Unfortunately. Where did you get that weapon you were pointing at my cameras tonight?"

"Swift gave it to me. He said he'd let me take you out 'cause it was an easy job to kill some chick living alone in the middle of nowhere, and then I'd get a bigger cut of the money. That fancy weapon was supposed to take out your cameras so I could just waltz in and..." He trailed off, and when he spoke again his voice trembled with despair. "He was fucking with me, wasn't he? That bastard took the easy jobs, and screwed me over."

I shrugged. "Well, if it's any consolation, he's dead and you're not. Yet. Who told you I'm a cop?"

"That guy just said so." Thorogood pointed his chin at Holt's motionless body.

Shooting a scornful look in that direction, I said, "You don't want to believe everything you hear. Did Swift say anything to you?"

"No!" The lie detector confirmed his reply. "If he'd told me up front, I woulda..." He trailed off.

"Would have what?"

"I don't know! I woulda... maybe... fuck, I *don't know*!"

Abandoning that line of questioning, I asked, "Who told

you where my cameras were, and how to use the weapon?"

"Swift said Volkswagen told him, when he gave him the weapon. He said Volkswagen knew where all your cameras were and that ray-gun thing would knock them out, so I could sneak into your place without getting caught." His face flushed. "The ray-gun was fake, wasn't it? It didn't even fucking work! He said you were just some chick living alone in the country, how hard could it be? He screwed me over-"

"Well, waah, waah. Sucks to be you." I pulled out my trank pistol and pointed it at him.

Thorogood thrashed against his restraints. "NO! *Don't*-"

I shot him.

"Come on, Holt," I said as I hurried for the door, making sure to exhale as I spoke.

Holt scrambled up, and we bailed out into the corridor.

When the door closed behind us, Holt cupped his crotch, shaking first one leg and then the other as he peeled the wet pants away from his skin. "Fuck, that gets chilly after a while."

I eyed him incredulously. "I can't believe you actually pissed yourself. Talk about getting into a role."

He grimaced. "Give me a break. I had a squeeze bottle of tea in my pants." He dipped into the elastic waistband and came out with the bottle.

Laughter seized me. "I thought you just had a giant hard-on, King Cocky," I said between giggles.

Holt snickered. "Thanks for noticing. And that's Emperor Dong to you."

When my laughter subsided, I slumped against the wall, rubbing my tired eyes. "Okay, I'm done. I need to put Thorogood's gun in lockup, and drop off the ray gun in Reggie's lab. Reggie already guessed Volslav had developed a handheld EM pulse pistol, so he'll be happy to get his hands on the real thing. And I'm really glad the techs put Faraday cages around all my cameras so it didn't knock them out this time." I sighed. "So what the hell are we going to do with Thorogood? He's basically just an idiot car thief. Maybe if we release him, he'll get the word out that I'm not a cop after all. Or lead us to the next hitman."

Holt shrugged. "Yeah, but let's hang onto him until tomorrow. Get the analysts to check his record; see if we come up with any more questions. It's the middle of the fucking night. No time to be making decisions."

"Dermott will probably release him tomorrow anyway," I said glumly. "Just to spite us both."

CHAPTER 45

The vibration of my phone yanked me from uneasy dreams. Heart pounding, I snatched it up only to relax at the sight of the text message.

John: *'Okay if we come in for shower/breakfast?'*

Groaning at the realization that it was morning already, I replied *'Sure'*, and trudged into the ensuite to take my own shower.

By the time I emerged, coffee scented the air. Wishing I actually drank the stuff, I threw on some clothes, donned my holsters, and sleepwalked out to the kitchen.

Kane looked up from the stove with a smile. "Good morning. How would you like your eggs?"

"Good morning." I managed a smile. "Just scrambled, thanks. Don't go to any trouble."

He pulled a disappointed face. "So Eggs Benedict is out?"

"'Fraid so, unless you can make it in under ten minutes. I have to be at Sirius in half an hour." I wandered over to the kettle with my eyelids at half-mast.

"That's freshly boiled," Kane said. "I didn't know whether you'd want green or herbal tea this morning."

"Green. I need a caffeine boost."

As I poured my cup, Kane gave me a sympathetic smile.

"Go and sit down. I'll start your toast when the eggs are almost ready."

"Thanks." I slumped into my chair, noting with appreciation that the peanut butter jar was already on the table in front of my place.

Hellhound emerged from the bathroom on a whiff of fresh soap, wearing nothing but soft faded jeans and looking even less awake than I was. Despite my exhaustion, I enjoyed the display of bulging tattooed muscles as he zombie-shuffled to the coffee pot.

Sinking into the chair across from me with a groan, he wrapped both hands around his mug and hung his head over it.

"Morning," I offered.

"Mornin'." His croak sounded barely human.

We drank our hot beverages in silence. A few minutes later, Kane slipped a plate of scrambled eggs and toast in front of me, and I gave him a grateful 'Thanks'.

He vanished into the bathroom, and I dug in. Hellhound drained his coffee mug and poured another, and by the time I had finished my breakfast and he had finished his second cup, I decided it wouldn't be too inconsiderate to speak.

"Did you get some sleep?" I asked.

"Yeah." He sucked back another gulp of coffee. "How'd ya do?" He eyed me keenly. "Nightmares?"

I shrugged. "The usual."

The sound of the bathroom door and the spicy scent of John's shower gel alerted me to incoming eye-candy. I swung around, hoping I'd be lucky enough to share my kitchen with two half-naked men.

Sadly, he was fully dressed, but at least his T-shirt was snug. And my God, he smelled delicious.

"Any word on the baby?" he asked.

Guilt twisted my belly. "I never even thought about it. I'm such a shitty friend." I jumped up and headed for the phone. "I'll call Spider right now."

"You're not a shitty friend," John said. "You spent last night protecting them, and you've only had four hours of sleep."

"Same as you," I pointed out as I dialled.

"It's of a little more interest to me than it is to you," he said gently. "That doesn't make you a bad friend."

As Spider answered, I turned to concentrate on the call. His voice vibrated with tension as he said, "Hi, Aydan."

"Hi. How's everything going?"

A sigh rattled the speaker. "The doctor says it's going fine. But Linda's exhausted and she's hurting so much and I don't know what to do! I wish I could help, but I'm just so... so... useless!"

"You're not useless," I comforted. "You're keeping Linda company and giving her encouragement, and that's what she needs from you right now. Hang in there. It won't be long now."

I grimaced. Sage words from a commitment-phobic woman who avoids babies like the plague.

Changing the subject to an area in which I actually had experience, I added, "We questioned the gunman last night, and it looks as though you should be safe to go home. Your name wasn't on the contract. It was only for John, Arnie, Stemp, and me."

"Oh, that's good," Spider said absently. A moment later, he blurted, "Jeez, no! Not good! It's awful that somebody's trying to kill you, I just meant-"

"It's okay, I know what you meant, and I'm really glad

you're not in the line of fire," I soothed. "I'll be coming into town soon. Can I bring you anything? Breakfast, or anything from home?"

Sounding distracted again, he mumbled, "Um... no... thanks." His voice firmed. "Sorry, I want to get back to Linda now, but thanks for calling. I'll let you know as soon as there's any news."

"Okay, tell Linda we're thinking of her." I disconnected and turned to John and Arnie. "No news yet." I shuddered. "God, what a barbaric process. Humans should just lay eggs."

"Don't even wanna think about it," Arnie said.

"Me, neither." I strapped on my waist pouch. "I have to go. I'm planning to be at Sirius today, but I'll let you know if that changes. What are you guys up to?"

"If you're going to Sirius, we'll keep the building under surveillance this morning," John said. "Their security cameras are good, but if we're moving around the perimeter, we can spot potential threats at a greater distance. We don't want a replay of Metz's remote controlled attack."

"Okay, but be careful. Remember, you're both still on the hit list."

Arnie frowned. "Yeah... 'bout that... I was s'posed to meet a client for my PI business in Calgary this afternoon. D'ya think I oughta cancel?"

I gave him a helpless shrug. "I don't know. We're down three hitmen, but that doesn't mean there aren't more. What if your so-called meeting turns out to be a murder attempt?"

"Doubt it." His frown deepened. "I had this meetin' set up before any a' this shit started, an' I hadta cancel an' reschedule once already. I hate to blow it off again. Client's a nice lady, an' she's pretty upset." He hesitated. "How 'bout this: Now that my SUV's busted up, I gotta go back to Calgary anyway an' get a rental. If Kane an' I take your half-ton down, I can get the rental an' meet my client in that. That oughta make me harder to spot."

"And I can be a decoy in the half-ton," Kane added. "If anybody identifies the truck, they'll come after me instead of you."

"Sounds like a plan," I agreed. "Except for the part where somebody comes after either of you. Let's skip that part."

I collected a hug and kiss from each of them and headed for the door, feeling awkward. Having them together in my house was just weird. The dirty jokes and sensual touches I shared with Arnie were replaced by chaste hugs and kisses; and the red-hot chemistry with John was dampened to self-conscious politeness.

Blowing out a frustrated sigh, I left.

Driving with only half my attention on the familiar road, I pondered. Surely Volslav must be running out of assassins by now. Thorogood was definitely scraping the bottom of the barrel.

But if they'd been willing to pay for three hitmen, four wasn't a stretch. One for each of us.

Thumping a fist against my steering wheel, I blew out a breath. Hell, it didn't matter how careful I was. If Volslav wanted me dead badly enough, I was going to get dead. The only thing keeping me alive right now was luck.

"Fuck it," I said, and steered for the Sirius parking lot. If I wasn't safe anywhere, I might as well have convenient parking.

I had only been at my desk long enough to check my email when my phone rang and the display showed the analyst-on-call extension.

I picked up. "Kelly."

A male voice said, "I have Ms. Stephanie Maldova on the line. Spider said you wanted to talk to her?"

"Yes, put her through. Thanks."

"Go ahead."

"Hello, Ms. Maldova?" I asked.

"Yes. Who am I speaking with?" Her voice was brisk and businesslike.

"Agent Aydan Kelly. You've received our warrant for information about Maria Harchman?"

"Yes." Her dispassionate tone revealed nothing.

"I understand you were the designated contact person for Maria Harchman while she was imprisoned at the Edmonton Institution, and you are also her executrix."

"Yes, that's correct."

Deciding on an oblique approach, I asked, "What can you tell me about Maria Harchman? Were you friends?"

"No, I represented her in her divorce after she was imprisoned. Since I had to meet with her frequently in prison during the divorce, she also engaged me to represent her interests to the board of directors of her stationery company, Glory Canadian Paper Products Limited. For convenience, she granted me power of attorney for decisions regarding the company, and named me her designated contact person at the prison. Ms. Harchman's mother was originally named executrix, but she lives overseas. Ms. Harchman updated her will after the divorce; and at that time she changed it to name me her executrix."

"Who are her beneficiaries?"

"Only one: Her mother."

"Do you think Maria Harchman was murdered?"

A heartbeat of silence on the line. Then, "The medical examiner ruled her death accidental."

"Yes. That wasn't what I asked."

Stephanie sighed. "It's possible. But it would be costly and time-consuming to challenge the medical examiner's findings; and nothing will bring Ms. Harchman back to life. Her mother chose not to pursue an inquiry."

"Did you know Maria was using the stationery company to launder money?"

Stephanie's response was typical lawyer-speak. "I only know that a warrant was served on the corporate headquarters and warehouse of GCPPL. The police searched the premises, but to my knowledge, no evidence of wrongdoing was found and no charges have been laid. There was nothing to indicate that GCPPL or Ms. Harchman were involved in any way with the money found at the Harchman estate. As I'm sure you're aware, it would be easy for anyone to cut the plastic strap on a carton of paper, substitute the contents, and then reclose the carton with a new plastic strap."

I suppressed a sigh. "Yeah. Still, though, I'd like to find out more about the company. What can you tell me?"

"Very little. Since the Estate of Maria Harchman is a majority shareholder in GCPPL, I have some basic knowledge about the company, but I don't foresee being involved much longer. It's in the best interests of the estate to liquidate quickly." A wry smile tinged her voice. "The longer it takes, the more the estate has to pay me. Some might consider that a golden opportunity; but as executrix I have a moral responsibility to make good financial decisions for the estate."

"Right," I agreed. "I'm sure her mother appreciates your

diligence. Can you suggest someone at GCPPL who could talk to me about their daily operations?"

"I'll email you the COO's contact information. May I have your email address?"

I gave it to her, and she replied, "Thank you. I'll send the information as soon as we're off the phone. Is there anything else I can help you with today, Agent Kelly?"

"Just one thing," I said casually. "Did Maria have any personal effects at the prison?"

"A few items of clothing and jewellery. As soon as the prison released her personal items to me, I shipped them to her mother in Bulgaria."

My heart gave a hard thump, and I held my voice steady. "Do you recall exactly what the items were? Could you describe them?"

"No, I'm sorry." She hesitated. "I don't mean to sound cold, but Maria was a client, not a friend. None of the items had any personal significance to me, so I can't describe them in detail. If it's important, the prison should still have a record of the items."

"Right," I agreed. "Sorry, I know you're busy but I have to ask you for one more thing. Could you please give me Maria's mother's name and address?"

"I don't have that information at my fingertips, but I'll look it up and email it to you along with the COO's contact information."

"Great, thanks for your time."

"You're welcome, Agent Kelly. If I can be of further assistance, please don't hesitate to call."

Holt had wandered in and flopped onto the sofa while I wrapped up the call. As soon as I hung up, he demanded, "Was that the lawyer? What did you find out?

I leaned back in my chair. "Not much. She didn't know Maria personally; she was just her divorce lawyer. They met pretty frequently during the divorce. Maria was a majority shareholder in the stationery company, so she gave Stephanie power of attorney for her business decisions, too, and named her as executrix when she redid her will."

"Huh. What about the necklace?"

"Sent to Maria's mother in Bulgaria. She's the sole beneficiary of the estate." I slouched lower in the chair with a sigh. "Stephanie is sending me the contact information, but it's going to be a pain in the ass to do anything about it. We'll have to get Interpol to send somebody over to pick up the necklace. And I forgot to ask if Maria's mother speaks English."

As I spoke, an idea dawned. Moonbeam and Karma were in Bulgaria. Katya spoke Bulgarian. This could work.

But how could I arrange it without revealing any secrets? Dammit...

A 'ding' from my computer dragged my attention back to my email.

"Good, here's the email already," I said as I clicked on it. "I like this Stephanie Maldova. She's efficient, and she's doing her best to wind up the estate quickly even though-"

Maria's mother's name jumped off the screen, striking me momentarily speechless.

Milena Georgieva Draganova.

The woman who had hired the hit on Katya.

CHAPTER 46

Holt sprang off the sofa and hurried to peer over my shoulder. "What?" He glanced from the screen to my face and back again. "What did you find?"

Shit, I couldn't tell him why I recognized Milena Draganova's name.

"Sorry, nothing." I infused my voice with exhaustion and rubbed my eyes. "I'm too tired to think and read at the same time. I was going to say, I'm impressed because Stephanie's doing her best to wind up the estate quickly even though she's getting paid by the hour."

Holt snorted and ambled back to the couch. "An ethical lawyer? That's pretty much an oxymoron. No wonder you were struck dumb."

"Most lawyers are ethical," I argued.

"You just keep on believing that, Pollyanna."

"You're such a cynical bastard." Relieved at the change in topic, I nudged the conversation elsewhere. "I'm going to call the COO of GCPPL."

"I have no idea what you just said."

"GCPPL. Glory Canadian Paper Products Limited, Maria's stationery company. I want to talk to their Chief Operations Officer and find out more about the company."

Holt shrugged. "Read the police case files. No need to

duplicate what they've already done. If they found cash in a box of paper, you can bet they've already investigated the company."

"Yeah, that's what Stephanie said; but the police were focused on the money. I'm more interested in the connection to Volslav. There's got to be somebody in that company that shipped out a special box once a month. If we can find that person, we might be able to follow them up the food chain and figure out who put out those hits."

Another thought pinged in my brain. What if Milena Draganova had been behind all of the hits, not just Katya's? Could she have been a silent partner in Volslav, running the organization from behind the scenes?

And did that mean that after we eliminated all the assassins she'd hired, we'd be safe because she was dead?

Or shit, what if she *wasn't* dead? What if she'd only faked her death?

But I couldn't talk to Holt about any of that, because I couldn't explain how I knew about Milena Draganova's murderous tendencies.

Realizing I was staring into space again, I hurriedly added, "You're right; I want to read the police file before I talk to the COO." I skimmed my list of emails. "I bet by now Megan's uploaded the police reports... yep, there's the file." I clicked on the folder. "Shit, it's huge."

Holt sighed and stood. "Might as well get started, then. How do you want to split it up?"

"First I'm going to go into the network and see if I can absorb anything from it. That often works better than reading, when I don't know what I'm looking for."

"Okay." Holt sat down again. "I'll come into VR, too. I can read files just as easily from a virtual terminal, and I can be your anchor at the same time. Don't forget to call Brock and tell him to throttle the connections for Stile and Mellor."

"Shit." I blew out a breath. "I really miss Spider when he's not here. Will you please call Brock while I go down and get my network key from the secured area?" I headed for the door.

When I burst into the secured area after enduring the claustrophobia of the time-delay chamber, I came face-to-face with Reggie. I let out a yelp and backpedalled, and he studied me with a raised eyebrow.

"Still having a tough time with your claustrophobia?" he asked sympathetically.

I straightened. "Of course not. I was just in a hurry."

He let out a skeptical snort, but changed the subject. "I was just about to call you. Thanks for the EMP pistol. Turns out Weiss invented that, too. Oh, and he dropped some names during our interview yesterday. I know you're on Volslav's trail, so I asked if they were part of Volslav and he said no; but I figured you should know."

"Great, thanks." I hesitated. "If it's not directly related to Volslav, I can't spare the time right now, but I'll get one of the analysts to talk to him. Is he still in the holding cell?"

"Yep."

I eyed Reggie's grin. "What are you not telling me?"

"Weiss is officially an employee. We got all the paperwork and lie detector interviews done yesterday, and his security clearances should be coming through today."

Sudden fear gripped me. "You didn't let him leave the building, did you? Somebody's trying to kill him."

Reggie's grin widened. "Don't worry, he won't leave. In fact, he's still in the cell. He likes it there. It's all white and gray, and the furniture is bolted down so nobody can move it out of perfect alignment. When we were negotiating the terms of his employment contract, I had to agree to give him a gray and white office with the furniture bolted down, just like his cell. And I barely managed to get out of having a prison toilet installed in the corner of his new office."

Laughter seized me. "Don't tell me, let me guess: He likes it because he's the only one who uses it, so he knows it's clean."

"Got it in one." Reggie shrugged. "Honestly, I would have caved on the toilet if I had to. He's going to be a huge asset to the Department."

Some of the day's tension slipped out of my shoulders. "That's great. Thank God *something's* going well."

Ten minutes later, I leaned back on the couch in my office and slipped into the virtual reality network. Holt's avatar popped into existence beside me, and we strode down virtual corridors to the file repository. I waved a computer terminal into existence and Holt sat down at it, holding out his hand.

"Good hunting," he said.

"Thanks." I took his hand and faded into invisibility, feeling guilty.

I wasn't lying to him. Just not telling him the whole truth. He'd be okay with that. He'd said himself that he couldn't always tell me the whole truth; or any of it. I wasn't screwing him over.

I still felt guilty. As I slipped into the data tunnels of the internal network, I made a fervent wish that Stemp's family situation would be resolved soon so I could stop lying.

I hesitated, then decided this was my chance to

investigate Milena Draganova. Even if Dermott somehow found out, I'd still be able to say under the lie detector that she was connected to the Volslav investigation.

Easing through Sirius's firewalls, I dove into the endless sea of internet data.

My search was long and frustrating. I found a few sentences in English, but they only fuelled my suspicions without providing useful information. Dammit. I'd have to get Trish to search in other languages.

Painstakingly retracing my way back through my scattered markers, I slipped back through Sirius's firewalls with a breath of relief.

Next, police files. I dove in, extending questing tendrils in all directions.

Sometime later, a tug on my consciousness interrupted my absorption. Retracting from the files, I popped into visibility in the virtual file room and inquired, "You rang?"

Holt grinned, his eyes alight with predatory fire. "I found something."

"Me, too. You first."

"According to the courier slips, copy paper was delivered to the Harchman estate via overnight courier once a month. The most recent carton of copy paper was delivered on June 21. The one before that was May 21. April 23 before that..."

My heart gave a thump. "Today's July twentieth."

"Yep, and it's Friday. So that means they're due for a delivery on Monday. And *that* means somebody at the paper company is probably preparing the special box today." Holt's teeth flashed in a shark-like grin.

"That's great..." My elation ebbed. "But there probably isn't a special box this month. They'd have to be pretty stupid to keep shipping it now. The police will be right on top of it."

"Maybe, maybe not," Holt argued. "The case never hit the news. The charity was discreet about contacting the Harchman kids, and the police kept a lid on it."

"Except for the part where they swarmed all over GCPPL's office and warehouse," I pointed out. "But what the hell, it's worth a try. And if they have done up a special box, I found something that'll help us spot it. GCPPL puts a plastic strap on each carton of their paper, around the short dimension of the box. But on the special boxes, the strap went lengthwise."

Holt grinned. "Time to call the cops and swarm the warehouse again. Let's roll."

As we strode down the virtual corridor to the network portal, my steps slowed.

Holt shot an impatient glance over his shoulder. "You coming?"

"Yeah." I grimaced. "Just not looking forward to rejoining my physical body. When I'm this tired, it hurts like hell."

"Oh. Right." His face softened. "Hang back for just a minute. I'll go out first and get my hands on those pressure points. Maybe if I hit them before you exit, it won't be so bad."

Hope dawned. "Thanks."

Holt's avatar vanished through the portal, and I counted to sixty before following.

Agony seized me for a bare instant, then vanished.

I eased one eye open. When nothing bad happened, I opened the other.

"Okay?" Holt frowned down at me from where he stood behind the sofa, still gripping my head.

I let out a slow relieved breath. "Yeah. It was like a bomb went off inside my head; just a quick blast and then it was over."

"Well, isn't that sweet." Dermott's acidic voice from the doorway jerked me upright.

Shit, of course he'd show up just when it looked as though Holt was caressing my face while we stared into each other's eyes. His next words confirmed my guess.

"Just so you know, Holt: She fucks every guy she works with. You're just one in a long line."

"That's another complaint to the HR department from me," Holt snapped as he came around the sofa and planted himself in front of Dermott, feet wide and arms akimbo. "What you just said is not only inappropriate, it's also untrue, which makes it slander. You should file another complaint, too, Kelly. And maybe a lawsuit."

"What do you want?" I asked Dermott instead of replying.

"A status report." He sneered at Holt. "Since you're too busy making eyes at each other to file one."

"Anger management," I murmured for Holt's ears only, then raised my voice. "We're going to call the Calgary police and get them to search the warehouse of Maria Harchman's stationery company again. If there's another box of money, it'll likely be packed today and shipped this weekend."

"Money?" Dermott glared at me. "What stationery company?"

"It'll all make sense when you read our reports." I turned to Holt. "I'll get Trish and Rebecca searching the internet."

Holt nodded. "Okay, I'll make the call to the police-"

"No, you won't," Dermott interrupted.

CHAPTER 47

Holt and I exchanged a glance. His jaw was jutting, and I gave him a tiny headshake.

"Why aren't we calling the police?" I asked Dermott in my mildest tone.

"Because you two are going to go and search the warehouse yourselves." Dermott gave us a triumphant look. "It's up to me as DCO whether to involve the police, and I say... no."

"It's a factory and warehouse," Holt said, the words straining out between his teeth. "Thousands of tons of cartons. We have hitmen on the loose here, and our time is better spent-"

"Safe and sound in a warehouse full of paper where no hitman will ever think to look for you." Dermott smirked. "Hurry up, off you go. It'll do you two good to get your hands dirty for a change." He turned on his heel and strode out.

Holt started after him, fists clenched; but I grabbed his arm. "He's not worth it."

The muscles under my hand were hard as rock. "I'm thinking maybe he is," Holt gritted. "How many times in your life do you get to do something you want more than anything else in the world?"

"Oh, you mean 'go to prison for life'?"

Holt let out a wordless growl and shook off my grip. "Fine. So we'll search the fucking warehouse. What are Kane and Hellhound up to? Can they help?"

"Arnie's busy later this afternoon, but he might be able to come for a while. John will probably help; and I'll call Ian, too."

"Don't call that asshole! The last thing we need is his so-called 'help'."

I sighed. "No, he's okay. I didn't get a chance to tell you earlier, but I talked to him; and he had a reason for what he's been doing."

"What reason?" Holt demanded.

I lowered my voice. "MI6 got a tip that Stemp was working with Volslav."

Holt stared in silence for a moment before his jaw hardened. "Fucking Dermott was the tipster," he gritted. "Tell me I'm wrong."

"Ian didn't say." I changed the subject before he could explode. "We'd better get going. I'll call the guys, and then we can go and get Trish up to speed."

When we convened in front of the warehouse in Calgary a couple of hours later, my heart sank. It was a big building. My back ached at the mere thought of hefting around fifty-pound cartons all afternoon. Hell, I was sweating just from walking across the parking lot in the blazing sun.

"Where's Rand?" Holt demanded.

I shrugged. "Did you really expect him to show? I left him a voicemail; but you can bet he's sitting in some air-conditioned bar, swilling champagne and chatting up the cocktail waitresses. No way he'd come out here and get his hands dirty with the common folk." I cast an apologetic glance at Arnie and John. "No offense."

Kane chuckled. "None taken. What's the plan?"

"The original search warrant has expired, but the board of directors offered us full access. The operations manager should be meeting us-" I broke off as a man in a hard hat emerged from the building and headed purposefully toward us. "That'll be him. He'll walk us around so the workers know who we are and why we're here. After that we can ask them to move pallets with the forklift if necessary, but the COO made it pretty clear that we're on our own with individual cartons."

"Marvellous," Holt grumbled. "Well, we might as well start with the shipping department. If they're planning to send it out today, they've only got a few hours left."

"If they haven't shipped it already," I pointed out.

"Let's hope they have," Kane rejoined. "It's easy to check courier slips. If we find any suspicious addresses, we can intercept the shipment."

Two hours later, I was exactly as sweaty as I had expected to be, and we'd found exactly what I'd expected to find: Nothing. No suspicious courier slips, no unusually-strapped cartons; only pallets and pallets of paper, and increasingly hostile expressions on the faces of the staff when we asked for help.

As I eased the kinks out of my back, Arnie came over. "Hey, darlin'. Sorry to bail on ya, but I gotta head out. I'll give ya a call when I'm done, an' if you're still here I'll come back an' help."

"Thanks." I gave him a hug and kiss. "I really appreciate

that."

As he turned away, worry niggled at me. What if somebody was lying in wait outside, ready to shoot him as soon as he emerged?

"Wait," I blurted. "I'll walk out with you. I want to grab a granola bar from my car." I waved to Kane and Holt, and Arnie and I headed for the exit together. At the door, he stopped and turned to smile down at me. "Ya ain't foolin' me, darlin'. I can see your trigger finger twitchin'. How d'ya wanna do this?"

I grinned. "You know me too well. Let's go out together and split sideways."

"'Kay. On three. One... two... three."

We stepped outside, dodging in opposite directions. No bullets greeted us, but we did garner an odd look from an incoming employee. After a quick survey of the surrounding vehicles and roofs, we headed for the parking lot.

"Okay now?" he said softly as we arrived at his rental.

I gave him a smile. "All good. Thanks for indulging me."

"No problem. Nice to know ya got my back." He held out his arms, and I tucked myself into his embrace. After a couple of slow and increasingly heated kisses, he sighed and tilted his forehead down to mine. "Guess we'll hafta save it for later, darlin'. I gotta go."

"Okay. Be careful."

I watched until his car turned onto the street and disappeared into traffic, then returned to my own vehicle to scrounge a heat-softened granola bar from my glove box.

Munching as I returned to the building, I was almost at the door when I spotted two big shipping container trucks backed up to the loading docks.

As I hurried into the building, Kane came over, eyeing

my frown. "Did something happen with Arnie?"

"No, he's fine."   I pointed to the forklifts ferrying wrapped pallets into the containers. "When did those trucks get here? I didn't notice them when I went out."

"I don't know. We were farther back in the warehouse. But if they're loading into shipping containers, that cargo is likely going overseas for export." As Holt joined the huddle, Kane added, "If we're going to check them, we'd better do it soon. They're half loaded already."

"Right," Holt agreed. "I'll tell the foreman we might need to reshuffle some pallets. You two take the left container; I'll take the right."

A few minutes later I was peering between pallets when Kane's urgent voice came from the far end of the container. "Here!"

My exhaustion forgotten, I hurried back into the dimness.

Kane shone his phone's flashlight at the pallet. "The strapping is wrapped lengthwise on all of these."

I shot him a grin. "Nailed them!"

As we turned back toward the warehouse, I glimpsed movement.

The container doors.

Swinging shut.

"HEY!"   Kane and I sprinted toward the rapidly-diminishing light. "WE'RE STILL-"

The doors slammed with a deafening clang, plunging us into complete darkness.

CHAPTER 48

"HEY! WE'RE STILL IN HERE!" Kane flicked on his flashlight app and we charged to the end of the container. "HEY! OPEN THE DOORS!"

No response.

We redoubled our efforts, shouting and banging on the doors.

The truck's engine growled and the floor vibrated.

I yanked out my phone and beamed its flashlight across the doors, scanning wildly. My throat seized, but I managed a hoarse whisper.

"There's no inside latch."

"No," Kane agreed. He didn't sound surprised.

"*Fuck!*" Staggering as the truck began to move, I hit speed dial for Holt, then stared wide-eyed at my screen. "No signal! Have you got anything?"

Kane consulted his phone, then shook his head. "No. Let's try different places in the container."

Swaying with the movement of the truck, we covered every inch, even crawling on top of the pallets.

At last I slid to the floor, panting in the oppressive heat. "Nothing. I got one bar a couple of times when I was on top of the pallets, but the call wouldn't connect."

Kane sat down opposite me, the light of his phone

silvering the sweat that dripped down his face. "Same here. I didn't realize these containers blocked cell phone signals so effectively."

"*Shit!*" I shot a frantic glance around our prison, pallets fading into darkness outside the small circle of our phones' illumination. "We're trapped! There's no way out of here!"

"Of course there is," Kane said confidently. "We just have to wait until the truck stops moving and go out through the doors."

"How?" I demanded. "There's no inside latch!"

"Take a breath," Kane said. "Breath with me, nice and slow. In... two... three... four-"

"You lied! You promised you'd never lie to me, and you just *lied!*"

"I didn't lie," he said gently. "When the truck stops moving and our captors open the doors, we'll be ready. We'll get out."

"Right." I swallowed hard. "Right. Sorry. I'm just a little..." I gulped overheated air, sweat slicking my skin and soaking my clothes. Fresh terror rolled over me in a wave of prickly heat. "Shit, this thing's in the sun. It's getting hotter by the minute. There's nothing to drink. If those doors don't open pretty soon, it won't matter if they ever do."

Kane let out a long sigh and slumped back against a pallet. "I'm sorry."

"For what? This isn't your fault." I sank my head into my hands with a groan. "It's mine. Oh, God. I *knew* I was going to get you killed sooner or later, dammit-"

"Stop." The word snapped out in Kane's drill-sergeant tone, jerking my head up. "Aydan, stop," he said more gently. "We're in this together. No guilt, no apologies. I'm here because this is what I chose."

I flopped back against the pallet beside him. "Doesn't matter. You're going to get just as dead."

"I don't intend to die. Or to let you die," he said firmly. "Let's plan our tactics for when they open the door."

Sucking in a breath and easing it out slowly, I fought back my panic. "Okay. You need a weapon." I handed him my tranquilizer pistol.

"I won't be able to shoot without knocking us out, too." Shrugging, he added, "But I'll carry a couple of loose darts. If we end up in close-quarters combat, I might be able to inject an assailant." He ejected the magazine and took out a couple of darts.

"Good plan." I touched my Glock's holster. "I won't be shooting in here, either. The ricochet would be deadly. But if I can get a shot out the door when it opens, I'll take it."

Our options were few, so our planning session took only minutes. Dripping sweat, we stacked cartons of paper to create a maze of obstacles that would provide cover for us and confusion for our enemies.

"That's the best we can do," Kane said, wiping his forehead on the shoulder of his T-shirt.

We both dropped to sit on the floor again, leaning back against the nearest pallet and gasping in the heat.

When I regained my breath, I said, "I guess they got Holt, too. I've been listening for sirens, but... nothing. Just normal traffic noise." I sighed and dropped my head onto my knees.

"Stay alert," John said softly.

"Why?" I thumped the vibrating floor. "We're still moving. Nobody's coming in until we stop. If we stop. They might drive across Canada without ever opening this tin can." I gulped, my throat dry.

"Lean back," he advised. "These boxes of paper are heavy and dense, and they're still holding some coolness from the warehouse."

I pressed back against the cardboard, suspecting he was only imagining the cooling effect but willing to take any placebo I could get.

The vibration and engine noise blurred into a soporific drone as our prison got steadily hotter. I sagged, my panic fading into heat-drugged stupor.

When the truck slowed and turned, it took a moment for me to realize what was happening.

"Aydan!" John shook my shoulder gently. "I think we're at our destination. Get ready."

"I'm ready." My heart pounded.

The truck slowed and stopped, then rolled forward, starting and stopping several more times. We crouched behind our barrier of cartons, weapons in hand, tensing every time the vehicle slowed.

After more turns and a final stop, deafening clangs made me tighten my sweat-slicked grip on my Glock. The sounds didn't come from the door latches, though. After a moment, my brain caught up. The container was being disconnected from the truck trailer.

A heavy clank from above made me duck involuntarily, and a moment later my stomach lurched as the container swayed.

"They're craning it off," Kane whispered. "This is it."

The swaying seemed to go on forever, and nausea squirmed in my stomach. "I wouldn't recommend this ride for people who get motion-sick," I muttered, and Kane gave me a half-hearted smile.

A *thud-clank* and the blessed cessation of movement

indicated we were down. Legs cramping in my crouch, I focused on the doors.

Nothing happened.

Long minutes later, I gave in to the discomfort and rose, keeping watch on the doors while I stretched out my legs. Kane did the same.

"What's taking them?" I whispered.

Kane shrugged and shook his head.

Heavy metallic clunks and clangs surrounded us, some from above and others sounding as though they came from below.

I finally stated the obvious. "We're in a freight yard."

Kane nodded.

As if to confirm my guess, the top of our container boomed with the contact of something big and heavy.

Something about the size and weight of a shipping container.

My knees weakened, and I slid down the wall to sit on the floor. "Nobody's coming, are they? We're stacked in a pile of containers. They're just going to leave us to die in here, and then they'll pretend it was an accident."

Kane sighed. "It looks that way. Let's make some noise. The gantry cranes are likely remotely operated, but there might be workers or truckers walking around outside." He hammered on the side of the container. "HEY! HELP! TRAPPED IN A CONTAINER!"

I added my fists and voice to his. "HELP! IN HERE!"

After several minutes, my throat was raw and my fists were bruised. I kicked the wall of the container one last time. "Might as well stop," I said as Kane drew breath to shout again. "We can't keep it up. Let's do it every five or ten minutes. It's too hot to work this hard."

He laid a hand on the metal wall. "The steel isn't as hot now. We're not in the sun anymore."

"Because we're in the middle of a giant stack of containers headed who knows where." I sank to the floor and buried my sweaty head in my even sweatier hands. "We'll be dead before it even gets loaded on the next leg of its trip. People can only survive about three days without water."

"Maybe they'll check the container," Kane said without conviction. "Containers are supposed to be full and the loads are supposed to be balanced. Ours is off-balance with all the pallets along one side, and the weight won't match the cargo manifest."

"Yeah," I agreed wryly. "They obviously noticed that when they craned it off the truck." Attempting to exhale my fear on a long sigh, I checked my phone again. "Still no signal. Shocker."

Kane straightened decisively. "We might as well try checking for a signal in every part of the container again. Just in case."

"Good point. I'd hate to die of my own stupidity."

A few minutes of crawling, reaching, and scrambling made it clear that we wouldn't be phoning for help.

Flopping down to sit on the floor again, I turned off my phone, plunging us into darkness. "Might as well save the phone batteries. I have a little LED flashlight in my waist pouch if we need light."

We sat in silence for a few minutes. Clicks and rustlings surrounded us, and my skin crawled as I imagined mice, spiders, or even snakes emerging from the tiny recesses of the pallets to creep over us in the darkness.

This darkness, where I would spend the final hours of

my life.

My mounting panic erupted in a convulsive twitch and shudder. Snatching out my phone, I flicked it on and swept the light over the floor around us.

No creepy-crawlies. I let out a breath and delved into my waist pouch. Turning on my tiny flashlight, I switched the phone off again.

"Those sounds are just the container contracting because of the temperature change," John said.

I gave him a sheepish smile. "I know that. Until it's pitch dark and I start imagining critters."

He chuckled. "Understandable." He checked his watch. "Arnie should be realizing something has happened to us by now."

"Thank God he left early," I agreed. "I just hope they didn't get him, too."

"Unlikely. This seemed opportunistic to me."

I frowned. "What do you mean?"

"It couldn't have been planned in advance. Nobody knew we were going to the warehouse until we got there." He shrugged. "And nobody could have predicted that we'd go inside these containers. I think somebody saw us go in, realized we were going to find the special boxes, and acted on impulse."

"Yeah..." I agreed hesitantly. "Except... Dermott knew. Dermott went out of his way to make sure Holt and I went to GCPPL this afternoon. And with the two-hour drive to Calgary plus a break for lunch..." I shrugged. "Three hours is lots of time to make a plan and set things up."

Kane stared at me. "You think Dermott is behind this?"

I blew out a resigned breath. "Honestly? No. I can't see it. He's a prick, but I don't think he's a traitor or murderer.

It's just a coincidence."

"I don't believe in coincidences."

"Me, neither; but sometimes they happen anyway." I got up and kicked the side of the container and yelled some more before resuming my seat, pretending calm.

After a few minutes of silence, Kane said, "Well, I guess this is as good a time as any. Aydan, there's something I've been wanting to talk to you about."

My heart froze in my chest. Claustrophobia, impending death, and a relationship conversation. A trifecta of terror.

"Don't panic," he said hurriedly. "I only want to tell you that I'm thinking of moving back to Silverside. I was meeting a real estate agent after our dinner at Fiorenza's. I intended to tell you then, but..."

"I was freaked out, and I shut you down." I rolled my shoulders, trying to ease my tension. "Sorry; and thanks for not pushing me then. But... you just moved to Calgary last winter to be close to Daniel. What will you do about that?"

"I'm working on it. But I want to be sure you won't feel uncomfortable if I move back."

"Of course not." I gave him a smile, feeling something inside me ease. Until this moment, I hadn't realized how vulnerable I had felt with John and Arnie living so far away. The relief was... terrifying.

I jumped up and vented my panic with kicks to the side of the container and cries for help. It was surprisingly cathartic.

After a few minutes I felt calm enough to speak again. I shuffled my feet for a few seconds before broaching an embarrassing and increasingly urgent topic. "So, um... speaking of awkward conversations..."

John stiffened. "What?"

"I need to pee."

CHAPTER 49

"Oh." John relaxed with a smile and a shrug. "Well, pick your spot."

"Thank you so much for not saying we should save our pee in case we have to drink it later."

He let out a laugh-strangled snort. "If Arnie's still alive, we'll be found before we have to drink our own urine; and if he's captured or dead, no amount of urine will save us. And even if we did want to save our urine..."

"Which I don't," I clarified firmly.

"Agreed." He glanced around us, spreading his hands. "What would we save it in?"

I followed his gaze. Boxes of paper. Nothing else. Even my trusty waist pouch didn't contain any waterproof vessels large enough to hold more than an ounce or two.

"Good point," I agreed.

"Besides, urine carries salts and toxins out of your body. Drinking it puts them back in your system and concentrates them if you're not drinking anything else. You'd still lose fluid through sweat, and you'd be poisoning yourself faster by drinking what amounts to an increasingly concentrated salt solution."

Laying a hand on the still-hot wall of the container, I sighed. "We're not even going to make it three days in this oven, are we?"

John hesitated.

"No lies," I reminded him.

Reluctantly, he shook his head. "Likely not. We've lost a lot of fluid already." Running a hand over his glistening forehead, he wiped it on his sweat-darkened T-shirt. "We're still losing a lot; and we'll continue to, until the air cools tonight. And it's supposed to be hot again tomorrow."

Claustrophobic terror seized me again, but I drew in a slow breath and forced a breezy tone. "Oh, well. Pee now, worry later." I headed for the doors. "I'm going to aim for the door seal. Maybe somebody will notice if our container starts dripping."

Kane laughed. "I love the way you think." Turning away from the direction of my intended latrine, he added, "I'll give you some privacy. Fire away."

Easier said than done, but at least I didn't sprinkle my pants or sneakers. Thinking squeamishly about the stinkier things we'd have to deal with if we were trapped in here much longer, I gave a mental shrug. At least we had lots of paper.

Which reminded me...

"We should open those boxes," I said as I returned to Kane's small circle of light. "Just in case we don't get rescued in time..." My throat tried to close at the thought, but I pushed on. "Sooner or later *somebody's* going to open this container. If it's the intended recipient, it probably won't matter; but if anybody else opens the container, I want them to find a pile of money along with our dead bodies. At least then the investigation will continue."

John rose. "Good point."

My sturdy knife made short work of the pallet wrap and

the plastic strap on one of the cartons. John opened it and extracted a ream of paper, holding out to me. "Care to do the honours?"

I slit the wrapping and he peeled it back.

Bundles of money tumbled out.

Letting out a long breath, I sank down cross-legged beside the box. "Well, there we go. I guess they decided to ship the rest of the cash to Bulgaria."

"Have you got a pen? Let's document what we know."

"Good idea." I delved into my waist pouch.

As we began scribbling notes, I hesitated.

Should I tell John about Maria's mother, even though I'd withheld the information from Holt?

"What are you thinking?" John asked. "You have that intent look."

I sighed. "I'm just deciding how much to tell you. It's really hard when you're not with the Department anymore."

His lips tightened. "I understand."

"Or..." I studied his face. "I could tell you everything, and trust that you won't tell Holt or Dermott. But that's laying a big burden of secrecy on you."

His expression softened. "It's up to you. It's no burden to me, and you can trust me to be discreet. But I would never ask you to compromise security."

I smiled. "I know. If you're okay with it, I'd like to give you the whole picture."

Almost the whole picture. Except the parts that involved Stemp and Katya and Anna. That, I would never reveal.

"Thank you for your trust," John said softly. "I can't tell you how much that means to me."

Somehow I managed to hide my spasm of guilt.

Several hours later, my flashlight was fading and we had covered page after page with notes and diagrams while we tried to puzzle out who was running Volslav's show.

"Maria's mother is still the most likely," I said. "She must have faked her death. Or maybe she paid the deposits for the hits on us and then got killed. The hitmen wouldn't know until they tried to collect their final payment."

"It's a good theory," John agreed. "But I'm still bothered by Dermott's vendetta against you. And his desire for Stemp's job. People have killed for much less. And remember, not only was he the only one who knew we'd be at the warehouse; he also knew exactly what time you and Holt would be at Weiss's house in Drumheller. He could have arranged the drive-by shooting, too."

"Yeah, but he wouldn't be able to pass the annual lie detector review if he was bent," I argued.

"How many times have you passed a lie detector interview through misdirection and sheer luck?"

I barked out a short uncomfortable laugh. "Okay, I'll give you that." I slumped as another thought occurred to me. "But it might not even be misdirection. If Dermott truly believes the Department would be better off without Stemp and me, he'd be completely honest when he said he hadn't done anything to violate his oath or his loyalty to the Department."

"We'd better document that, too."

At last, Kane rose, stretching and rubbing his eyes. "I'm done. Now I need to sleep on it." He hesitated. "I guess it's my turn to water the door seal."

Feeling as though the sides of my throat had been glued together, I sucked my cheeks in a futile attempt to quench my raging thirst with what little spit I had left.

"Watch your step," I croaked. "There's a puddle. But at least your aim will be better than mine." I rubbed my arms. "I'm going to make a bed. It's finally getting chilly in here, and I don't want to sleep on the bare floor."

Kane disappeared into the gloom at the other end of the container while I busied myself constructing a low barrier out of cartons. When he returned I was crumpling paper into balls and tossing them into the enclosed space.

"Good idea." He smiled and joined in.

By the time we had filled the bed-sized void with springy balls of crumpled paper sandwiched between flattened cardboard boxes, I could barely control my claustrophobia.

This might be the last night of my life. Trapped in a pitch-dark steel prison with no escape.

Don't-panic-*don't-panic*...

John finished laying out a final layer of cardboard, then turned to me. "There. Try it."

I stepped onto the surrounding ring of cartons and rolled onto the makeshift mattress. Faking calm, I said, "Not bad. At least we won't be lying on the bare floor." Squirming over, I added, "Come to bed."

He rolled cautiously in beside me, sinking with a crunch as the cardboard and paper compressed.

"Whoa!" My sheet of cardboard slid down the slope, depositing me against Kane's hard body. From inches away, I gazed into his eyes, dilated black in the dimness. "Hi."

"Hi yourself," he said, his voice deeper than it had been a few minutes ago.

The heat of his body radiated into mine. A flush of

arousal drove back my discomfort.

"So, um..." My hoarse voice sounded too loud in the silence. "Is this another one of those situations where we have wild monkey sex because we're about to die?"

His velvet baritone tickled my ear. "Do you want it to be?"

"The dying part, no." I swallowed, my heart thumping so hard that he must be able to hear it. "The wild monkey sex... I could probably be persuaded."

"It's too bad there are no wild monkeys in here, then," he teased.

"You'll do." I caressed the hard heat of his sculpted pecs. "You'll definitely-"

His lips cut off the rest of my sentence.

Hunger exploded between us, driving our bodies together while our tongues tangled in a ravenous kiss. I ran greedy hands over his shoulders and chest, memorizing the mountains of muscle with my palms.

With a harsh indrawn breath, John pulled away to look into my eyes. "I don't have any condoms with me. Do you?"

I blinked away the blur of lust. "No. I wasn't expecting to get lucky today."

His smile was wry as he indicated our surroundings with a wave of his hand. "If you can call this 'lucky'."

"Yeah. So... what do you want to do? The last time we were about to die, you didn't feel comfortable having unprotected sex. And this time I don't see a convenient night table with somebody else's condoms in it."

He hesitated. "No..."

When he didn't say anything else, I prompted, "So... do you mean 'no, there's no night table', or just 'no'?"

John sighed. "I'm probably crazy, but... I'm afraid it's

'thanks, but no thanks'. I'm sorry."

"No problem." I kept my voice light. "Are you okay with cuddling?"

"Absolutely." He held out his arms and I snuggled into his embrace. Laying his cheek on top of my head, he added, "I'm not rejecting you. I want you more than you can imagine."

The hard ridge pressing against my thigh underscored his sincerity, but I resisted the urge to grind against it.

"Don't worry, I get it," I said instead. "It's not safe sex if you only use protection when it's convenient."

I could feel his grimace against the top of my head. "It's not the safety aspect. I know you and Arnie always use condoms, and I trust you. Last time, I didn't feel comfortable because I'd just..." He trailed off.

"Had sex with another woman. It's okay to say it."

His arms tightened around me. "A woman I didn't trust at all. But this time I know I have a clean bill of health. It's just that... if my last lovemaking with you has to be wallowing in a pile of garbage, covered with dirt and reeking of stale sweat... I just... can't." He shifted, easing his pelvis away from my thigh. "Well, obviously I can, but..."

"It's okay, I get it."

"Plus, I can't help thinking about what they'll find in the forensic examination if we die in here. Our decomposing bodies, pools of urine, semen and vaginal fluid on a pile of stained cardboard..."

"EWWW!" I pushed him away, laughing. "Okay, we're done here."

He chuckled. "Thanks for understanding."

"No problem." I settled into his arms again.

Silence fell.

"Aydan," he said against my hair. "If I do move back to Silverside, would you consider... dating me?"

I tried not to tense. "You mean... *exclusively*?" The word came out in a squeak as my throat closed with instinctive fear.

"No," he said quickly. "I would never ask you to change your relationship with Arnie. I just want to spend more casual time with you. No commitments, no expectations."

I drew a slow, calming breath. "So... you mean... just... do things together regularly? Like normal people?"

He nodded. "It wouldn't even have to be one-on-one. We could do things with a group of friends, too."

"Um... do you have a group of friends?"

"No. You?"

"No." I huffed out a laugh. "Pathetic."

"Understandable," John corrected. "You get isolated in this job."

"Yeah..." I said slowly. "And honestly? I want it that way. Anybody who gets close to me is at risk, and that's not acceptable."

"Understood. But I'm capable of dealing with the risks. And we've been seen together often enough that it can't really get any riskier for me."

I snorted and waved a hand at our prison. "Case in point."

"Yes. So... what do you say to some casual dates?"

The terrified voice in my head screamed '*Run like hell!*'

But it was time I stopped running from my fears.

I held my voice steady with all my will. "I think... I'd like to give it a try."

A heavy thump shook me out of a fitful doze. I scrabbled for my flashlight in the pitch darkness, cutting my hand on a cardboard edge.

"*Fuck!*" I hissed. "What's happening?"

"I think they lifted the container off us," Kane whispered.

Finally locating my flashlight, I flicked it on. We scrambled into position behind the cartons.

A deafening clang from above made me flinch. My empty stomach protested as our container rocked and swayed, and I swallowed nausea.

At last a clunk and stability indicated that we were down.

But where?

On a truck that would start a cross-country drive?

A man's voice called from outside. "Police! Anybody in the container?"

Kane and I exchanged a wide-eyed glance.

"Trap?" I hissed.

He gave me a tense shrug. "Stay down and cover me."

"Let me-"

"No. You've got the firearm."

Dammit, he was right. If I gave him my gun and he shot someone, he could end up in prison.

I nodded and hunkered down behind the cartons, gripping my Glock.

CHAPTER 50

"Help!" Kane shouted. "I'm in here! Open the container!" He banged on the side of the container. "Help! Open up!"

The other voice responded immediately. "Hang on, buddy, we'll have you out in a minute!"

As the latches grated and the doors swung open, I crouched lower and peered through the gap we'd left between the cartons. High-powered lights scoured the inside of the container, making me blink and squint.

Kane moved forward, only a silhouette with his hands held up and away from his body. The posture looked placating, but I knew his every movement would be carefully calculated, ready to launch into lethal action if necessary.

"Who are you?" he asked. "Where am I?"

"Police. You're at the Intermodal depot in Calgary."

Kane eased forward far enough to peer out of the container, then lowered his hands. "It's safe, Aydan. It's really the police."

Letting out a giant sigh of relief, I holstered my gun and slipped out from behind the cartons, my hands in the air just in case. When I stepped outside, the red and blue flashing lights felt like a celebration.

"Do you need medical attention?" the constable asked.

When we both shook our heads, he added, "How did this happen?"

"Long story," I said. "If it's okay with you, I'll just reach into my waist pouch and show you some ID...?" He nodded, and I showed him my Department ID. "How did you find us?" I asked. "Who called you?"

"I don't have any details. Dispatch just sent us over here with two container identification numbers and told us to check them for people trapped inside. We happened to be the closest unit."

"Well, thanks. I can't tell you how glad I am to be out of there. You said two containers. Did you find a man in the other one?"

"Yes." Holt's disgusted voice spoke before the constable could respond. "I'm here, too." He strode into the headlights, trailed by the other police officer. Holt addressed both of them. "Thanks for getting us out. This is one of our current investigations, so we'll take it from here."

"Actually..." I countered. "We'll need a security detail on this container. And protect the latch handles so we can check for fingerprints."

Holt's face lit up. "You found something?"

"You bet we did." I gave him a grin before turning back to our rescuing constable. "Were you wearing gloves when you opened the container?"

He stiffened. "No. Did I destroy evidence?"

"I don't know." As his shoulders slumped, I added, "Don't worry, there are likely dozens of prints. It would have been a long shot regardless."

"I'll make sure you get a copy of my prints for comparison."

"Thanks. Can you keep this sealed and guarded until we

can get a team here? We'll send for one right away."

Holt put in, "We need you to seal off the warehouse, too, until we can get a team over there. And find and detain some truck drivers."

The constables and I exchanged information while Holt called the Department. When everything had been arranged, the first constable angled his chin toward a hard-hatted man hovering outside our perimeter.

"That's the shift manager. He wants you to go up to the office and fill in an incident report before you leave."

Holt let out a martyred sigh. "The first of the fucking mountain of paperwork."

"As long as he gives me water, I'll fill out as much paperwork as he wants," I said as I raised my hand in thanks to the constable and headed for Hard Hat Man. "Let's go."

My phone had been vibrating steadily with incoming texts and voicemails, and I pulled it out as we walked. I wasn't surprised to see Arnie's number over and over. Without bothering to check the messages, I dialled him back.

He picked up on the first ring. "Aydan?"

"Hi. I'm sorry I missed all your calls and texts. We were locked in a shipping container and it blocked the signal."

His exhalation rattled the speaker. "Thank Christ! Fuck, darlin'." His voice was hoarser than usual, and his swallow carried clearly over the line. "Fuck," he repeated. "Am I ever glad to hear your voice."

"I'm glad to hear yours, too. We figured you'd be hot on our trail if you were still okay, but we didn't know..." Suddenly my voice was hoarse, too. "I'm really glad you're okay."

"I'm fine. An' I'm fuckin' glad Rand was here. He's the one that kicked things into gear."

Hard-Hat Man eyed me impatiently from the driver's seat of a half-ton crew cab as I trailed over, absorbed in the conversation. Kane and Holt were already seated in the back, so I got in the passenger side.

"Tell me what happened at your end," I said to Arnie as our driver pulled a U-turn. "How did you find us?"

"Sorry I didn't find ya sooner, but my meetin' ran long an' then I hadta head out right away. Cheatin' husband; an' it turned out tonight's the asshole's usual night to get some. I called an' got your voicemail, but when I hadn't heard back from ya in an hour, I called an' texted again. Gave ya another half-hour an' then headed back to the warehouse. Your car an' half-ton were in the lot, but nobody in the warehouse knew where ya were."

I snorted. "Or nobody was saying."

"Yeah. I called the Department, but couldn't get through to Dermott. Then I raised as much hell as I dared at the warehouse, but a guy that looks like me..." I could practically hear his shrug. "They were gonna call the cops, so I left. Figured I might wanna call the cops myself; an' gettin' arrested wasn't gonna help that any. But when I got back to the parkin' lot, Rand was there. He'd been tryin' to call ya, too."

"He actually showed up." I shook my head. "Will wonders never cease?"

"He wasn't there to help shift boxes. He'd been tryin' to call ya, an' gettin' nothin' but voicemail, too. He pulled some strings through MI6 an' got us in to search the warehouse. When we didn't find ya, I remembered seein' those trucks loadin' when I left. We checked with the duty manager, an' half the cargo that was s'posed to be on the trucks was still on the loadin' dock. He tracked down the container IDs.

Dunno what we woulda done if ya weren't in there."

I hugged the phone closer. "I knew you'd figure it out. You're brilliant."

"Thanks, darlin'; but it was Rand that got the cops involved an' got ya out."

"Well, I'll call and thank him, too; but without you we'd be dead. Where are you?"

"Still at the warehouse, but now that I know you an' Kane are okay, I'm gonna go back an' see if I can catch ol' Weasel-Dick in the act. What're you two gonna do?"

"Drink a bathtub full of water, eat half a cow..." A huge yawn swallowed the rest of my words.

"An' head to a hotel an' sleep for a coupla days," Arnie suggested.

"Long hot shower first, but after that I plan to be dead to the world for a while. I'll text you when we get to a hotel. You can meet us there."

"Nah, I really wanna nail this asshole tonight. Text me in the mornin', an' I might head over an' crash for a while if it's still before check-out time."

"We'll pay for a couple of nights," I decided. "I'm going to want to go back to the warehouse in the morning. You can sleep the day away in the room tomorrow if you want."

"Sounds good. See ya later." His voice softened. "Love ya, darlin'."

"I love you, too. Be careful."

"Told ya before, Careful's my middle name."

I laughed and hung up.

Switching to voicemail, I listened to the first two messages from Arnie and a jubilant one from Spider. I hit pause and twisted to smile at Kane behind me. "Spider and Linda have a new daughter. Isabella Rose, weighing in at seven pounds, six ounces; and nineteen inches long. Mother and baby are doing fine."

John's face softened, his smile touched with wistfulness. "That's wonderful."

I nodded, hiding my surge of fear at the thought of being responsible for a tiny helpless infant. A shudder shook me, and I concealed it by turning around to concentrate on my voicemail again.

There were more increasingly worried messages from Arnie, a triumphant 'Found something! Call me!' from Trish Belling, and three words from Ian: *'Please call me.'*

Trying to tamp down my annoyance at Ian's vagueness, I eyed my watch. Two-thirty in the morning, but he was probably still awake if he'd been at the warehouse with Arnie. I hit the callback button.

Our driver pulled up in front of a low building and parked. As I got out of the truck, Ian's tired voice spoke from my phone.

"Rand."

Not trusting the unsecured line, I said simply, "It's me. You called?"

"Can you talk?"

"No." Yawning, I trailed after Hard Hat Man.

"Are you safe?" Ian asked tensely.

"Yes. Thanks for helping."

"Glad to. When can we meet?"

"Can..." Another gargantuan yawn interrupted me, and I tried again. "Can it wait until tomorrow morning?"

"It's urgent."

"Life-threatening?"

He hesitated. "Probably not tonight, as long as nobody knows where you are."

"I'm going straight to a hotel and straight to bed. I'm not even going to call in."

"Good. Talk to me before you do. I'll text you a meeting location tomorrow morning. Ten AM. Come alone."

"Okay." I hung up.

The incident report forms were blessedly short, and Hard Hat Man gave us water. After guzzling two bottles I felt almost human, but my stomach was growling when we got into the taxi we'd called.

John and I got in the back, leaving the front passenger seat to Holt. Halfway to the warehouse, my fatigue-sodden brain disgorged an idea. I reached forward to tap Holt on the shoulder, motioning for John to lean in.

Lowering my voice, I said, "Let's grab our overnight stuff and leave our vehicles at the warehouse. The employees would know about the search for us, but they wouldn't know we'd been found. If our guy comes to work in the morning and sees our vehicles still there, he'll figure he's in the clear. We might catch him by surprise when we show up."

When we finally disembarked at a hotel, I eyed the all-night restaurant beside it with relief. "You guys go and check in if you want," I said to Holt and Kane. "I need food. Can I get you anything?"

Holt shook his head. "Meet you in the hotel restaurant at nine AM for a strategy session." He headed for the lobby without waiting for an answer.

"I'll come with you," Kane said to me. "I'm hungry, too."

As we turned toward the restaurant I shot him a look, but he wore a neutral expression. Either he hadn't intended any double entendre, or he was far better at hiding his feelings than I was.

Or maybe I just had sex on the brain. Not surprising,

considering what had been pressed against my thigh only a few hours ago.

Another sidelong glance at Kane did nothing to cool that memory. He had cleaned most of the dirt off his skin at the depot office, but he'd missed a few smudges. How could anyone make 'sweaty and dirty' look that good?

In short order we were settled at a table, and I forgot everything else as I tore into my breakfast burrito. "Thank God for all-night breakfast," I mumbled through a mouthful.

Kane smiled and nodded as he bit into his sandwich.

A few minutes later I finished the last bite and sagged back in my seat with a sigh. "That was amazing." Plucking at my dirty clothes, I added, "And the only things more amazing will be a hot shower, a soft bed, and clean clothes."

"Agreed." John hesitated. "Are we getting separate rooms?"

Taken aback, I stammered, "Um... sure. If that's what you want."

He studied me. "What do you want?"

"I, um... I guess I just assumed we'd..." My face heated. "Never mind. Whatever you want is fine."

"But what do you want?" he repeated.

I was too fucking tired for mind games. If he wanted his own room, I wasn't going to beg him to sleep with me.

"Separate rooms are fine. Let's go." I got up and headed for the door.

"Aydan." He hurried after me, taking my hand as I strode out. "Wait." He tugged me gently to a halt on the sidewalk, turning me to face him. "I wasn't rejecting you. I just didn't want to presume."

I shrugged, too worn out to get into it with him. "It's no big deal. Let's just call it a night. We can talk about it tomorrow if you want."

"Aydan..." John tipped his face to the sky as if seeking divine intervention, but when he faced me again he was smiling and his voice was warm. "Let me be clear: That was only a 'no' to rooting around in a pile of garbage next to pools of urine. It's a resounding 'yes' to just about any other scenario you could name." He spread his hands, his voice deepening. "I would love to share a room, and... other things... with you tonight. But only if it's what you want, too. I'm trying not to impose my wishes on you."

"Oh." I blinked, shifting mental gears with an effort. "So... you're saying I just mind-fucked myself again?"

John laughed and drew me into his arms. "This is why I want to date you."

"Seriously?" I pulled away to frown up at him. "You actually want to deal with this fucked-up-ness? Maybe I don't want to date you after all. You're obviously nuts."

He laughed again and put his arm around my shoulders, turning us toward the hotel and setting us in motion. "I'm not nuts. I want to date you because the only way to deal with these misunderstandings is to work through them, and come out the other side trusting each other a bit more. And we can only do that if we see each other more often, when we're not in crisis mode."

"Huh." I looped an arm around his hips. "You're 'way too smart for your own good."

"I don't care about my own good." His voice deepened. "But I care about all the good things we can do together."

"Mmm." I cuddled closer. "Tell me more."

"As soon as we get that room. Come on." He picked up the pace and we jogged the last few yards to the hotel.

CHAPTER 51

The check-in process seemed to take forever. John kept his arm around me, the heat of his body setting mine on fire. I slid my hand down the ridges of muscle along his backbone, fighting the temptation to move my hand lower. I sneaked a peek over my shoulder at the mirror behind us.

Goddamn, John had an amazing ass. Rock-hard and perfectly sculpted; just begging to be groped. Very soon I'd be digging my nails into it while he...

"...Aydan?"

I blinked out of my lust-induced reverie. "Uh?"

"What are the license numbers for the car and half-ton?" John repeated. "For the parking passes, after we pick up the vehicles tomorrow."

"Oh. Right." I turned a liar's smile on the desk clerk. "Sorry. Really tired."

At last the paperwork was complete and we headed for the elevator. When the doors closed behind us, I let my hand wander.

"Mmm." John's voice came out as deep as a growl. Bending to place his lips next to my ear, he murmured, "There's a security camera." His warm breath poured a shower of shivers down my spine. The shivers turned into sparks when he added a tiny nip to my earlobe.

"So you're saying..." I turned to face him, gliding my hand over his chest and making small fingertip-circles around his nipple through the T-shirt. "...I shouldn't rip your clothes off and bang you up against the wall right now?"

His eyes darkened as he caught my hand and pressed it against his chest. "Only if you can do it in the ten seconds before-"

A ding interrupted him.

"...the doors open," he finished as the elevator stopped and the doors parted.

"That might be a bit quick, even for me," I admitted as we stepped into the corridor.

As soon as the hotel room door closed behind us, we crashed together. Dropping my backpack, I pressed the length of my body against his muscular heat. His lips came down on mine and I moaned, opening to his kiss and clutching his mountainous shoulders. Liquid heat bloomed between my legs as I ground against the hardness in his jeans.

Pulling away, he gasped, "Shower first."

"Why?" I reclaimed his lips. "We're only going to get sweatier."

"Shower," he growled, his hands clamping on my ass as he body-pushed me into the bathroom, still kissing me.

"Mm, why didn't you-" My words short-circuited as he stripped off his T-shirt. "...say so," I mumbled, nibbling a luscious slab of salt-seasoned shoulder. "God, you taste good."

John groaned, fisting a hand in my hair and planting hot kisses across my throat and down my neck. "Clothes." His grip shifted to my T-shirt. "Off." He pulled it over my head.

I arched my back, letting my lacy bra do the talking.

"God, Aydan..." He cupped my breasts, burying his face in my cleavage. "So sexy." One hand glided around to my back, deftly unfastening hooks. As the bra released he pushed it up and drew my nipple into his mouth. My breath stuttered as he sucked, flaring hot sensation through me with teeth and tongue.

Starved for more, I attacked the button of his jeans with lust-trembling hands and slid the zipper down. Dipping inside his briefs, I wrapped my hand around velvet steel.

He gasped, pulling me with him as he backed toward the walk-in shower. "Shower." He reached in and twisted the controls, his gaze never leaving me. "Naked." Pushing the bra straps down my arms, he tossed it aside and paused as if drinking me in. "Short words," he mumbled. "All I can manage. This is what you do to me."

He unfastened my jeans and crouched to work them down my legs, delivering a nuzzle and nip to my inner thigh that sent a shock of need through me.

"Shower first," I panted, my knees trembling as he nibbled higher.

John stood, his eyes glazed, and I shoved off my jeans and underwear. He let out an inarticulate growl as he did the same.

His erection sprang free, and lust flooded my belly at the sight. Wide shoulders, biceps like rocks, corrugated abs, perfect V-shaped torso arrowing down to muscular thighs and that magnificent-

Pulling me against him, he backed into the shower, then jerked with a gasp as the water hit him. "Cold!" He adjusted the temperature and then stepped us backward under the warm spray.

Devouring his mouth, I pressed against him, catching my

breath at the sensuous slide of skin against slick skin. Turning us, I backed up against the shower wall and hooked one leg behind his thighs to pull him closer.

John hissed out a breath, looping his hands under my ass to boost me higher. On one tiptoe, I tightened my other leg's grip, grinding against his erection. My breath stalled as a tilt of my hips notched him just... *there...*

"Condom," he growled. "In my bag." He pulled away and practically dove out of the shower for the backpack he'd dropped by the door.

In seconds he was back, rolling on the condom and watching me with dilated eyes. I cupped my breasts and offered them to him.

"Touch yourself." His baritone was gravelly with hunger.

I shuddered as that low note hit my ears and shot straight down between my legs.

"Like this?" My voice was husky with desire as I fondled my breasts, watching him watch me. My vision blurred with the shocks of pleasure as I tugged and rolled my nipples between my fingertips. "Or... like this?" I slid a hand down my body, gasping as I drew a finger through the slippery heat.

"Yes." His eyes were half-closed, his chest rising and falling rapidly as his erection strained the condom. "Yes."

I sucked in an uneven breath. "Need you." When he didn't move, my voice rose in a desperate entreaty. "Please. *Now!*"

He let out a growl and charged, gripping my ass and lifting me off the floor as he pinned me against the wall. Wrapping my legs around his waist, I opened for the deep hard plunge I expected.

It didn't come.

Instead, John gazed into my eyes, barely entering me. I squirmed, whimpering an abject plea.

Inch by slow inch, he pressed in as I writhed with pleasure and need.

"More," I gasped. "*Please!*"

At last he filled me, so big and hard and hot that I clenched around him, on the verge of orgasm already.

"Aydan..." His words strained out between gritted teeth. "I won't last..."

"You don't have to." I tightened my legs around him. "*Now!*"

He rocked into a slow deliberate rhythm. Each stroke pumped more sensation into my body, the tide rising higher and hotter. Every nerve blazed to life.

"Harder!" I bit down on his shoulder, my nails scoring his back.

He shifted his grip and I rolled my hips to meet him as he thrust into me again and again.

The lightning-storm gathered, coiling my muscles into the glorious tension before release.

Musk-spiced salt on my lips, rigid muscle under my hands, hot-hard-deep-

Right-there-

Electric orgasm crackled through my body, yanking my spine into an arch. "*God-John-NOW-HARD!*"

My mind shattered as he slammed into me, driving me higher with every thrust. His body was granite under my greedy hands, hot steel between my legs. Wordless cries tore from my throat as wave after wave shook me, catapulting me beyond thought.

John went rigid, roaring his release as he strained into me.

Ecstasy swept me away, the bounds of my body dissolving in an inferno of sensation.

At last I floated back to awareness.

Hot slick muscle under my palms.

Our ragged panting.

The splash of the shower.

John shifted, triggering another orgasm. Gasping and shuddering, I clung to him, arms locked around his shoulders and legs around his hips.

"Good God," he murmured in my ear. I shivered at the deep vibration, the stimulus sending another clench through my body. John twitched and sucked in a breath.

"Sorry," I croaked, and unwrapped my legs.

"Never apologize for blowing my mind," he growled, steadying me as my feet slithered on the wet tile. "That was... just..." He let out a breath, dropping his forehead to my shoulder. "Wow."

I leaned into him, my rubbery legs barely holding me. "'Way beyond 'wow'. I hope I didn't hurt your back."

He chuckled. "Are you referring to the scratches? Or the bites? Or the spur marks from your heels? All of which were intensely pleasurable, by the way."

"Oh." I sidestepped and peered at his back with a wince. "I didn't quite draw blood, but I definitely marked my territory. Sor-"

John laid a fingertip against my lips. "Do *not* apologize." He kissed me unhurriedly. "You're amazing." He drew away far enough to look into my eyes. "And exhausted, unless I miss my guess. Let's wash up and get to bed."

"Good plan," I agreed as my eyelids suddenly drooped.

The remainder of our shower blurred into languid kisses and soapy sensuous stroking. By the time we plodded out of the bathroom, my muscles felt like wet noodles.

"What time do you want to get up?" John asked as I fell into the nearest of the two beds.

I squinted at the clock. "God, nearly four-thirty," I mumbled, my eyes already closing. "Make it a quarter to nine."

"Done." He set his phone's alarm, then slipped under the sheets. He held out his arms, and I cuddled into his embrace.

As his body softened into sleep, I eased away.

He stiffened. "Are you all right?"

"Fine."

In the dim glow of the bedside clock, I could see his frown.

I added, "Sorry, I just need..." I made an awkward gesture toward my side of the bed. "...space. To sleep. Sorry."

He smiled. "It's all right, I remembered that. No need to apologize."

"Thanks." I kissed him. "Good night."

As I settled on the blissfully cool sheets, the memory of Ian's voice saying '*urgent*' sent a shiver of misgiving down my spine. And his momentary hesitation when I asked if it was life or death...

Maybe I should go and...

The ring of my burner phone jerked me awake. Eyes half-closed, I dragged myself out of bed and fumbled the phone out of my waist pouch. "Hello?"

Moonbeam's usually-gentle voice held an urgent edge. "Do you know the whereabouts of Cosmic River Stone?"

Suddenly I was wide awake, my heart thumping. "No. I'm in Calgary. What's happening?"

"He has missed a check-in."

Tension seized my shoulders. "When?"

"Over an hour ago."

"Shit." I squinted at the bedside clock.

Eight AM. Shit, shit, *shit!*

Somehow I kept my voice calm. "Let me see what I can find out. I'll call you back as soon as I can."

"Thank you, dear." I knew how concerned she was when she hung up without offering the Earth Spirit's blessing.

Dammit. Stemp wouldn't miss a check-in. This was bad.

I yanked out my personal cell phone and hit the speed dial for Lola.

"Aydan, what's wrong?" Kane's sleep-gravelled baritone interrupted my worrying.

I held up an 'in-a-minute' finger to Kane as Lola's cheery voice spoke in my ear. "Good morning, Aydan! How are you this beautiful day?"

Her buoyancy was such a contrast to my mood that I was momentarily struck dumb. Fortunately, it gave me an instant to recall that not everyone's life was a shit-show.

Faking an upbeat tone, I replied, "Just thought I'd check in with the brand-new great-grandmother. Congratulations!"

A delighted laugh bubbled out of the speaker. "Thanks, honey! I'm tickled pink! Literally, pink, since it's a girl. Isabella Rose." She sighed. "What a lovely name for such a beautiful little girl. Oh, Aydan, she's such a perfect little cherub!"

I forced a smile into my voice. "I'm so happy for you, and for Spider and Linda, too. I haven't called them yet, but

I will." Making a mental note to do that and hoping I wouldn't forget, I added, "I won't keep you, but I do have a quick question. I tried to call Charles this morning, but I didn't get an answer. Do you know if he's home?"

"Oh, heavens, I don't know. I was at the hospital until late last evening, and I haven't checked in with CRAPS yet this morning. Bud would know, though. Do you have his number?"

"Could you give it to me, please?"

I scribbled it down and said, "Thanks, I'll give him a call." Hoping to keep her focused on happy thoughts, I injected a teasing note into my voice. "Don't wear out that baby with all your cuddling. She has to last quite a few decades, you know."

Lola laughed. "That's the best thing about babies. Grandmas can't cuddle them too much."

I managed a chuckle. "Well, then, knock yourself out. 'Bye for now."

I tapped in Bud's number next. When he answered, I said, "Good morning, Bud, it's Aydan Kelly calling. I hope I didn't wake you."

"Heck, no, Miss Kelly." He drew a wheezy breath. "I'm always up with the birds."

"Must be your army training," I teased.

"Army, and farming. Six AM is sleeping in." He chuckled, but it turned into a coughing fit. After a few worrisome moments he mastered it and croaked, "Excuse me."

"Of course, and I won't make you talk too much. I just wanted to ask if you'd seen Charles this morning."

"No, he left..." He drew a wheezy breath. "With a friend..." Wheeze. "...last evening."

The back of my neck prickled. "What friend?"

"I don't rightly know." Wheeze. "Anthony said..." Wheeze. "Charlie and his friend..." Wheeze. "...came out of Charlie's house..." Wheeze. "...around eleven PM."

I fought to hide my anxiety. "Did Charles look okay?"

Obviously I hadn't fooled Bud. Tension sprang into his voice, his speech still punctuated by gasps for breath. "Anthony said they had... a few pleasant words... and went on their way. Why, what's wrong?"

"It's probably nothing to worry about. I tried to call him this morning and couldn't raise him, that's all."

I thumped my forehead. Shit, I'd better actually try calling Stemp. Maybe something was wrong with Moonbeam's phone. We might be worrying needlessly.

My foolish hope evaporated when Bud spoke again. "Now that you mention it... something's not right. Charlie would have... given me the signal... if he was leaving. But his blinds are still down."

Forcing a casual tone, I replied, "Well, maybe time got away from him last night. He'll likely be back later today."

Bud's voice was grim. "Time doesn't get away... from Charlie. He's the most punctual man... I ever met. I'm going over there... and if he's not there... and there's no note... I'm calling the police."

I sighed. "I guess there's no point in telling you to be careful, or take someone with you?"

"I'll take someone with me." Even though his voice was shaky with age and illness, it was hard as flint. "My friend Mr. Remington. Loaded with double-aught buck."

CHAPTER 52

Squeezing my eyes shut in a silent prayer for Bud's safety, I said, "Be careful. Call me back at this number and let me know what you find. If I don't hear from you in fifteen minutes, I'll call the police."

"Thanks, Miss Kelly. You sit tight now. 'Bye."

As soon as I disconnected from Bud, I punched in Stemp's number. Pacing back and forth while it rang, I willed him to answer.

Come on. Pick up.

I imagined his precise voice saying 'Thank you for your concern; however, it is unwarranted.'

The phone rang a final time before flipping to voicemail.

"Shit!" I punched disconnect, then rooted through my waist pouch for the list of burner numbers Stemp had given me. As I tapped in the first number, I muttered, "Pick up, dammit. Come on..."

After the twelfth ring, I gave up and switched to the next number. Twelve rings later, I switched to the final one.

"Answer your fucking phone," I gritted.

Eighteen rings later, the vibration of an incoming call made me jerk the phone away from my ear to check the call display.

Stemp's home number.

Stomach clenching, I hit Talk and snapped, "Hello?"

"Bud here." He sounded even more out of breath than usual. "At Charlie's. Looks like... there was... a fight in... the back entry. Called the police."

I did my best to hide my emotions, but even I could hear the defeat in my voice. "Thanks, Bud. Please keep me posted."

"I will... Miss Kelly. You take... care now."

"You, too. 'Bye."

After disconnecting, I pulled out a secured phone and hit the speed dial. When Megan answered, I identified myself and asked to speak to Dermott.

"I'm sorry, he doesn't come in on weekends."

"Shit, I forgot it's Saturday. It's urgent, though. Could you please connect me to his home number?"

"Calling now."

Several long moments later, Megan came back on the line, sounding strained. "I'm putting you through now, Agent Kelly. Please go ahead."

"What the fuck?" Dermott's snarl issued from the speaker before I could open my mouth. "You better have a damn good reason for calling this fucking early on a Saturday!"

Somehow I managed not to snap back at him. "Stemp's been abducted." I explained the circumstances.

"So he walked out under his own power, just a few hours ago." Scorn dripped from Dermott's voice. "Doesn't sound like abduction to me. Sounds more like a crooked bastard skipping town to avoid the NSIRA inquiry. Hell, he probably even staged those assassination attempts on himself, to make it more convincing when he finally disappeared."

"He was abducted! His neighbour, Bud Weems, found

evidence of a struggle!"

Dermott snorted. "Staged, too. And Weems is just an old fart with too much time on his hands and a desperate need to feel relevant."

"Bud is a decorated war veteran," I hissed. "He put his life on the line for our country, and he's still ready to sacrifice it if necessary. He's a better man than you'll ever be."

"I don't give a shit what he did sixty fucking years ago," Dermott barked. "Right now he's an old fart making a mountain out of a molehill!"

"He's not! We need to get a team over to Stemp's right away!"

"What team? You and Holt are the only agents based in Silverside. Where the hell are you, anyway?"

"Calgary. Where you sent us." I bit my tongue to hold back inflammatory words. "And I meant, send a forensic team to Stemp's."

"Let the police decide if it's worth following up. No point in sending a forensic team if there's no crime scene in the first place."

Rage surged up and straight out my mouth. "Yeah, you'll just ignore the whole damn thing, and hope he dies so you can take his job! I don't know why the hell I thought you'd actually do something!"

Dermott's voice was suddenly quiet. "What the hell is that supposed to mean?"

With a violent sweep of my arm, I flung the phone at the wall. It exploded into plastic shrapnel, and I sank down onto the edge of the bed and dropped my head into my hands.

"Aydan?" Kane's hand made a warm circle on my back.

"Stemp's been abducted, and Dermott won't do anything about it." My words came out devoid of hope. "Stemp walked past the CRAPS patrol last night; hasn't been seen since; there's evidence of a fight in his house; and he's not answering any of his phones. And he missed a scheduled call with Moonbeam this morning. He'd never do that."

"He might," Kane countered. "If something more pressing came up. He's not the most... considerate person in the world."

"He'd *never* worry his parents like that," I snapped.

Kane blinked. "All right. You obviously know him better than I do." He hesitated. "Is that why you have several phone numbers for him? Is he... are you...?"

"For chrissake!" I glared at him. "Why does everybody think I'm screwing him? We're *friends*, for fucksakes! Not even friends; we don't talk or do anything outside of work. I just... he doesn't *have* anybody else!"

Kane came around the bed and sat down next to me, putting an arm around my shoulders. "Only you. Always looking out for everyone." He pressed his lips to my temple. "I didn't mean to upset you. I'm sorry."

"It's okay." I sighed and leaned into him. "Apparently that's where everybody's mind goes. Lola thinks I'm having an affair with him, too. It gets annoying, but I didn't mean to take it out on you. Sorry."

"Why would Lola think you're involved with Stemp?"

"Moonbeam invited me over to Stemp's place for dinner a couple of times. And..." I gave him a wry grimace. "Lola is Lola."

Kane chuckled. "That's true." Sobering, he added, "How can I help?"

"I don't think you can; but thanks. Dermott won't authorize a forensic team from the Department, but I'm going to call Peters and Birch at the Drumheller RCMP so they know Bud's not just going off half-cocked. They can handle it until I can get back to Silverside."

"Will you get in trouble for contacting the RCMP? That's the Director's decision; and Dermott is looking for any excuse to accuse you of interfering in police cases for your own personal reasons."

"I don't give a shit!" I snapped. "We're talking about Stemp's life here. Dermott can kiss my lily-white ass!"

John made a 'calm-down' gesture. "I didn't mean to suggest-"

I interrupted, "It's okay, I know you're just looking out for me, so thanks; but there's really no other choice. You'd do the same, wouldn't you?"

He sighed. "Yes."

"Thought so. So... we need to meet Holt at nine; and investigate the warehouse; and I have to meet Ian at ten. It'll take a while for the police to get a forensic team out to Stemp's, if they even bother; but I hope I can get back there this afternoon and take over."

"I could go back to Silverside now. I can't interfere with the police investigation, but I can talk to the CRAPS members and keep you updated. And I might be able to have a social chat with Peters or Birch if either of them is on the scene. They might give me an inside track."

"That would be great. Thanks."

Kane hesitated. "Have you considered taking this up the chain of command?"

"I'll have to talk it over with Holt. Dermott pushes every single one of my buttons, so it's hard to tell whether I'm overreacting."

"You're not," Kane said firmly. "And speaking of Holt..." He glanced at the clock. "We're due at the restaurant."

"Right, I'll call the RCMP right away. And I'll text Arnie. He'll be ready to sleep by now." I clenched a fist in my hair and tugged. "Shit, and I have to call Trish. She left me a message yesterday; plus I want her to get the team to start digging for anything she can find on Stemp. You go down and meet Holt; I'll be there as soon as I can."

He departed and I made my calls, making the final one to Megan from a secured phone.

"Hi, it's Aydan. Do you know if Trish Belling is working today?"

"Let me check." After a short wait she returned to the line. "Since her promotion, she's only scheduled for nine to five Monday to Friday; but she's in today anyway. I'll put you through."

When Trish picked up, I said, "Hi Trish, Aydan here. Sorry I couldn't get back to you yesterday. I had a situation."

"No problem. So, I found information! First, I interviewed Rupert Weiss and tracked down the names he'd mentioned; and one of them was connected to Milena Georgieva Draganova. Milena Draganova is Maria Harchman's mom, and Maria's dad was a Bulgarian crime boss. He was killed when Maria was fourteen. Apparently that's when Milena took over the crime business, and brought Maria in when she came of age. I haven't found hard evidence yet, but my gut feeling is that Maria's mom was a silent partner or advisor for Volslav. It also looks as though she hired a bunch of hits just before she died. One here in Bulgaria..." She paused dramatically, and when she spoke again, her voice was smug. "...and four in Canada."

I did a fist pump. "Got her! Do we know who was hired to do the hits?"

"No; but Milena's bank account showed several big

withdrawals around the time when the hits were taken out."

My glee vanished. "Shit. I bet I know where one of the hitmen was last night." I told her about Stemp's disappearance.

Tension strained her voice. "Crap! I'll call in the team and we'll start searching for any CCTV footage or anything else that might help find Director Stemp. One more thing about Milena Draganova... She was killed last week, but her bank account's still active. There are regular cash deposits that probably came from the stationery company, but there was a cash withdrawal after Milena died. Same amount as the previous withdrawals. I bet that was the final payment for when they thought John Kane had been killed. Half up front; half on completion."

"Right, but who made the withdrawal if Milena was already dead? Did she fake her death?"

"I wondered that, too; but I can't read the autopsy report because Rebecca doesn't speak Bulgarian. And I haven't had time to trace it yet. I'll keep digging."

When I joined Kane and Holt in the restaurant, Holt didn't waste time on small talk. "Where do you want to start at the warehouse?" he asked as I sat down.

We strategized while we ate, and I brought him up to speed on Trish's news and Stemp's apparent abduction.

"Fuck." Holt rubbed his forehead wearily. "You know he's probably dead, right?"

My heart plummeted, but I argued, "Maybe not. Why would they bother to walk him out of the house if they wanted him dead? It would be a whole lot easier to just kill him inside."

"Maybe he wasn't abducted at all," Kane pointed out. "The CRAPS patrol said they had a pleasant conversation. Surely the patrollers would have noticed if Stemp was injured or distressed."

"Stemp would pretend everything was fine, just to keep the CRAPS members safe." My heart squeezed at the thought of Stemp, protecting the vulnerable seniors with cool disregard for his own safety. He would have known he had no hope. Nobody to sound the alarm; nobody to rescue him.

I burst out, "We've got to get back there!"

Holt frowned. "Maybe Kane's right, and Stemp just left with a friend."

"He didn't," I snapped. "If he had, he would have signalled Bud." I didn't add that as far as I knew, Stemp didn't have any friends. God, now I felt even worse.

"Can you handle the warehouse and question the truck drivers?" I asked Holt. "I promised to meet Ian in..." I consulted my watch. "...half an hour... but I want to go back to Silverside right afterward."

"You're meeting Rand? What the hell does he want?" Holt demanded.

"No idea; but he says it's urgent."

Holt snorted. "Which means he's bored and yanking your chain."

"No, this time I believe him."

Holt raised a skeptical eyebrow, but asked, "Do you want me to come with you?"

"No, it's more important for you to get to the warehouse-" I broke off as my phone vibrated with an incoming text. "That'll be Ian." Checking the message, I let out a breath of relief. "Good, our meeting location is only fifteen minutes away." I stuffed the last bite of toast in my mouth and mumbled around it, "I need to get going. We good?"

Holt nodded. "Let's do a text check-in every half hour."

"Okay. John; you, too."

We all updated our phone numbers, and Kane and I headed for the exit. As we reached the door, my phone vibrated again.

I checked the text and relaxed. "It's Arnie. He's waiting for us..." We exited the restaurant and I waved at the bulky figure slouched in one of the lobby chairs. "...in the lobby."

Hellhound rose as we approached, and I hurried over to hug him. Worriedly studying his grayish pallor and the lines of fatigue scoring his face, I exclaimed, "Good God, when was the last time you slept?"

"Dunno." He attempted a smile, hesitating as if doing the math. "Guess I slept a few hours, a coupla nights ago."

Wrapping an arm around him, I propelled him toward the elevator. "You're going straight to bed."

He chuckled tiredly as the three of us stepped inside. "That an order?"

"You'd better believe it."

"Did you catch the cheating husband?" Kane asked.

Hellhound grinned. "Yep. Got some real nice pics. Don't think ol' Weasel-Dick's gonna wanna put 'em in the fam'ly album, though." He sobered. "Glad it's done. I hate infidelity cases."

The elevator opened at our floor, and we headed for our room.

Inside, I gave Arnie a rapid rundown of events to date. "...and now I have to get going," I finished. "Promise me you'll sleep as long as you can, and text me when you're up and ready to leave the room. John and Greg and I are doing half-hour check-ins, and I'd like you to do the same after you wake up."

"I promise, darlin'." He gave me a hug and kiss, and tossed a casual salute to Kane. "Be safe, both a' ya."

In the hallway, Kane turned to me, frowning. "Are you sure you don't want backup for your meeting with Rand?"

"No, he said to come alone. I trust him; and the sooner you get to Silverside to keep an eye on things, the happier I'll be." I slid my arms around him. "But be careful. There's still at least one hitman on the job."

"I will. You be careful, too." He lowered his lips to mine for a slow gentle kiss.

When I walked into the restaurant at Ian's hotel, he rose from his table with his usual flirtatious 'good morning'; but it seemed forced. As soon as we were seated, he leaned in and lowered his voice.

"You were right. Brent Dermott is crooked."

I frowned. "I didn't say he was crooked."

"You said he wanted you and Stemp dead."

"I meant-"

"Look at this," he interrupted, and took out his smartphone. After cueing up a video, he handed the phone to me.

I touched the play button and studied the footage of Dermott at a small table, leaning forward in a tête-à-tête with an attractive blonde over coffee. "This is the Greenhorn Café. When was this, and who's he with?"

"I haven't the foggiest notion who she is; and if you don't recognize her, either, it means your Department is in serious trouble." Fear clenched my guts as he went on, "I recorded this yesterday around three o'clock. Read their lips."

"I don't know how to lip-read. What are they saying?"

Ian reclaimed his phone and restarted the video, frowning in concentration. "She says, 'Did you release the prisoner'; and he says, 'Yeah'. Then she says, 'Is Kelly out of the way'; and he says, 'Yeah. Holt's becoming a problem, too. I sent them both down to'..." Ian paused the video. "I can't catch the next word."

"GCPPL," I supplied, my heart thumping. "Glory Canadian Paper Products Limited. The warehouse."

"Ah, of course." He returned his attention to the screen. "...'down to GCPPL. That'll fix them. And it'll keep them away from Stemp.'"

Ian shot me a look. "So, do you still believe Dermott is on your side?"

CHAPTER 53

"Shit! Why didn't you tell me this earlier?" I demanded.

"I tried to call you immediately, but only got your voicemail. Then I drove down to Calgary and initiated a search for you. When I did finally speak to you last night, I told you it was urgent." Ian raised a supercilious eyebrow. "I don't know what that word means to you, but in the Queen's English, it means-"

"Sorry, you're right; it's not your fault." My throat tightened, and I held my voice level. "I'm just upset because they got Stemp last night."

Ian's eyes widened. "Dead?"

"Abducted. I hope he's not dead."

"I'm so sorry, Storm. If I had realized, I would have insisted on meeting you last night."

"It's okay. It wouldn't have changed anything. We still wouldn't have known Stemp was missing until this morning." Fury boiled up like lava in my belly. "Goddammit, I want to kill Dermott with my bare hands! But at least now we can question him. Maybe find a place to start looking for Stemp." I swallowed hard and faced the bitter reality. "But if it was a hit, Stemp was dead before we even got out of the shipping container last night."

Ian grimaced agreement.

I sighed. "Anyway, thank you for doing this, and for rescuing us last night. Do they say anything else in the recording?"

"Nothing relevant. She thanks him for his loyalty, blah, blah."

"Can you text me the video right now?"

"To what number?"

I recited it to him, and a moment later one of my secured phones vibrated as the file arrived.

As soon as I had the video, I hit speed dial. Conscious of our public location, I put my finger in my ear as though trying to block out the restaurant noise. With both elbows bracketing my head and my face turned down to my lap, nobody should be able to hear or lip-read me.

When Megan answered, I said, "Please connect me with General Briggs. It's an emergency. No matter what he's doing, this is more important."

Tension flared into her voice. "Right away. Please hold." Long minutes later, she came back on the line. "Please go ahead."

"Briggs here." His clipped words evoked a memory of his steady gaze and effortless authority, and the tension in my shoulders eased.

"It's Aydan Kelly," I said. "I have a video of Brent Dermott discussing what appears to be confidential information with a woman I don't recognize, in a public place. If you don't recognize her either, I think we should detain and question Dermott. I want to send the video to you directly because I don't know if there's been a security breach."

"Send it to this number." He recited it, and I forwarded the video.

"I don't lip-read, so I don't know exactly what was said," I cautioned. "Agent Rand from MI6 translated it for me."

"What was his translation?"

"Hold on, I'll let you speak to him." I put my hand over the microphone pickup as I held the phone out to Ian, lowering my voice. "It's General Briggs. You can trust him."

Ian shot me a dubious look, but accepted the phone and said, "Rand here." After Ian had repeated his lip-reading, he said, "I'll give you back to her", and returned the phone to me.

"Aydan here," I said. "What do you think?"

"I personally know everyone in the Department who is authorized for that level of disclosure, and I don't recognize this woman. I'll have Dermott detained immediately; and I'll send this video to an analyst I trust, to double-check the lip-reading and start a facial recognition search on the woman. Where are you?"

"In Calgary, but I'm leaving for Silverside right away. I'll be there in two hours. Did you know that Charles Stemp was abducted last night around eleven o'clock?"

A quiet word that might have been an expletive preceded Briggs's reply. "No. Dermott didn't report that."

"I only found out an hour ago. I've got the RCMP and a team of analysts working on it. I hope to find out more when I get back to Silverside."

"I'll meet you in Silverside at thirteen hundred hours. If possible, please arrange to have the lie detector available to question Dermott."

"Yes, sir."

I shook my head at myself. As an agent with the civilian branch of the Department, I didn't have to observe military formalities; but the force of Briggs's personality made 'sir' pop out automatically.

"One more thing, Agent Kelly. I'm appointing you Acting Director, effective immediately."

Shock froze my vocal cords. Then my voice came out in a squeak. "Me?"

If my wimpy response gave Briggs second thoughts, he showed no sign. "You have a top-level security clearance; and you're the only person I can trust at the moment. I'll inform the staff at Sirius as soon as we have Dermott in custody. See you at thirteen hundred."

"Y-Yes, sir." I disconnected with a trembling hand.

Ian eyed me expectantly. "So?"

Not quite ready to address my terrifying temporary promotion, I kept it simple. "Dermott is being locked down even as we speak. Thank you."

"You're welcome. But if you'd like to express your undying gratitude..." He puckered up theatrically.

I snorted. "My undying gratitude will have to do."

"Come on, Storm. Just one little kiss. That's all I ask."

"No, it's not. It's only the first thing you'll ask." I stood. "I have to go."

He rose, too. "I'll come with you."

"I appreciate the offer, but Holt needs backup more than I do. I don't want him alone at the warehouse. Would you mind going over there instead?"

Ian sighed. "He's not nearly as attractive as you. But sadly, he probably does need the backup more. Let him know I'm on my way, won't you?"

"Sure. And will you fill him in on the situation with Dermott? And do text check-ins every half hour. Just in c-"

My phone vibrated.

Consulting it, I said, "That's Holt's first check-in." I

texted him back, letting him know Ian would be arriving to help him soon and omitting the news that I was now technically his boss. After hitting send, I returned my attention to Ian. "Do you have burner numbers? I'll give you mine."

We exchanged information and headed for the door.

As I got into my car, my phone vibrated again with Kane's first check-in. I replied that I was just leaving for Silverside, then switched to a fresh secured phone and called Trish.

When she answered, I said, "Would you please send a forensic team over to Stemp's house, and let the RCMP know they should give everything they've found so far to us?"

"Uh... sure." She hesitated. "Should I... did you already clear it with Dermott?"

I opted for a partial truth. "General Briggs authorized it a few minutes ago."

Her breath of relief was audible. "Thank goodness. I'll get on it right away."

I disconnected, enabled my hands-free, and then used one of my burner phones to dial Kane's burner number before pulling onto the road.

He answered immediately, sounding tense.

Anxiety clutched at my gut. "It's me. What's wrong?"

"Nothing. Is everything all right with you?"

"Yeah, I'm just outside Calgary. I need to give you an update. That's why I called your burner."

"Oh, good." His voice relaxed into its usual smooth rumble. "What's new?"

When I had finished giving him the details, the hiss of his exhalation carried clearly over the line. "Dammit! So it was Dermott all along. I wonder how much intel he's leaked."

I sighed. "I still can't believe I read him so wrong. I really didn't think he was a traitor."

"Well, he fooled an infallible lie detector and a lot of experienced agents," Kane said grimly. "Don't beat yourself up."

Letting out a noncommittal grunt, I knuckled my gritty eyes. "Anything new with you?"

"No. Same old highway. I'm only forty-five minutes ahead of you. Should I stop and wait for you to catch up?"

"No, keep going. The sooner you get to Bud's, the better. I'll check in with you when I get to Silverside, and I have to meet General Briggs at Sirius at one o'clock."

Silence fell.

Kane broke it. "I'm fighting sleep. Do you want to keep talking to help stay awake?"

"Sure, that would be great."

Or would it?

I added warily, "What do you want to talk about?"

John chuckled. "Well, I guess we could have our fight now."

More tension slammed into my muscles. "What fight? What's wrong?"

"Nothing, that I know of. But our usual pattern is to have sex and then fight; usually about commitment or your relationship with Arnie. I press, you get defensive and angry, and off we go. I hope I didn't trigger you this time, but..." I could hear the smile in his voice. "What will it be? Let me have it."

My relief whooshed out in a gusty laugh. "I've got nothing. It must be your turn to get angry and defensive."

"Hmm. Let me see... no, all I've got is a euphoric

afterglow."

I grinned. "Me, too." The words slipped out before I could censor them.

John's voice deepened. "I'm glad." After an awkward pause, he added, "Are you panicking about me getting too close yet?"

"Yep, right on schedule," I quavered. "Are you sure you don't want to start a fight? I'd like to hide behind some self-righteous anger now."

"Sorry, can't oblige." He mercifully changed the subject. "Tell me about your '53 Chevy restoration. Did you ever hear back from that body guy?"

After a long conversation interrupted every half hour by check-ins from Holt and Rand, Kane said, "I'm pulling into Silverside now, so I'd better hang up. See you soon."

"Be careful!"

"I will." He hesitated. "I mean this in the most non-threatening way possible, so don't panic; but... I love you."

I managed a smile in spite of myself. "Thanks. I love you, too. No commitment. 'Bye."

Without the distraction of his conversation, I found myself clenching the steering wheel in a white-knuckled grip as I stewed about Dermott's betrayal and worried over Stemp.

Poor Charles. If he was still alive, he'd been in enemy hands for over twelve hours. I shuddered as memories of torture swooped in, drenched in blood and reeking of terror.

Maybe it would be better if he was dead.

But he would have died alone, knowing nobody was coming to save him. My heart clenched.

No. He had to be alive. His family needed him.

I needed him, dammit. In the Director's office, cool and dependable and three steps ahead of everybody.

Blowing out a breath, I fought the dark thoughts.

Keep your head in the game.

In Silverside at last, I studied every vehicle and pedestrian for potential hitmen while I drove to Stemp's house. The sight of the police cruiser and crime-scene tape made me draw a breath of relief.

As I got out of my car, Kane strode over.

"Did you find out anything?" I asked.

"Not much. The CRAPS patrol gave me a description of Stemp's 'friend' that's so general it could fit nearly every male in Silverside. Sandra Peters is attending, but she didn't offer me any intel and I didn't press. She's interviewing Bud and the other neighbours now. She was glad when the forensic team arrived and told her the Department was taking over."

"Oh, good, the team's here?"

"They arrived about ten minutes ago."

"I'll go in and talk to them." I headed for the house.

John caught my arm. "Remember, you're surrounded by snoopy seniors." He tilted his chin subtly toward Bud's front window, where several watching figures were visible. "Don't blow your cover."

I sighed. "Shit. Thanks. I should have thought of that."

He gave me a smile. "You're tired, and you've got a lot on your mind."

"That's no excuse." I took out a secured phone and hit the speed dial. "Hi, Megan? I'm outside Stemp's house, and I need Constable Peters to escort me inside so I don't blow my cover. Could you please get in touch with her and arrange it? I'm in a bit of a rush, so the sooner the better."

"I'll do it right away."

Less than five minutes later, Constable Peters came out of Bud's house and strode over. "Hi, Aydan. I hear you've had a promotion."

I winced. "Extremely temporary, I hope. Can you make it look as though you're escorting me into the house to check something?"

"Sure. Come on." She motioned toward the house, and I obediently fell into step beside her.

At the front door, she lifted the police tape and ducked underneath. Standing in the open doorway, she called, "Hello!"

A tech rocketed around the corner, clad from head to toe in disposable protective gear. "Stay out!" She jerked to halt. "Oh. Agent Kel... sorry, um... Director...?"

I managed not to wince this time. "Hi. I need to check Stemp's security cameras. I'll suit up before I come in, but you'll find my fingerprints in here anyway."

"Okay..." She eyed me warily. "Where?"

I sighed. "All over the place. You might find some of my hair, too." I tugged a long lock. "I shed like crazy."

Her expression turned embarrassed as her gaze slid sideways.

Shit, I needed a T-shirt that said '*No, I'm not screwing my boss*'.

I added, "You'll likely find Agent Holt's prints, too. We searched the entire property inside and out about a year and a half ago."

She relaxed. "Oh, okay. The van's out back. You can grab some gear from there. Just don't come through the back door; that's where we're working right now."

"Thanks. Have you found anything yet?"

"Maybe. We won't know until we've taken it all back to the lab and processed it."

I sighed. "Right, stupid question. Sorry. Be right back."

When Constable Peters and I returned, kitted out in disposable coveralls, booties, gloves, and hair nets, the tech met us at the door. "I'll follow you so I know where you've been and what you've touched."

"Thanks. I appreciate you being so careful."

Surprise flickered across her face. "Most agents get mad."

I gave her a smile. "Nope. Let's go. Yell if you see me reach for something I shouldn't."

As we trooped down the basement stairs, I sent a fervent prayer skyward. *Please let Stemp's abductor show up on the videos.*

I held my breath as I jiggled the mouse to wake Stemp's security computer.

Come on. Show me who took him.

The screen lit up.

My heart sank.

CHAPTER 54

"Shit!" I stared at the grid of black squares on Stemp's computer screen.

"What's wrong?" Constable Peters asked.

"The cameras are offline." I glared at the screen. "He had motion-activated cameras blanketing all the approaches to his house. Damn it to hell!" Dropping into the desk chair, I opened the camera application and checked the timestamps. "The system went down at eleven o'clock. Maybe..." I rewound the footage to ten-thirty and hit fast-forward. We watched in silence as the various cameras blinked on to capture people walking by, then blinked off again.

My heart leaped. *"There!"*

I froze the view and studied the blurry figure. Then I advanced the recording slowly, watching as a black-clad man crept toward Stemp's back gate.

Had Stemp missed seeing this? Maybe he'd been distracted, on the phone with one of the CRAPS members?

My pulse pounded as the intruder slipped through the gate and approached the back door. There was something in his hand...

He glanced toward the camera and the recording ended.

I sprang to my feet. "A clear shot of his face! Got him!"

"Why would the recording end there?" Peters asked. "The intruder didn't do anything to disrupt it."

"Not that we can see in the frame," I agreed. "But all the other footage ends at the same time. As if the master feed was cut..."

Suspicion flared into certainty. The EMI-generating 'ray gun' could do that, but it should have been safe in Reggie's lab last night. Maybe the assassin had another.

"I have to go." Turning to the tech, I added, "I want to copy this video onto my USB stick. That shouldn't be a problem, should it?"

"No; you're not disturbing any more evidence than you did by touching the mouse and keyboard and sitting in the chair."

"Good." I plugged in the tiny flash drive that I carried on my key ring.

A few minutes later the video was safely transferred, and the tech escorted us out of the house.

"Can I hand this case off to the Department now?" Constable Peters asked.

"I'd rather you finished your interviews first. We'll take over after you've handled the public-facing stuff."

"Okay." She headed back to Bud's house.

As I stripped off my protective gear, Lola hurried out of Bud's house and made a beeline for me. Kane moved to intercept her; but I already knew that unless he intended to physically restrain her, it was no use. Once she was focused, nothing short of heavy artillery would stop Lola.

Seconds later, she arrived and flung her arms around me. "Oh, honey, I'm so sorry this is happening. How are you holding up?"

Her heartfelt concern lodged a thick lump in my throat.

"Okay," I croaked, blinking back the burning behind my eyes. "But I'm really worried about him."

Her hug tightened. "I know, honey. We are, too. Just stay positive. He'll be okay, you'll see."

I swallowed hard. "Thanks."

As Kane approached, Lola lowered her voice. "They wouldn't let any of us near the house. Did they let you in because you're his girlfriend?"

Trying not to clench my teeth, I kept my tone casual. "I'm not his girlfriend, remember? It was just a bookkeeping thing. They wanted me to look at his computer and see if I could spot anything unusual."

"Oh. Right, bookkeeping." She drew back to look up into my eyes. "And?"

"And I didn't find anything." Sucking in a deep breath, I squared my shoulders. "I have to go. I have a one o'clock meeting."

A stop at the Melted Spoon netted me a sandwich to go, and I gobbled it one-handed while I drove the few blocks to Sirius. It was probably tasty; but if it had been cardboard I wouldn't have noticed.

I made a complete circuit of the block around Sirius, eyeing all the parked cars and other possible points of attack. I didn't spot anything sinister, but by the time I parked in the lot my heart was pounding. After a final visual sweep of the area, I jumped out of my car and ran for the entrance.

At the security wicket, Leo greeted me with a grin. "Good afternoon, Director."

I grimaced. "Don't start."

His smile vanished. "What do you mean?"

He looked so crestfallen that my heart smote me. "Sorry. But it's only temporary. The sooner Stemp is back, the happier I'll be."

"Oh." He dropped the sign-in sheet and my fob in the turntable and rotated it. "Well, everybody is thrilled that you're taking over from Dermott." As I signed in, he leaned closer, lowering his voice. "So what's the scoop? General Briggs contacted me himself and told me to rescind Dermott's clearances; and less than a minute later the Head of Security marched Dermott down to the secured area in handcuffs."

I sighed. "You know I can't tell you anything. Especially now that I'm..." The title stuck in my throat.

"Director!" Leo grinned, his cheerfulness restored. "Let me know if there's anything I can do to help."

"Thanks. Is General Briggs here yet?"

"No." Leo glanced behind me at the sound of the opening door, and I spun to follow his gaze as he corrected, "Yes."

Briggs strode across the lobby, his ramrod posture and weathered face reminding me of granite. If not for the smile lines around his eyes and mouth, he'd be completely terrifying.

He gave me a brisk nod. "Director."

I gulped. "Yes, sir?"

Damn, I'd done it again with the 'sir'.

Briggs politely ignored my slipup; or maybe he was so used to the title that he didn't even notice. "Were you able to reserve the lie detector?" He casually returned Leo's salute without removing his attention from me.

"Yes..." I couldn't help it. "...sir. Dr. Travers has it. I have to drop off some data to one of the analysts upstairs, and then I'll go down to the secured area and get set up."

"Good. I'll be down in a few minutes."

I nodded and made for the stairs before I could 'sir' him again.

Trish was in her office, absorbed by her computer screen. I tapped on her open door, and she twitched and sucked in a startled breath. "Oh! Hi, Aydan."

"Sorry, I didn't mean scare you." I came in and handed her the USB stick. "Thank you so much for being here on your day off. Here's a video of the guy who abducted Stemp. Can you get it to the team and start a facial recognition search?"

"Absolutely." She plugged the device into her computer, transferred the file, and handed the device back to me. "Done."

"Thanks."

As I turned to leave, she added, "Hey, Aydan, it's great to have you as Director."

I flinched, mumbled "Thanks", and fled.

When I hurried into Jack's lab in the secured area a few minutes later, she looked up from her computer with a smile. "Aydan! What wonderful news! Congratulations on your promotion!"

Somehow I suppressed my groan. "Thanks. I hope it's very short-lived."

"You want *Dermott* back in charge?"

Her expression was such a mix of horror and incredulity that I had to chuckle despite my chagrin. "Not particularly, but I really want him to be innocent."

She shook her head as she handed over the lie detector. "You're a better person than I."

"I'm really not. It's just that if he's guilty, the security breach will be a disaster."

"I suppose you're right." She sighed. "Good luck."

I arrived at the meeting room just as Dermott was being marched down the hall by two guards. Nodding to General Briggs as I slipped into the room, I rounded the table so I could sit with my back to the wall. As I placed the lie detector case on the table, the guards brought Dermott in.

His face twisted in a sneer. "Oh, look, I'm getting my day in kangaroo court." He scowled at Briggs. "Whatever she said about me, she's lying. Ask me anything you like, and the lie detector will prove I'm innocent."

Briggs addressed the guards. "Put him in the chair and cuff him to it." They obeyed. As they straightened, Briggs added, "Wait outside until we call you."

The guards did a smart about-face and filed out. Ignoring Dermott's hate-filled glower, I fastened the lie detector's electrodes around his temples.

When I was done, Briggs raised his voice slightly. "Begin recording." The security camera's red light blinked on, and Briggs eyed Dermott. "This session is being recorded. This isn't an official proceeding, and you're not currently under arrest. We received notice of a possible security breach, and you're being detained so we can ask you some questions under the lie detector."

"Why the hell are you questioning *me*?" Dermott spat. He shot me a glare. "*She's* the one you should be questioning!"

As though he hadn't spoken, Briggs went on, "However, if you say anything that registers as a lie; or if you refuse to answer, you'll be immediately suspended pending a full NSIRA inquiry, and you may face criminal charges." He turned to me. "I don't know the official Police Warning. Director, will you do the honours?"

I had barely opened my mouth when Dermott exploded

in a bellow. "*DIRECTOR?* You *promoted* the bitch? She's a fucking self-serving traitor who's been colluding with Stemp all along, you *idiot!* I can't believe... how did she get to you? Are you fucking her, too?"

Briggs went still. When he spoke again, his voice was dangerously quiet. "The police warning, please, Director."

I swallowed in an attempt to get some saliva into my desert-dry throat. "Brent Shirley Dermott, you're being detained-"

Dermott's deluge of profanity drowned out most of my words, but I faced the camera and recited the entire warning without raising my voice. It wouldn't take a genius to lip-read me; and I didn't want to show weakness in front of General Briggs. He might only be an inch taller than me, but good God, the man was intimidating.

Dermott and I ran down at about the same time. Silence fell.

A long silence.

I clamped my teeth on my tongue to prevent myself from blurting something stupid.

Briggs finally spoke. "Please answer yes or no. Is your name Brent Shirley Dermott?"

"Yes," Dermott growled, and the lie detector shone green.

"Do you understand the warnings you have just been read?"

"Yes." If Dermott's glare was a laser, I'd be dismembered.

"Do you want to have a lawyer present?"

"What the hell good would it do me?" Dermott snarled. "This is obviously a setup."

"Yes or no, please."

Briggs's dispassionate voice reminded me of Stemp, and my heart clutched. Please let him be okay.

"No, I don't want a fucking lawyer," Dermott snapped. "Get on with it."

Briggs gave a short nod and turned on the projector. The wall screen lit up. "You were observed yesterday afternoon in the Greenhorn Café having a conversation with an unidentified woman." Briggs pressed the Play button. "Our lip-readers translated your conversation." As the video played, the words displayed in subtitles.

Dermott's jaw dropped and his face went white, then red.

The video ended, and Briggs said evenly, "Please tell us who that woman was and explain the context of your conversation."

"I... I..." Dermott glanced at me, then quickly away. "Not in front of *her*."

"Director Kelly needs this information in order to do her job." Briggs was as expressionless as before, but I was sure he was needling Dermott by repeating my temporary title.

It was working. Dermott turned burgundy and a vein bulged in his forehead. "I can't," he gritted through clenched teeth. "It's a matter of national security."

Briggs eyed him. "Director Kelly is in charge of national security."

"And putting her in charge was fucking stupid!" Dermott barked. "Get her out of here, and I'll explain it to you!"

Something was off. Dermott was a bully and a coward. He didn't seem scared enough to be guilty. But if I left the room, who knew what poison he'd spew? Briggs wouldn't necessarily believe him; but I didn't dare-

"You can explain it to us both," General Briggs said. Transferring his gaze to the camera in the corner, he added,

"Let the record show that I take full responsibility for any security breach that might occur as a result of conducting this interview in front of Director Kelly."

Dermott growled, "You're making a huge mistake. But fuck it, I can see you've already sold out to her. So, fine. You can go down with her." He shot me a gloating grin. "Kelly's under official investigation, and I'm coordinating directly with the Department of National Defense. The woman in the video is Nicole Jacobsen, the Associate Deputy Minister."

Briggs frowned. "No, she's not."

Dermott's shit-eating grin wavered. "Not... what?"

"Director Kelly isn't under investigation. And the woman you were speaking with isn't Nicole Jacobsen."

Dermott paled. "Y-Yes, she..." He straightened, jaw jutting. "You know damn well Kelly's been under investigation since January! I had a team of analysts reporting to the Deputy Minister himself!"

"That investigation ended last month." Briggs skewered Dermott with his iron gaze. "Which you know, because you forwarded the final report yourself. And the real Associate Deputy Minister uses a wheelchair."

The colour drained from Dermott's face. "But... but... this investigation of Kelly was parallel to the other one. The DND one I'm coordinating has been going on since mid-February."

"No." Briggs's voice was rock-hard. "It hasn't. There is no other investigation."

Dermott slumped as though his spine had turned to jelly. His voice was a hoarse whisper.

"Oh, shit."

CHAPTER 55

"How did she get to you?" General Briggs's voice snapped out like a whip. "How much information have you disclosed?"

Dermott flinched. "I... I... let me think..." He paused, staring into space, then gulped. "She phoned me at home. Sometime in the middle of February; I can't remember exactly what day. She said she was Nicole Jacobsen, Associate Deputy Minister of National Defense, and she said the DND suspected Stemp and Kelly of leaking intel from the Department. She said that's why she was contacting me at home. She didn't trust the Department's internal communications."

"And you believed her." Briggs's voice was expressionless.

Dermott flushed. "No, I fucking didn't! I told her I'd need verification. She said she was impressed with my cautiousness, and told me to phone the Deputy Minister of National Defense to verify her identity and confirm that they were investigating." His bluster vanished as he shook his head. "I don't know how she did it. I hung up from her call, looked up the correct number, and dialled it. They must have somehow hijacked my phone line."

I sighed. "It's a new scam called line-trapping. Spider

told me about it a few months ago. You hang up from the scammer's original call, but the scammer doesn't disconnect. Then you pick up the phone right away to dial the legitimate number, but the scammer is still on the line. They play a recording of a dial tone, and then after you dial, they pretend to be the place you've called."

General Briggs fixed Dermott with an icy stare. "You didn't call from a secured phone?"

Dermott flushed. "She said it was urgent. And she'd just called me on that line. I didn't even think, I just..." His shoulders sagged. "Shit. She put me on hold, pretended to transfer me a few times... I was on the line for nearly half an hour, thinking I was waiting to talk to the Deputy Minister himself. I finally talked to a guy who pretended to be him. He said they wanted me to report to Nicole secretly from outside the office because the Department's internal communications might be compromised."

I groaned. "And you believed it because you've been suspicious of Stemp ever since he took the ultrasound weapon to Europe; and you knew I was already being investigated. No wonder you've been so hostile."

"Sorry," Dermott mumbled.

"What information did you disclose?" Briggs demanded.

Dermott squeezed his eyes shut and then reopened them as though fighting a headache. "At first I only gave her what I knew about Stemp and Kelly, which really only amounted to their activities because I didn't have proof of anything. But then Nicole... fuck, whoever she is... she brought up the Volslav investigation. She gave me information up front that wasn't public knowledge, so I believed she was legit."

Ice formed in my belly. "And she knew the information because she's Volslav! Shit!" Fighting spiralling panic, I refocused. "Is everything you've said so far in this interview true?"

"Yes."

The green light shone. The portent of doom.

Briggs was already on the phone. After a terse conversation, he hung up and faced us. "No results yet from the facial recognition search I initiated."

"She looks like Nicole Jacobsen." Dermott sounded as though he wanted to cry. "I double-checked her Department ID."

"Are you trained in facial recognition techniques?" Briggs snapped.

Dermott flushed. "No."

"Did you use the Department's facial-recognition program?"

"No." Dermott's reply was barely audible. "I thought the system was compromised."

Briggs's voice was dry ice. "And you didn't notice that the fake Nicole wasn't in a wheelchair."

Dermott straightened and locked eyes with Briggs. "I'll take responsibility for the facial recognition slipup; but the wheelchair doesn't show up in Nicole's Department ID photo. I couldn't have known."

"Fake-Nicole obviously didn't know, either," I said, stifling my urge to kick the table and scream blame-filled obscenities. "If she had, you can bet she'd have showed up in a wheelchair." I held my voice level. "So I'm assuming Volslav has all the intel we've given you in our reports, up until yesterday afternoon?"

"No." Dermott didn't meet my eyes. "I was behind on the reports."

Hope edged into my heart. "What was the latest thing

you told her?"

"Just what you saw in the video. That I'd released the hitman, and sent you and Holt down to search the stationery warehouse."

"Did you tell her about the necklaces, and that we suspected Maria's mother?"

"She'd mentioned Tawny Harchman's necklace back in March, so I didn't think twice about telling her about Weiss and his two necklaces. I didn't say anything about Maria's mother." His gaze dropped. "I haven't actually read that report yet."

I sighed. "I'd better call Stephanie Maldova. Fake-Nicole probably tracked her down and called her, too; and if she did, Stephanie would have told her she'd sent Maria's necklace to..." I trailed off. "Shit. I bet Volslav already has Maria's necklace. I bet that's why there was a break-in at Maria's mother's place. *Dammit!* We *need* that fourth necklace!" The rest of Dermott's confession finally registered, and I slumped in my chair. "And you released the guy who tried to kill me?"

"Yeah," Dermott mumbled. In the short disapproving silence that followed, he straightened with a return of his usual bluster. "You couldn't have gotten a conviction! You lied to him, didn't read his rights..." He glanced at Briggs's granite face and fell silent.

"It was a sting," I said, trying to keep the accusation out of my voice. "We were hoping he'd lead us to his boss when we let him go." Refocusing, I added, "Have you told us everything you disclosed to the fake Nicole?"

"Yeah..." The yellow light flashed, and Dermott sighed. "I've told you everything I can remember right now. I'll keep thinking about it, and check back through the reports. If I remember anything else I'll let you know right away."

"Is that true?"

He gave me a wry grimace. "Yeah." The green light shone.

I turned to General Briggs. "That's all the questions I have for now. Do you have any?"

"Yes." He leaned forward, pinning Dermott with a steely gaze. "Why didn't you contact me when you received the original phone call from the fake Nicole?"

Dermott blinked. "I... uh, didn't think of it. Nicole said the investigation was being handled by the Deputy Minister's office. You're Chief of Defense. Military, not civilian."

"True. But I'm part of your direct chain of command. And you know me by sight." Briggs's voice was implacable. "So it would have been a good cross-check to call me. Wouldn't it."

Dermott gulped. "Yes, sir."

Briggs eyed him for an excruciating moment before asking, "How much did your personal animosity toward Director Kelly and your belief in our..." He hesitated, obviously looking for a tactful word. "...involvement... contribute to your decision not to call me?"

Dermott's throat bobbed again as his gaze skated away. Then he straightened, glanced at me, and met Briggs's eyes. His voice was hoarse but firm. "Some. I didn't actually think you were fu-" He coughed and rephrased. "...uh... involved... until I walked in here today and got the wrong idea. Kelly and I locked horns last winter, but we talked it through and I tried to let it go. But when the fake Nicole told me Kelly was crooked, I thought she'd been playing me all along." His fists clenched on the chair arms. "I was so fucking pissed! I fucking *hate* traitors!"

"And now you are one." Briggs's words cut the air.

Dermott blanched.

"Unintentionally." The qualifier surprised me when it jumped out of my mouth. As both men turned to me, I added, "It's too late to point fingers. Let's just fix this."

"How?" Dermott's question came out sounding like a challenge, but I could see sincerity in his eyes.

Both men looked to me.

Shit.

"Um... First of all, is everything you just said true?"

"Yes."

The green light confirmed Dermott's honesty, and my exhausted brain booted up the beginning of a strategy. "Do you have a way of contacting Fake Nicole?"

"She contacts me."

Just as my heart began to sink, Dermott added, "But she gave me a phone number. Only to be used if there's a big development."

I let out a breath of relief. "Good. Did she tell you what kind of development she was looking for?"

"No."

"Okay, so you can tell her..."

I pondered. What would be irresistible to Volslav?

A slow grin spread over my face. "You'll tell her I've been showing too much interest in the three necklaces and you're afraid I might steal them. Tell her you want to take the necklaces to the Minister's office in Ottawa for safekeeping. I bet she'll offer to deliver them for you. And when she shows up to get them..." My grin widened. "She's ours."

Briggs nodded. "That could work. She shouldn't be expecting any tricks from Dermott after nearly five months of his cooperation."

"But if she figures it out, she'll kill me." Fear quivered in Dermott's voice.

"We'll make it as safe as possible for you," I said absently, my mind already engaged in planning.

Briggs rose. "I'll leave you to work out the details. But first..." He faced the camera and spoke clearly. "Brent Shirley Dermott, I'm relieving you of duty. You're not under arrest, but you are suspended pending a full NSIRA inquiry. Your security clearances are revoked. We'll release you from custody, but if you don't cooperate completely with the Department and Director Kelly, you may face criminal charges. Do you understand and accept these terms?"

"Yes," Dermott growled. The lie detector shone green.

"End recording." The red light blinked off, and Briggs added, "I'll send a guard in to release you." Briggs turned to me. "Director, keep me informed."

"Yes, sir." Fortunately he had already turned for the door, so he didn't see my grimace when I realized I'd called him 'sir' again.

Briggs departed. A guard came in and removed Dermott's restraints, then left.

Dermott and I sat in silence, avoiding each other's eyes.

"Sorry," he muttered finally.

"It's okay. You thought you were doing the right thing." I changed the subject. "Do we have any agents available besides Holt and me?"

"No. Richardson and Wheeler are tied up in Calgary, Germain's in Ontario, Francis is overseas, and Vale's been undercover so long he doesn't even remember who he really is."

"Vale? I've never heard anybody mention him before."

Dermott shrugged. "He was undercover long before you got here. Even if we could pry him out of hiding, he's completely fucking squirrelly. Forget him. It's just you and Holt."

I sighed. "I guess I'd better call Holt, then. Maybe Agent Rand will help, too."

"That asshole? Talk about squirrelly! No way I'm putting my life in *his* hands."

I nearly snapped, 'You'll do whatever you're damn well told', but I managed to bite my tongue before the words popped out.

"I'll put Holt on speaker," I said instead. "That way we can brainstorm."

A nasty grin formed on Dermott's face. "I can hardly wait to hear what he says when he finds out *you* got appointed Acting Director."

"Try not to be an asshole," I said tiredly, and dialled Holt's burner. Dermott flushed and opened his mouth to retort, but I shot him a warning scowl as Holt answered.

"Hi, it's Aydan," I said. "I'm here with Dermott and we've got you on speaker."

A wary pause greeted my words. "Why?"

"Volslav pulled an elaborate scam on Dermott. A woman has been pretending to be the Associate Deputy Minister, and he's been giving her intel since mid-February."

A deluge of profanity crackled through the speaker, and I raised my voice to be heard as I finished, "I think we can contain it, and Dermott's going to help take her down with a sting."

Another pause.

"And you trust him?" Holt demanded incredulously.

I sighed. "Yeah." I managed not to add, 'sort of', and

finished, "He passed the lie detector."

"Thanks for the vote of confidence, asshole," Dermott growled, then caught my eye and amended, "I was talking to Holt." Before Holt could reply, he went on, "By the way, Briggs suspended me and made Kelly Acting Director. You report to her now."

He delivered the news in a dispassionate tone; but there was a malicious glint in his eyes.

"Oh. 'Kay." Only a slight hiccup in the word 'okay' betrayed Holt's reaction. "So what's the plan?" he added.

"What's your status there?" I asked.

"We interviewed the truck drivers and they swear they didn't realize anything was wrong. A dock worker told them to head out; and they did. We have two dock workers in custody, but there might be more. We need to do more interviews, and we'll probably detain a few more people."

"You might have to put the interviews on hold. The sooner we sting Volslav, the better." I outlined the bare bones of my plan.

"Where do you want to do it?" Holt asked.

"I'm thinking somewhere in Calgary. It's more anonymous; and-" Urgent rapping on the door interrupted me. "Hang on." I got up and opened the door, tensing at the sight of Trish's pale face. "What's wrong?" I demanded.

"I just got off the phone with the RCMP in Kananaskis. There was an accident sometime last night. A car went over the cliff above Grassi Lakes. They've just retrieved it. It was a rental, registered to Charles Stemp."

My heart stopped. "Is he..."

"They haven't found Director Stemp or his body, but they're still searching the scene. The RCMP think the car was stolen. The driver was killed. They sent me a photo, and facial recognition says he's a probable match for the intruder at Stemp's house."

I swallowed, fighting the tightness in my throat. "*Probable* match?"

She gave me an unhappy grimace. "The cliff was over a hundred metres high. The corpse was pretty banged up."

"Oh."

"But that's not the worst of it." Trish clenched her hands together, the skin whitening from the force of her grip. "There was blood in the trunk. Lots of blood. And a bullet hole. Like somebody had been stuffed in the trunk and shot."

"Shit!" Fear for Stemp chilled my heart and hardened my voice into a bark that made Trish twitch. "Get that car! Get every scrap of evidence into our lab! Top priority!"

"Right away!" She turned and ran.

CHAPTER 56

My gut churning, I closed the meeting room door and returned to the table.

"What's happening?" Holt demanded over the speaker.

I brought him and Dermott up to speed in a few sentences, then added, "We have to do this sting today! If Stemp's injured, he's on borrowed time. We need to bring in Fake Nicole and question her."

After a short silence, Holt spoke, his tone softer than usual. "Look, I know you don't want to give up. But you don't stuff somebody in the trunk and shoot them if you plan on keeping them alive."

Biting back a furious rejoinder, I took a breath and let it out slowly. "I know, but if there's even a slim chance, we owe it to Stemp to try."

"Agreed." Holt's voice firmed, switching into planning mode. "Okay, we're going to want a couple of hours to set up; so pick a location. Rand and I will go over right away and get eyes on it before Dermott makes the phone call. That way Volslav won't have time to set up an ambush. We'll stay in place until you get there."

Dermott gulped. "Y-You think... what if they just shoot me and grab the necklaces?"

I sighed. "It'll be broad daylight in a public place.

Volslav has always played it smart. Fake Nicole won't want to attract attention."

"Let's make it a coffee shop with a decent-sized parking lot so we have room to manoeuvre," Holt said. "We'll take her down when she's leaving, after she gets the necklaces from Dermott. We'll need a sharpshooter to hit her with a trank dart from a distance. The Calgary facility has a surveillance van disguised as an ambulance, so we can park it in the lot before she gets there. Nobody will hear the shot, so it'll look like she's collapsed. Our guys can run out and load her into the back of the ambulance and drive away."

"I don't want anybody with a rifle working in broad daylight," I objected. "I don't even want to take a chance on drawing a trank pistol. Remember, we're in public. If anybody sees a firearm, it'll be mass panic. Plus, if Volslav spots it, they might open fire with real ammo. We can't take the chance when we're surrounded by civilians."

"Well, we need to take her down somehow," Holt said. "Call Hellhound. He always makes his kill, and he's done some pretty weird shit to get the job done."

A memory tickled my brain.

"Cigar blowgun," I said.

"What?"

"He killed a guy once with a blowgun disguised as a cigar. That would work perfectly for this; we can just use a trank dart instead."

"Okay, you can-"

The phone's call-waiting tone interrupted us.

"Shit," I muttered. "Greg, I have to put you on hold. I've got another call."

When I switched to the other line, Megan's crisp voice said, "Director, I have Constable Peters from the RCMP on the line for you."

"Thanks, go ahead."

The line clicked, and Peters's no-nonsense voice spoke. "Found a dead body I thought you'd want to know about."

My heart froze and the phone receiver emitted a small creak under the sudden force of my grip. "Who is it?" My voice came out paper-thin.

"His ID says Max Thorogood." Relief flooded me as she went on, "He was shot execution-style, so..." Grim humour edged her voice. "I figured it was probably related to your case. The blood's dry and he's cold and stiff so I'm guessing he's been dead at least twelve hours, probably longer. Do you want him in your lab?"

"Might as well; we're getting quite a collection here. I'll switch you back to Megan to make the arrangements."

With that done, I picked up Holt's line again. "Hi, I'm back. Looks like the last of our hitmen bit the dust. Somebody shot Thorogood."

"Huh. You sure there were only four?"

"I'm assuming. Maria's mother only paid for four hits in Canada."

Holt grunted. "Well, somebody offed Thorogood, so there's at least one killer still out there." He returned to the subject at hand. "So, I'll coordinate with the Calgary team while you coordinate with Helmand. You okay with involving Rand if he's willing to help?"

"Sure, we'll need everybody we can get."

"Kane, too."

"He's a civilian now," I objected.

"So what? He was a top agent, and we need the manpower. And Command will be thrilled if you get him on the job again, even if it's just for a little while." When I hesitated, Holt prodded, "All hands on deck, right?"

I sighed. "Yeah. Call me back when you have everything arranged with the Calgary team. By then I'll have a location."

A few tension-filled hours later, I eyed the monitor screens inside the fake ambulance with my heart thumping. Worry writhed like venomous snakes in my belly. I pushed a psychic message to Stemp with all my strength.

Hang on. We're coming.

On one of the monitors, I watched Ian stretch out his legs comfortably in the corner of the coffee shop as he drank his coffee. He replaced the cup on the table and returned to typing on the laptop in front of him.

Another camera in the opposite corner of the coffee shop showed Holt pretending to talk on his phone, anonymous in a full beard, camo pants, and a redneck baseball cap.

Clad in safety gear, John's broad-shouldered figure swept the wand of a power washer steadily back and forth, working his way toward the coffee shop.

Hellhound was out of range of the cameras, so I spoke over the open comm. "Arnie, are you in position?"

The fat rumble of his Harley-Davidson assured me that he was ready before he even spoke. "Ready to roll, darlin'."

I had saved our most important and least dependable team member for last. "Brent, any last-minute questions?"

The view on one of the monitors jiggled and swung as Dermott removed the sunglasses containing the camera and turned them to face himself in the driver's seat of his car. He wiped sweat off his pale face and croaked, "I g-guess... I'm ready...?"

Dammit, the poor bastard was scared shitless. Fake

Nicole would know something was up the instant she saw him.

"Brent," I said, keeping my tone calm and neutral. "You'll do fine. When you get into the coffee shop, buy a clear soft drink and sip it. Hold your stomach and pretend you're feeling sick. When Fake Nicole gets there, tell her you ate something for lunch that didn't agree with you. If you get stuck for something to say, groan or belch or sip your drink to buy time."

The tension in his face eased. "Okay."

"Put on your glasses and go in. Greg and Ian are right there, and the rest of us are only a few seconds away. You'll be fine."

God, I was such a hypocrite, blowing sunshine up his ass while I sat here safe and sound inside the fake ambulance. But, dammit, Briggs had given me a direct order: *'The Director stays in the van to coordinate.'*

Under the appraising eyes of the three tac team members dressed as paramedics, I fought the urge to jump up and pace in the cramped space beside the stretcher.

Dermott headed for the coffee shop.

What if Volslav sent a team with automatic weapons to simply mow him down and grab the necklaces?

My muscles tightened with the need to jump out of the van and do... something. Anything. Shit, this was worse than being in danger myself.

"Fake Nicole's coming, about a minute out," one of our spotters reported from the street. "She's driving a silver Ford Escape. There's nobody in the passenger seat, but the back windows are tinted; so somebody could be hiding there."

Dermott's onboard camera showed his hands trembling

as he paid for his drink. When he seated himself in the place we'd selected for him, I had to remind myself to breathe.

The silver Escape pulled in and parked, and Fake Nicole got out and strode confidently into the coffee shop. She gave Dermott a cheery wave as she stepped up to the counter to order a drink.

My teeth ached. Easing the clenched muscles in my jaw, I scanned the rest of the monitors.

Greg and Ian looked oblivious. Kane moved closer to the coffee shop, his shoulders slouched with the boredom of a mindless job. Dermott hunched miserably at his table, hugging his midsection.

The roar of a Harley penetrated the van, and Arnie's bike rumbled into a parking slot a couple of spaces away from Fake Nicole's vehicle. He swung down the kickstand and made a show of dismounting and stretching. Then he dawdled around the bike, removing his leather jacket and doffing his helmet. He was rummaging in one of his saddlebags when movement on the monitors yanked my attention back to the coffee shop.

Fake Nicole sat down across from Dermott, studying him dubiously. "Is everything okay?" she asked.

"Ye-" Dermott's voice came out in a thin croak, and he cleared his throat. "Yeah. Ate something. A... a burrito. Earlier. Stomach's upset." He gulped his drink and belched. "Sorry."

Fake Nicole's friendliness cooled as she eased back in her seat. "Well, I guess it's a good thing you won't have to get on the plane to Ottawa, then. You look like you need to lie down, so I won't keep you. Do you have the necklaces?"

"Yeah." Dermott produced the envelope and slid it across to her with a shaking hand. "Thanks for taking care of this."

"I'm happy to. National security is my top priority." She eyed the sweat-stained envelope before picking it up by a corner and stowing it in her handbag. "Well..." She rose and patted him squeamishly on the shoulder. "I hope you feel better soon."

As she headed for the door, Holt's voice snapped through the open comm. *"Don't drink that!"*

Shit, had Dermott already taken another gulp of his drink?

Nothing I could do about it. Somehow my voice came out steady. "Arnie, now."

He extracted a fat cigar from his saddlebag and plied a lighter, releasing a puff of smoke as he turned toward the coffee shop.

Fake Nicole emerged and made a beeline for her vehicle as Arnie strolled toward her. Beside me, the fake paramedics tensed.

Arnie didn't alter his easy gait; didn't even look at Fake Nicole as he puffed on his cigar. When she stumbled and collapsed, he rushed over and crouched beside her. "Hey, lady, ya okay?" When she didn't respond, he threw a wild glance around the parking lot, stubbing out his 'cigar' and tucking it in his pocket. "SOMEBODY CALL 911!" He patted Fake Nicole's hand ineffectually and yelled in the direction of the van. "HEY! AMBULANCE GUYS! HELP!"

Kane put down his pressure-washer and hurried over as the tac team sprang out, bringing the stretcher.

Holt's voice crackled with alarm. "Ambulance! A man has collapsed! Hurry, he's having a seizure!"

Wait, what?

A *man?*

I jerked my attention back to the monitors, my blood turning to ice at the sight of Dermott sprawled on the floor of the coffee shop, convulsing.

CHAPTER 57

Ian shoved people and chairs out of the way and dove to his knees beside Dermott while Holt relayed details to the emergency operator.

Outside in the parking lot, the fake paramedics trussed Fake Nicole into the stretcher while Kane and Hellhound faded into the growing group of wide-eyed spectators.

I yanked my scattered wits together. "Ian, stay with Brent and keep me posted on his status. As soon as Greg's off the phone, tell him to pull out. John, get Fake Nicole's keys and take her vehicle. Arnie, bug out on your bike. Everyone meet at the secured facility."

John made a show of picking up Fake Nicole's fallen handbag and putting it onto the stretcher. Even watching on the camera, I wouldn't have noticed him stealing her keys if I hadn't known he was doing it.

The fake paramedics whisked the stretcher back to our van and shoved it into place.

"Go!" I snapped as soon as the doors closed behind them.

Our driver accelerated out of the parking lot.

Switching to back to the comm, I demanded, "Ian, did you see what happened?"

His whispered words came out uneven as he struggled to

keep Dermott's head from smashing into the floor during his spasms. "No, Fake Nicole blocked my view with her body. Holt must have seen her put something in Dermott's drink." He hesitated. "If it's this fast-acting, it's probably cyanide. Usually fatal."

"Fuck!" Glaring at Fake Nicole's peaceful face on the stretcher pillow, I fought the urge to throttle her before she regained consciousness. "Thanks, Ian. Do you remember how to get to the Calgary base?"

"Yes, I'll meet you later." He fell silent to concentrate on Dermott.

I pulled on gloves and grabbed Fake Nicole's handbag, upending it over the stretcher. A small handgun bounced out and I swore and corralled it, touching it as little as possible.

"Have we got evidence bags?" I asked.

One of the men handed me one, and I bagged Fake Nicole's gun. Picking up her wallet with my fingertips, I opened it.

"*FUCK!*"

At my infuriated bellow, the tac team tensed. "What's wrong?" the nearest man demanded.

"Stephanie Fucking Maldova!" I met their confused frowns with a disgusted headshake and added, "Never mind. What's our time?"

"Seven minutes total elapsed on the tranquilizer. ETA at base, three minutes."

"Thanks." The feeds had gone blank as we exceeded the range of the transmitters, so I used a secured phone to contact Holt. At his 'yeah', I said, "It's me. Status?"

"Dermott's in the ambulance. I'm on my way to base. ETA five minutes."

"I just checked Fake Nicole's ID. She's Stephanie Maldova, Maria's damn lawyer. Finally, it all makes sense. She could have confidential conversations with Maria in prison, and relay information between Maria and Tawny. Then I bet she got greedy after Tawny died. Eliminate Maria, and it was all hers."

"And eliminate Maria's mother," Holt said.

"Right..." Another thought hit me. "I bet she was using Maria's mother as a fall guy. Gal. Whatever. Got her to arrange the hits and pay for them, so Stephanie's hands and bank account stayed clean."

"And then Maria's mother gets murdered in a so-called burglary," Holt finished. "Smooth."

"I'll call Trish. And then I'm going to get answers out of Fake Nicole."

I made my call, disconnecting as we pulled into the secured underground parking garage. As we parked, I told the team, "Search Fake Nicole and transfer her to a cell. I'll be right behind you." I barely waited for them to nod before I sprang out of the van and ran for the technology lab.

When I panted up to the cells a couple of minutes later, the guard pointed toward the phone. "There's a call holding for you."

I jabbed a finger at Fake Nicole. "If she starts to wake up, break a dart in front of her nose. I want her to stay unconscious, but only for a few more minutes." Grabbing the phone receiver, I barked, "Kelly!"

"It's Trish here, and I've got Spider with me."

My heart lurched. "Any news on Stemp?"

"No. They searched the area around the car crash site but there was no sign of him. I had them fly the car and body here to our lab..."

I gulped. Apparently when the Director said 'top priority', no expenses were spared.

Trish was still talking. "...found a gun with the driver's fingerprints on it, and two bullets missing from its magazine. They say the blood in the trunk was likely spilled hours before the car crashed. They're doing a rush DNA test on it and we should have results soon." She hesitated. "But... the blood in the trunk is AB negative. Less than one percent of North Americans have that type." The tremor in her voice warned me to brace myself. "Director Stemp's blood type is AB negative. And there was a lot of blood. The doctor says... even if the wound wasn't instantly fatal, the victim wouldn't survive that much blood loss without emergency medical treatment."

I swallowed hard, and somehow my voice came out level. "Anything else?"

"Spider's been working his magic on the money transfers between bank accounts. It looks as though Stephanie Maldova has been accessing Maria's mother's bank account. By the timing, it looks as though Tawny decided to bring Stephanie into Volslav a few months after Dawn and Yana died."

Too worried about Stemp to feel triumph about my correct guesswork, I said, "Good work, you two." Holt jogged up just as Stephanie twitched and moaned, and I added, "I have to go."

The guard held a tranquilizer dart under Stephanie's nose, but I waved him off and hurried into the cell.

"What are you doing?" Holt demanded as I peeled the backing off one of the self-adhesive network keys I'd grabbed from the tech lab.

I stuck the tiny circuitry to the back of Stephanie's neck,

then gripped the other key as I plopped down to sit on the floor. Leaning back against the wall, I replied, "Messing with her in VR."

"I'll come in with-"

"No. She only put hits out on Stemp, Kane, Hellhound, and me. I don't want you associated with me."

Stephanie stirred and groaned.

Holt tried again. "Wait, let's-"

"Stemp *can't* wait," I hissed, and dove into virtual reality.

In seconds, I had created a plain white room with a single chair. Stephanie's avatar wavered into existence, and I dragged her into the chair and yanked the restraints tight around her wrists and ankles before stepping back several paces.

Drawing a deep breath, I fought the urge to enact a vicious torture scenario and force her to tell me where Stemp was.

Be smart. More to the point, be *legal*.

And don't let her realize how important Stemp is...

When Stephanie's eyelids fluttered open, I gave her my best wolf-smile. "Hello, Stephanie. Or should I call you Nicole?"

She shrugged, her eyes narrowing as if to bring me into focus.

"How do you like my drugs?" I asked. "You might feel a bit sleepy now, but soon you'll be telling me everything I ever wanted to know."

She raised her chin. "I don't have to talk to you. I want a lawyer."

I snorted. "Do you see any lawyers around here?"

"I see a cop. That means I get a lawyer."

I let my smile widen. "You'd think so, wouldn't you? My

bosses think I'm straight, too, but they don't realize my Arlene Widdenback cover is actually real. So, sorry; no lawyer. Are you feeling talkative yet?"

Stephanie gave me a contemptuous lift of her eyebrow and stayed silent.

"That's okay, we've got lots of time," I lied.

Dammit, dammit, we have *no* time!

Faking calm, I went on, "You really should have picked a better organization to take over. Volslav is hard on your health." I cocked a grin at her. "First Yana bit the big one..."

The body of Yana Orlov appeared on the floor at my feet, her beautiful dark eyes glazed, her head twisted at an unnatural angle.

Shit, I hadn't intended to do that.

Focus.

Stephanie's eyes widened as she studied the corpse.

Covering my mistake, I faked puzzlement. "What are you... oh. I guess the hallucinations are starting. I always wonder what people see when I give them this drug. But they never tell me. All they do is scream. Anyhow..." I gave a carefree shrug. "First Yana bought it. Then Dawn. That was ugly. She was tortured to death in a butcher shop, you know."

Dawn's ravaged corpse materialized next to Yana, leaking blood from horrific wounds.

God, I hadn't needed to see that again. It haunted my nightmares often enough. But at least it seemed to be working on Stephanie. She was holding a good poker face, but I saw her swallow.

I put on a regretful voice. "And then there was Tawny. I had to shoot her myself. It's so hard to get good help these days."

Sure enough, Tawny's body appeared. Too-tight-too-bright clothes, grossly inflated lips and boobs, and a lot of bullet holes.

"I guess you took care of Maria for me, though," I allowed. "Thanks for that."

Maria Harchman popped into existence dressed in prison scrubs, glowering at Stephanie. "You stupid little bitch!" she snapped. "How dare you kill me!"

Okay, I hadn't done that. Stephanie's imagination must be animating Maria's construct. And now I knew for sure that Stephanie had murdered Maria.

Tawny Harchman pulled herself to her feet, leaking gore. "Look what she did to me," she hissed at Stephanie. "This is all your fault!"

The other two corpses animated as well, converging on Stephanie. Not my doing, but maybe Stephanie would loosen her own tongue.

Her mouth dropped open, and she strained back in the chair.

"How do you like the hallucinations so far?" I inquired. "I can give you the antidote any time you're willing to answer some questions."

"This is bullshit," she gritted. Tawny reached for her and she jerked back with a small shriek. "Get away from me!"

"So, you had Maria's mother killed, too," I said conversationally. "Was it her idea or yours to put contracts out on me and my boys?"

Stephanie pressed her lips together.

"You might as well tell me," I urged. "I've taken over all your bank accounts and assets. Even if you somehow get away from me, you're penniless." I shrugged. "But if you give me some answers, I might decide to let you go just so I can watch Dermott chase you to the ends of the earth. He's pissed."

Dawn's corpse shambled over and held a lacerated wrist over Stephanie's head, dripping blood on her elegant coiffure.

"Ew!" Stephanie jerked away, fighting her bonds.

"I can make this stop anytime," I reminded her. "All you have to do is answer a few questions. Let's start with an easy one. Where's Charles Stemp?"

Tawny's corpse smirked and leaned over to bleed on Stephanie's expensive-looking suede pumps. I held my breath, using all my self-control to keep from wrapping my hands around Stephanie's throat and screaming '*TELL ME!*'

Stephanie glared at me, her eyes glowing with hatred and triumph. "Dead," she hissed. "He's long dead. Just like you."

A man burst through the door, swinging up a submachine gun. The volley of bullets caught me square in the chest.

Transfixed, I stared down at the torn flesh and gushing blood where my heart had been.

CHAPTER 58

Healing my injuries and disintegrating my attacker with a wave of my hand, I snapped, "Nice try, bitch!"

Stephanie let out a cold brittle laugh as the corpses vanished. "I knew this was virtual reality. I never met Yana or Dawn. No idea what they looked like, so I couldn't possibly hallucinate them."

A whirlwind of knives exploded out of nothingness, and I let them slice through me.

"Don't bother," I growled. "The external parameters prevent any harm to me."

Stephanie gave me a superior smirk. "But not to me, I bet." Her smirk turned poisonous. "Good luck finding your friend now. Bye-bye, bitch."

Machine-Gun Man popped into existence again, and this time the bullets ripped through Stephanie.

Her avatar vanished.

"*SHIT!*" I folded sim-space and sprang through the portal.

I jerked upright in the real world. Holt was already starting CPR on Stephanie. A guard rushed in carrying the automatic defibrillator kit.

My mind filled with silent screams as I watched the two men work over Stephanie's motionless body.

Dead. He's long dead.

She was lying. Trying to get to me.

But even if Stemp was still alive, her suicide might have taken him to the grave with her. Now I had no idea where to look for him.

Medical personnel rushed into the cell, taking over from Holt and the guard.

Holt came over to stand beside me. "It was a good try," he said awkwardly. "You couldn't have done anything else."

I didn't reply.

We waited in silence until Stephanie was officially pronounced dead. Straightening my aching shoulders, I said, "We need to-"

"Phone call for you, Director," the guard interrupted.

"This better be good news." I went over and accepted the receiver from him.

"Aydan?" Spider's wobbly voice chilled my heart.

"What's wrong?"

"W-We... got a phone call... from the Calgary police. They knew we were looking for Stemp..." His gulp carried clearly over the line.

My knees gave way and I sank onto the corner of the guard's desk. "What is it, Spider?" Somehow steady words came out instead of the frantic shrieks locked inside my chest.

"One of the Calgary veterinary clinics... they're closed on weekends... but one of the vets had to go in and pick up something. Th-They... have a resomation chamber."

"I don't know what that is."

Please don't tell me.

"It's... they call it 'natural water cremation'. Instead of cremating dead pets with fire, they... dissolve them. In a big computer-controlled tank."

I couldn't speak.

Spider struggled on. "The vet found... blood. Drag marks, on the floor. And the resomation chamber had been activated. She called the police. When they opened the chamber, there were... human remains."

My voice came out in a croak. "Identifiable?"

"Resomation destroys everything but bones, and the tank had completed its cycle. But it doesn't destroy synthetic fibres or plastic... like..." He swallowed. "Driver's licenses and credit cards. The body... skeleton..." He hesitated, then his words came out in a choked rush. "Stemp's wallet was in there, with all his identification."

My stomach rolled, but somehow words came out. "We'll need a DNA test."

"Resomation destroys all DNA. But the Medical Examiner's office is checking dental records. I told them to make it top priority. They should know in an hour or so. They'll call me with the results, but if you want to go over..."

"I'll go." I hung up without a goodbye.

Holt eyed me, grim-faced. "They found him."

"Maybe."

"Probably," he corrected, studying my expression.

I sighed. "But maybe not. I'm going to the Medical Examiner's office."

CHAPTER 59

As I turned to leave, the phone rang again. The guard answered, then called, "Director!"

I went back to reluctantly accept the receiver. "Kelly."

"Rand here."

"How's Dermott?" I asked, afraid to hear the answer.

"Fine." Ian's voice was pure disgust. "The bloody wanker was faking it. He noticed Fake Nicole dropping something into his drink and he decided to play dead. He's hiding in the hospital, hoping you'll put him in the witness protection program."

"He..." I clamped my mouth shut so my outrage couldn't erupt.

Stemp might be dead. Not just dead, horribly *dissolved*.

And Dermott, that useless self-centred coward... was unharmed.

After a long moment of silence, I spoke, holding my voice steady with all my will. "Thanks, Ian. I'll deal with him later." I replaced the receiver gently in its cradle.

"How's Dermott?" Holt's expression was half fear, half determination.

"Fine. He was faking it."

Holt gaped at me for an instant before exploding, "That fucker! I'm going to kill that fucking asshole!"

I couldn't deal with his emotions, too.

I walked away.

An hour passed in a blur while I waited in the Medical Examiner's office. When Ben Salmer came in, his grim expression told me all I needed to know.

"I'm sorry," he said. "The examiner says some of the jaw and facial bones were shattered, probably by a fatal gunshot; but the remaining teeth and jaw segments are a match to Charles Randall Stemp."

My body jerked as every fibre of my being screamed a silent '*NO!*'

My voice came out flat and empty. "Could you be wrong?"

His sympathetic grimace destroyed my last vestige of hope. "Mr. Stemp had very unusual work done on one of his molars. It was hollow with a cosmetic veneer, so a tiny object could be hidden inside. That tooth was present. And the remaining dental pattern matched."

"So... it's him." My words came out as heavy as my aching heart. "*Was* him."

Salmer nodded. "I'm afraid so."

Numb.

Hold the numbness. Don't feel the pain.

"How long before you can release his remains?"

"No more analysis can be done. There's no DNA left, only bones. As soon as his next of kin choose a funeral home, we can release the remains to them."

"Thank you for doing this so quickly." I hauled myself to my feet and stumbled blindly for the door.

The men were in the waiting room, but I couldn't face

them yet. I ducked into the ladies' washroom.

Inside a cubicle, I curled into an aching ball. Moonbeam and Karma and Skidmark would be devastated. They'd had such a short time to enjoy their son after their long estrangement. And how awful for Katya to survive an assassination attempt, only to lose her husband.

And Anna. Poor little fatherless Anna.

A painful lump lodged in my throat, but tears wouldn't come.

I didn't deserve to grieve. They had trusted me to keep him safe, and I had failed.

Dragging myself to my feet, I washed my hands and trudged out.

In the reception area, I broke the news to the men, avoiding their compassionate eyes. Their hugs were no comfort.

Stemp would never give or receive another hug.

"Come on, darlin'," Arnie said gently. "Let's go get somethin' to eat, an' then we can all go back to my place an' have a wake for him."

"Nobody goes home." My words came out flat. "Somebody shot Max Thorogood, so there's still at least one hitman out there. I'm not losing anybody else."

The men exchanged a glance. Arnie tried again. "We get that, darlin', but it could be days or weeks 'fore ya find out who offed Thorogood. Maybe never."

"You're not going home tonight. None of you. I'll have you locked up if I have to."

Ian cleared his throat. "If I may..." He hesitated at the sight of my 'do-not-mess-with-me-now' look, then pushed on. "I completely agree with you, Storm, and I have a solution. I have a suite at the Palliser. We can go there and order room service..." As I opened my mouth to lambaste him he quickly amended, "I meant, we can *all* go there. Safety in numbers, you know. Nobody goes home. Everybody gets food and a safe place to sleep."

"That's a good idea," John said gently. "You need rest and food. We all do."

Too worn out and heartsick to think any more, I gave in. "Okay. Thanks. I have to call his parents. I'll be back in a bit."

Alone again in Ben Salmer's office, I took out the list of burner numbers and stared at it. Which of them should I call? Whose heart would I break first?

The numbers blurred, and I scrubbed angrily at my eyes. Looking away from the list, I lowered my fingertip onto it. Without giving myself a chance to hesitate, I dialled the number.

Skidmark's voice sounded weary. "Yeah?"

"It's me." I gulped. "Aydan. I... I..." My throat closed.

His voice softened. "We already got the bad news, girlie. Cops called us."

"I'm so sorry." Emotion roughened my voice, but I fought it under control. "You should have heard it from me. I'm so sorry."

He sighed. "Don't beat yourself up. You did the best you could."

"Not good enough."

"Sometimes it's not, no matter how hard you try. It's shitty, but you know we get it. We've all been there."

His compassion made me feel even worse. Tears clogged my throat.

As if realizing I couldn't speak, he added, "There is one thing you could do for us, if you don't mind."

I cleared my throat and managed a croak. "Name it."

"Could you bring him home to us? We don't want to send him to a funeral home."

Swallow.

Breathe.

"Of course." My voice wasn't steady, but I did my best. "They can release his... him... anytime."

"We'll book you a flight tomorrow."

"No, I'll pay for the plane ticket; I-"

"We'll get it," he overrode me gently. "Your flight will leave at one-thirty, if that's okay with you. We're tied up here on the commune, so we'll rent a car for you, too. Everybody knows why you're coming, so they understand we're making an exception to the 'no vehicles' rule. Just drive right up to the garage. I'll email you the flight and rental details."

Words failed me again. "Okay."

"Girlie, don't grieve too hard. We all know the risks that come with the job."

He disconnected, leaving me deeply ashamed that he had put aside his own pain to comfort the woman who had let his son die.

The suite at the Palliser was sumptuous. It felt like an insult to Stemp's memory to be surrounded by such luxury. I huddled in the corner of the sofa, letting the men's conversation flow around me while I ate without tasting and drank beer after beer.

Time slowed and the room blurred. Gentle hands tucked a blanket around me.

At three AM, my brimming bladder yanked me to

miserable wakefulness. Head throbbing, I trudged to the bathroom, downed several glasses of water, and crept back to my nest on the sofa.

Morning was ugly. The men moved quietly around the suite while I huddled under my blanket, my stomach churning with nausea that had nothing to do with a hangover.

The sofa dipped with Arnie's weight, and he lifted the blanket away from my face. "Hey, darlin'. I got coffee an' a big greasy plateful a' eggs an' sausages an' hashbrowns for ya."

I sat up, leaning into his strength for a moment. "Thanks."

As I shovelled the food in, John surveyed me. "I thought you only drink green or herbal tea."

I gulped a bitter black mouthful from the mug, shuddering as it burned its way to my belly. "That's right. Unless I've had too much to drink the night before. Then I need coffee and grease."

"I didn't know that." His intent expression indicated that he was filing the new information in memory.

"Now you do." A small smile touched my lips. Maybe I'd feel smothered later, but right now my battered heart was grateful for his care and attention.

The moment shattered when my burner phone vibrated. Yanking it and my bug detector out of my waist pouch, I blew out a breath at the sight of the bug detector's green light.

I accepted the call with a generic, "Yeah."

"It's Spider. Can you talk?"

"Yes."

He let out a breath. "I have updates."

"Anything I can't reveal to Greg, John, Arnie, or Ian?"

"Um..." He paused as if in thought. "No, they've been involved all along. This is just tying up loose ends, nothing classified. You can put me on speaker if you want."

I toggled the button and laid the phone on the coffee table, beckoning to the men. They gathered around, and I added, "Go ahead, Spider. We're all here."

"Okay." He sounded subdued. "I think we've got it all figured out. I wish..." The sound of his swallow carried over the speaker. "I wish it had been in time to save Director Stemp."

My throat tightened. "Me, too. What have you got?"

"We were right about Stephanie being brought in as a new partner and then getting greedy. She also threatened Rupert Weiss not to talk to anyone, and started an intimidation campaign so he'd be afraid to work for anyone else. And it looks like she framed Maria's mother, too, and then hired someone to kill her in the guise of a break-in." Spider hesitated. "This might not be related, but there was another hit taken out on somebody else in Bulgaria. The woman's name was Elena Dobrev. We can't trace her, so it's probably an alias."

It probably was. My heart clenched at the thought of Katya, hiding behind identity after identity in her attempt to stay alive. I'd have to ask if she was okay, when I saw Moonbeam and Karma and Skidmark.

Grief slammed me again. In just a few hours, I'd have to face them.

Spider was still talking. "...Stephanie had Maria's necklace, and it gave me everything I needed to find and decode Volslav's master file. And Stephanie also had a necklace that contained updated records. Police and Interpol are making arrests across North America and

Europe. The full report will be on your desk tomorrow morning. The lab techs pulled an all-nighter, and they've confirmed that the gun that was found with Stemp's stolen car is the one that fired the bullet that..." His voice wavered. "...killed him. The prints on that gun matched the driver. The bullet that killed the last hitman came from the gun you found in Stephanie's purse."

I sat back, trying to unravel everything in my mind. "So that's why Stephanie had an in-person meeting with Dermott in Silverside. She didn't care about seeing him; she just wanted to be there so she could get rid of Max Thorogood."

"It looks that way. She was cleaning up loose ends. There was luggage in her car, and she had an airline ticket to Bulgaria in her purse. The departure time was three hours after she would have gotten the necklaces from Dermott." He sighed. "So that's it. Volslav's finished. Maria's mother is actually dead; I got confirmation from Interpol this morning. And all the hitmen are dead. Everyone's safe."

Except Stemp.

I didn't say that out loud.

"That's all for now, unless you have questions," Spider added.

I cast an interrogative glance around the table, encountering headshakes all around. "No, Spider, you've done your usual outstanding job. Thanks for coming in to help."

"Trish did most of it," he demurred. "I only finished up. She was exhausted, so I sent her home."

I read between the lines. "So you pulled an all-nighter last night." He didn't deny it, and I added, "Thank you so much. Now go home, get some sleep, and enjoy your new daughter. I'm giving you a week off."

Did I still have the authority to do that?

Screw it.

I added, "And tell Trish to take time off to make up for working on her day off yesterday, too."

"Thanks, Aydan. I'll tell her. Are you coming home today?"

The lump in my throat was back. "No, I'm flying to British Columbia. Stemp's parents asked me to bring his... remains."

"Oh." Spider swallowed. "Please give them my deepest sympathy."

CHAPTER 60

Needing solitude, I said my goodbyes and left the men at the hotel.

When I got to the Medical Examiner's office, Salmer was out and a tech met me instead. When I showed my Department ID and explained that I was taking custody of the remains, the tech nodded briskly.

"Cremains of Charles Randall Stemp? Got 'em all packed up for you. Hang on." He left, returning less than a minute later with a small nondescript cardboard box. Plopping it unceremoniously on the counter, he shoved a digital clipboard at me. "Sign here."

Angry words threatened to spew out, but I bit them down and signed. When I thought I could trust myself to be civil, I held my voice under control. "Isn't there something a little... nicer... to carry him in? I'm taking him home to his family."

The tech eyed me as though I'd asked for gold-plated toilet paper. "It's a CTA-approved transportation vessel." He spun the box and pointed at the crookedly-applied black and white label. "If you're carrying it on, this is what the airline needs. They have to be able to x-ray it."

I didn't trust myself to say anything else. Carrying the box carefully, I made my way back to the parking lot. There,

I hovered beside my car.

This seemed so disrespectful. An insult to the reserved, dignified man I had known. What if I put the box on the passenger's seat and then had to slam on the brakes?

But I couldn't put him in the trunk. Not when he'd been stuffed in a trunk, shot and killed...

Blinking the moisture from my eyes, I placed the box gently on the passenger seat and tightened the lap belt around it as best I could.

On the long drive to the airport, the box reproached me with its silent stillness.

"I'm so, so sorry," I said to it. "I tried... so hard..." Tears choked my words. I wiped my eyes, pressed my lips together, and completed the drive in silence.

The two-hour flight seemed longer than usual, but at last I disembarked with my solemn burden. Soon after navigating the lineup at the rental counter, I was driving again with the box as my silent passenger.

As the road narrowed to the seldom-used track leading to the commune, I stiffened my spine. Get it together. Moonbeam and Karma and Skidmark would expect no less.

I didn't encounter any commune members as I drove up the hill to the garage, and I was grateful. Maybe they'd been told to stay away, allowing Charles to complete his final journey without spectators.

Pulling to a stop in front of the dilapidated garage, I cut the engine and squeezed my eyes shut.

Be brave.

When I opened my eyes, Skidmark was emerging from the garage. He made his way slowly toward my car, looking his age for the first time since I'd known him. I got out and went to meet him.

"I'm... so sorry," I choked.

His face softened. "Aw, girlie. It's okay."

"He's..." I motioned at the passenger seat.

"Walk with me." He turned away, and I followed.

We walked slowly through the woods toward the hillside bench that overlooked the commune. They must be holding the ceremony there.

I stiffened my spine. Be brave.

Music floated to us on the breeze, the sweet notes of a single violin.

My heart clutched. Stemp would never practice the violin again. I was certain he had been better at it than he claimed. He would have demanded perfection of himself.

Gulping at the lump in my throat, I forced my emotions down again.

We emerged at the lookout behind a bearded, sarong-clad violinist. As the man turned, Skidmark stepped forward to perform introductions. "Storm Cloud Dancer, this is Dharma Peace-Singer. He'll be doing the Celebration of Life."

The bearded man offered me a bow. I did my best to summon a smile as he straightened, his own smile crinkling his eyes.

His piercing amber eyes.

Surrounded by black and purple bruises.

All the air left my body. Somehow I managed to gasp, "Y-You're..."

Stemp nodded, smiling.

I launched myself at him, flinging my arms around him and hugging him with all my strength. "*Ohmigod!* You're okay, you're alive, you're..."

To my utter mortification, I burst into tears.

Stemp's arms came around me, holding me while I sobbed out my trauma and guilt and joy.

Fighting my way back to control, I pulled away, wiping my face with the hem of my T-shirt. "Sorry," I mumbled. "I just..." I had to swallow again. "I'm really glad you're alive."

"We all are." Moonbeam and Karma emerged from the trail, followed by a beautiful dark-haired woman and a little girl with Stemp's amber eyes.

The woman and girl embraced Stemp while his three parents engulfed me in a group hug, rocking and murmuring comfort when a few more sniffles escaped me.

"We are so sorry you had to go through that," Moonbeam said softly as we pulled apart at last. "We didn't dare communicate without a secure channel. Even the burner phones were too risky."

"Sorry, girlie," Skidmark added. "I'd have told you right away, but we had to make it look good in case any of the commune members were watching."

"Please accept my most heartfelt apologies, too," Stemp said. "I would have spared you this turmoil if I could. I tried to use our usual protocol, but..."

I gulped and wiped my eyes again. "I haven't been home."

"So I gathered." He smiled at Katya and Anna, holding them close. "Storm Cloud Dancer, I'd like you to meet my wife, Sunray Precious Jewel, and my daughter, Summer Starsong."

I held out my hand to Katya. "I'm so happy to finally meet you."

She took it in both hands, her smile illuminating her face. "And I, you." Her words were graced with the slightest hint of an accent.

Moonbeam spoke up. "I think Dharma Peace-Singer and Storm Cloud Dancer have things to discuss." As Stemp's family detached themselves from him, Moonbeam added to me, "Whenever you're ready, please come to our tent."

I nodded, still struggling with my emotions.

When the others had vanished down the path, Stemp gestured to the bench. "Please, sit."

I collapsed onto it, taking comfort from the sun-warmed wood at my back. "Tell me everything."

Stemp seated himself beside me. "Again, I must apologize. If there had been any other option..."

"It's okay. You had to do it this way."

"True. Thank you for understanding." He turned a troubled gaze on me. "I moved to Silverside nearly eight years ago, knowing that when the time was right I would fake my death and disappear. I intended to remain aloof from the community, so that no one would mourn my passing." A bittersweet smile softened the corners of his mouth under the fake beard. "But there was Bud. And then, you. I am so sorry. I never wanted to cause you pain."

"It's okay," I repeated. "And I'm so glad you're finally safe and together with your family. I just wish I could tell Bud. He'll be grieving."

Pain crimped Stemp's eyes. "Yes. Bud will grieve. If I could change that, I would; but I cannot." He gave me a steady look. "You owe me no loyalty, but it would be a great favour to me if you would keep my secret."

I sighed. "I will. I won't even tell Arnie and John. I know they would never blab, but... it's a big responsibility. I don't want to burden them."

"As I have burdened you."

I reached over and squeezed his hand. "This isn't a

burden. It's a relief." Questions finally bubbled up through my emotional overload. "So... if you're alive... then who's in the box in my car?"

Stemp leaned back in the bench with a chuckle. "The assassin who tried to kill my wife."

"But... the dental records... and all the blood that matched your rare blood type..."

"Yes. DNA tests will confirm that it is indeed my blood in the trunk of that car. Several pints of it, the loss of which would be sufficient to kill a man. The bloody drag marks at the veterinary clinic will also match my DNA."

I stared at him. "You've been banking your blood."

"Yes. And employing a creative and discreet dentist overseas, so that I could produce a jawbone and teeth that match my dental records here in Canada. Then all I needed was a corpse and a way to eliminate its DNA."

I gaped at him. "Of course! If I'd thought about it... why would your killer bother breaking into a veterinary clinic to dispose of your body?"

He nodded. "Indeed."

"But what about the guy who stole your rental car and supposedly shot you? Who was he?"

"He was the assassin who was sent to murder me." A small grim smile hardened Stemp's face. "Which was most convenient. After the attempt on Katya's life overseas, Moonbeam and Karma took the would-be assassin into custody. That was when we decided it was time to extract Katya and Anna, and for me to make my exit from Silverside. The assassin would serve as my dead body. They drugged him, disguised him as a senile stroke victim, and brought him back to Canada in a wheelchair with a fake passport. But..."

His smile warmed me. "I knew you would not rest until my murderer was found. And even if I contacted you and told you I had faked my death, you would still be compelled to waste Department time and resources in an official investigation."

"Shit, you're right. And if there were any inconsistencies, the whole thing could unravel."

"Indeed. So when that incompetent assassin arrived on my doorstep, he was a gift from heaven." Stemp's smile turned wry. "Or, since I am now Dharma Peace-Singer, I should say 'a gift from the Earth Spirit'. In any case, I made sure his face was visible in my video recordings so you could identify him, then disabled the cameras and forced him to leave with me. My parents and I broke into the veterinary office to stage my resomation using the body of Assassin Number One, and then drove out to Kananaskis and staged the car accident of Assassin Number Two."

I let out a long breath. "An open-and-shut case. No further investigation required. You're fucking brilliant."

"Thank you."

"And you and your family are safe," I added. "We finally have all of Volslav's records, and the last member of Volslav is dead. This time it's really over." I outlined everything that had happened.

When I finished speaking, a small silence fell between us.

"So..." I ventured. "Are you here to stay?"

"Yes."

Fear shook me. How would we manage without his incisive mind at the helm? Oh, God, they wouldn't promote Dermott, would they? No. Surely not now. Headquarters would assign us a new Director. But what if he or she was worse than Dermott?

I blocked out the worrisome thoughts and refocused as Stemp went on, "Sunray Precious Jewel and I will take over leadership of the commune after a few years, when it is plausible that my parents would want to relinquish their responsibilities."

"And will you carry on their... other responsibilities?" I asked.

Stemp smiled. "Yes. The commune will remain a watchdog for homegrown terrorist activities."

"So you finally did it. The prodigal son returns."

"And I am glad to be here. And..." His voice softened. "I am glad you are here. Are you able to stay for a short time? Sunray Precious Jewel would like to get to know you; and my parents delight in your company." He inclined his head graciously. "As do I."

"Thank you." I slumped, utterly drained. "I'd like to stay for a couple of days. I need a break."

He rose with a smile. "Shall we tell my parents? They will be most pleased."

I stood, too, straightening slowly as the weight of guilt and grief receded. "I need to call the Department; and John and Arnie, too."

"Very well. I will meet you at my parents' tent." Stemp strode off down the path, and I took out my cell phone.

I left a message for General Briggs saying I was taking a few days off. After a moment's hesitation I hit the speed dial for John, mentally rehearsing my weasel words.

John answered on the second ring. "Aydan?"

"Hi. I just wanted to let you know that I made it to the commune okay. Can you let Arnie know, too?"

"Of course." His voice softened. "How are Stemp's

parents?"

Somehow I managed to push out a deceptive truth without choking on it. "I think they'll be okay."

"They're remarkable people." He hesitated. "When do you get back? I can meet you at the airport if you like."

"That would be nice. I'll call you when I've booked my return ticket. I'll likely be here a few days."

The merry sound of a violin floated up to my perch, and somehow I managed to keep the smile out of my voice.

"I'm going to stay for Stemp's Celebration of Life."

Book 18 is coming!

Visit my Books page at dianehenders.com/books for progress updates and announcements.

A Request

Thanks for reading!

If you enjoyed this book, I'd really appreciate it if you'd take a moment to review it online.

Here are some suggestions for the "star" ratings:

Five stars: Loved the book and can hardly wait for the next one.

Four stars: Liked the book and plan to read the next one.

Three stars: The book was okay. Might read the next one.

Two stars: Didn't like the book. Probably won't read the next one.

One star: Hated the book. Would never read another in the series.

You can help prospective readers by writing a few sentences about what you liked or disliked about the book.

Thanks for taking the time to do a review!

About Me

Before I started writing fiction, I had a checkered career: technical writer, computer geek, and interior designer. I'm good at two out of three of those. Fortunately, I had the sense to quit the one I sucked at (interior design).

When my mid-life crisis hit, I took up muay thai and started writing thrillers featuring a middle-aged female protagonist. ('Walter Mitty', you say? Nope, never heard of him.)

Writing and kicking the hell out of stuff seemed more productive than more typical mid-life-crisis activities like getting a divorce, buying a Harley Crossbones, and cruising across the country picking up men in sleazy bars; especially since it's winter most months of the year here in Canada.

It's much more comfortable to sit at my computer. And Harleys are expensive. Come to think of it, so are beer and gasoline.

Oh, and I still love my husband. There's that. So I stuck with the writing.

Diane Henders

And here's my "professional" bio, in case you need something more suitable for mixed company:

Diane Henders is the Kindle best-selling author of the NEVER SAY SPY series: Sexy thrillers packed with tension, laughs, profanity, and sometimes warm fuzzies.

The first book in the series, NEVER SAY SPY, has had over 450,000 downloads to date, and stayed on Kindle's 'Women Sleuths' Top 100 list for 60 consecutive months.

Diane enjoys target shooting, gardening, auto mechanics, painting (art, not walls), music, and martial arts; and loves food and drink almost as much as she loves her husband. They live in the wilds of British Columbia, Canada, where they get all the adrenaline rush they could ever want by growing fruit trees in bear country.

Want to know what else is roiling around in the cesspit of my mind? Drop by my blog and website at dianehenders.com, check out the extras, and don't forget to leave a comment in the guest book to say hi – I love hearing from you! Or you can connect with me on Facebook at:
https://www.facebook.com/authordianehenders.
See you there!